# Beyond
### THE
# Breakwater

# Praise for Radclyffe's Fiction

"...well-plotted...lovely romance...I couldn't turn the pages fast enough!" – Ann Bannon, author of *The Beebo Brinker Chronicles*.

"...well-honed storytelling skills...solid prose and sure-handedness of the narrative..." – Elizabeth Flynn, *Lambda Book Report*

"...a thoughtful and thought-provoking tale...deftly handled in nuanced and textured prose that is both intelligent and deeply personal. The sex is exciting, the story is daring, the characters are well-developed and interesting – in short, Radclyffe has once again pulled together all the ingredients of a genuine page-turner..." – Cameron Abbott, author of *To the Edge* and *An Inexpressible State of Grace*

"With ample angst, realistic and exciting medical emergencies, winsome secondary characters, and a sprinkling of humor...a terrific romance...one of the best I have read in the last three years. Highly recommended." – Author Lori L. Lake, Book Reviewer for the *Independent Gay Writer*

"Radclyffe employs...a lean, trim, and tight writing style...rich with meticulously developed characterizations and realistic dialogue..." – Arlene Germain, *Lambda Book Report*

"...one writer who creates believably great characters that are just as strong as mainstream publishing's Kay Scarpetta or Kinsey Milhone...If you're looking for a great romance, read anything by Radclyffe." – Sherry Stinson, editor, *Outlook Press*

# *Beyond*
## THE
# *Breakwater*

*by*

### RADCLYₗFFE

2004

**BEYOND THE BREAKWATER**

© 2003 By Radclyffe. All Rights Reserved.

ISBN 1-933110-06-6

This Trade Paperback Original Is Published By
Bold Strokes Books, Inc.,
Philadelphia, PA, USA

First Edition: September 2003
Second Printing: Ocober, 2004 Bold Strokes Books, Inc.
Third Printing: December, 2004 Bold Strokes Books, Inc.

---

**Credits**

Executive Editor: Stacia Seaman
Editor: Laney Roberts
Production Design: J. Barre Greystone
Cover Photo: Radclyffe
Cover Design By Sheri (GRAPHICARTIST2020@HOTMAIL.COM)

# By the Author

## Romances

| | |
|---|---|
| Safe Harbor | Tomorrow's Promise |
| Beyond the Breakwater | Passion's Bright Fury |
| Innocent Hearts | Love's Masquerade |
| Love's Melody Lost | shadowland |
| Love's Tender Warriors | Fated Love |

## Honor Series

Above All, Honor

Honor Bound

Love & Honor

Honor Guards

## Justice Series

A Matter of Trust (prequel)

Shield of Justice

In Pursuit of Justice

Justice in the Shadows

Change Of Pace: *Erotic Interludes*
*(A Short Story Collection)*

# Acknowledgments

This seems like the perfect time to be writing this foreword since I am in Provincetown and have daily walked by many of the places in this book. As always, the town and the natural beauty of the land and sea and the famous "Provincetown light" inspire. I have never wanted to be able to paint or write poetry as much as I have when I am here. This book is special to me for many reasons: because of the setting, because it continues the story begun in my first published work, and because the characters have carved a permanent place in my heart. I owe a debt of thanks to all the readers who asked for this sequel.

Thanks go to my editors, Laney Roberts and Stacia Seaman, for their patience, professionalism, and willingness to live with my quirks; my beta readers, Athos, JB, Jane, Tomboy, and Diane, for their review of the early manuscript; and to HS and all the members of the Radlist for their enthusiastic support and unflagging belief in me.

The cover photograph is the lighthouse at Wood End in Provincetown. Once again, Sheri has captured the spirit of the story with another superb cover.

Every day, Lee graciously and without complaint makes room in her life for these characters, these stories, and the demands they make on our time. Every day, I am grateful for her. *Amo te.*

# Dedication

For Lee,
For Always and Beyond

## CHAPTER ONE

### September, Provincetown, MA

D r. Victoria King tilted her face to the sun and let the swift ocean current carry her to shore. She rested her paddle across the front of the seventeen-foot-long, twenty-one-inch-wide red kayak and squinted in the early morning haze toward the beach at Herring Cove. Men and women perched on the undulating curve of sand marking the border between earth and water, casting baited lines to tempt the sea bass to their last meal. In the black ribbon of parking lot sandwiched between the dunes and the shore, vacationers were just beginning to stir, opening the windows and doors of their mobile homes and airing out their sea-dampened linens and clothes.

Tory was so used to seeing the idyllic tableau, she barely took note as her craft glided the last few feet and touched bottom in the frothing water at the ocean's edge. But then, she wasn't watching the locals *or* the end-of-the-season tourists. There was only one thing for which she was searching.

Smiling, she found it.

As it had almost every morning for the last two years, a police cruiser sat amongst the battered trucks belonging to the early-morning anglers and the huge Winnebagos of intrepid travelers. And, as it never failed to do, the sight of the vehicle settled her world even as a swift surge of pleasure raced along her spine.

Carefully, she pulled her legs from inside her shell and swung a foot over each side, straddling the kayak as she stood up in the shallow foam. Once she had her balance, she moved to the needle-thin front and pulled the boat onto land. The fiberglass construction was amazingly light, making it easy for her to maneuver it over the sand unaided.

As she unzipped her life vest and tossed it into her boat, the sound of a car door thudding closed penetrated the roar of the waves. Looking up, she stopped what she was doing to watch the tall, lean, uniformed figure walk toward her across the shell-littered sand, a blazing grin on her handsome face. Tory was used to seeing the deputy sheriff's cruiser on the shore every morning, too, as natural a part of her personal landscape now as the dunes and the sea and the clear blue skies. But seeing the dark-haired, blue-eyed woman made her heart flutter just as it had the very first time they had met.

There were moments like this, after they'd been apart, when Reese would appear and Tory would wonder fleetingly if perhaps she had conjured her. Because, after all, women don't walk out of your dreams and right into your life. And because, after all this time, her heart still fluttered. *Walk slowly, so I can watch.*

Reese must have read Tory's mind, or maybe she just read the gleam in her eye, but she took her time crossing the beach, one dark eyebrow quirked to match her cocky grin.

"Good morning, Sheriff," Tory called on the wind, her eyes roaming the trim body in the immaculately pressed and polished uniform, moving slowly from the broad shoulders over the faint swell of breasts to the narrow hips and long, muscular thighs. Reese had left her hat in the patrol car, and the wind ruffled her thick black just short-of-short hair, giving her that slightly wild look that Tory loved. *God, you're gorgeous.*

"Good morning, Doctor," Reese replied easily, stopping a few feet away, shoulders squared in that unconscious military posture that was second nature to her. She knew Tory was watching her, *wanting* her, and she liked it. Her skin tingled under the stiff cotton of her khakis everywhere Tory's glance fell, the visual caress as tangible as a touch. The two feet of air between them shimmered like the currents above blacktop on a hot summer's day. "Nice out there today?"

"Mmm. Yeah, it was."

Reese smiled. Tory's clear, lightly tanned skin was flushed from the wind off the water and the exertion of her recent paddle. The T-shirt she had worn under her PFD was damp with sweat and spray, the thin material subtly outlining her firm, high breasts. Her mid-thigh-length shorts hugged slender, toned legs. Even the scarred and damaged calf held a trace of valiant beauty.

"Give you a hand?" Reese's voice was husky. *You are so very lovely.*

"Anytime." Tory let Reese take the kayak up the beach, following with paddle and drybag, but falling slightly behind as her unsteady gait in the sand hampered her progress. Still, the lightweight high-impact plastic brace on her right ankle was far better than the full metal one she had needed until recently, and she wasn't complaining, especially now that she rarely, if ever, needed her cane. If it had been anyone other than Reese, though, she would have refused the aid. She had managed such things on her own for so long that it was second nature for her to decline assistance.

She caught up to Reese by the side of her Jeep and opened the back. Tossing the items she carried inside, she then turned and found the sheriff leaning against the side of the vehicle, watching her... watching her with that particular sparkle in her eye that suggested she was considering things one couldn't do in public. Things Tory really didn't want to think about at eight in the morning when she had forty patients waiting in her office.

Flushing, Tory looked away and reached for the rear of the kayak. "Ready?"

"Any time you say, love." Except Reese wasn't looking at the kayak.

Tory reached for the lift strap on the end of the boat. "Stop."

"Oh, I don't think so." Reese's voice was playful.

"Just help me with this and try to behave."

"Anything you want."

Tory laughed, and together they lifted the craft to the roof rack and secured it. As they stood facing one another by the side of the vehicle, their eyes met and they moved close enough that their hands touched. Tory slid her fingers under the starched cuff of Reese's shirt, lightly encircling her wrist.

"Busy day today?" Reese brushed the auburn collar-length hair back from Tory's face with her fingertips, letting her hand linger against her lover's cheek.

"Uh-huh," Tory murmured, pressing her face to Reese's palm as she rested her free hand on the taller woman's chest. "You?"

"Routine," the sheriff replied, watching the green eyes deepen to the color of the ocean in August. "I won't be late. Can we have dinner?"

"Probably. Call me when you finish your shift, and I'll see where I am with my patients."

"You think Randy will let me interrupt your office hours, even for dinner?" Reese referred to Tory's clinic majordomo with genuine deference. "He doesn't like it when I interfere with your schedule."

"He'll make room for you if he knows what's good for him."

Reese laughed. "I'll tell him you said that."

"Mmm, okay." Tory ran a finger down the buttons on Reese's shirt, thinking about the hard muscles and soft smooth skin underneath. She thought about waking with her that morning and how much she had wanted her right then and knowing that there wasn't time—knowing that she would want her all day, knowing that in the evening there *would* be time. "I love you."

Reese lowered her head and brushed her lips over Tory's, her hand beneath Tory's hair caressing the back of her neck. "Me, too," she whispered against her lover's ear. "I don't suppose you could get away at lunch?"

"Now you're pushing it, Sheriff." Tory's laughter was rich and full as she pressed both palms against Reese's chest and pushed, backing her up a step. "No, I can't. And it won't hurt you to wait."

"I'm suffering already."

"Go to work," Tory ordered as she stepped away. Reese had a dangerous glint in her deep blue eyes, the kind of spark that promised flames. Tory was afraid that if they touched again they'd kiss for real, and then she wouldn't be able to concentrate all day. Twelve hours was an eternity when your body was on fire.

"When?" Reese persisted, but she didn't move. She didn't dare. *You always do this to me—make me so hot I can't think.*

"Later. Now go." Tory slid into the Jeep, pulled the door closed, and started the ignition with shaking hands. After two years, she had expected the passion to lessen, the heat to cool, but neither had. She glanced into the rearview mirror as she drove away. Watching Reese stride to her patrol car, she hoped that they never would.

❖

Later turned out to be eleven o'clock that night.

Tory's patient schedule had been disrupted while she sutured a series of nasty lacerations on the forehead of a cyclist who had blown a tire coming down Route 6 from Truro. He'd catapulted into the guardrail, and he looked it. By the time she got home, her head ached, she was exhausted, and sex was the last thing on her mind.

"Did you ever get dinner?" Reese, in jeans and a faded green T-shirt with *USMC* stenciled on the left chest, met her lover on the rear deck of the house they shared overlooking Provincetown Harbor.

"No." Tory sighed as she flopped into a deck chair, absently petting the huge brindle mastiff that lumbered to her side. "Hey, Jed," she whispered faintly. Looking up at Reese, she added wryly, "Some date night, huh? Sorry."

"You're forgiven." Reese leaned in for a kiss. "Relax a minute. I'll be right back."

Tory closed her eyes, and when she jerked awake a few moments later, there was a tray table beside her with a glass of wine and a sandwich. Suddenly, she was ravenous.

"Oh, yes," she breathed, casting a grateful glance at the woman who leaned against the deck rail a few feet away. Moonlight and the soft glow from the kitchen behind them illuminated Reese's strikingly beautiful Black Irish coloring and sculpted features. Sandwich nearly forgotten, Tory had to swallow around the fist of desire in her throat before she could speak. "Thanks."

"My pleasure." Reese watched Tory consume the late meal, trying not to let her worry show. As the town's only year-round doctor, Tory worked long hours and was always on call, and she often forgot to eat or didn't get enough sleep. "Better?" she asked when Tory set her glass down with a satisfied groan.

"Almost."

Reese raised an eyebrow. "Something else?"

"Uh-huh." Tory held out a hand, and Reese moved to take it. Tory tugged her lover down onto the lounge chair beside her, turning so that they rested face to face. Threading her arms around Reese's waist, she pressed close, pushing one thigh between Reese's. "This."

It began with just a kiss—a kiss to say *welcome home,* a kiss to say *I missed you,* a kiss to say *I love you.* It became something more urgent as flesh met flesh and passions stirred. Tory worked her hand between them and pulled the T-shirt from Reese's jeans, resting her palm on the curve of rib as it arched above Reese's taut stomach. She ran her nails lightly down the center of Reese's abdomen, smiling against Reese's lips as muscles flickered.

Reese kissed her way from Tory's mouth along the line of her jaw to the smooth skin of her neck, biting lightly until she drew soft cries from her lover's throat. Their hearts pounded, beating a familiar rhythm that echoed in each other's blood as they explored one another with mouths and lips and demanding hands.

"Love," Reese gasped as she felt Tory's fingers slip down the front of her jeans. She didn't remember opening her fly, but one of them must have. "Careful there. I've waited all day."

"And your point is…?" Tory murmured thickly, pushing lower, finding heat, as she leaned up on the other arm so she could watch Reese's face. *"I've* been waiting all day, too. Now, I'm done waiting."

"Ah, God…you know I'll go fast if you touch me like that."

"I'm not worried." Tory's fingers found the hardness she sought, and as she pressed steadily, Reese moaned. "You're always good for more than one."

Through a haze of want, Tory watched; she loved to see Reese like this—growing so still under her hands, body arched slightly, head tilted back, pupils wide and dark. After all this time, Tory knew just how to touch her to keep her on the edge, knew the telltale flutter of her lids, the stutter of breath in her chest, the faint cry barely uttered. She knew and she held Reese there on the brink, moving her fingers slowly, carefully, one gentle stroke after another.

"Tory…love," Reese whispered as the pleasure escaped the confines of the places Tory touched and cascaded outward to burn through her blood and roll down her legs, muscles clenching with the force of nerves and vessels turning to fire. She pressed her forehead to Tory's shoulder and shuddered helplessly, lost and forever found.

As many times as she had watched Reese surrender to her touch, Tory was never prepared for the beauty of it. Awestruck, humbled beyond words, she bit her lip to keep from falling with her, wanting to remember each precious second. But she couldn't keep from thrusting against Reese's thigh, her body having long since moved beyond her control. Trying desperately to ignore the pressure building between her legs, she clung to her lover, gasping.

Dimly, Reese heard Tory's ragged breathing against her ear, and even as she continued to shiver with the last ripples of release, she reached for her. "I want to be inside you."

"Yes." Tory lifted her hips, helping Reese push her slacks down. "Yes. Yes."

It was quick, because she was so close. One second, Reese was gliding over her, opening her, and then she was inside her, owning her. Tory cried out once, sharply, and then she was coming. Over and over and over, she closed around Reese's fingers, each spasm knifing through her with a terrible wonder. When she could make a sound, she could find no words. She simply turned her sweat-damp face to Reese's chest and hung on.

❖

The chill roused Tory from her unintentional slumber. The night was very dark around them, and the wind from the water was sharp and crisp. In the distance, the foghorn off Long Point echoed plaintively. Tory stirred, running her fingers over Reese's chest.

"Hey, Sheriff."

"Mmm?"

"Bedtime."

Reese stretched languidly, settling Tory closer against her, nestling her face in the soft hair. "Do we have to?"

"It will be freezing out here in a few hours."

"Okay," Reese conceded, but when she moved to get up, Tory suddenly held her tighter. Surprised by the fierce grip, she asked, "What's wrong, Tor?"

"Nothing." Tory shook her head and fiddled with the button on Reese's jeans, uncharacteristically uncertain. "You know I'll be thirty-nine in November."

"Uh-huh." Reese waited.

Tory took a deep breath. "I was thinking it's time for us to have a baby." She began to worry when Reese was quiet for a very long time. Maybe her timing was lousy. Maybe two years wasn't long enough. Or maybe she didn't know Reese as well as she thought she did. "Reese?"

"You know," Reese said softly, her voice husky and low. "Five minutes ago, I would have said that life couldn't get any better." She kissed Tory, gentle as a promise. "It's so nice to be wrong."

Tory closed her eyes and pressed her face to Reese's neck, sighing softly as strong, sure arms tightened around her. After all this time, she had expected the passion to lessen and the fires to cool. For the first time, she truly allowed herself to believe that they never would.

## December, Provincetown, MA

Reese reached for another folder and shook some of the tension out of her shoulders. She'd been hunched over her desk for over an hour filling out requisition forms for equipment that needed to be replaced as well as completing paperwork on an early-morning domestic disturbance complaint. At the outset of winter, Provincetown was deathly quiet. The small community on the very tip of Cape Cod had been a thriving fishing village a hundred years before, and some of the inhabitants still worked the boats that ventured out into the Atlantic every day. But the primary source of income for many was tourism. And tourism was decidedly seasonal.

The three thousand or so year-round inhabitants were pretty well dug in for the winter, with most of the shops and even the small Cinema Arts Theatre in the center of town having closed for the off-season. The number of law enforcement personnel had been trimmed down to the bare minimum, too, which meant that Reese was one of only a handful of full-time officers available. She didn't mind the long shifts, but things were so damn slow that any kind of call was a welcome break in the mind-numbing routine. The thirty minutes it had taken her earlier that morning to calm down an irate housewife who had discovered that her husband had sold her prized antique porcelain chamber pot to pay off a poker debt had been a relief from the obligatory desk work.

When the front door opened, admitting a gust of cold air, she looked up, grateful for the diversion. Sheriff Nelson Parker walked in. A burly man in his late forties, he approached six feet and was carrying a few extra pounds around his middle. His dark hair was still thick without a trace of gray, and his eyes were the color of a winter sky.

"Hey, Chief."

"Morning, Reese." Nelson brushed a light dusting of snow from the shoulders of his red and black checked hunting jacket and then shrugged it off. He hooked the jacket over a coat tree and put his Stetson on an adjoining shelf. "Anything happening?"

"Not much," Reese said with resignation. She was working twelve-hour shifts with another officer, seven to seven, and two other pairs split the evening and night hours. "A couple of minor calls, but nothing serious. Night shift had nothing to report."

"Well," he settled behind his desk, "that's about right for this time of year. Remember when you first started, I warned you about how dull this place can be in the winter."

"I remember." Reese glanced out the window at the slate-colored sky and then shifted her gaze inside. "You were right then, and nothing's changed since."

The sheriff's department main office was a single large room. There was a tiny seating area separated by a wooden railing from the small collection of desks and chairs where the officers and clerical staff sat. Behind Reese, a door led to the rear of the building to two small holding cells, which almost never saw any use.

"Summertime makes up for it, though. Plus, it's so beautiful here, even now, that I don't mind the quiet." Reese stretched and sighed. "Most of the time."

"There is something awfully pretty about the dunes in the winter." Nelson reached for his own stack of paperwork. "Have you heard from Bri lately?"

Surprised, Reese shook her head. "Not since Thanksgiving when she and Caroline were here. Why?"

"No reason," Nelson said nonchalantly. He was mildly embarrassed to admit that his daughter had not phoned him in several weeks and had failed to return his calls when he had tried her number in Manhattan. Sometimes it bothered him that Brianna and Reese were close in a way that he and his daughter were not. He knew that Bri confided in his second in command in a way that she rarely did with him. And he knew why. As hard as he had tried, he couldn't really understand what life was like for her.

In truth, he supposed their closeness made sense, since Bri and Reese were practically cut from the same mold—stubborn and strong and brave. Hell, they even looked alike—both dark-haired with wild blue eyes, almost too handsome for women. But there was something in Bri's eyes that he'd never seen in Reese's. There was a simmering anger that had begun in Bri's early teens and hadn't abated even when she went away to school. Maybe the rage had been further fueled by the events of two summers before. Thinking about that summer, something he tried not to do, he unconsciously winced.

"Nelson? You sure everything's okay?"

"Yeah, I'm sure." He cleared his throat. "You know how twenty-year-olds are. They don't think much about calling home."

"Right." Reese nodded, although she didn't really know what he meant. When she'd been twenty, she'd been in college, too, but she'd also been in the Naval ROTC, on track to be a marine officer. Raised by a career marine officer, she'd never imagined any other future—that's what her father *expected* her to be and what she expected of herself. She hadn't had the kind of youth many had; she'd certainly never had a lover, male or female, when she was Bri's age. "If I hear from her, I'll tell her to report in."

Reese knew there was more on his mind, but she hesitated to inquire. She and her boss were friends, but she and his daughter shared a special bond that had been forged shortly after Reese had come to Provincetown. Bri had been a wild teenager at the time, and she and Reese had developed a friendship when Reese began training her in the martial arts. The connection had grown as Bri gradually adopted Reese as not only her mentor, but as her role model.

"No. Forget it," Nelson said with a wave of his hand. With the other, he searched in his desk drawer for a roll of Tums and, finding a loose one, popped it into his mouth. "She'll just figure I'm checking up on her."

"Aren't you?" Reese asked with a laugh.

After a second, Nelson's somber expression faded. "Yeah, I suppose."

At that moment, the door opened yet again, and a middle-aged woman entered carrying a shopping bag in one arm. Of average height, she wore her wavy gray hair tied back with a multicolored scarf and sported a knit suit beneath a long down coat. After removing her outerwear, she rummaged in the bag and set a box of donuts by Nelson's elbow.

"God, I can't wait till this winter is over."

"You've got quite a wait there, Gladys." Nelson smiled at the sheriff's department office manager. Fishing a sugared donut from the box, he added, "Thanks."

"Yes, well, I can always hope." She smiled at both of the officers as she wended her way between the desks toward the large workstation in one corner with the room's only computer. During her day shift, she monitored the local and regional police activity, relayed messages to the officers in the field, and performed whatever computer checks needed to be done quickly.

"How's that lovely partner of yours, Reese?" Gladys settled herself at her station. "I haven't seen much of her lately."

"Uh, fine." Reese blushed. Even after two years, she couldn't quite get used to the easy familiarity of the small town's local inhabitants. Everyone seemed to know everyone else's business and didn't mind asking for the information if they didn't. "Tory is working in Boston today."

"Is she still flying over there three days a week?"

"Yep." Reese nodded. "She doesn't need to keep the clinic open here full-time during the winter, and she likes doing the emergency room shifts. She says it keeps her current with the newest techniques."

"Well, she oughta jump at the chance to take it easy," Nelson remarked. "The summer is always busy enough for two or three doctors."

"True enough." Reese thought about tourist season and the incredible changes it wrought on the town almost overnight. From Memorial Day weekend until after Labor Day, the population swelled tenfold with an enormous influx of day travelers and vacationers. Tory was continually busy providing emergency medical care, often working eighteen-hour days for the entire four months. Reese had yet to convince her to hire a temporary physician associate to help out. *Maybe by summer, if—*

The ringing of the phone interrupted her musings, and Reese picked it up on the second ring. "Sheriff's department, Conlon."

"Honey?"

"Tor?" Reese's heart started pounding double-time. It was rare for Tory to call her at work, particularly when staffing a shift at the Boston City Hospital emergency room. "What's the matter?"

"Nothing," Tory assured hastily. "I just need you to come to Boston."

"Now?"

Tory laughed, and the sound stirred a small fire in Reese's depths.

"How about late this afternoon?" Tory clarified.

"Uh…my shift isn't up until seven." Reese hesitated, glancing at the other occupants in the room as she lowered her voice. "Is it, you know, time?"

"That's what my thermometer says. I've talked to Wendy, and she can see us at six."

Reese could sense that both Nelson and Gladys were watching yet pretending not to. She curled over the phone as if that would make some difference. "I'll get someone to fill in for me."

"Is everyone listening?"

"Uh-huh."

"It's okay to tell them, you know. It's not like we'll be able to keep it a secret."

"Isn't it...well...bad luck or something to talk about it before?"

Tory laughed again, and the heat in her voice was almost palpable over the phone line. "Do you know how much I love you?"

"Cut it out," Reese said in a husky murmur. "I'm supposed to be working here."

"Yeah, well...your services are required elsewhere. Get your butt on a plane, Sheriff."

"I'll be there soon."

When she hung up, both Nelson and Gladys were frankly staring.

"I need to take the afternoon off," Reese said abruptly.

"Sure." Nelson was clearly surprised at the unusual request. "Gladys can call Smith or Lyons to come in. God knows, they both owe you time."

"Thanks." Reese stood and walked to the coat tree beside the door. She shrugged into her green nylon flight jacket and pulled her brimmed uniform cap down over her eyes in a familiar gesture.

"Is everything okay?" Gladys knew that Nelson wouldn't pry even though he was obviously dying to know what was going on, too.

"Yes. Perfect." Reese opened the door, stepped through, and then stuck her head back in. "I just need to get to Boston so Tory and I can make a baby."

Grinning, she closed the door on the explosion of surprised questions.

❖

"You made it! Great." Wendy Deutsch greeted Reese and Tory in her waiting room. With light blond hair and lashes and a slight but athletic build, she looked young enough to be a med student. She wasn't, though; she was the head of the reproductive medicine division at Boston Hospital and one of Tory's best friends from medical school. "Are you two all set?"

Tory, suddenly and inexplicably frightened, turned to Reese, searching the handsome face as she reached for her hand. *Reese... honey? Of course we're ready, right? We've talked about it—about how it would change our lives, about how it would shape our future, about what would be hard and what would be wonderful. Because this is it; now is the tim—*

"I love you, Victoria King," Reese murmured, her entire being focused on Tory. "I will always love you."

And that was the ultimate truth, and the ultimate answer.

"Yes," Tory stated firmly, entwining her fingers with Reese's and smiling into her eyes. "We're ready."

"Come on back, then." Wendy led the way into a dimly lit room.

There was a beige carpet on the floor, which struck Tory as odd. She was used to the harsh lights and institutional tiles of examining rooms. And the air was warm, with a hint of vanilla teasing at the edges of her awareness. *Nothing cold, nothing sterile, nothing clinical about it.*

"You both get settled, and I'll be right back." With that, Wendy left them alone.

Slowly, Tory undressed. Reese took each garment and folded it carefully, placing the clothes on a small table against one wall. She bundled Tory into a white terrycloth robe that had been left for her.

"Cold, love?" Reese asked gently.

"No, I'm fine." Tory eased up onto the table, glad that the surface was covered with a soft cotton sheet.

Reese covered her with another sheet, then pulled a chair close to the head of the table and sat down. She threaded the fingers of one hand into Tory's hair and took Tory's hand with the other. Tory turned her head so that their faces were only inches apart.

"Are you sure this won't hurt?" Reese was unable to hide her concern. *You mean everything to me.*

"Yes, I'm sure. I won't feel anything."

There was a knock on the door. "Okay to come in?"

The two women smiled, and Tory called, "Yes, we're ready."

Tory continued to look into Reese's eyes, listening with only part of her mind to the doctor quietly arranging a tray. When

Wendy softly instructed her to slide down and lift her legs into the supports, she complied without breaking the eye contact. She felt only Reese's hand, strong and warm, enclosing hers.

After a moment, Wendy murmured, "Here we go."

Reese touched her forehead to Tory's, and together they whispered, "I love you."

## CHAPTER TWO

### January, East Village, Manhattan, NY

The rail-thin young man with short, spiked hair wore a shapeless black T-shirt and equally formless black denim pants that hung precariously from his nonexistent rear end. In the tiny kitchen of a fourth floor walk-up, he approached a petite blond, also dressed in black jeans that actually fit her trim form along with a midriff-baring white crop-top that exposed a softly curved belly adorned with a silver navel ring.

"Great party, Carre. Any more beer?"

"In the fridge." The three studs in the rim of Caroline Clark's left ear glinted as she turned to refill a bowl of pretzels from a bag on the counter. "It's nice to get the midyear projects over, huh?"

"For sure. Did you hear about Paris yet?"

"Just that they got all my application materials." Caroline's smile faded slightly as she thought of spending her junior year abroad. She *wanted* to go because the chance to study and paint in France was a dream come true. But when she actually pictured herself there, so far away from everything she knew, everyone she loved…"My adviser thinks it should be fine, but if I don't get the financial aid, I'm not going to be able to go."

"No sweat. You'll get it." He reached around her to open the refrigerator. "What about Bri? She going, too?"

Caroline hesitated. "I…we…haven't really talked about it." *Every time I do try to bring it up, Bri changes the subject or just says, "That's great, babe. Go for it."*

"Where is she tonight, anyhow? She's missing all the fun."

"At the dojo." Caroline glanced at the clock uneasily. It was after eleven p.m., and Bri's class ended at nine-thirty. *She knew I was having friends over from school tonight.* Caroline tried to ignore the stab of hurt at her lover's absence. Now that she thought about it, Bri had been even quieter than usual the last few weeks. She seemed to be training more and more, if that were humanly possible, and coming home later and later. For the first time in the four years they'd been together, Caroline felt uncertain of what was happening between them.

"What?" Caroline suddenly realized that her friend James was still speaking.

"The black belt thing...that's happening soon for her, right?"

"Oh. Yes. Sometime this year."

"Man, that's amazing." James leaned against the counter and fished a handful of potato chips from an open bag beside him, then took a swallow of his beer. He and Caroline moved closer together as another woman squeezed in beside them, muttering that she was looking for ice. "She, like, practices every day, doesn't she?"

"Almost." Lately, it seemed that Bri's training was the most important thing in her life. Caroline knew for a fact that the martial arts were much more important to Bri than college. And not for the first time, she thought that Bri had come to Manhattan only to be with her. *Perhaps if we had stayed in Provincetown, Bri would have been just as happy. Maybe more.*

When they'd talked about going away to college, Bri had simply said that she would go anywhere that Caroline wanted to go. So, when Caroline received the scholarship to the Parsons School of Design in Manhattan, it had seemed like an ideal solution. Manhattan wasn't that far from Cape Cod, so they could still get home easily. There were plenty of schools where Bri could enroll, and Reese Conlon knew of a dojo where Bri could train. Bri had settled on John Jay University, because it was affordable and offered a solid curriculum in criminology. She wanted to go into law enforcement, like her father and Reese.

It was great timing when she and Bri found the tiny apartment in Alphabet City, the student/artist enclave in the East Village, and life had seemed perfect. For her, it still was.

"I'd better get back out there." Caroline grabbed a bottle of beer for herself and moved toward the front room.

"Later," James called as he reached for more chips.

The front door was just closing behind Bri as Caroline walked into the crowded living room, which also happened to be their bedroom when the sofa bed was pulled out. Caroline stepped over extended legs and threaded her way around the bowls and bottles on the floor until she reached her lover. Standing on tiptoe, she slipped one arm around Bri's shoulder and gave her a quick kiss on the mouth.

"Hi."

Bri, taller than Caroline by a head, was in her usual outfit— tight, threadbare blue jeans, multizippered leather jacket, and heavy black motorcycle boots. She put both arms around her girlfriend and pulled her close, squeezing gently. Caroline always smelled like the shampoo she used, some combination of fruit and spices. Just the scent of her could make Bri wet.

"Hey, babe. How's it going?"

"Okay. Missed you."

"Sorry." Bri let Caroline go and shrugged out of her jacket. The black T-shirt was stretched tight across her muscled chest and shoulders, her breasts smooth shadows beneath the thin cotton. Narrow-hipped and broad-shouldered, hard-bodied from the daily practice of jujitsu, she exuded danger and a seething sexuality.

"Come on." Caroline took her hand. "You want something? A beer?"

"Sure." Bri allowed herself to be pulled though the crowd. She was relieved that Caroline hadn't asked her why she was late, but she'd seen the hurt in those deep green eyes just the same. *Fuck. I have to tell her soon.*

❖

By two a.m., everyone had gone. Discarded bottles and half-empty bowls of snacks lay scattered around the room, but the apartment had survived the crush of partyers in fairly good shape. Caroline and Bri were nestled on the couch where they had collapsed after bidding good night to the last of the art students. The room lights were off, and a few candles provided the only illumination. Bri, cradling Caroline in her arms, leaned against the corner of the sofa with the smaller woman lying between her outstretched legs.

"I guess we should open the bed," Bri murmured, nuzzling her lips in Caroline's fragrant hair. She rubbed her palm slowly up and down Caroline's bare stomach, brushing the navel ring back and forth. Every now and then, she tugged it lazily between her fingers. "Carre? Babe? You awake?"

"Mm-hmm." Caroline turned on her side and snuggled her hips between Bri's thighs. "It's awfully nice just like this."

"Oh, yeah?"

"Yeah."

Bri tilted Caroline's chin up with a finger and found her lips, exploring with the tip of her tongue along the sensitive inner surfaces. They'd kissed thousands of times, but every time she was struck anew by the incredible softness of Caroline's lips. Within seconds, Bri felt herself swell and grow hard.

"I love to kiss you," Bri whispered.

"Mmm. Me, too." Caroline rested her hand on Bri's chest, rhythmically brushing her thumb across the peak of her lover's taut nipple. She knew that would make Bri crazy.

After a minute, Bri was primed. "Come on, babe. Let's open the bed and get out of our clothes."

"Not yet," Caroline said with gentle firmness. "I'm too comfortable. Just kiss me for a little while longer."

Bri knew what Caroline was doing, and as much as it frustrated her, it excited her tremendously, too. *Carre likes to tease me. She always has.* They'd barely been sixteen when they'd met, but Caroline had always been confident. She wanted Bri, and she didn't care who knew it. That had always made Bri feel like a king.

Surrendering to the sweet torture, Bri groaned and kissed Caroline hard, her tongue inside the warm mouth now. Minutes—hours—passed, she couldn't tell how long. Her head was light, her legs heavy, and her breath hissed from her chest in uneven gasps. Somewhere in the midst of their kisses, Caroline had turned on her stomach between Bri's open thighs, and now she thrust her hips into Bri in time with their questing tongues.

Clasping Caroline's butt in her hands, Bri pulled her hard against her crotch, trying unsuccessfully to satisfy the pressure building precariously inside. She sighed against Caroline's mouth. "You feel so good."

The only response was a soft whimper.

The sound of Caroline's pleasure snapped the tenuous threads of Bri's control, and she wrapped one strong arm around Caroline's waist and twisted until the smaller woman was beneath her. She grasped the lower edge of the diminutive crop top, pushed it up, and lowered her mouth to the soft, full breast.

Caroline arched and cried out as Bri sucked the nipple into her mouth. She fisted her hands in Bri's hair, pulling frantically as the pleasure streaked from her breast through her belly. "Bri...ooh, you always make me so hot."

Never moving her lips from Caroline's breast, Bri eased away enough to get her hand between them. Deftly, she opened Caroline's jeans and began to push them down over her hips.

"Oh, yes. Hurry." Caroline lifted her hips, grasped her jeans with one hand, and helped bare her body. Then with her lips pressed to Bri's ear, she begged, "I'm so excited. Make me come, baby."

Bri groaned. Nothing had ever made her feel at once so powerful and so hopelessly inadequate. That Caroline would want her, would trust her so completely, nearly broke her heart. She pressed her forehead to Caroline's breast, murmuring fervently, "I love you so damn much."

"I know...I know...oh, love me now." Eyes closed, head twisting helplessly against the arm of the sofa, Caroline pushed Bri down with trembling hands.

Moving fast, Bri knelt on the floor, her palms beneath Caroline's hips, pulling her forward to the edge of the couch and lifting her easily on her powerful forearms. "Babe, I love you."

"Please, do it. Please." Caroline lifted her hips beseechingly.

Then Bri lowered her head and stroked the slick folds with her tongue, holding tightly as Caroline jerked at the first light touch. When she took the distended clitoris between her lips, Caroline's cries echoed the thundering of her own fierce passion. With her mouth, with her hands, with her lips, she paid homage to the love that had saved her sanity and shaped her life.

As Caroline climaxed, trembling and whimpering, Bri groaned with the answering surge between her own thighs. She rocked her pelvis against the sofa, the seam of her jeans riding over her clitoris. The faint pressure was more than enough to trigger her oversensitive nerve endings, and she came instantly, shuddering with the force of it. Her hoarse cries mingled with her lover's last soft moans.

"Bri? Honey?" Caroline questioned weakly, trailing her fingers over Bri's face. Bri's cheek was pressed to her stomach, and Caroline's hand came away wet. "Are you crying?"

"No," Bri lied.

Caroline sat up and leaned forward, her arms resting on Bri's broad shoulders. "Oh, baby. Yes, you are."

"It's nothing." Kneeling, encircled in Caroline's embrace, Bri looked away. "Don't worry."

"I don't think you've done that since the first time. Remember?"

Caroline's voice was gentle, and Bri thought of the warm summer nights in the dunes—innocently making love beneath the stars with the sounds of the surf in the background. "Yes," she said quietly. "I remember."

"What's wrong?"

"Nothing," Bri insisted again.

"You *have* to tell me." Caroline gave Bri a small shake. "Something hasn't been right for a long time. Ever since Christmas."

"I don't know how to explain."

Caroline's heart lurched. Suddenly, unimaginably, she was frightened of something that Bri might say. Her hands tightened on Bri's shoulders, and she lowered her face so that she could see her expression in the flickering candlelight. "Is there…another girl?"

"No! Jesus." Bri put her palms on either side of Caroline's face and kissed her swiftly. "Never."

"Then what?"

"I want to quit school."

"In the middle of the school year?" Caroline jerked back. "Why?"

"I don't know…college, it's just not for me." She didn't know quite how to tell Caroline that she'd never really been happy in Manhattan. Caroline loved it there, loved the excitement of being with other artists like herself. But Bri felt lost, out of place, far from the wild seas and barren shores of Cape Cod. Just walking the beach in Herring Cove settled her restlessness. And being in school, pursuing a degree that every day seemed less and less to represent what she wanted out of life, was making her miserable. She just wanted to be a small-town cop, like Reese. "I don't need to spend four years studying to do what I want to do."

"I know you want to be a sheriff, but I thought you said college would give you more opportunities later." Caroline was trying not to sound scared, but she was.

"I've changed my mind."

"But why quit *now*?"

"Because I don't want to be here next year while you're in France." She hadn't wanted to say that. But it was the truth.

"Oh." The sound was small, surprised.

Neither of them said anything for long moments, until finally Bri got to her feet and moved as far away as the small room would allow. She leaned against the doorway that joined the kitchen and the living room and pushed her hands into the back pockets of her jeans.

"I won't go then," Caroline said quietly as she hastily rearranged her clothing. Brushing a hand through her disheveled hair, she smiled tremulously. "Why didn't you tell me before?"

"Because I *want* you to go," Bri said forcefully. "*You* want to go. Fuck…you *should* go."

Bri turned and walked into the kitchen, then jerked open the small refrigerator door and pulled out a bottle of beer. Viciously, she twisted off the top and threw it into the trash. She turned to find Caroline framed in the doorway, staring at her with wounded eyes. "I can't go with you, Carre. You know that."

"What would you do?"

Bri looked away.

"Bri?"

"I applied to the sheriff's department training academy on the Cape. If I start with the next incoming class, I'll graduate in time to work this summer."

"When does that start?"

Bri hesitated. "In a few weeks."

"You're going to move back home?"

"Yeah."

Caroline couldn't hide her shock. She felt as if she had just plummeted into another world. They had barely spent a day apart since they were sixteen years old. From the minute she'd had awareness of her own sexual longings, those desires had been centered on Brianna Parker. She'd never imagined a life with anyone else, and she couldn't conceive of being away from Bri, even for a few weeks. She'd known that the year in Paris was going to be hard for them both, but she had hoped that somehow they would find a way to work it out. Now, it seemed that Bri had made other plans—plans that didn't include her at all.

"When did you apply?" Caroline's voice was eerily calm.

"Just before Christmas."

"You didn't tell me." It was a statement, not an accusation.

"I didn't want you to change your mind about Paris."

"Oh, Bri." Caroline hadn't meant to cry, but the tears came before she could stop them. She felt so sad, and so helpless to change events that already seemed to be moving too fast.

Stunned, Bri put the beer bottle on the counter and rapidly crossed the room. She pulled Caroline into her arms and buried her face in her hair. "I'm sorry. Please, don't cry."

"Can we talk about this tomorrow?" Caroline pressed hard against Bri's body, needing the solid reassurance of her presence.

"Sure. Anything you want." Bri kissed Caroline's forehead. "It will be okay, babe."

But somehow, they both knew that wasn't true.

❖

Less than two weeks later, Bri and Caroline stood together in the chill January wind on the sidewalk in front of their apartment building. Bri strapped her loaded saddlebags onto the back of her

Harley with methodical care. She wasn't taking much—extra jeans, a few books, her *gis*. And she was leaving *everything* behind. "You should go inside. It's freezing out here."

"I'm okay." Shivering, Caroline crossed her arms over her chest, but it wasn't the frigid air that chilled her. She was still having trouble believing that when she went to bed that night, she would be lying down alone and waking up without Bri beside her. "I don't care about Paris."

She'd said it before, a hundred times, a *thousand* times, in the last two weeks, trying to convince her stubborn lover that a year of studying in France didn't matter to her. But Bri wouldn't budge, insisting that Caroline shouldn't miss the opportunity, and Caroline didn't know what else to say. She couldn't beg her to stay in Manhattan, not when she'd finally realized how miserable Bri had been for months. Bri wanted to go home, wanted to get a job, and Caroline wanted to finish school.

"I know you want to do this sheriff thing now, and not two years from now. It's okay. I want you to do it, too, if that's really what—"

"Look, I'll come home when I can. And once school ends, you'll be moving back to the Cape for the summer. That's only four months." Bri's chest ached. The tears in Caroline's eyes were killing her.

"But if I stay here next year," Caroline continued hurriedly as if Bri hadn't spoken, "I'll be able to see you every other weekend or so. At least once a month."

"How? Take the train or the goddamn bus for six hours each way?" Bri yanked on her heavy riding gloves. "I don't know *when* we could afford a car."

"Still, it would be better than a whole yea—"

"We'll have this summer together. By the time you have to leave in the fall, we'll be used to the idea." Bri straddled the bike and tried to think of something that would take the hurt out of Caroline's eyes. *It's not just Paris. It's not just next year. Don't you know that? Your art is really good, babe. Everyone knows it. And this is your chance. You have to do whatever it takes, and it sure isn't going to be spending your life in Provincetown. If I stay here, I'm only going to hold you back.*

Caroline rushed across the sidewalk and threw her arms around Bri's leather-jacketed shoulders. She buried her face in Bri's neck, her words muffled against her lover's cold skin. "I love you. I don't want us to be apart."

"Oh, babe." Bri wrapped the smaller woman in a bone-crushing embrace, pressing her face to the top of Caroline's head. Much more of this and she was going to crack. It felt like her chest was going to explode, it hurt so much. "We just have to do this. Promise me if you get the scholarship, you'll go."

"Bri," Caroline pleaded, her fists clutching the stiff leather.

"Promise."

Caroline nodded wordlessly as Bri brushed a kiss into her hair. "Go inside, Carre. I don't want you to watch me ride away."

"Call me when you get there?"

For one terrifying moment, Bri didn't think she could let her go. She had a horrible feeling that she would never hold her again. *Oh Jesus, what am I going to do without you?* Hoarsely, she managed a barely audible, "Sure."

Reluctantly, Caroline stepped away, her jade green eyes locked on Bri's midnight blue ones. She was crying now, but she didn't feel the tears freezing on her cheeks. "I'm not going to let you leave me."

"I'm not," Bri whispered, but she feared she might be lying to them both.

# CHAPTER THREE

## February, Provincetown, MA

Reese leaned on the railing of the postage-stamp-sized deck behind the Galleria, a relatively new two-story enclave of boutiques on Commercial Street in the middle of town, watching the fishing boats leave Provincetown Harbor for their morning run. The air smelled of seashells and jellyfish, and in the distance, the waves frothed against the breakwater, a huge rock barrier that prevented the ocean's wrath from pummeling the harbor shoreline. She'd looked on the scene hundreds of times since she had come to Provincetown almost three years before, searching for home. And she'd found it here by the timeless sea in the arms of a woman whose love had defined her destiny. Never had she imagined it was possible to feel so content.

A gruff voice from behind interrupted her reverie. "What are you doing working already?"

Reese turned, rested her hips against the rail, and nodded to her boss. "You're up awfully early, Chief."

"Don't call me Chief," he groused, handing her a steaming cup of coffee. "I saw the cruiser out front. It's another hour before the day shift starts."

"I took Tory to the airport for her 5:30 flight to Boston." Reese sipped the coffee and regarded him silently. He didn't look as if he'd been sleeping very well. The bags under his eyes were heavier, and his complexion had lost some of its healthy ruddy tone. "I figured I might as well do a run through town on my way in."

"Have you heard from my kid?"

"She called me two days ago. Gave me an update on the first few days of her training."

"Is it going okay?"

"So far. You know she never says much. I'm sure she'll do fine."

"You know, she didn't tell them she was my daughter when she applied." He snorted. "I called the head training instructor up there, and he had no idea."

"You surprised?"

"Nah. You know how independent she's always been."

"Can't imagine where she gets it from."

He grumbled something unintelligible. Bri hadn't called *him*, but then, thinking back, he figured that was pretty much his fault.

*He pulled the cruiser into his driveway and stared at the big black Harley parked in front of his garage.* What the hell?

*She was in the kitchen, perched on a stool with a glass of orange juice and half a hoagie splayed on a paper wrapper in front of her. Same jeans, same boots, same slicked-back black hair. Same hoodlum jacket, too. Christ, he was glad to see her.*

*"Bri?"*

*"Hey, Dad."*

*He tossed an arm around her shoulder and squeezed, brushing his cheek quickly across the top of her head. She seemed thinner, harder, and there was a look in her eyes that he hadn't seen in a long, long time. A lost look. His heart turned over, and his stomach started burning.*

*"It's Wednesday. What are you doing here?"*

*She shrugged.*

*He shed his parka to the back of a chair and walked to the refrigerator. He rummaged around, found a beer, and popped the top. Then he leaned on the counter and stared at his only child.*

*"You okay?"*

*"Yeah." It came out a bit strangled, and she cleared her throat. "Yeah. Fine."*

*"Caroline with you?"*

*Bri shook her head.*

*Sipping the beer he couldn't even taste, his mind raced.*

If she needs money, she probably would have called. Of course, she never asks for money. Hardly ever asks for anything. Couldn't be trouble with Caroline's old man. That asshole is long out of the picture—the guy hasn't had anything to do with the kids since he slapped Caroline around for being involved with Bri and then tossed her out of the house. Trouble with the law? Nah—not my kid. So, if it isn't money or—

*The burning in his gut climbed into his chest. "Are you sick?"*

*"What?" Bri stared at him. "No."*

*"Then what the hell are you doing here in the middle of the week in the middle of school?" He might have asked a little loudly, but she'd scared the crap out of him.*

"I quit."

Nelson's mouth dropped open. "Are you nuts?"

She shrugged again.

"Does Caroline know?" Caroline was the only one who'd ever been able to handle his headstrong daughter. She'd never let Bri do anything crazy. "Where is she?"

"In Manhattan."

*"Did she quit, too?"*

*"No." Bri's voice was tight again. "I moved out."*

Okay, relax. Try to get the facts. Don't yell at her. *He crushed the beer can without even realizing it. "Jesus H. Christ, Brianna! What in hell are you thinking?"*

*She got up fast and headed toward the back door.*

*"Bri, wait! Jesus…just…wait, okay?"*

Her hand was on the doorknob, but Bri didn't open the door. With her back to him, she said, "I'm starting at the Sheriff's Department Training Academy on Monday."

*"Just like that?" he asked as quietly as he could, which wasn't very. "You just walk away from school? Did you walk away from Car—"*

*But he was talking to himself by then, and all he could hear by the time he made it to the door was the thudding of his heart and the roar of her motorcycle fading into the night.*

Nelson cleared his throat. "She, uh…say where she was staying?"

"Chief," Reese said quietly, "I'm kind of in a bind here. Like I said, she didn't say much."

"And if she did, you wouldn't tell me?" he snapped.

Unconsciously, Reese squared her shoulders. "No, sir. Probably not."

His eyes blazed for an instant, and he stiffened. "Oh, for Christ's sake, Conlon. Lose the 'sir' bullshit."

Reese said nothing, but his display of temper surprised her. The only time she could ever remember him being out of control was the night that Bri had been assaulted. And then, realizing that, everything made sense. *He's scared for her.*

Taking a deep breath, Reese relaxed her shoulders. "She told me she was sharing a place with a couple of other cadets in Barnstable. It sounds like she's okay."

"Okay," he muttered, looking beyond Reese to the harbor. "How in hell can she be *okay*?"

"She's got a plan, Nelson. She got herself into the academy. It's not like she's doing anything wrong."

"It doesn't make sense. To leave school? Jesus, to leave *Caroline*?" He met Reese's eyes, and his were filled with uncertainty. "You haven't seen her. She's got that look in her eyes like she had before Caroline settled her down. Like there was something broken inside of her."

"You need to call her, then. Talk to her."

"Yeah, I did great with that last time." He stuffed his hands into his pants pockets. "Jesus, why is it so hard to talk to your own kid?"

"Probably because she means so much to you."

After all this time, his second in command still surprised him. She was usually so quiet, revealing almost nothing about herself, that he often got to thinking of her as just another one of his men. She was bigger than most of the guys, absolutely a lot more fit, and probably the bravest. She'd give her life for any one of them without a second's hesitation. Every man on the force was proud to work with her.

But she *wasn't* one of the men, despite displaying so many of those traits that allowed him to be comfortable with her in a way that he might be with another man; she was a woman. And every now and then, when she'd say something that a man would never say to him, he realized it. "I think about her being hurt, you know? And it makes me want to...break things." *And cry at the same time.* He looked away, embarrassed by the admission.

Reese thought about Tory being harmed. The pain was so intense, it actually made her feel ill. "Yeah, I know."

"You'll probably know a lot better when you have a kid of your own," Nelson said gruffly.

"Probably." Reese grinned.

Sighing, Nelson joined her at the rail, close beside her but still not quite touching. Together they faced the sea, and at length he asked, "How is that...situation...going?"

"No word yet." Reese wasn't totally comfortable talking about the baby thing—not because of embarrassment but due to a lingering superstition. She just didn't want anything to go wrong. She and Tory hadn't talked about it explicitly, but she knew that Tory wasn't exactly the ideal age to be getting pregnant. But Tory said it was safe. *Promised* it was safe. "Sometimes, Tory says, you have to try more than once."

"Huh. Doesn't sound a whole lot different," Nelson acknowledged, purposely not looking at Reese. "Everybody thinks it's easy the...you know, the...regular way. But it isn't...not all the time."

She waited.

"Brianna...it was a long time before her. We'd kind of given up." His voice had gotten rougher, and he cleared his throat. "She was like a present, when she came along."

"I can imagine that she was," Reese said softly. "It's kind of terrifying, isn't it?"

"Damn right, it is." Nelson laughed. "And you haven't even gotten started yet."

"Look," Reese offered, imagining his worry. "I'll give Bri a call."

"Okay. Yeah. Thanks. You don't need to say I was asking."

"Nope, I won't. I figure the two of you will get tired of out-stubborning each other sooner or later, and then you can talk to her yourself."

He grumbled, but a small smile almost broke through before he stifled it.

"Well, I've got to get to work, Chief." She clapped him on the shoulder and then tapped the brim of her cap. "I'm gonna take a ride through town before I hit the office."

"Sure." He watched her walk away and silently counted himself lucky that she was part of his daughter's life.

❖

The rest of the day passed uneventfully, and at just after seven p.m., Reese stood outside the tiny airport watching the sky. The wind had picked up, and the day that had begun with a teasing breath of spring had turned cold again. Just a reminder that nothing was predictable on the Cape. In the distance, she could make out the faint drone of an airplane. Smiling, she searched the black canvas overhead that was the night sky until she could distinguish the lights of the approaching craft from the stars.

Five minutes later, the twin-engine twelve-seater taxied to a stop a hundred feet away. Six people disembarked, one of them Victoria King. Reese walked out to meet her.

"How you doing?" Reese took Tory's hand and leaned over to give her a quick kiss on the cheek.

"I'm fine," Tory said with a smile. "How was your day?"

"Not bad. Let me take your briefcase."

Tory laughed. "I've got it. How about taking me out to dinner, though?"

"Sure." Reese held open the door to the one-room terminal. "Anyplace special?"

"You pick." Tory threaded her arm through Reese's as they crossed the nearly empty waiting area.

"Lorraine's is open. Feel like Mexican?" Once outside in the tiny parking lot, Reese opened the passenger door of her Blazer and waited while Tory climbed in.

"Perfect."

Fifteen minutes later, they were settled in a booth in one of the few restaurants that was open year-round, perusing menus that they knew practically by heart. After they had ordered, Reese reached across the table and took Tory's hand.

"You had a long day. Was it busy?"

"The usual," Tory replied. "Mostly walk-ins interspersed with the occasional acute medical condition—chest pain, asthma attacks, uncontrolled diabetes. There was a gunshot wound in the middle of the afternoon that kept us jumping for a while."

"How much longer do you plan to work three days a week over there?" Reese leaned back to allow the waitress to set the appetizers in front of them.

"I had planned on another few months." Having heard the concern in the deep voice, Tory studied Reese across the candlelit table. "Why?"

Reese shrugged. "It's a pretty hectic schedule."

"Well, actually, I'm going to tell them I want to cut back to half-shifts in the ER starting in March."

"Really?" Although the news was welcome, Reese was surprised. Nothing in her memory had ever prompted Tory to cut back on her work schedule, even when Reese urged her to do it. "How come?"

Reaching for a nacho, Tory said, "There's a lot of work to be done at my clinic before the season starts. I need to inventory the supplies, set up schedules for the employees, and I still have to arrange interviews with a couple of physicians for the interim position."

"Makes sense," Reese said with a wave of relief. She tried hard not to interfere with Tory's work, but she couldn't help but worry about Tory's demanding schedule.

"Besides," Tory added casually, "I'm pregnant."

Reese dropped her fork. "Holy God!"

"Wendy confirmed it this afternoon." Tory grinned. "We did it, honey."

In the next instant, Reese was on her feet and moving around the side of the table. She took Tory's face in both hands and kissed her thoroughly. Then, unmindful of the few patrons who watched and the waitress standing a few feet away with loaded plates balanced on one arm, she knelt on the floor by Tory's side and took both Tory's hands in hers.

"You know my heart is yours," she said softly, running her finger over the scrolled gold band on Tory's left hand. She wore one to match. "But I want everyone else to know how very much I love you. Will you marry me?"

"A wedding?"

"Yes."

"In town—at the meeting house?" Tory, too, forgot they had an audience.

"Yes, there or anywhere you want."

"Oh, sweetheart, I would be so happy to." Tory's eyes welled with tears as she stared into the deep blue ones gazing at her with open devotion. As she leaned over to kiss her kneeling partner, she heard the muted sound of clapping, and thought, not for the first time, how blessed she had been the day Reese walked into her life.

❖

Reese couldn't remember a thing about the rest of the meal or the drive home. It was just after ten when they started a fire in the bedroom fireplace and settled under the covers. She turned on her side, her head on the pillow a few inches from Tory's, and whispered, "It's going to take me a while to believe it."

"Are you okay with it?" Tory hoped her trepidation didn't show in her voice. Despite the weeks they had spent talking and planning, she knew that oftentimes the reality threw couples into turmoil.

"Oh, yeah." Reese caressed Tory's cheek with her fingertips, her throat so tight she could hardly swallow. "I'm so high, I feel like I'm flying."

Tory ran her fingers through Reese's hair and moved closer, until their bodies touched all along their lengths. "You never let me down, you know?"

"I'll try not to, ever," Reese murmured. She stroked her palm over Tory's shoulder and down her arm to her hand, squeezing her fingers briefly. Then, she rested her hand on the arch of her lover's hip, making slow, gentle circles with her fingertips. "I love you, Tor."

"Mmm." Tory leaned nearer still and brushed her lips over Reese's. "Me, too." She enjoyed the gentleness of her lover's mouth as her fingers played over the hard muscles of Reese's chest and shoulders. Reese was such a wonderful contradiction of strength and secret softness, and touching her never failed to stir Tory's desire. Tonight, she wanted, needed, to be as close to her as possible. When she felt Reese's tongue slide smoothly across her own, she moaned. She edged her thigh between Reese's legs, her stomach clenching briefly as the smooth, warm skin pressed to her own heated center. She knew she was wet, and she rocked her hips gently to increase the contact against her exquisitely sensitive nerve endings. "Can you feel me?"

"Oh, yes," Reese gasped, her voice a register lower than normal.

"God, I could come doing this."

"Go ahead." Reese slid a hand between their bodies and cupped Tory's breast, finding the nipple and squeezing gently to the cadence of her lover's surging hips. "I love it when you do that."

"Maybe later," Tory managed, struggling not to lose control. "I want *you* to make me come the first time."

Reese groaned and pressed her forehead to Tory's. The throaty sound of Tory's need sent a pulse of excitement streaking through her depths. Her clitoris twitched madly in response. "Jesus."

Tory's only response was a faint whimper as she caught the fingers sweetly torturing her breast and drew Reese's hand down along her stomach toward the space between her legs. When Reese gently brushed the damp curls at the base of her belly, she arched her back and pressed against Reese's palm. And when fingers gently fondled the stiff bundle of nerves, she moaned, "Oh, honey…that's so nice."

"You're so beautiful." Reese moved her lips along the edge of Tory's jaw. Tory's neck was arched, exposing her throat, and a pulse beat wildly at the base. Reese pressed her lips to that point, marveling at the thrill of life and passion beneath the skin. Her own heart beat furiously, her stomach tight with wonder, as she slowly massaged Tory's clitoris.

When Tory couldn't stand the pleasure any longer, she grasped Reese's wrist and pressed her lover's hand further between her legs. "I'm…going to come. I want you…inside."

"Tory, love," Reese gasped. "Is it…okay?"

Whimpering, beginning to crest, Tory didn't answer but guided her lover where she needed her. Before Reese was fully inside of her, Tory's muscles clenched forcefully, and she climaxed. She clutched Reese's shoulders, growing rigid with the first forceful contraction, and then shuddered with each wave of aftershock.

Reese closed her eyes, forgetting to breathe as Tory trembled in her arms. They must have drifted together in the twilight of passion, because the fire had nearly burned down when Reese opened her eyes again. Tory's cheek was pressed to her breast, and her fingers were still between Tory's thighs. Carefully, she withdrew.

"That was wonderful," Tory mumbled.

"Yeah, it was." Reese kissed the top of Tory's head. "Are you warm enough?"

"Mm-hmm."

"I should set the alarm."

Tory tilted her head and kissed the tip of Reese's chin. "In a minute. How're you doing?"

"Great."

"Just great?" Tory ran a finger down the center of Reese's belly and didn't stop until she found the answer to her question.

"Jesus, Tor." Reese stiffened as if she had been electrified and jerked as Tory flicked her finger teasingly against the base of her clitoris. "Do that a few more times and I'll…oh…"

"I know exactly what you'll do," Tory said with a satisfied smile, never letting up on the steady rhythm. "And…I…know… exactly…when."

Reese's hips pumped once, hard, and she shouted as the orgasm crashed through her. Distantly, she heard Tory's joyful laughter.

"Are you sure," Reese asked breathlessly as the last surge of pleasure rolled through her, "that this is okay?"

"Okay?" Tory vaguely remembered that Reese had asked something similar sometime earlier. "Why wouldn't it be?"

"You know," Reese said weakly, trying to gather her wits when her brain had just been turned to mush. "The baby."

"The baby?" Tory leaned on one elbow and stared at her lover. "What about…oh! *Sex* and the baby."

"Yeah."

"Sweetheart, I don't think it would be very good for the baby if I lost my mind while pregnant." Tory kissed her slightly befuddled lover soundly on the mouth. "Which is exactly what would happen if we stopped making love. Don't worry; this is just what the doctor ordered."

"Oh, good," Reese murmured as she wrapped her arms around Tory and closed her eyes.

❖

Reese was awakened what seemed like five minutes later by an insistent pounding on the front door. Jed, fast asleep at the foot of their bed, snored peacefully. She rolled over and peered at the bedside clock. 5:43 a.m.

"Holy hell," she muttered under her breath, trying to ease out of bed without awakening Tory. It was unusual for the doctor not to awaken at the first sound of the phone or the prospect of someone being at the door. *She must be beat.*

"Reese?" Tory mumbled as she stretched out her hand and found the vacant space where Reese had just been. Instantly alert, she sat up, holding the sheet against her body with one arm. "Honey, what is it?"

"Don't know." Reese hurriedly pulled on a pair of jeans and searched a nearby chair for a T-shirt. As she pulled one over her head, she added, "I'll go check. You don't need to get up, love."

Turning on lights as she passed through the living room, Reese reached the front door and looked through the beveled glass window to the front porch. There was just enough light to make out the features of the two people peering back at her. She pulled the door open hastily. "Mom? Jean?"

Kate Mahoney and her lover, Jean Purdy, swept past Reese and into the living room. Kate made a beeline for Tory, who was just coming down the stairs from the second floor wearing one of Reese's uniform shirts and a baggy pair of sweatpants. She'd also slipped on her ankle brace and wore scuffed slippers on her feet.

"Is everything okay?" Tory stopped on the bottom step and reached for the banister, trying to ignore a faint wave of nausea. *Oh, no. This can't be starting yet.*

"Is it true?" Kate asked excitedly.

"Uh…" Reese muttered as she followed the procession toward her startled lover. "It's not even six o'clock in the morning, Mom."

Never taking her eyes off Tory, Kate replied dismissively, "I wanted to catch you before you went to work. You two are always up this early."

"It's Sunday," Reese pointed out, although no one seemed to be listening.

"Honey," Jean, a compact, middle-aged woman with kindly eyes, said soothingly as she stepped up behind the tall, blue-eyed woman who bore a striking resemblance to Reese. "They just woke up. Maybe we should come back later."

"Well? Are we going to be grandmothers?" Kate demanded of Tory.

Reese made a choking sound as Tory's face broke into a wide smile.

"News certainly does travel quickly." Tory, feeling steadier now, walked toward Kate. "And the answer is, yes, you most definitely are."

Amidst the chaos of happy exclamations, Kate threw her arms around Tory, and Jean hugged Reese.

"How did you find out so soon?" Reese grinned as she extricated Tory from her mother's embrace. "*I* didn't even know until last night."

"Darling, when someone gets on her knees in the middle of a restaurant in Provincetown, people notice. Especially when it's a couple like you two, and *especially* when we've all been waiting for the happy news."

"I should have known," Reese grumbled, wondering if it had been the waitress or one of the diners who had spread the word. "Once Gladys finds out, she'll probably put out a state-wide bulletin."

Tory slipped her arm around Reese's waist and snuggled close to her. "I told you there would be no keeping it a secret, honey."

Reese kissed the top of Tory's head while her mother and Jean beamed. "Do you two want breakfast?"

"I've got an even better idea." Kate took Jean's hand. "You two go back to bed, and we'll bring you breakfast."

Reese paled. *Everyone is insane. Is this normal?*

"That's not necessary." Tory laughed. "But thank—"

"Of course, it's not necessary," Jean said quietly. "But you've made us so very happy. Now that we're here, it would make us even happier to do something for you."

"And then you can tell us just how you managed it." Kate had a devilish glint in her eye.

"*Mom,*" Reese said warningly.

Kate kissed her daughter swiftly on the cheek. "Never mind, Reese. I don't really want to know *all* the details."

"Don't tease her before coffee, Kate, please." With a laugh, Tory tugged Reese toward the stairs. "Come on, honey. They just made us an offer we can't refuse. Let's go back to bed."

Recognizing when she'd been outmaneuvered, Reese acquiesced good-naturedly. She climbed the stairs, an arm still around Tory's waist to provide support should Tory need it.

"Sorry about that," Reese whispered when they were back in bed. She propped her back against the pillows, drew Tory down against her side, and wrapped an arm around her shoulders.

"I don't mind." Tory rested her cheek against Reese's chest as she threaded one arm around her waist. "It was pretty endearing."

"I never realized my mother was so anxious for grandchildren." Reese rubbed her cheek against the top of Tory's head, breathing in the sweet, distinctive scent that always made her feel at home. "God, you feel good."

"Mmm, so do you." Tory felt the first stirring of desire, and then swiftly reminded herself that her in-laws were downstairs. "I hate to say this, but it will be nice to have babysitters in the immediate area."

"Now there's an advantage I hadn't considered. Good thing they decided to stay up here year round." Reese laughed, running her hand gently up and down Tory's back. "I guess I can forgive them for dragging us out of bed."

"Honey," Tory said contemplatively. "What are you going to tell your father?" As she expected, Reese stiffened. Tory ran her palm softly back and forth over Reese's chest. "I'm not rushing you, sweetheart. It's completely up to you."

"The general has managed to deal with the fact that I'm a lesbian by ignoring it," Reese said quietly. "I've let him, because my relationship with him has always been more military than familial. I guess I've probably let him, too, because I haven't wanted to be coerced into resigning my commission."

"I know how much the Corps means to you." Tory took a deep breath. "Is the baby going to be a problem?"

"No, never," Reese said quickly, tightening her arms around her lover. "I only meant that if I force him to acknowledge our relationship, he might invoke regulations."

"The 'don't ask, don't tell' thing?"

"Yes."

"Oh, honey. I'm sorry."

"You have nothing to be sorry for." Reese put two fingers beneath Tory's chin and gently tilted her face up until their eyes met. "You've made me happier than I ever imagined I could be. Now, with the baby coming, life is even more wonderful. You and this child are the only things that matter to me."

"But the Mari—"

"I gave most of my life to the Marine Corps. Now, I'm just yours."

"Oh, sweetheart." Tory shifted until she was lying in Reese's arms, facing her. She brought her mouth close to Reese's, holding her gaze. "I love you."

As often happened when the depth of their love, at once comforting and wild, rose up to confront them, the rest of the world receded. Reese was about to bestow a kiss when a knock sounded on the door. One of them groaned.

"I was just getting started," Reese whispered.

"Mmm. So was I." Tory kissed her quickly, then rolled away. "Look out when you get home tonight, Sheriff."

Laughing, Reese took her hand. "Come on in, Grandmoms."

❖

"So, Sheriff," a gravelly voice said. "There're some rumors going around town about you."

Reese pushed out the seated bench press bar, counted off another rep under her breath, and glanced at the iron-gray-haired woman beside her. The owner of the gym, a sturdy fiftyish woman whose tanned and finely lined skin spoke of a lifetime of sun and wind, grinned at her. "Oh, yeah?"

"Yep." Marge Price handed Reese a towel. "I've had it from several reliable sources that you've gone and gotten our very own Dr. King with child."

It was Reese's turn to grin. "Well, that would be a loose interpretation of the facts."

As Reese rose from the bench and stretched, Marge looked her over with an appreciative expression. "So it's true, huh?"

"Yes," Reese said with just a touch of wonder. "It's true."

"Well, I'll be damned." Marge clapped Reese on the shoulder and smiled broadly. "It seems like yesterday I was trying to figure out whether you were gay or not, and now you're starting a family."

"It'll be three years in just a few months," Reese pointed out as she picked up a pair of twenty-five-pound dumbbells. She began her biceps curls. "But sometimes it feels like only a few days."

"I'm really tickled for you both. In fact, everyone is. You know, in a town this small, something like this is quite an event."

"Great." Reese tried to hide her discomfort. Somehow, the idea of the entire town being privy to something so personal made her uneasy. She had barely gotten used to the idea herself.

"What?" Marge tilted her head and squinted at Reese.

"Nothing."

"Bullshit. What's bothering you, Sheriff?"

"It's just that this is personal." Reese racked the dumbbells, picked up a curl bar, and began doing upright rows. "Our having the baby, I mean."

Marge laughed. "It might be personal, but it sure isn't going to be private. Everyone knows Victoria King. At sometime or other, Tory has taken care of almost everyone in this town. She's a special person."

"I know," Reese said proudly.

"And so are you."

"Yeah, well…"

"Don't pretend you don't know how important you are to folks around here." Marge handed her a plastic bottle of water. "You make this place a safe place to live, and that means a lot."

Reese blushed. "I'm just—"

"Yeah, yeah. I know. You're just doing your job." Marge shook her head. "Jesus. Still the Boy Scout."

"Well, maybe," Reese said with a small shake of her head. "But I don't exactly feel prepared for what's happening."

They were alone in the gym, and Marge settled on a flat weight bench across from Reese, who was now doing forearm curls. "You mean the baby?"

"Yes."

"Well, Tory's a doctor. She should pretty much know how to take care of things."

Reese shook her head as she set the weights aside. She ran the towel briskly over her wet hair and then crumpled it in her fists, resting her elbows on her spread knees. Meeting Marge's eyes, she said quietly, "I mean about taking care of Tory."

"While she's pregnant, you mean?"

"Right." Reese nodded solemnly. "I don't know anything about this. Remember, until a little while ago, I was a marine."

"Tory will tell you everything you need to know."

"No," Reese said with a small smile. "Tory will tell me whatever she thinks won't worry me."

"Cripes." Marge blew out an exasperated breath. "I've never known two people who spent as much time worrying about each other."

"Isn't that part of loving someone?" Reese looked confused.

It was said so innocently that Marge merely shook her head. "Yes, I suppose it is. So what are you worried about?"

"She's going to be almost six months pregnant when the season starts in May." Reese spoke softly and stared at the towel she was twisting between her fists. "You know how hard she works during the summer. I'm afraid…" She had to stop to clear her throat. "She can't work eighteen-hour days much longer."

"Have you talked to her about it?"

"Some. She's talking about hiring another doc to help out over the summer, but she keeps finding reasons not to interview anyone."

"I'm not surprised. She's a perfectionist." Marge brushed a strong hand through her short hair. "Listen. The most important thing for you to do is be there for her, no matter what she needs. I have two sisters, and believe me, I love them. On the other hand, being around them when they were pregnant wasn't always fun."

"I know things will be different," Reese said mildly. "I just wish I knew how."

"Well, you won't know until it happens. Just remember that Tory loves you and will be counting on you to be steady. You have to make sure her world doesn't tilt."

"That's a tall order," Reese said softly.

"And you're just the one to fill it."

## CHAPTER FOUR

### February, Barnstable, MA

It was after nine p.m. on Friday night, and the parking lot that separated the administrative buildings from the training facility at the sheriff's department main headquarters was almost empty. Reese parked her Blazer around the side of the gymnasium, where light filtered into the night through several windows set high up in the wall. Most of the building was dark. She reached over the seat into the back of her SUV and grabbed her gym bag, then exited the vehicle and walked to the building's side entrance. She slid her ID card through the lock sensor, and when it snicked open, she shouldered her way through. Immediately inside, a long corridor ran the length of the building, and she walked down the deserted hallway to the last door on the right.

There was only one person in a room the size of a basketball court.

"Hi, Bri." Reese hadn't heard from the younger woman in three weeks. Nelson hadn't heard from her at all. Finally, Reese had called her, and they'd agreed to get together.

Bri turned away from the hanging bag that she had been lightly punching to loosen up her arms. None of her relief at seeing Reese showed in her face. "Hey."

"How are things going?" Reese asked as she stripped off her windbreaker. She pulled her black canvas drawstring pants from her bag and tossed them on the bottom step of a short set of bleachers, then sat down to unlace her work boots. She removed them along with her socks, then stood and stepped out of her jeans in one fluid motion.

Bri looked away. Even though she'd seen Reese without clothes in the gym before, she wasn't entirely comfortable with the faint stir of arousal the sight of the well-built body produced. It was probably normal, but she didn't really have any way of knowing. There'd only ever been Caroline in her life. *Carre. Jesus, I miss you.*

*"I miss you, Bri." Caroline's voice was small and sad.*

*Bri's heart ached from hearing the hurt and knowing she had put it there. "I know, babe. Me, too." Her own voice was thick in her throat. She slid down the wall beneath the pay phone in a corner of the building that housed the classrooms, her stomach in knots. She'd had to call, even though she only had five minutes between classes. She was just so lonely. "How's school?"*

*"Okay. The same—you know."*

*"Your painting going okay?" Bri wondered when it had gotten so hard to talk to the woman who had been her lover and best friend for four years.*

*"Uh-huh."*

*"Have you heard anything about the scholarship?"*

*"Not yet." Caroline's voice trailed off, then came back strong. "So, are you working hard?"*

*"Yeah. I'm taking some classes with the night-school group. That way I can meet my minimum hours requirement faster."*

*"Can you come home this weekend?" The hopeful note in Caroline's voice was obvious.*

Home.

*"I can't, babe," Bri said softly. "I signed up for weapons training on Saturday mornings."*

*"Oh."*

*"I'm sorr—"*

*"No," Caroline said hastily. "That's okay. I knew you'd be busy."*

*"You'll be here Memorial Day, right?"*

*"That just seems so far away."*

Oh, fuck, don't cry. *Bri swallowed the lump in her throat.* "Do you need money...for the bus? I sent the rent check already."

*"No...I...Bri..." She was crying. "I have to go."*

*"I love you, babe,"* Bri whispered, *one hand fisted in her hair, her head down almost on her knees. "Please, don't cr—"*

*"Hey! Parker! You coming to class or not?"* a rough male voice demanded.

*"Yes, sir."* Bri jumped to her feet. *"I gotta go, babe. Carre?"*

*But the line was already dead.*

"Bri?"

"Sorry. What?" Bri blushed.

"The academy. Everything okay?" Reese tied her pants, shrugged into her *gi* jacket, and wrapped the gold embroidered black belt around her waist with practiced efficiency.

"Yeah, sure. Fine."

"Good."

Reese walked to the edge of the mat and bowed toward the spot where the *kamiza*, or ceremonial altar, would be if this were a true dojo. After she stepped onto the mat and knelt, as did Bri, they bowed to one another. Then, as they had done five or six days a week for the year and a half before Bri had left for college, they trained.

In Japanese, Reese would first announce the attack followed by the defense, and they would alternate each position. Otherwise, no words were exchanged as they kept their eyes focused on one another—circling, blocking, and eventually throwing each other to the mat. Once down, each executed wrist, elbow, and shoulder locks designed to immobilize or dislocate. At the end of an hour and a half, Reese called a halt, and they once again knelt and bowed. Then Reese led Bri to the edge of the mat where they bowed once more and stepped off.

"Thank you, *sensei*," Bri said quietly. Together they walked to the bleachers and began to remove and stow their uniforms.

"You've learned a lot since you've been gone," Reese remarked.

"As soon as I graduate from the academy, I'll be able to train regularly." Bri's voice was pitched low.

"I hope you don't mind, but I talked to Moriyama *sensei* about you resuming your training with me." At Bri's quick glance, she added with a grin, "After all, I was only *loaning* you to him while you were in New York."

Bri's eyes sparkled for the first time that evening. "Thanks."

"I don't see any reason why we can't keep you on schedule. You can either test for *shodan* in New York with Moriyama's class later this year, or you can test here with me."

"How would that work?"

"I'll bring in a test board. There are people I can call." Reese shrugged. "We don't need to decide that now. You've got enough things to worry about. First priority is getting through the academy with good scores so you can have a shot at picking your field training placement."

"I know. I'm busting my as...butt in class."

"Good. See that you keep it up."

"Yes, ma'am." When Bri realized that Reese would probably head back to Provincetown any minute, she was almost desperate. "Listen, we could shower here and then maybe go out for a drink. If you have time?"

Reese regarded the young woman intently. Bri's dark blue eyes were shadowed, and despite her formidable physique, she looked gaunt. "If you don't mind a little healthy sweat, I don't. I'm pretty hungry. Let's skip a shower. Any place near there we can grab a bite?"

Bri's grateful smile tugged at Reese's heart, but she resisted the urge to throw an arm around the younger woman's shoulder and hug her. There was a brittle look in Bri's eyes that suggested she was just hanging on to the last remnants of control. A lifetime in the Marine Corps had taught Reese that sometimes comfort could break a person. "What do you say?"

"Yeah," Bri replied eagerly. "There's a tavern out on 6A about ten minutes from here."

"Let's go, then," Reese said briskly. "And Bri?"

"Yeah?"

"Soda for you in the bar."

Bri flushed. "Yes, ma'am. Absolutely."

Nine minutes later, they made their way to a booth at the back of a beer joint that was packed with locals and academy trainees. A few guys and several women called to Bri in friendly welcome as she and Reese squeezed their way through the crowded bar toward the few open spots at the far end of the room. If Reese wasn't mistaken, at least one of the young women eyed Bri with an appreciative glance that was definitely more than friendly. If Bri noticed the interested appraisal, she gave no sign of it.

Once seated, Bri gave her order to a young woman in tight blue jeans and an even tighter T-shirt that showed off perky breasts, who appeared with a pad and pencil at the ready. "Hamburger, fries, and a root beer."

"Make that two," Reese added. "Along with whatever beer you have on tap."

"I'm really glad you came," Bri said shyly. It was still difficult for her to relate to the woman who had been her teacher first as simply a friend now. That's what Reese had become to not only Bri and Caroline during their senior year in high school but also several of the town's other gay youths.

They'd all started out spending time together as students at Reese's dojo, which had been in Reese's converted garage before Reese had sold her house and moved into Tory's home just on the outskirts of Provincetown. After that, Reese had rented a building on the east end of Bradford that had once been a seafood shanty. Now, it was the Provincetown Martial Arts Center—P-MAC to its students, who ranged in number from three to eight depending on the time of year. Reese and Tory, who trained and taught there as well, had become friends and role models to the often marginalized teenagers.

"That's okay. I wanted to see you." Reese took the mug of beer that the waitress offered. "Find out how you were doing."

Bri sipped her soda. "The academy's not that bad. There's a lot of material to be covered in a short time, but most of it is just common sense."

"You shouldn't have any trouble with the physical aspects of the training."

"Not so far." Bri couldn't hide a satisfied grin. "A lot of the guys think that the women can't handle themselves in that area, you know?"

"I've seen a bit of that in the military and in the sheriff's department," Reese said mildly. Their food arrived, and she took a minute to add ketchup to her burger. "Did you straighten them out on that point?"

"Let's just say there're a couple of guys in my class walking around with sore shoulders."

"Good. You can handle yourself. Don't be afraid to show it."

Bri nodded, feeling almost happy for the first time since she'd left Caroline. "No problem."

"It'll be good to have you back in the dojo," Reese remarked. "Once you're through the academy, we'll need to talk about you teaching one of the junior classes."

"Yeah, I'd like that. Isn't Tory teaching a class in self-defense now?"

"Yes. But I don't know how much longer she'll be teaching."

"Why?" Bri's expression was suddenly serious. "Is there something wrong?"

"Nope." Reese couldn't keep from smiling. "She's pregnant."

Bri's hand stopped halfway to her mouth, the hamburger forgotten. Her blue eyes grew so round they looked almost black. "No fucking way," she said in a reverent whisper.

"It's true."

"Wow."

"Yes," Reese confided. "That's exactly how I feel, too."

"Does my dad know?"

"Sure. I told him right away. We've known for a couple of weeks."

"What did he say?" Bri knew he tried hard to understand about her and Caroline, and he had been there for them when they hadn't had anywhere else to turn. Still, she could tell when she talked to him that he didn't really get it. Sometimes, she thought that he didn't really take them seriously. As if being young meant you couldn't really be in love.

"I think he said something along the lines of what you just did," Reese replied with a laugh. "He seems fine with it."

"Good."

"You might want to give him a call sometime, Bri." Reese pushed away the remnants of her meal.

Bri stiffened reflexively, but when she looked at Reese, she saw only the familiar, steady gaze. Reese had always been straight with her and had always treated her like an adult. Reese was everything she admired. "Yeah, I know."

Reese nodded, waiting.

"I knew he was going to be pissed about me leaving school. I just didn't want to get into it again with him."

"He won't understand unless you explain it to him."

"I don't know what to say," Bri said softly, the pain that was always stuck in the center of her chest rising up to choke her. Her hands trembled, and she put them quickly underneath the table so that Reese wouldn't see it. *I don't understand it all myself. Just that I had to leave.*

"Why don't you try practicing first with me," Reese suggested easily.

Bri fisted her hands and stared at the tabletop. "I always wanted to be a cop."

"I know." Reese remembered the day Bri had shyly confided the fact to her after one of their classes. "But what made you leave school now?"

"I…it wasn't working out."

"School?" Reese was surprised. Nelson had said Bri was doing well, and she knew that Bri was more than capable of handling the course load.

"Yeah. Look," Bri said hastily, afraid that if she continued everything might come pouring out. "I just got tired of talking about the law. I wanted to start *doing* something about it."

"Fair enough. When the pressure around here lets up a little bit, maybe you can tell your dad that. That sounds like something Nelson could understand."

"Okay. Sure."

They counted out cash to cover the check and the tip and then wended their way back through the crowd toward the door. Outside, they walked briskly in companionable silence back to the training center where Reese had left her SUV.

"Things will get busy at home pretty soon preparing for the season," Reese said, leaning one shoulder against the driver's door of the black Blazer. "With Tory…you know, being pregnant…I don't know when I'll be able to get back this way again."

Bri's stomach lurched, but she kept her expression blank.

"Call me." Reese clapped Bri on the shoulder. "Come for a visit whenever you can, and we'll train. Okay?"

"Thanks, I will."

Reese studied Bri's face, trying to get a glimpse of what was happening inside her. All she could see were hints of her pain. The memory of the shadows in the younger woman's eyes haunted her all the way home.

❖

With a sinking sensation in the pit of her stomach, Bri watched the taillights of Reese's Blazer disappear into the night. Suddenly at loose ends, she shoved her hands into the pockets of her leather jacket and looked around the deserted parking lot. The options were few. She could go back inside the gym and work out until she felt tired enough to sleep, or she could head back down the road to the tavern and at least be in the company of other people. That might take her mind off the empty feeling that snaked through her body. Not wanting to think about that, she strode quickly to her cycle, swung one long leg over the low-slung tank, and fit her key to the ignition. Ignoring the helmet strapped to the rear, she kick-started the engine, slammed into gear, and tore off into the dark.

A few minutes later, she settled on a stool at one end of the still-crowded bar and ordered a club soda. She wasn't thinking about much of anything at all, just aimlessly turning the glass on the bar, wondering what Caroline was doing, when a soft female voice spoke very close to her ear.

"You're back awfully soon."

Bri swiveled on the seat and met the eyes of one of her academy classmates, a softly beautiful dark-haired young woman about her own age. They'd nodded to one another in class but had never engaged in conversation.

"There's not much to do around here on the weekend," Bri said noncommittally.

"You've got that right. Do you mind if I keep you company for a while?"

"No, suit yourself." Bri was oddly uncomfortable, and uncertain why. Maybe it was just that she wasn't used to casual conversations with strangers.

"I'm Allie Tremont." Her voice was faintly Southern-accented and a delicate hand reached out.

"Bri Parker." The handshake was surprisingly firm, Allie's skin smooth and warm.

"Uh-huh. I know," Allie replied. "Where are you from?"

"I'm a local. Provincetown. You?"

"South Carolina. Bet you can't tell, though."

"Uh…" Bri grinned. "A little."

"My mom got a job at Woods Hole Marine Biological Laboratory near Falmouth when I was a junior in high school. So I'm sorta local, too."

They both laughed. After a moment, Bri offered, "Can I get you a drink or something?"

"I'm okay with this one." Allie lifted her bottle of beer. "So what do you think of the academy so far?"

"It's about like I expected." In truth, Bri didn't pay much attention to her classmates. Her entire focus was on the material and what she needed to do to meet the academic and training requirements for graduation. Because many of the cadets had come from previous jobs and had diverse educational backgrounds, the training program was very flexible and allowed the trainees a great deal of independence when arranging their schedules. Bri had mapped out a course of study that would get her through in the shortest possible time.

"The guys don't seem to give you much trouble," Allie observed wryly.

"Are they bothering you?" Bri regarded her companion seriously and was surprised to notice how dark her eyes were, almost liquid. Then she realized she was staring and quickly studied her soda.

"Not really." The young woman's tone, however, lacked conviction.

"But someone *said* something to you?"

"Not exactly. Just the usual offhand remarks about women not being strong enough to handle a physical confrontation. That kind of crap."

"Hand-to-hand combat isn't about how big you are," Bri said intently. "Or how strong. It's about how you use the resources that you have."

"I heard that you're some kind of martial arts master."

"Hardly." Bri laughed to hide her embarrassment. Luckily, it was too dark for Allie to see her blush. "I've had some training, but I have a lot more to learn."

The young woman casually put her hand on Bri's wrist below the cuff of her jacket, then leaned closer to talk. "I saw you in the physical training section the other day. You knocked that big blond guy, Jacobs, on his ass like he was a feather."

"That's because the idiot rushed me. With that kind of move, they have so much forward momentum that if you simply sidestep and redirect, they'll go right over. It's totally a matter of using your own center of gravity against theirs."

"So, do you think you could work out with me sometime? Like a training partner, maybe?"

Bri glanced down at the fingers lightly curled around her forearm and was suddenly uncertain. She didn't have many friends; she never had. Just Caroline and a few of the kids who hung out at Reese's dojo. Most of the friends they'd made in Manhattan were Caroline's classmates from art school. She'd never wanted anyone else's company. Caroline was enough. The pang of loneliness that shot through Bri made her breath catch, and she looked away.

"I'd pay you back. I'm a pretty good cook."

"Sure…I guess so." Bri looked back and tried to smile. The fingers on her arm were warm. "I mean, I don't know that I can teach you anything that you won't get from the instructors. But, I guess that would be okay."

"Great." Allie gave her a winning smile. She didn't move her hand.

## CHAPTER FIVE

It was well after midnight when Reese pulled into the driveway beside her home. The house was dark, but Tory's Jeep was gone. Immediately, Reese reversed her vehicle and backed out onto the road, gravel spewing from beneath the SUV's tires. She headed west along the narrow strip of highway between Provincetown Harbor on the left and the outskirts of town on the right. Within a minute, she was heading down Bradford, and after another thirty seconds, she turned onto the side road that fronted the East End Health Clinic. The building was dark; the parking lot empty.

*Damn it. Where is she?*

Reese pulled over, extracted her cell phone from the glove compartment, and punched in the number to the sheriff's department. One of her officers answered. "Lyons, it's Conlon."

"Yo, Reese. What's up?"

"Is there any kind of medical emergency in town that you're aware of?" Her heart was thudding erratically, but nothing showed in her voice. *Maybe she's sick. Maybe something happened, and she couldn't reach me. Jesus, maybe—*

"There's a big two-car crash on Route 6 coming west from Pilgrim Heights. Smith called for the EMTs about forty minutes ago."

"Did anyone call Tory?"

"Don't know. Not from here, but maybe the squad did. They will, you know, if it's a messy one."

*I know. Everyone calls her when there's trouble.* "Thanks, Jeff."

Reese put the SUV into gear and sped toward the main highway that ran the length of Cape Cod. Five minutes later, she parked on the narrow shoulder behind a sheriff's cruiser, a fire truck, two EMS vans, and Tory's Jeep Cherokee. Emergency lights strobed wildly from the tops of all the vehicles, sending colored light beams streaking disjointedly across the blacktop and into the starless night sky. The sound of radio chatter crackling from open doors of vehicles and people shouting directions added to the chaotic atmosphere.

Hurriedly, Reese grabbed her Mag-Lite from the emergency kit in the rear of the Blazer and clipped her badge to her belt. Then she made her way around the road cones, stepped over the flares that crisscrossed the highway, and walked between the haphazardly parked cars and trucks toward the center of activity. There, she got a clear view of a minivan resting against the guardrail, its front end a crumpled mass of metal and shattered glass. Oil and other fluids pooled under the frame in glistening dark puddles. The street-side doors stood ajar, apparently having sprung from their hinges as a result of the collision or having been pried open with the hydraulic Jaws of Life. The other vehicle was nowhere in sight, and neither was Tory.

"Is Dr. King here?" Reese asked the first EMT she identified. The man was bent over a victim who was strapped to a stretcher. Reese couldn't tell through the blood on the patient's face if this one was a man or woman.

Without looking up, the technician said sharply, "She's down with the second car, I think."

Reese looked around and didn't see another vehicle. *Down? Down where?*

Following the skid marks on the highway, Reese reconstructed the accident in her mind. *One vehicle traveling east—doing sixty from the looks of it—crosses the median and slams the minivan head on. Poor bastards in that never had a chance. Guard rail stops the minivan, and the other vehicle veers off...fuck!...into the salt marsh.*

Stomach churning, she found the section of guardrail that had been breached and shone her light down the steep embankment. A trail of crushed reeds, pond grass, and scrub brush outlined the errant car's path. The vehicle itself lay upside down in the salt pond that ran alongside the highway. The front end was under water up to the windshield and steam billowed from the cracked engine. Emergency lights had been erected, and a clot of people milled around, maneuvering stretchers and assorted emergency equipment. One of the firefighters appeared to be attaching a towline to the back of the vehicle. No sign of Tory. Maybe the EMT was wrong, and she wasn't down there, after all.

Sliding, nearly falling, Reese made her way down the damp, muddy bank. *How in the hell could Tory get down here? I can't even stand up.*

"Smith!" Reese finally saw someone she recognized. She approached her officer as quickly as the treacherous footing would allow. "Where's Tory?"

"Reese, what are you doing here?" The young man gave her a heartfelt smile. Ever since she had been instrumental in saving his life during a shootout, he had been her staunchest supporter. "You don't need to be here, boss. We've got it pretty much under control. There's just one more victim to extricate. The rest have been transported already."

Reese clamped down on her anger, because she knew he had no idea the terror she was feeling. Very succinctly, she repeated, "Where is Dr. King?"

"Oh, she's in the car."

"How long?" The words snapped like live wires.

"Huh? Oh...I dunno. Twenty minutes maybe?"

"Son of a bitch," she shot out to no one in particular. She pushed her way past him and through the firefighters and EMTs crowding around the capsized vehicle.

*That water has got to be freezing. Jesus, God, she needs to get out of there.*

Ignoring the biting cold as she slogged through icy water up to her mid-calves, Reese bent down to peer through the shattered driver's side window. Tory was crouched over in the front seat compartment of the Cadillac, her emergency medical kit open beside her and a battery-powered hazard light hanging from a loose piece of metal on what was once the vehicle's floor. She appeared to be working on someone who was obscured from Reese's vision by a tangle of electrical wires and engine parts. "Dr. King? Problem?"

"Reese?" Tory could barely move in the compressed space of what had once been the big luxury car's passenger area. She didn't know how long she'd been there, but it felt like forever. Turning her head as much as possible, she spared her lover a quick glance before turning back to her task. "The driver has a crushed larynx. The EMTs couldn't ventilate him so I had to trach him in here. Just got an airway."

"What's his condition?"

"Unconscious and critical. I'm bagging him by hand, but there's a lot of resistance. He must have at least one lung down." Her teeth were chattering, and it was difficult to talk. "I can't tell what his oxygenation status is. Too damn dark in here to read a pulse oximeter, even if I had one."

"Can one of the EMTs take your place?" Reese couldn't see Tory's face clearly, but she could hear the strain in her voice. Just seeing her in there made Reese's guts churn. "Tor?"

"He's too unstable. I can't trust this tube not to come out, either," Tory replied distractedly. "Tell the fire captain he can winch whenever he's ready."

"No way. Not with you in there," Reese said adamantly. "That's a twenty percent incline up to the road. This car's going to twist all over the place when they start pulling it up."

"No choice. This guy doesn't have much time."

Reese turned and shouted, "Get the fire captain down here!"

A minute later, a fifty-year-old man—average height, solid and sturdy—tramped through the marsh toward Reese. "Sheriff Conlon. I didn't see you before."

"Peterson. Just got here." Reese was brusque. "What's the status on this vehicle extrication?"

"We're just about ready. We've been waiting for the doctor to give us the go-ahead."

"What about the structural integrity of the car? Dr. King says she needs to stay inside with the victim while you haul this thing out of here."

"Well, it'll be one helluva bumpy ride, but they made those old Caddies to stand up to almost anything." He shrugged. "She'll get knocked around some. Probably get a few bruises, but the frame will hold."

"Give me a minute. Do *not* move this vehicle until I give the word."

He hesitated, but there must have been something in the tone of her voice that convinced him. "Okay, but make it fast. We need to get this scene cleared up."

Reese bent over to look inside again. "Tory," she said in a voice too low for anyone else to hear. "You can't stay in there during the extrication. It's going to be rough. *Too* rough…especially for you now."

"I'll brace myself. I'll be okay." Tory took a long shuddering breath, and then admitted what she hadn't wanted Reese to know. "There's a lot of water in here, and I'm getting really cold. So is my patient. Get us out of here, Sheriff."

Rapidly, Reese assessed what she knew of the situation. More importantly, she considered what she knew of her lover. There was no way she was going to get Tory to climb out of that car if her patient was in danger. Which left only one solution.

"Two minutes!" Reese yelled back over her shoulder as she grabbed the top edge of the vehicle, which was in actuality part of the undercarriage in its now upside-down position, and levered her legs through the open window.

"Reese, what in God's name are you doing?"

"I'm going to give you a cushion, Doctor." Reese twisted her larger frame back and forth until she had one leg on either side of Tory's body.

Now that she was inside, Reese could make out the driver's legs underneath the steering column and his head jammed under the dashboard on the passenger side. Tory was holding the tracheostomy tube in place with one hand and squeezing a portable oxygen bag with the other.

"There isn't enough room," Tory protested.

"That's the point." Reese grunted as she wedged herself into the corner formed by the floor of the car above them and the side wall. Tory was now effectively insulated from the frame by Reese's body.

"Be careful, Sheriff, there are metal shards sticking out everywhere."

A powerful engine roared somewhere above them, and the car shuddered.

"Brace your legs on something and push back into me," Reese instructed as she wrapped her arms tightly around Tory's waist from behind.

Precipitously, the car tilted, and they were thrown forward. Reese shot her right arm out straight to stop their fall, ignoring a sharp stab of pain as something jagged tore through her jacket just below her elbow. As the car rocked violently from side to side, she cradled her lover to her chest.

"Hold on to me!"

"I can't," Tory shouted. "I have to secure this trach tube."

The car continued to bounce up and down as it was winched up the side of the embankment. Reese absorbed most of the shock on her shoulders and back as she curled protectively around Tory's body. What seemed an interminable time later, but which was in reality only a minute or two, the car leveled out and the earsplitting rattles and bone-jolting vibrations stopped.

"Are you all right?" Reese asked anxiously.

"Yes." Tory's voice was muffled due to their awkward jackknifed position.

Reese rested her cheek against the back of Tory's head and closed her eyes for a second. "Are you sure?"

"I'm all right, honey. Just help me move him."

By that time, firefighters and EMTs were working to separate enough of the frame to ease out the victim. Reese shifted again until she could reach down as far as the driver's body.

"I can hold that, Tor. You need to get out of here and get warm. You're shaking all over and practically freezing. I can feel it."

"I'll be oka—"

"God damn it, Tory. Get out of this fucking car." Reese's voice was flat as she got the fingers of one hand around the trach tube and took the compression bag with the other. "Do it now, or I'll have someone remove you. You're done here."

Tory stared at Reese's face in the flickering glow of the emergency lights, and she saw the expression she'd only seen a few times before. Once had been just before Reese had gone alone into the field of fire to rescue a fallen fellow officer, and the other had been the night someone had assaulted Brianna Parker. There was cold fury in the set of her starkly handsome features and an absolute determination as unyielding as stone.

"Be sure and advise me if there's any change in his condition, Sheriff." Tory quietly eased her cramped, stiff body toward the broken-out window.

"Understood, Doctor," Reese said without looking at her. "Smith!"

"Right here, Reese." He stood just outside the vehicle.

"Take Dr. King to the EMS truck and have someone look at her. Get her warmed up. *Now.*"

"Roger that, boss."

Ten minutes later, Reese found Tory in the back of an EMS van, sitting on the edge of the open rear compartment. She was wrapped in a thermal heating unit and held a steaming cup of tea in her hands.

"How are you doing?" Reese asked softly, stopping a foot in front of her. She wanted to take Tory into her arms. Not only was it not the place for it, but also she wasn't certain that Tory would want it. There was no welcome in those green eyes.

"You pulled rank on me back there, Sheriff," Tory said, ignoring the question. Her expression was carefully neutral.

"Yes." It was a statement, and although the word was delivered quietly, there was no apology in her tone.

"Did they get him out?"

"Yes, about three minutes ago." Reese blew out a breath. *At least she's speaking to me.* "The EMTs are preparing him for transport now. Someone will be back to give you a report soon, I imagine."

"You know that when there's an injured party in the field, my authority is paramount." Tory ran a hand through her hair, struggling with her temper because she wasn't entirely certain what she was angry about. "I can't have our relationship interfering with my ability to do my work."

"It wasn't about us, Tory."

"Wasn't it?" She didn't like the fact that Reese had ordered her out of the vehicle, even though she knew she would have been in serious trouble had she stayed much longer. She was *still* cold, but her blood pressure had been within normal limits when the EMT checked her out. Other than some temporary physical discomfort, there hadn't been any risk to her or the baby. *But Reese couldn't know that.*

"No, it wasn't. You're right that you're in charge of emergency medical decisions—up to a point," Reese said wearily, fighting a wave of sudden dizziness. She blinked her vision clear. "But when both the victim *and* the emergency personnel are in danger, then the authority passes to me. There can only be one commander in the field."

"And that's you, I take it?"

"In a situation like this, yes."

It was an argument they would probably have again, Tory reflected. Reese was used to command, and she was good at it. Nevertheless, Tory wasn't accustomed to having her own authority questioned. But it was too late at night, she was too tired to argue, and she hated to be at odds with Reese. The patient was stabilized, which was all that really mattered, so she relented.

"I appreciate your position."

"I'm sorry I lost my temper, love." Reese brushed the backs of her fingers over Tory's cheek. "You didn't deserve that."

"It's okay, sweetheart."

"I'm still sorry."

"You're soaking wet, Reese. You should go ho—" Tory's eyes narrowed as she examined the large wet patches on her lover's clothes. The ones on her right arm and leg actually seemed to be getting larger as they talked. Her heart gave a sudden painful thud. "My God, you're bleeding!"

"Yeah, I guess." In the last several minutes, Reese had become aware of a variety of aches and pains. Her right forearm throbbed and burned, and she was having a little trouble putting her full weight on her right leg. It felt like it was about to give out. "I think I might have gotten snagged here and there on pieces of the car when they were pulling us out."

"Why didn't you say something sooner?" Alarmed, Tory set the cup aside, threw off the blanket, and got hastily to her feet. She was a little unsteady, but fortunately, her braced leg held. She'd left her cane in the Jeep. "I need to look at you. Climb up into the van where there's some light."

"Look, can we do this later? I have to check—"

"Now, Reese." Tory's voice was now one of absolute command, but her fingers were still gentle as she brushed them briefly along Reese's jaw. "Honey, you're hurt. Don't fight me on this."

Reese blew out a breath and nodded. "Sorry, you're right. I'll just tell Smith I'm leaving the scene to him. He can secure my vehicle later."

Turning, Reese stumbled slightly and Tory was instantly at her side, threading an arm around her waist. "Sweetheart, you're not going to make it. You need to be off that leg right now. Don't argue."

"Okay," Reese muttered, struggling with a fresh wave of dizziness. "But let's go to the clinic. I don't want to do this out here, and I can call in from there."

Tory didn't question her stoic lover's motives, because her only concern was assessing the injury and controlling the damage. "My Jeep is right here. Let's go."

"Fine."

Tory found Reese's easy acquiescence worrisome. The fact that she allowed Tory to open the door and help her inside only made Tory worry more.

Fortunately, at that time of night there was no traffic, and in less than five minutes, Tory pulled into the parking lot in front of the clinic. When Reese pushed open the door to get out, Tory simply said, "Don't even try it. Wait for me."

Once again, Reese complied, and together, they made their way carefully up the gravel drive to the small landing in front of the main door. Reese leaned heavily against the wall as Tory sorted through her keys and unlocked the door.

"Still doing okay?" Tory asked quietly as they maneuvered through the deserted clinic toward the examining rooms in the rear.

"Fine." Reese grunted through gritted teeth. For some reason, her arm and leg seemed to be burning worse now. Her stomach was a little queasy, too.

The pain on Reese's face made Tory's insides twist, but she kept her discomfort to herself. When they reached the largest examining room, which also doubled as a procedure room, Tory reached inside and flipped on the wall switch. "Lean against the table until I can help you get your clothes off."

Hurriedly, Tory washed her hands at the small sink in one corner, then moved to where Reese rested with a hip up on the examining counter. Willing her hands not to shake, she unbuttoned Reese's shirt. "Where're you hurt, honey?"

"Mostly my right arm and leg. The rest of the damage is just bumps and bruises, I think." Reese was having more and more difficulty moving the injured extremities, and it was laborious to get her shirt off. As Tory eased the material down over the injured right arm, Reese drew in her breath sharply at the swift streak of pain that shot up toward her shoulder.

"Sorry," Tory murmured, finally removing the garment. She tossed it aside, leaving Reese clad in the undershirt she'd worn beneath it. Tory bit back a cry of alarm when she saw the jagged tear in Reese's forearm that was deep enough to expose the muscle compartment. Blood oozed steadily from the dark ragged tear, but thankfully, there was no indication of bright red arterial bleeding.

"Christ, that's sensitive," Reese grunted. As her head spun suddenly, she grabbed the edge of the table with her uninjured hand to steady herself.

"It's the salt from the marsh water," Tory said flatly. "That's what's stinging. Let's get these trousers off so I can see your leg."

Gingerly, Reese unbuckled her belt and lowered her fly. "I think you're going to have to do it for me, honey. Sorry."

"It's okay. Put your hand on my shoulder and lean on me a little."

Tory bit her lip when she saw the jagged star-shaped puncture wound on the outside of Reese's right thigh. It looked as if it had been made by the sheared-off top of the gearshift. Further examining it, she realized that it had probably happened when they had pitched forward during the car's bumpy ascent up the steep bank to the roadbed. It was lucky that neither she nor Reese had been speared in some vital body part during the rocky ride.

"I've got to get you up on the table so I can clean out these wounds. The one on your arm is going to need sutures."

As she spoke, Tory worked at separating herself emotionally from the fact that she was looking at her partner's torn and bruised body. Thinking about Reese in pain was not going to help her accomplish what needed to be done. For an instant, she flashed on what might have happened if Reese had not gotten into the vehicle to help shelter her from the trauma. Frowning, she shook the nightmare images from her mind.

"What's wrong, Tor?" Reese asked as she watched Tory examining her.

"I hate to see you hurt," Tory confessed quietly.

"It's not too bad. Don't worry, love."

"You don't get it, do you, Sheriff?" Tory smiled up at her with a quick shake of her head. "I worry about you because I love you. It comes with the territory."

"I know. Try to remember that when I'm being overly protective, okay?" Reese took a deep breath. "Like tonight. I was scared out of my mind when I saw you in that upturned car in the marsh."

"Okay," Tory said softly. Then she leaned down and pressed her lips to Reese's forehead for an instant of much needed contact. When she straightened, her expression was soft with love, but her eyes were firm with purpose. "Now, don't talk to me anymore. Just do what I tell you to do. Do you think you can handle that for a few minutes?"

"That's a tall order, Doctor."

"Stretch yourself, Sheriff. I'm sure you can manage."

❖

By the time Tory was finished, they were both awash with sweat.

"I'm sorry. I know that hurt." Tory stripped off her gloves and brushed her hand over Reese's cheek. Almost to herself, she murmured, "You're so pale."

"It's okay." Reese tried to smile, but her stomach felt like it had been tied into knots. "It had to be done. I'm glad it was you."

"I'd rather it not be anyone at all sewing you up." Tory sighed, knowing that nothing would stop Reese from doing whatever she felt needed to be done in the line of duty, and tried to put the worries from her mind. She crossed the room, unlocked the drug cabinet, and searched around inside for a minute. After filling a paper cup with water at the sink, she returned to Reese and held out several colored tablets in her hand, along with the cup. "Take these."

"What are they?" Reese was suspicious of all things pill-shaped.

"Antibiotics and a pain pill. Believe me, you're going to need them when the lidocaine wears off."

"Thanks." Reese complied without protest.

"Let's get you home."

"That sounds like a great idea."

With Tory's help, Reese climbed wearily down from the table, and the two of them walked slowly from the clinic to Tory's Jeep. Reese called Lyons with instructions for Smith, then closed her eyes. Ten minutes later, they reversed the process and, arms around one another, made their way inside. Tory let Jed out while Reese continued up to their bedroom.

"Can you get undressed by yourself?" Tory asked when she appeared a few moments later. "I really need to take a shower."

"I do, too."

"Not yet. I want you to keep the wounds dry tonight. You can shower in the morning."

"Okay." Reese nodded and sat tiredly on the edge of the bed. "You go ahead. I can manage."

For a few seconds, Tory studied Reese intently. She'd seen her injured before, but she'd never seen her appear quite so drained. "I'll only be a few minutes. If you're sure."

"I'm all right, love." Reese smiled faintly. "Don't worry."

As soon as she could, Tory returned to the bedroom, wearing only an oversized T-shirt. The room lights were still on, and Reese was lying on her back on the bed, still in her T-shirt and trousers. Fast asleep.

Carefully, Tory removed Reese's shoes and socks, unbuckled her belt and slid it free, and pulled her shirt from beneath the waistband of her pants. She didn't bother trying to undress her further because Reese barely moved for the entire process. Also exhausted, Tory simply stretched out beside her lover and pulled the comforter from the bottom of the bed over them both. Within seconds, she, too, was asleep.

The insistent buzzing of the alarm finally penetrated Tory's consciousness. She rolled over and peered at the clock, then settled back with a sigh. "Reese...honey, it's time to get up." When there was no response, she gently shook Reese's shoulder. "Reese?"

"Tor," Reese mumbled weakly. "I can't."

"What?"

"I don't...feel very...well." Reese barely managed to get the words out before she rolled to the side of the bed and vomited onto the floor. "Sor—"

"Reese!" In a flash, Tory bolted upright and leaned over to stare. What she saw made her heart nearly stop. Reese's eyes were unfocused, her color gray, and her skin slick with sweat. Worse, her breathing was shallow and rapid. *My God, she looks septic!*

"I need to check your wounds," Tory said as calmly as she could manage. She slid from the bed, grabbed her cane from its customary spot by the night table, and went to the bathroom where she kept a small emergency kit. Returning with gloves and clean dressings, she said, "Let me see your arm, honey."

Reese didn't move but lay with her eyes closed, unresisting, while Tory unwrapped the gauze from her forearm.

Before Tory had even exposed the entire laceration, she could discern the redness and swelling extending from the wound nearly four inches up Reese's arm. *Cellulitis. To be this bad, this soon, it's got to be a virulent organism.* Without hesitation, she snatched up the bedside phone and punched 911.

"This is Dr. King. I need an ambulance immediately."

She gave them the address, slammed down the phone, then rushed to get dressed. In a minute, she was back at Reese's side with a cool towel, which she used to wipe her pallid face. "Reese— sweetheart, can you hear me?"

"Tor?" Reese's lids flickered open, and she looked up in confusion. "Wha...what's wrong?"

"You've got an infection, honey. I need to take you to the emergency room so we can evaluate you. It's going to be okay."

"Nelson...should call..."

"I'll call him a little later. It's okay. Don't worry about work." Tory glanced at the clock. Ten minutes. *Where are they?*

Then, in the distance, she heard the siren and breathed a sigh of relief. Loath to leave Reese, she raced downstairs, opened the front door wide, and signaled with her arm for the EMTs to come inside. "We're upstairs," she called as she hurried back to Reese.

Thankfully, Reese appeared slightly more coherent when the emergency technicians arrived. Enough to protest, "I don't need... an ambulance."

"Probably not," Tory said gently as she held Reese's uninjured hand. "But it will be easier on me if I don't have to drive to the hospital."

"Okay," Reese replied softly. However, when she sat up, she gasped sharply, pressed her hand to her midsection, and promptly vomited again.

"Let's get her on the stretcher," Tory ordered. "She needs IV hydration and a loading dose of broad-spectrum antibiotics. Come on. Let's move it!"

With practiced proficiency, the two male EMTs shifted Reese to the gurney, strapped her on, and pushed her from the room. Tory stayed as close to the side of the moving stretcher as she could. Then she climbed into the back of the van and settled near Reese's head as one of the techs, a burly redhead, rapidly started an intravenous line in Reese's left arm.

"What do you want to give her, Doc?" As he spoke, he wrapped a blood pressure cuff around her bicep and took a rapid reading. "Ninety over forty. Heart rate's one-seventy. She's pretty dehydrated."

"Run the saline wide open. Then give her a gram of Ancef and a hundred milligrams of gentamycin. We need to cover all our bases, because I don't know what this is."

The tech deftly sorted through the drug box and began administering the antibiotics.

"I need to culture this wound right now," Tory said as the ambulance screamed east on Route 6 toward the nearest hospital, in Hyannis. Her mind was racing, veering toward near-crippling panic. She forced herself to think about the problem and not about the fact that it was Reese lying unresponsive in the back of an ambulance. "Get me a prep tray and some instruments."

The tech's eyebrows lifted in surprise, but he voiced no objection. He handed Tory sterile gloves and prepared to assist.

Meanwhile, Tory removed the dressings on Reese's arm once again, carefully prepped the area with antiseptic solution, and snipped out several of the sutures she had placed the night before. When she gently squeezed the area, Reese moaned, thrashed weakly on the stretcher, and tried to pull away. Tory did not look at her face.

"I don't see any pus in there, do you?" The EMT peered curiously over her shoulder.

"No. It's too soon for an abscess. This is a soft tissue infection."

"Strep?" His concern was evident in his tone. "Jesus, do you think it's necrotizing fasciitis?"

"I don't *know*." Tory carefully pushed a sterile culture swab into the depths of the wound. Reese stiffened at the swift jolt of pain, and Tory's stomach clenched. "I'm sorry, baby."

"S'okay," Reese mumbled before she faded away again.

"I don't have my cell phone with me. Can you connect me to the hospital?" Tory questioned.

"Sure." He tapped on the sliding glass panel between the front cab and the treatment section in the rear. "Ken, pass me the radio." He handed it to Tory and pointed to the button on the side. "Push to talk, let go to receive. I'll get someone in triage for you."

After he gave the person in the emergency room their ETA, he handed the transmitter to Tory. She did as directed and spoke firmly, with no hint in her voice of the terror she felt.

"This is Dr. Victoria King. I have a septic patient coming in. I need an infectious disease consultant and a surgeon standing by."

An eternity later, the EMS van careened into the ambulance bay of the regional hospital. Within seconds, they were inside, and a swarm of nurses and ER doctors descended upon them. By the time Tory was done giving a synopsis of the injury and presenting symptoms, Reese had been hooked up to monitors and additional IV lines. Throughout it all, Tory never left her side.

"I'm Jill Baker. Infectious disease," a short, trim African-American woman in a conservative blazer and slacks announced as she approached the bed. "What have we got?"

"Victoria King." Tory shook her hand and then repeated the details of the previous night and morning. As she spoke, Baker shook her head.

"Foreign body punctures combined with salt marsh contamination. Jesus. Whatever happened to good old-fashioned dog bites?" The infectious disease specialist surveyed the monitors, frowned, and reached for Reese's injured arm. "No hypotensive episodes? Nothing to indicate shock?"

"No." Tory's throat was dry, and she suddenly felt light-headed. "I'm sorry. I need to sit for a second."

"Here," a deep alto voice said from behind her as a firm hand took her arm. "There's a seat right over here."

"Thanks," Tory mumbled, fighting a wave of nausea as she settled onto a stool and put her head down. She was struggling so hard not to pass out, she barely heard the swift intake of breath from the woman beside her.

"Tory?"

When she could look up without her vision dimming, Tory found herself staring into the face of a stranger who had once been her whole world. She was Tory's age, still fit, and still roguishly attractive. She'd been a lady-killer when they'd been lovers. And undoubtedly she still was.

"Hello, K.T."

"Are you all right?" The dark-eyed, dark-haired woman's expression was one of concern and surprise. She grabbed the arm of a passing tech without moving her eyes from Tory's face. "Bring us some orange juice, will you?"

"I'm fine, really." Tory chanced an upright position. "What are you doing here?"

"Moonlighting. I'm the surgeon on call. What's going on? Why are you—"

"I think it's *Vibrio*," Jill Baker interrupted as she walked over to them. "She's got a rip-roaring cellulitis that's climbing up her arm, GI symptoms, and mental confusion. It all fits with an acute marine bacterial infection."

"What the hell is that?" K.T. O'Bannon, uncharacteristically, was in the dark.

"It's a salt-water organism. Some of them can produce a fulminant infection within hours and eat just about anything in their path while they're at it."

"Does she need to be debrided in the OR?" the surgeon asked curtly.

"Probably." Baker lowered her voice. "If it's the *vulnificus* variety, it can be fatal if you don't remove the involved tissue right away."

Tory's head pounded, not with dizziness but with mind-numbing fear. She walked away from them and went to Reese's side. "Hiya, Sheriff," she said when she saw that Reese's eyes were open, and thankfully, clear again. She brushed her fingertips over Reese's face.

"Hey," Reese said hoarsely, holding up the hand with the IV taped to it. "How you doin'?"

"I'm okay." Tory's throat was tight with tears she would not shed as she wrapped her hand around her lover's.

"What's going on? I don't remember much of how we got here."

"You've got a bad infection in your arm. How do *you* feel?"

"Head hurts." Reese frowned. "My insides feel like I swallowed nails. Can't say as I feel much in my arm." She saw Tory pale. "Tor? What is it? You better tell me now...I'm getting pretty foggy again."

"You may need surgery, honey. To remove the infected tissue."

"Surgery?" Reese tried to sit up, but failed.

The sight of her normally strong, commanding partner so weak and ill scared Tory to her depths. Her eyes flooded, and she looked away.

"Tory, please," Reese said urgently, summoning all of her strength. "This is my weapon arm. You can't let them cut pieces out of it."

"You're more important than any job." Tory's voice was rough, her eyes dark pools of anguish.

"Don't cr—oh, fuck…I'm gonna throw—"

Tory grabbed a basin just in time as Reese vomited again. She slipped her arm beneath Reese's shoulder and held her as close as the hospital bed would allow. "It's okay, honey. It's okay."

"Please," Reese muttered when she could catch her breath. "Don't let them operate." Then she leaned back, closed her eyes, and slipped into darkness.

## CHAPTER SIX

B ri examined the clock beside her bed for the fourth time in less than ten minutes. Naked, she rolled onto her back and stared at the ceiling. *It's too early to call. Carre never gets up this early.*

It was hard getting used to waking up without Caroline beside her. Hell, it was hard doing everything without her. It had been especially weird riding the Harley with a woman pressed against her, arms around her waist, a cheek resting lightly against her shoulder, who hadn't been Caroline.

She'd dropped Allie off at her place after they'd left the tavern around one a.m. Allie had said she could walk home or grab a ride with someone else, but Bri had insisted on taking her. It was funny, but watching Allie walk away had left her with an empty feeling. And that didn't make any sense, because she didn't even know her. When she got home, even though it was late, she had called Caroline. And no one had answered.

*You wanted to do this. You knew it would be hard. There's no point in complaining now. Just suck it up, Parker.* Sighing, Bri rolled onto her side, buried her face in her pillow, and tried to sleep.

*Fuck.* She got up, pulled on sweats and a T-shirt, and padded barefoot out into the living room, where the only phone in the apartment was located. There were two other bedrooms, both occupied by academy trainees like her, bargain basement furniture in all the rooms, threadbare rugs, and not much else. The place had no personality, no personal touches, and not much to recommend it other than the fact that it was cheap and the roof didn't leak. Fortunately, if she were lucky, she wouldn't be here long.

She slumped onto the end of the lumpy couch and reached for the phone. After seven rings, she was about to hang up when she heard Caroline's sleepy voice.

"Hello?"

"Babe? Sorry, did I wake you?"

"Bri? Hi, yeah. That's okay." Caroline laughed. "I'm awake now. What's going on?"

"Nothing," Bri said quietly. "I just…wanted to talk to you. I tried calling last night…"

"Oh." There was a beat of silence. "I was out with some of the kids from school. I…I got the scholarship."

Bri closed her eyes. Took a deep breath. "That's great, babe. I'm really proud of you."

"I tried to call you, but I guess I missed you."

"Yeah. I was with Reese." Bri straightened her shoulders. "So listen, we should do something to celebrate. I'll come down today. I can be there by dinnertime."

"What about your class?"

"I'll skip it."

"Really?"

"Sure." The surprise in Caroline's voice tugged at Bri's heart. *Do you think I don't miss you?*

"That would be so great. I miss you."

"Me, too." Bri heard a muffled voice in the background. "Is somebody there?"

"Oh. That's James. It was really late when the party broke up last night, and he walked me home."

"And stayed over?"

"Uh-huh."

Bri had a sick feeling in the pit of her stomach. You could spit from one side of that apartment to the other. Everything was turned upside down, and all she could feel was the dark ache of loss. The words were out before she even had time to think.

"Where did *he* sleep?"

"What? Bri!"

"Well, Jesus, Carre—what am I supposed to think?"

"You're supposed to think I love *you*. And in case you've forgotten, I like girls." Caroline's voice rose, tight with anger. "It's pretty clear you've forgotten that the only girl I ever wanted was you. No wonder it was so easy for you to leave."

"Easy?" Bri whispered, so quietly her voice did not carry over the line.

"I'm going to go now, Bri, because I don't want to fight. Call me later."

Bri closed her eyes as a soft click broke the connection. *Stupid. Jesus, what's wrong with you?*

She got up and headed for the shower, determined to ride to New York City and apologize. As she stood under the hot spray, trying to purge the misery from her mind and heart, a pounding on the bathroom door penetrated her awareness. She stuck her head outside the shower curtain. "What?"

The door opened a crack and a male voice called, "Parker, your old man's on the phone."

"Tell him I'll call him back," Bri yelled, surprised.

"He says it's an emergency."

Heart pounding, Bri stepped from the shower and grabbed for a towel.

❖

Tory glanced at the clock on the opposite side of the brightly lit emergency room. She couldn't believe it was only ten o'clock in the morning. It felt as if the day had been endless. She jumped, startled by the voice beside her.

"Tory, I need someone to sign an operative consent." K.T.'s voice was calm and gentle. "I don't think she's competent. Do you know how we can reach her next of kin?"

"I have medical power of attorney." Tory leaned against the aluminum guardrail that stood between her and Reese like the bars of a jail cell, her left hand curled tightly over the top rung, her right softly stroking Reese's forehead. She didn't look at the surgeon standing next her.

"*You* do?"

"Yes. She's my lover."

There was a moment's silence, then K.T. said flatly, "Fine. I'll get the papers."

"No. Not yet." Tory turned and met K.T.'s eyes. "Her vital signs are stable. She just got the loading doses of chloramphenicol an hour ago. I want to wait until Jill has had a chance to look at the gram stain."

"Why?" the surgeon asked impatiently.

"Because this might be a limited infection, and another dose of antibiotics might bring it under control without surgery."

"And if we wait, and it *isn't* a mild form of the organism, she could lose her arm. She could die."

"K.T., she's a sheriff and a lieutenant colonel in the Marine Corps. She needs the use of that arm to be who she is." A wave of agony passed through Tory. "I have to be sure."

"I'll be as conservative with the resection as I can," K.T. insisted.

"Can you promise me that you won't resect the extensor muscles in her forearm? Because if you do, she'll never hold a gun again."

"You *know* I can't promise that. It depends on what it looks like when I get in there."

"Yes, and you can't always tell if the tissue is healthy or not just by looking at it. And surgical teaching says *when in doubt, cut it out*. I lived with you through your surgical residency, remember?"

"God damn it, you're letting your emotions affect your judgment." K.T. took Tory's elbow and moved her several feet away from Reese's bedside. "You're not thinking like a doctor. You shouldn't be making this decision."

"I *am* a doctor," Tory said sharply. "*And* I'm her lover. I'll let you know after I've talked to Jill."

"Jesus," K.T. cursed. "You're just as stubborn as ever."

"And you're—"

"Tory!" Bri called as she hurried across the room. After her father had informed her that Reese was in the hospital, she'd pulled on her clothes and jumped on her motorcycle. It had taken her less than an hour to get to the hospital.

Tory looked over at the handsome youth in leather motorcycle pants, black jacket, and white T-shirt. An inexplicable wave of relief washed through her. Maybe it was simply the fact that Bri had always reminded her of Reese in her single-mindedness and her uncommon sense of valor. She held out her hand, which Bri took. To her surprise, Bri leaned close and kissed her on the cheek. *Oh, Bri. You've grown up, haven't you?*

"Thanks for coming, Bri."

"I left as soon as my dad called me. He said he'd be here as soon as he stopped at your place to check on Jed."

"Great." Tory's tone was distracted as she indicated K.T. with a nod. "Bri, this is Dr. O'Bannon, one of Reese's doctors."

Bri briefly shook K.T.'s hand but her gaze was on Reese. "How is she?"

"In and out. She's sleeping right now." Tory squeezed Bri's hand. "I called Jean and Kate, but they must be away because I only got their answering machine."

"I'll call my dad again in a few minutes. He can probably track them down." Bri couldn't take her eyes from Reese. The sight of her in the hospital bed sent a jolt of terror straight through Bri's chest. Carefully, she kept her expression blank. "Can I…is it okay if I…"

"Go talk to her for a minute," Tory said gently. "She might not answer, but she'll hear your voice. I need to hunt down one of the other doctors."

Hearing the exhaustion in Tory's voice, Bri studied her with concern. "Have you had anything to eat this morning?"

"What?" Tory asked, momentarily confused.

"You haven't, have you?" Bri put her hands in the pockets of her leather jacket and hunched her shoulders slightly. "Look, I'll bring you something from the cafeteria. Toast or something. Is coffee okay?"

The sight of Bri, so very much like Reese, searching desperately for a way to take care of her brought a sudden flood of tears to Tory's eyes. With a shaking hand, she brushed away the few that escaped before she could contain them. She cleared her throat and smiled. "I guess I should skip the coffee. But some juice and toast would be great. Thanks, sweetie."

Bri blushed and ducked her head. "I'll be right back."

K.T. watched Bri walk away. "She's hot."

"She's a child," Tory said acerbically.

"I don't think so." She gave Tory a speculative glance. "Still living in Provincetown?"

"Yes. Bri's father is the sheriff there and Reese's boss."

"Why did the kid ask if coffee was okay? I remember it used to be an addiction with you. Is something wrong? Ulcers or something?"

"No." Tory hesitated. "I'm pregnant."

K.T.'s gasp of surprise was audible. "Jesus Christ, Tory. Stop fooling around, then. Let me operate and make sure your partner's around to see the baby."

Tory's face lost the last remnants of color, but she refused to give in to the sudden wave of dizziness. "You never could see the shades of gray, could you? I'm going to find Jill Baker and see what she thinks. I'll give you my decision after that."

Then she walked to the bed, leaned over, kissed Reese on the lips, and strode away without looking back at the astonished surgeon.

❖

Tory found Jill Baker in the pathology laboratory, bent over a microscope, a frown of intense concentration wrinkling her smooth forehead.

"What have you found?"

Without looking up, the infectious disease specialist answered, "It's a gram negative, just like we expected. At least we know the antibiotics are correct."

"Is there any way to tell if it's the virulent form or the self-limited variety?" Tory tried to keep her voice even and hoped that her rising panic wasn't evident. As each second passed, and the clock ticked down on the chance of keeping Reese out of the operating room, her anxiety escalated.

"No, I'm sorry. Not from this. We need to wait for the culture and sensitivity results to come back." Jill's eyes were sympathetic, but her tone held the matter-of-fact delivery of every physician who knew that nothing less than the truth would suffice.

"How long before you know which it is?" Tory knew, but she hoped for a miracle.

"Twelve hours at best, more likely twenty-four." Jill shrugged. "Bacteria grow at their own pace."

"If it's *Vibrio vulnificus,* she doesn't have twelve hours, does she?" Tory put one hand on the counter, determined not to let anyone see her falter.

"If that's what it is, she doesn't even have six." Jill's gaze slid from Tory's tormented green eyes to the scrolled gold band encircling her left ring finger, the exact match to the one on the sheriff's hand. "What would you say if you didn't know anything about her except the medical facts?"

Tory looked away and attempted the impossible task of putting Reese's face from her mind. After a moment of calling upon every defense she'd ever learned as a doctor to gain some emotional distance, she was able to think objectively—assessing, categorizing, analyzing the timetable, reviewing the sequence of symptoms. She took a deep breath.

"I'd say that everything points to the rapid onset of cellulitis, most probably the product of an ocean-borne pathogen. In all likelihood, there was systemic spread almost immediately, which accounts for her toxic presentation and associated gastrointestinal symptoms. I can precisely pinpoint the time of infection, and considering that it's been almost twelve hours, the progression is not escalating particularly rapidly."

"Very good," Baker said with a grin. "And your conclusion?"

"It's more likely to be the non-fulminant variety; otherwise, her condition should have deteriorated by now to the point of shock and multiorgan system failure." Her voice shook as the magnitude of that truth pierced her precarious emotional shields. It took her a second before she could continue. "There's no evidence of disseminated intravascular coagulation on her last blood panel, and there are no distant or satellite lesions."

"Want a job? We could use another ID attending around here."

"No thanks." Tory gave a shaky laugh. "What if we wait on the surgery, and I'm wrong?"

"Being cautious is the sign of a good physician. Second-guessing yourself, though, is dangerous." Jill's expression was solemn. "Let's try a little old-fashioned medicine. Let's go look at the wound again. If the cellulitis hasn't progressed, and she still looks stable, I say we sit on it for another couple of hours."

"O'Bannon's going to go crazy."

Jill lifted one elegant shoulder. "Let her. *Her* ego can handle it."

Tory took a deep breath. "Okay."

❖

K.T. was gone when Tory and Jill returned, having been called away by an emergency in the trauma unit. Bri was sitting by Reese's bedside, perched on a tall stool, a tray bearing English muffins and cardboard cartons of juice balanced on her knee.

"Look who's here," Bri said happily as Tory approached, inclining her head toward the bed.

Tory leaned over the rail and gazed into the bluest eyes she'd ever seen. "Hello, sweetheart," she murmured, her heart aching at the shadows of pain that lingered in Reese's face.

"Hi, love. Sorry, I keep…fading." Reese turned her head slightly. "Bri says she has breakfast."

"Yes." Tory brightened with a smile. "But not for you just yet. Are you hungry?"

"Not really." Reese grimaced. "I'm just happy not to be heaving. You go ahead and eat."

Tory petted Reese's hair, stroked her face, unable to bear not touching her. "In a minute." She glanced to the side as Jill joined her at the bedside. "Honey, this is Jill Baker. She's an infectious disease specialist. She needs to look at your arm."

"Okay," Reese said weakly. "Just looking, right, Doc?"

"No sharp instruments, Sheriff." Jill flashed a smile, lifting both hands to prove her point.

Reese kept her eyes on Tory's face as the other doctor unwrapped her arm. She knew she would be able to see the truth in her lover's eyes. When Jill gently probed with a gloved hand, Reese winced and immediately, Tory's eyes darkened. "I'm okay, Tor. It doesn't hurt too much."

"I know, sweetheart." Tory's fingers trembled in Reese's hair. "What do you think, Jill?"

"It's no worse."

Tory closed her eyes, nearly weak with relief. When she opened them, Reese's questioning gaze was fixed on hers. "That's good, honey."

"No surgery then?"

"Maybe *I* should decide that," K.T. announced dryly as she moved in next to Jill and reached for Reese's arm. Her dark eyes were steady on Reese's blue ones. "I'm Dr. O'Bannon. I'm a surgeon."

"Doctor," Reese said with a hint of her old authority in her voice. "I hope I won't need your services."

K.T. didn't respond as she lifted and turned Reese's arm, then probed upward toward her shoulder. "Hurt up here?"

"No."

"Make a fist."

Reese tried, but couldn't quite close her fingers.

"That bother you anywhere?"

"Just feels stiff." Reese frowned. "Mostly I feel really beat. I can't seem to stay awake."

"That's the effect of the dehydration and the bacterial toxins." K.T. never took her eyes from the wound. After a moment, she gently placed Reese's arm back on the bed. Then she grasped the guardrail in both hands and leaned over slightly so that her face was all that Reese could see. "I don't see very much change in the physical appearance of your arm in the last four hours. That may be a good thing, or it might not. The safest thing would be to take you to the operating room, remove the rest of the sutures, irrigate the wound, and excise any dead tissue."

"How would that affect the function of my arm?" Reese worked hard to concentrate and stay alert. The headache was slowly returning, and with it, an overwhelming urge to close her eyes.

"Maybe not at all."

"Maybe?"

The surgeon blew out a slightly exasperated breath. "I cannot tell you for sure until I see what the tissue looks like."

"Worst-case...scenario?"

"Sensory loss, primarily in the upper aspect of your hand, weakness of wrist extension, decreased grip strength."

Reese's eyes flicked to Tory. "Can we wait?"

"Honey—"

"Sheriff Conlon," K.T. interrupted. "If we go now, we minimize the risk—"

"K.T., let me talk to her alone for a minute." Tory's tone left no room for discussion.

Reese jerked slightly and shifted her gaze back to the surgeon. The familiarity in Tory's voice was too much to be coincidence. *So you're the idiot who let her go.*

"I have a patient to check on in the trauma unit," K.T. said stiffly. "I'll be back shortly."

"Reese, sweetheart," Tory said softly, "I know how important it is for you to have the full use of your arm. But we can't take any chances. I…I can't risk losing you."

"I would never willingly do anything that might take me away from you." Reese lifted her left hand, and when Tory grasped it, she entwined her fingers with her lover's. "But if there's a possibility that we can ride this out without the surgery, I want to try."

"Jill feels we can wait a couple more hours." Tory knew that she was making perhaps the most important decision of her life. Searching her heart and mind, she settled herself. "I agree with her."

"Okay then. We wait." Reese sighed and closed her eyes. "If you don't mind…I think I'll sleep for a bit."

Tory laid Reese's hand down on the bed and brushed her fingers over Reese's hair, then kissed her. "I'll be right here, sweetheart. You just rest."

❖

Shortly, Reese was transferred from the emergency room upstairs to the intermediate intensive care unit for observation. The isolation room was equipped with the standard hospital bed, freestanding bedside table, and several chairs. In addition, a small sofa had been provided in the event that family members wanted to stay for extended periods of time. It was easier for visitors to remain in the patient's room rather than the regular waiting room, thereby avoiding the cumbersome process of scrubbing and donning cover gowns every time they reentered the room.

"You don't have to stay, Bri." Tory leaned her head against the back of the sofa and closed her eyes.

"I *want* to wait." Bri settled on the sofa next to her. "If that's okay?"

"Sure."

It was noon. Twelve hours since she had gotten the call from the EMTs about a multivehicular accident with victims trapped in the wreckage. It was a call like so many other late-night calls she had gotten in the seven years she'd been Provincetown's year-round doctor. She and Reese had responded to innumerable calls for police and medical assistance over the time they'd been a couple, and they were used to working together. It had all seemed so routine the night before, but then that's how many life-altering events began— as something so ordinary. And now, she was waiting while Reese's future, and possibly her life, hung in the balance.

"Just a few weeks ago, we found out about the baby." Tory's voice broke on the words. "Now…"

"Tory," Bri whispered softly as she edged closer on the sofa, alarmed by the tears trickling from beneath Tory's closed lids. Tentatively, she placed her hand on the weeping woman's shoulder. "She's going to be okay."

Tory struggled with the rush of emotions, but she was so tired and so terrified that before she could stop herself, she'd turned into the warm body next to hers. Bri's arms came around her and Tory held on, pressing her face to the strong shoulder as she wrapped one arm around Bri's waist. She felt a soft cheek against her hair and the whisper of breath against her ear as she let the tears come.

"She'll be fine," Bri murmured and pulled her close.


When Nelson Parker arrived at the hospital and asked for the whereabouts of his deputy sheriff, he was directed to a room in the intermediate care unit on the second floor. The door was closed when he arrived, and looking up and down the hall, he saw no one around. Carefully, he pushed the door open and peeked in.

The room was dim. At first, all he could make out was the single hospital bed in the center of the room holding a sheet-covered form. His gaze drifted to the small sofa tucked into one corner, and his eyes widened. His daughter sat with a woman cradled in her arms, her chin resting on the top of the tousled auburn hair. He and Bri stared at one another for an instant, and then he slowly closed the door.

Nelson leaned with his back against the wall and replayed the image in his mind. He was reminded every few months how little he understood his daughter. Bri was his child; he remembered a million images of her growing up, the kind of snapshot moments he supposed most men had of their children. But he didn't know who she had become. In fact, he didn't have any point of reference to even imagine who she was. Victoria King was one of the strongest women he'd ever met, and his daughter was in there holding her, sheltering her, it looked like. He felt inexplicably proud.

The door opened softly, and Bri stepped out. "Hi, Dad."

"Hi, Bri," he said gruffly, his throat a little scratchy. "How's Reese?"

"She's been asleep since they brought her up here, maybe two hours ago. The doctors are supposed to look at her again soon."

"She...uh...she's pretty sick?"

Bri swallowed hard. "Yeah."

"Christ," he growled. "How's Tory taking it?"

"She's worn out. She's been asleep, too."

"You okay?"

"Yeah." Bri looked away. *I'm fucking scared out of my mind.*

Nelson squeezed her shoulder with one huge hand, then slid his arm around her and pulled her close. He hugged her for a second, amazed as always by her solid strength. "Reese is tough."

"Yeah," Bri said again. *She'd never leave Tory. But people do leave, don't they? We lost Mom.*

Bri stepped away. "I oughta get Tory some lunch. She forgets, and you know...with her being...you know. Well, Reese would be pissed if we let Tory get sick."

"You go back in." Nelson jumped at the chance to do something, anything, remotely useful. He did *not* want to walk in

there and see Reese on the edge. He didn't think he could take it.
"I'll get Tory a sandwich. That would be good, right?"

"Yeah. And juice. Juice seems to be okay."

"Great. Got it," the chief said as he hurried away.

Bri glanced at the clock down the hall at the nurses' station.
Almost three p.m. She thought about calling Caroline. Caroline
would tell her that Reese would be fine and make her believe it.
Caroline had always been able to do that—make her see the light
in the dark, no matter how bad it seemed. Bri closed her eyes and
leaned her head back against the wall. *I wish you were here. I wish
you knew how much I need you.*

After a minute, she opened her eyes, straightened her
shoulders, and slipped back into the hospital room.

❖

Reese opened her eyes, blinked, and focused on the faces
leaning over her. The surgeon was closest to her, her dark eyes
opaque, her austerely handsome features expressionless. Tory
stood across from her. Focusing on those tender green eyes, Reese
smiled. "Is this the only show in town?"

A flicker of joy flared in Tory's eyes, the first sign of happiness
in hours. The corner of her mouth lifted in a soft smile. "Apparently,
Sheriff, you're it."

"It's good to see you," Reese whispered, lifting her free hand,
which Tory immediately grasped. Then, Reese turned toward K.T.
O'Bannon. "How do things look, Doc?"

"Stable." K.T.'s gaze was on Reese's arm. Then she seemed to
reconsider. "Actually, a bit better than that. I think the cellulitis has
receded and the swelling is a little less."

"I guess that means you and I won't be getting together
then."

K.T.'s dark eyes rose to meet the deep blue ones. She smiled
faintly. "I guess not." Then she glanced across Reese's body to Tory.
"Can we speak outside?"

Tory looked as if she were about to object, but Reese squeezed
her hand reassuringly. "Go ahead, love."

After a second's hesitation, Tory nodded. "I'll be right back."

Once outside, Tory studied K.T., who leaned with one shoulder against the wall, waiting for her. The surgeon wore only hospital scrubs with no lab coat. Her beeper was clipped to the right hip and several pens protruded from her breast pocket. She was still lean and faintly tanned. She looked much the way Tory remembered her, with only a few added lines around her eyes to mark the passage of time. She was still heart-stoppingly beautiful, with that same dangerous glint in her eyes, as if she knew it. Looking at her, Tory's memories of their years together were clouded by the mists of half-truths and lost dreams. The emotions that had once been so achingly close to the surface whenever she thought of K.T.'s smile, her touch, were gone.

"What is it?" Tory regarded K.T. uneasily. "Did you see something that worried you when you examined her?"

"No, nothing like that," K.T. clarified quickly. "I just wanted you to know that I'll be here for another twelve hours. If there's any change, call me. I'll come take another look."

"Thanks." Tory allowed herself to hope. *Maybe the nightmare really is over.* "I appreciate you spending so much time with us. I know how busy it gets when you're the only one on call."

"That's okay." K.T. shrugged. Then, her voice pitched low, she added, "I'm glad things turned out this way. As much as I love to operate, I'm glad I didn't have to this time."

"So am I. I know you weren't happy when I wanted to wait."

"The both of you would have been hard to take on."

Tory smiled. "Reese is not someone you want to challenge at any time, even when she's flat on her back."

"I haven't even seen her at her best, and I believe you." Uncharacteristically, K.T. looked away for a heartbeat, and then brought her eyes back to Tory's. "I still miss you."

Tory's lips parted in surprise. They hadn't seen each other since separating nearly seven years before. The first few years after that had been agonizingly difficult for Tory. She'd been through medical school and residency with K.T., and she had planned on a lifetime with her. When all that had changed, she'd lost faith in love and even worse, in herself.

Determined to reclaim her life, Tory had left Boston. First, she had regained her identity and sense of purpose by establishing her medical practice in Provincetown. She'd rebuilt her life while keeping her heart locked safely away. Then Reese had come along and made it impossible for her *not* to believe in love again. Reese had brought hope back into her heart, and because of Reese's love, her life was filled with joy and promise.

"Take care of yourself, K.T.," Tory said quietly. "I need to get back to Reese."

As Tory turned away, the deep, sensuous voice she knew so well murmured, "If I called you, could I see you?"

"No."

Without looking back, Tory walked through the door and let it swing closed behind her.

❖

"Everything okay?" Reese watched her lover approach. She'd been fading in and out for what felt like days, but she remembered realizing who the surgeon had to be—Tory's ex-lover. *Do you still hurt, love?*

Tory pulled a chair close to the bedside and lowered the rail that separated them. She placed both hands around Reese's below the intravenous line, lifted it, and pressed her lips to the top of Reese's hand. "Everything is wonderful."

"O'Bannon's your K.T., right?"

Tory stiffened slightly, then shook her head gently. "No, honey. Not anymore."

"You feeling all right?"

"I am now. Now that you're better." Tory lifted Reese's fingers and brushed them against her cheek, then turned her face and kissed each one. "How do *you* feel?"

"Like I've been on maneuvers for four days straight in a swamp somewhere without water. My head hurts, my insides are empty, and I don't think I could stand up if the room was on fire." Reese grinned weakly. "But compared to this morning, I feel like a million bucks."

"You're going to be fine."

"I can think a little bit clearer now, and I seem to have most of the feeling back in my right hand. I'm just so damn weak."

*You'll get over this. You have to, because I need you so much.*
Tory closed her eyes as a sudden rush of emotions swamped her.
Then she couldn't stop the tears, even though she wanted to. "Oh,
God, Reese."

"Tory," Reese whispered. "It's okay, love."

"I was so scared," Tory murmured, her eyes still closed. "I don't
know how I would manage without you. I can't even imagine…"

"I love you. I will not leave you." Reese moved their joined
hands until her fingers touched the tears. "Besides, we have a baby
coming, and I intend to be there for every second of the fun."

Tory leaned closer and rested her head against Reese's
shoulder. "Fun. *Ha.*" But her spirits lifted at the sound of Reese's
steady heartbeat beneath her cheek.

"I can't wait." Reese wrapped her free arm protectively around
Tory's shoulders and held her as close as she could. "You should go
home, love. You need to get some rest. Especially now."

"No."

"Tory, please. Everyone agrees I'm going to be okay, and I
don't want anything to happen to you. Please."

"Later, I promise. I'll go home in a little while." She lifted her
gaze, her green eyes still swimming with tears. "I just need to be
with you a little longer. I need to feel safe again."

"Okay." Reese's fingers softly stroked Tory's face. "Okay,
love. Whatever you want. Always."

They both jumped as a knock sounded at the door. Then it
slowly swung open and Bri peered around the corner. Her face lit
up when she saw that Reese was awake. "Hey! You okay?"

"Yeah, pretty much. Come on in."

Suddenly shy, Bri came slowly forward until she stood on the
side of the bed opposite Tory, her hands in the front pockets of her
low-riding pants. "I'm glad you're okay."

"Me too, kiddo." Reese smiled. "You know, I seem to
remember you managed to find some food earlier. Any chance of
repeating that trick?"

"Sure, if it's okay." Bri looked to Tory questioningly.

"Now that we know she's not going to need surgery, I don't
see any reason she can't eat. I'll check with Jill Baker. She's the
attending."

"How about Bri hunts down some hoagies, and by the time she gets back, we'll have our answer?" Reese suggested. *You look ready to collapse, love. Hoagies will have to do until I can get you to go home.*

"You mind, Bri?" Tory hated to impose yet again on their young friend.

"Hell, no. Anything, as long as I don't have to eat what they have in the hospital cafeteria again."

They all laughed and Bri hurried out.

"She's been here all day," Tory said quietly. "Nelson was here earlier, too."

"He see Bri?" Reese's eyes fluttered closed, and she fought them open.

"Yes. They seemed okay."

"Good. I'm glad Bri...was here for you."

"She's been great. It's hard to believe that she's not a kid anymore."

"Yeah," Reese agreed. "She is and she isn't, you know? She's not a kid, but she's still...so damn young." She sighed and closed her eyes. "I'm a little...worried...about her."

"Rest for a while, honey. I'll wake you when Bri gets back with the sandwiches."

"Maybe just for a few minutes," Reese murmured as she drifted off into healing slumber.

## CHAPTER SEVEN

A week later, Kate Mahoney looked up from the newspaper and regarded her daughter with amused consternation. "Reese, darling, I don't think that's exactly what Tory meant when she said you should rest today."

"If I rest any more, I'm going to be comatose." Reese awkwardly pried open a can of primer with her left hand. The right was tucked into a sling across her chest. She wiped her hand on her faded fatigue pants and glanced at her mother in frustration. "I've been home from the hospital for four days, and I'm perfectly fine. If there were any real paperwork to do, I'd beg Nelson to put me on desk duty. But until the end of the month, there's hardly enough of that to keep *him* busy in the office."

"I know you're bored," Kate sympathized. "But somehow, painting a room does not seem like resting."

"It's therapy. She said I could use my hand."

"No. What she *said* was that you could start gentle strengthening exercises. I doubt very much that includes wielding a paintbrush."

"Did Tory assign you to spy on me?" Reese regarded her mother with faint suspicion. Kate and Jean had been in Boston for a weekend of shopping and theater-going when Reese had been admitted to the hospital. Upon their return and subsequent discovery of Reese's illness, they had taken turns spending time at the hospital. Reese had been enormously grateful when Kate convinced Tory to go home in the evenings rather than spending all of her time with Reese. But now she wanted everyone, including her mother, to leave her in peace.

"No," Kate said with a laugh. "I just happen to like your company. I know once the season starts, you're going to be too busy even to visit."

"Shouldn't you be working in the gallery? Don't you have paintings to hang or something?"

"The gallery is in good shape. Jean is taking care of the all the details for the opening." Kate smiled benignly. "I have absolutely nothing on my schedule."

"I'm not going to do anything foolish." Reese stirred the paint and sighed. "I don't want anything to keep me from getting back to work as soon as possible."

"Tory said it would be a month," Kate reminded Reese gently.

"It needs to be a little sooner," Reese said determinedly. "The stitches will be out in another week, and there's no reason I can't start getting some of the strength back in my arm now."

"If you use it too much, too quickly, you'll just prolong the swelling."

Reese raised an eyebrow. "Is the house bugged? Tory said something just like that this morning."

"No, but I lived with your father for fifteen years, and I've seen my share of physical injuries. Marines tend to get banged up a good deal, as you may recall."

For a moment, silence descended between them. They rarely talked about Reese's father, because the terms of Kate's divorce from him had stipulated her separation from Reese as well. Reese had spent her teenage years and young adulthood with no contact at all with her mother. Had Reese not made a life-altering decision to leave active duty and move to Provincetown, she and Kate might never have had the chance to get to know each other.

"I suppose I'm as bad a patient as he was," Reese muttered. She knew that in many ways she was like her father, and sometimes that bothered her. She respected him, even admired him, as an officer. But she didn't want to be like him as a person. She looked at Kate questioningly. "Do you think we're a lot alike?"

"Only in the sense that neither of you were ever willing to admit there was something you couldn't do." Kate looked away, a distant expression in her eyes.

Reese leaned back on her heels and asked softly, "Do you hate him?"

"No," Kate replied without hesitation. "I don't *like* him, but I don't believe he ever did anything to intentionally hurt you. Hurt me, yes. But not you. That I would never forgive."

"He never tried to understand you."

"I doubt that he could. He can't change who he is any more than I can who I am."

"He could learn to accept some things." Reese's voice held a hint of bitterness.

"Like the fact that his ex-wife and his daughter are lesbians?"

"Maybe." Reese's smile was brittle. "Or maybe just that there are more ways to live than *his* way."

"I won't defend him to you, Reese. Not when he took nearly twenty years that I might have spent knowing you."

"Tory thinks I should tell him about the baby."

"Do you want to?"

"I don't know." Reese leaned her shoulder against the wall and rubbed her eyes. "I'm not sure what the point would be. He hasn't accepted my relationship with Tory, so he certainly isn't going to accept our child."

"Perhaps it isn't his acceptance, but you telling him that matters."

"I'm not sure I know what you mean." Reese considered the prospect solemnly.

"You and Tory are about to experience something wonderful, something precious," Kate said gently. "He's your father, one of the most significant people in your life. You need to tell him for your own sake and let him deal with his feelings the best way he can. Because if you don't, it diminishes you *and* your relationship with Tory."

"Like hiding being gay to avoid a court-martial?"

"Reese, I know how much that bothers you. But, how does the saying go? You have to pick your battles?"

Reese grinned. "Uh-huh."

"Well, when you choose not to reveal your sexuality to General Conlon, it's a professional necessity. Not telling your *father* about your child is personal, and in my opinion, much more critical."

"Being a marine's a lot simpler. The rules are clearer, and the strategic decisions a lot easier to make."

"Yes, indeed." Kate smiled. "I think you're doing wonderfully as a civilian, by the way."

"I hope so, because Tory means more to me than anything else ever could. And now…" Reese swallowed and met her mother's eyes. "I think I'm going to need a fair amount of advice about this parenting thing."

"I'm sure you and Tory won't have any trouble at all. I intend to do nothing except spoil him or her, which is a grandmother's right."

"Well, as long as you're available for an emergency rescue mission if I get into trouble," Reese remarked, hunting for the paintbrush.

"You can count on that."

❖

Tory stopped mid-stride in the middle of the dining room and cocked her head. "Why do I smell fresh paint?"

Reese swiveled on the stool at the breakfast counter and smiled. Tory had been in the clinic all day. Thirteen interminable hours. "Welcome home, love."

"Let me repeat," Tory said as she crossed the room. "Who's been painting?"

"Uh, I thought I'd get started on the nursery."

"You did." It was a statement, not a question. Tory leaned her cane against the counter and regarded Reese expressionlessly. Normally, Reese was a recruiting poster example of good health and physical fitness. Now, a trace of illness still lingered. The shadows under her eyes had faded but had not disappeared completely. Her color was better, but she was still pale. She hadn't been out of the hospital long enough for Tory's fear to have completely subsided. "I'm going to kill you."

"Could you kiss me first?" Reese murmured, extending her good hand.

Tory moved between Reese's parted legs, resting her palm on Reese's thigh for support. "Hmm, I suppose."

"Then I'll go happy." Reese slid her arm around Tory's waist and pulled her near, then dipped her head to claim soft lips. Eyes closed, she lost herself in the familiar sensation of supple warmth and tender welcome. It had been too long since they had touched this way. Tory's breasts brushed her own, and, as always, the pressure of Tory's body started Reese's blood humming. She groaned faintly and worked the back of Tory's blouse free from her slacks. Her palm found the hollow at the base of her lover's spine, and she spread her fingers over the swell of hips below, urging Tory closer still.

"Reese..." Tory sighed as she released the kiss. "I don't think..."

"Shh. I've missed you." Reese's voice was deep and mellow. She took Tory's mouth again, more insistently this time, probing deeper with her tongue, sucking on the full lower lip until Tory moaned. Reese closed her thighs, holding Tory captive against her.

"Your ar—"

"Is fine," Reese whispered and moved her lips to the sweet spot below Tory's jaw, kissing her way down to the faint hollow between her collarbones. She drew her fingers from Tory's back, around her side, and up underneath the front of her blouse. When she encountered the thin silk brassiere and the hard nipple beneath, she flicked her thumb across the taut peak. Tory surged against her, a sharp cry resonating from her throat. The sound of her pleasure made Reese stiffen and throb. "Ah, God, you are so perfect."

"They're so sensitive now." Tory arched her neck, her eyes closed. "I can feel it all the way inside me when you do that."

Reese rested her forehead against the crook of Tory's neck, working the full nipples between her fingers, one and then the other. Tory's breasts lay heavy in her palm, a weighty fullness so sensuous it stole her breath. Listening to Tory's breathing quicken, she teased her until Tory's hands in her hair forced her head up.

"Am I hurting you?" Reese quickly searched Tory's face.

"No," Tory managed hoarsely. "It feels so good I think you could make me come."

"Do you want to try?" Reese whispered through a throat tight with desire. She never stopped the rhythmic squeezing, watching Tory's green eyes darken with arousal.

"Mmm, no. I want to lie down so you can touch me everywhere."

Reese groaned as another jolt of excitement tore through her. Pleasing Tory always drove her to the edge, and often when Tory climaxed, she would too, spontaneously, just from hearing her lover's cries. "Bedroom?"

"Yes, now, before I can't walk at all."

They managed to climb the stairs to their bedroom without losing contact, their arms around each other's waists.

Once at the bedside, Tory turned on the lamp and, with her voice pitched low, directed, "Sit down."

Wordlessly, Reese did as she was bid. Although aware of the steady pounding in her depths, of the building pressure demanding relief, she would not move until Tory allowed it. Tory's pleasure was her greatest satisfaction.

"Watch me," Tory murmured as she unbuttoned her blouse, her eyes on Reese's face. She slid it off, let it fall to the floor. "I love the way you want me."

"So much." Reese forced the words out as her hand trembled on her thigh. She caught her breath as Tory reached behind, released the clasp on her bra, and freed her breasts. They were fuller now, lush in a way that was primordially female. Watching Tory's hands brush lightly over them, linger briefly on the swollen nipples, then slide down her abdomen, made Reese's stomach clench. A pulse beat frantically between her thighs.

"Touch me," Tory breathed, stepping closer and reaching for Reese's left hand. She drew the fingers to her breast, closing her eyes at the shock of pleasure as Reese gently squeezed. While Reese teased her, Tory unbuttoned her own slacks and pushed them down along with her underclothes. Resting one hand on Reese's shoulder, she stepped free, exposing herself to her lover's view.

"You're more beautiful every day." Reese lightly smoothed her palm down Tory's gently curving abdomen. When her fingers brushed the soft hair at the base of her belly, Tory's hips jerked.

"Time for me to lie down," Tory said huskily, her fingers fluttering over Reese's cheek. "Be careful with your arm, sweetheart."

"I'm fine." Reese shifted to make room on the bed, leaning her right shoulder against the pillows as she turned on her side. "Lie close to me."

"Yes." Tory lay on her back, her eyes on Reese's face. "Go slow."

"I will."

Knowing fingers traced Tory's breasts, the slope of her ribs, the faint curve of her hip. Everywhere, Tory's skin tingled; every sensation seemed to center between her thighs. When Reese brushed her hand the length of Tory's leg, then up the inside, Tory's hips lifted in invitation. But Reese did not touch her where she so desperately needed to be touched, moving instead to the other leg, stroking lightly up and down until Tory quivered with urgency.

"Slow enough?"

"Mmm…"

"Now?"

"Oh, please."

Smiling, her breath barely moving in her chest, Reese drew a fingertip high between her lover's legs, parting swollen folds, and gasped as a flood of moisture rose to her touch.

"Yes." Tory sighed.

"Don't close your eyes," Reese demanded softly as she slid her fingers around Tory's clitoris, squeezing gently. She fondled her until the rolling rhythm of Tory's hips signaled she was on the edge. Then Reese moved lower, easing inside, drawing a guttural moan from her lover. She thrust slowly, watching Tory's pupils grow huge.

"Oh God," Tory cried. "You have me so close."

"Help me," Reese urged, deep in her now.

Tory slid her hand down her own abdomen, her eyes locked on Reese's. The first flick of her fingertips over naked nerve endings brought her hips off the bed and wrenched a cry from her throat.

Reese groaned.

Tory kept her eyes open as long she could, watching her own pleasure reflected in Reese's face. When the pressure built too high to resist release, she pressed harder, her hand and Reese's moving together, driving her to orgasm.

Long moments later, Tory sighed contentedly. "Maybe you could just stay home and be my sex slave."

"Hmm. Okay." Reese nuzzled Tory's ear, grinning inwardly. "But sex slaves don't cook."

"Is that so?" Tory turned languidly on her side. She licked a bead of sweat from Reese's neck as she reached for her fly. "Let's check."

# CHAPTER EIGHT

"**W**ell! Now things will get back to normal around here," Gladys announced with a huge smile as Reese entered the office. "How are you feeling, honey?"

"Just fine, really." Reese blushed faintly and glanced at Nelson, who just shrugged.

"Desk duty," Nelson grumbled. "That's what the doctor said."

"What, have you got my report card there or something?" Reese balanced her cap on a stack of folders resting precariously near the edge of her desk. Ignoring his snort, she sauntered across the room to a counter along one wall that held the coffeepot. She lifted the cloudy pot, swirled the murky contents, and eyed it speculatively. "How old is this?"

"Don't look at me." Gladys pointedly turned her chair away. "I don't drink that poison."

"I made it just…yesterday afternoon," Nelson admitted sheepishly. The stuff *had* tasted a little like battery acid that morning. Just thinking about it sent him searching in his desk drawer for his antacids.

"I think making coffee is probably considered desk duty," Reese said with a sigh. "And for your information, the *doctor* said I can work as long as I don't stress my arm."

"And I know your doctor, and I sure as hell don't plan to get on her bad side." Nelson still hadn't forgotten the one time Tory had threatened him with bodily harm, and he'd known then that not only had she meant it, but also she was capable of doing it. "Three weeks is awfully fast to come back to work." *Especially after being flat on your back and scaring the bejesus out of everyone.* He didn't like to think about it even now. The only good thing to come out of the whole deal was that Bri seemed to be speaking to him again. At least a little.

"Three weeks is an awfully long time to be sitting around the house going crazy, too," Reese grumbled.

She filled the paper filter with coffee, settled it into the plastic chamber, and slid it home. After punching the on button, she turned and gave the room a contented once-over. Nothing had changed, except that the pile of paperwork on her desk seemed to have managed several generations of reproduction while she'd been gone. "And if we don't get the hiring done and all the paperwork in order before the end of this month, we're going to be behind for the rest of the summer."

Nelson chewed the chalky tablet absently, fingering a dog-eared piece of paper as he read it for at least the tenth time. Then he passed it from his desk to Reese's. "That's the first order of business. What you decide to do about it is up to you."

"What is it?" Reese's curiosity was piqued as she settled behind her desk. The chair creaked in its familiar fashion, which brought a smile to her face.

"I've got to sit in on one of those damn town council meetings," Nelson announced as he rose abruptly. In less than a minute, he had fished his hat and jacket from the rack by the door and walked out, leaving Reese to stare after him in surprise.

When she raised a questioning eyebrow at Gladys, the older woman merely shrugged her shoulders. "I don't have any idea what's going on with that man. But something is surely bothering him, and I can only think of a couple of things that might be."

Reese nodded contemplatively and turned her attention to the document Nelson had passed to her. It was an official inquiry, addressed to her, that had undoubtedly been opened in her absence to ensure that some important business had not gone unattended. She skimmed it quickly and thought she understood at least one reason for Nelson's disquiet.

Reese phoned ahead to the clinic as she drove. They still had plenty of time before their flight, but it never hurt to give Tory a little advance warning. When the phone was answered by an extremely harried receptionist, she figured Tory was backed up with her schedule.

"East End Health Clinic, hold please." A moment later, Randy returned. "How may I help you?"

"Hi Randy, it's Reese. How's Tory doing?"

"If she hurries, she'll only be a little late." He laughed distractedly. "So, I would say it's business as usual."

"Did she have lunch?"

"I ordered it, Reese, I swear." Randy's tone vacillated between irritation and frustration. "But I can't make her eat it."

Reese sighed, curbing her temper with effort. It wasn't Randy's fault if Tory worked too hard, and it certainly wasn't his responsibility to see that she took a lunch break. "Do me a favor, will you? Have Sally pack it up, and I'll see that she eats it on the plane."

"Uh-huh…"

His voice faded away and she heard a muffled, "Excuse me… don't let him eat that pen, please."

"It's important." Reese said it loudly enough to get his attention.

"I know, Reese," Randy replied, affronted.

"I'm sorry. I'm just a little…"

"Never mind. We love her, too. Look, I'm up to my behind here—"

"Right. Thanks again. I'll wait outside."

At only a few moments past their appointed rendezvous time, Tory exited through the front door of her one-story medical office building and hurried across the parking lot to Reese's cruiser. She carried her briefcase in one hand and a paper bag in the other.

"You can't harass my staff in the middle of office hours, Sheriff," Tory remarked threateningly as she slid into the front seat.

"Says who? *I'm* the law around here."

Tory leaned over and kissed Reese on the mouth, then glanced pointedly at Reese's right arm and frowned. "How are you feeling, really? And I don't want a two-word answer."

Reese grinned. "Being pregnant makes you cranky."

"You haven't *seen* cranky yet, sweetheart. Now, let's have a progress report."

"No swelling, no numbness, and…just a little stiff and sore."

"Good." Tory leaned back with a sigh and closed her eyes.

"You okay?" Reese glanced over in concern.

Tory rested her left hand on Reese's thigh and patted her gently. "It was hectic this morning, that's all."

"Do you have your lunch?"

Smiling, Tory turned her head and opened her eyes. "Yes, I do. As per your instructions. Whatever it is you do to Randy, you make him nervous. There was no way he was letting me out of the building without it. I was afraid he was going to do a full body search."

Reese grinned. "If he tries that, I'll *really* make him nervous."

❖

Forty-five minutes later, *Reese* was nervous. "Tell me again what this is going to show."

They were seated on facing chairs in one corner of Wendy Deutsch's waiting room. There were two other couples in the room, the female members of each pair conspicuously pregnant.

Tory rested her hand on Reese's knee. The thick khaki fabric of her uniform pants was as reassuringly solid as Reese herself. "It will give Wendy, and us, some information about the baby— how it's developing. If we didn't know exactly when the date of conception was, it would help determine fetal age, too."

Reese cleared her throat, ignoring the faint churning in her stomach. "So, it's routine."

"Almost eighty percent of pregnant women have an ultrasound performed at some point during their pregnancy," Tory assured her. "And for high-ri—uh, for women over thirty-five, it's absolutely standard."

*High risk. She doesn't think I know?* Reese covered Tory's hand with hers and squeezed gently. "And we'll be able to see its… parts?"

"What parts would you be referring to?" Tory couldn't smother a laugh. "Besides, I thought you said you didn't care."

"That's not what I meant," Reese grumbled in mock indignation. "The head and the heart and the spine. *Those* parts."

"Very good, Sheriff. Yes, at eleven weeks we can see the heart beat and with a good image, we can tell if the neural crest elements—the brain and spinal cord—are developing normally."

*God, what if...* But that was like wondering what an upcoming battle would be like. What it might be like to be shot or killed. Pointless musings about an eventuality that might never arise. Reese straightened her shoulders, and, with the long-ingrained gesture, her nervousness disappeared. "Will you be able to tell its sex, if you see it?"

"Well, if I see *it,* I'll know. But not seeing a penis doesn't mean it's not a boy. It just means it doesn't show."

"But *I* won't be able to tell," Reese pointed out in a rare show of pique. "I've seen those pictures in your books. They look like a bunch of blanks in a snowstorm."

"I'll make sure you see, if you want to."

"If you know, I want to know."

"Deal." Tory extended her hand to seal the bargain.

Reese smiled and took Tory's hand, but she didn't shake it. She folded it between both of hers and leaned forward to murmur, "I love you."

"I lo—"

"You two all set?" Wendy's nurse interrupted as she approached with a chart in one hand.

"Yes," they said in unison.

Forty minutes later, Tory was dressed again, and she and Reese waited in one of the consultation rooms for Wendy to return with the printouts of the ultrasound examination.

"So, what do you think about names?" Reese's blue eyes were dancing. "Something nice and strong to go with King, like yours. Victoria Conlon King. Great name for a girl. Oh, but Victoria's already taken. And we already have too many Kates and Catherines in the family. My mother, your sister. Maybe—"

"Reese, sweetheart," Tory said calmly. "We don't *know* it's a girl."

"Well, yeah, but we saw *everything*. So if it was there, we would've seen—"

The door opened and Wendy came in. "Okay," she said briskly as she walked around the cluttered desk and sat down. She extended her hand with the Polaroids. "Here you go. Baby's first pictures."

Grinning, Reese took them, then glanced down as she shuffled through the images. Suddenly, all the black and white splotches looked miraculously like arms and legs and facial expressions.

"Everything seems fine with the fetus," Wendy commented neutrally.

*Fine with the fetus, but...*Reese looked up instantly, her eyes darkening, searching and intent. She glanced at Tory, whose expression was unreadable.

"Your blood pressure is just a tad high, Tory."

"Yes, I know," Tory replied evenly. "I've been charting it for the last few weeks. It's been running a bit above normal, but today is about the highest it's been. I guess I was a little nervous."

"Understandable, and nothing to get alarmed about, although it bears watching. Keep a log. Call me if it starts reading higher. For now, limit your salt intake. And no caffeine at all."

Tory groaned.

"Sorry." Wendy grinned. "Regular exercise and plenty of rest."

"Can I keep kayaking?"

"I don't see why not."

"What about the dojo?" It was a quiet inquiry from Reese. "Should she quit?"

"Not until the last trimester," Wendy replied. "I wouldn't let an inexperienced student throw you, Tory, but ordinary workouts should be fine."

"Okay." Tory watched Reese, who had gotten very still. A muscle bunched at the base of her jaw. *Ah, damn. I didn't handle this very well.*

"Good." Wendy stood. "Then I'll see you in two weeks. I've got to run. Call me any time."

After Wendy left, Reese asked flatly, "Why didn't you tell me?"

Tory debated several answers, but there was really only one thing she could say. "I didn't want you to worry."

"Don't do that again, okay?" Reese reached over and took Tory's hand.

"No," Tory murmured, lifting Reese's hand to her lips. "I won't."

❖

The taxi ride to the airport was quiet, and Tory napped on the short flight back to the tiny Provincetown airport.

"Do you want to go out for dinner?" Tory had only a scant memory of the bag lunch.

"It's been a long day," Reese commented quietly as they settled into the car. "Let's go home, and I'll cook."

"Perfect."

When they reached the house, Jed's exuberant barking welcomed them, and Tory grabbed his lead from the hook just inside the door. "How about I take him for a walk while you start dinner?"

"Great. He'll like that." On the threshold, Reese leaned over to kiss Tory lightly on the cheek. "You've got at least forty-five minutes."

Tory ran her fingers lightly down Reese's arm. "See you soon."

Reese watched Tory disappear down the path to the harbor and wondered what was bothering her. And when she would share it.

❖

The beach was deserted. The evening air was cold enough to require a jacket, but warm enough to promise summer around the corner. Tory carried Jed's lead and let him run ahead. She walked along the water's edge, watching the last memory of sunlight shimmer and die across the water.

"Hey, Jedi, we're going to have a baby," she whispered. "What do you think, huh? Pretty amazing."

He didn't answer, but his large form in the gathering night was a comfort. As shadows turned to darkness around her, she watched stars flicker on overhead. "Pretty scary, too."

Her stomach was queasy from the events of the afternoon, and it wasn't just the news about the hypertension. She'd seen that coming for a while and already had some practice trying to put her worries about it aside. Most of the time, she succeeded. Keeping *Reese* from worrying might prove to be a bigger challenge.

Most unexpectedly, it was the ultrasound that had thrown her. Watching the tiny movements, listening to the rapid beat of a microscopic heart, had impressed even her scientific mind with the magnitude of what was happening inside her body. As much as she'd thought herself prepared for the changes that were coming, there were still moments when she was almost overwhelmed. There were suddenly so many things she needed to balance—her personal needs for professional fulfillment, her responsibility to Reese, the physical demands of her pregnancy. In the midst of happiness, she would suddenly feel uncertain, wondering how she was going to manage everything. Just thinking about the incredible challenge and responsibility of raising a child sometimes made her feel inadequate.

*People have been doing it for millennia, right? Reese and I love each other, and we want this baby. That's what counts, right? God, what is wrong with me? I'm never like this.*

Jed came bounding over, a look of supreme contentment in his eyes. Unfortunately, his happiness was a direct result of the abandoned horseshoe crab shell he carried joyfully in his big jaws.

"Ick. Gross. Drop that, Jed," she scolded, secretly happy to be distracted from her concerns.

He regarded her as if she had momentarily lost her mind and sat in the sand on his haunches, turning his head from side to side as the carapace crunched with each small movement.

"I'm not going to fight with you, Jedi. *Drop it.*"

With a morose droop in his enormous shoulders, he relinquished his treasure, depositing it at her feet reluctantly.

"Good boy," she praised as she patted his head. "We should probably head home. Reese will have dinner ready soon."

As she looked over her shoulder, she saw the lights of their home flickering through the small pines that separated the rear deck from the beach. Knowing that Reese was back there filled her with a sense of assurance and comfort. Each time she found herself struggling with doubt or fear, she had only to think of Reese to realize that whatever challenge awaited her, she would not face it alone.

*She's truly the rock upon which my world stands.*

A few moments later, Tory let herself in through the sliding doors from the deck. Jed bounded ahead and skidded clumsily around the breakfast bar into the cooking area, nearly clipping Reese behind the knees.

"Hey! Get out of here, you oaf," Reese yelled. Turning with a spatula in one hand, she smiled at Tory. "Is there a reason he smells like week-old fish?"

"Dead sea treasures."

"Lovely." Reese slid a plate with appetizers onto the counter. "You can nibble on these while I finish dinner."

"Thanks." Tory settled onto a stool.

"I got a request from the academy today to accept a new cadet for field training in May."

"Really? You want to?"

"Yeah, I do." Reese nibbled on a carrot stick. "But I'm not sure how well Nelson will handle it."

"Why would he mind?"

"It's Bri."

"Oh." Tory paused. "Will he be jealous?"

Reese looked surprised. "I never though of that. I was worried he'd think it was a conflict politically. You know, because Bri's his daughter."

"I'd think it would be okay as long as you were doing her evaluations."

"Good," Reese said as she stir-fried greens for pasta. "Because I'll feel better if she's with me those first few months."

"I love you," Tory murmured.

Stopping in mid-motion, Reese raised an eyebrow. The tone of her lover's voice had not been casual. "You okay?"

"Mostly." Tory extended her right hand on the countertop and Reese took it. "Sometimes, you know, I get a little…" She sighed and shook her head. "It all just sort of hits me."

"Yeah, me, too. But you know what?"

"What?"

Reese released her hand, walked around the breakfast island, and circled her arms around Tory. "Everything is going to be just fine."

Tory threaded her arms around Reese's waist, rested her head against the broad chest, and closed her eyes. With her cheek pressed to her lover's heart and the heat of the familiar body enclosing her, she couldn't conjure up a single worry. Quietly, she murmured, "I knew that."

❖

"God, it feels good to get into bed," Reese observed with a contented sigh. She stretched out her arm and Tory snuggled close, the movement automatic after hundreds of nights together.

"Yes, so good." Tory smoothed her hand over Reese's chest, then down the center of her abdomen. Drifting, pleasantly tired, she trailed her fingers over the edge of a hipbone and down one hard-muscled thigh. When Reese curled her right arm around Tory's body, Tory felt the long ridge of the healing scar brush along her skin. A quick thrust of fear swept through her as she realized anew what she had nearly lost. In the next breath, she envisioned walking on the beach earlier and how just *thinking* about Reese had settled her. She remembered, too, what life had been like before Reese had come into her world, bringing such pure and selfless love.

*Everything. You're everything.*

Tory pressed her lips to Reese's shoulder, reveling in the heat of her skin. Her heartbeat quickened, as did her passion. "Reese?"

"Hmm?"

"You tired?"

There was a beat of silence, then a soft chuckle. "Is that an invitation?"

Tory shifted until she was lying on top. Her legs fit perfectly between Reese's; her fingers curled possessively over Reese's shoulders. "Could be."

"Feels like."

Laughing softly, Tory leaned down and kissed Reese, slowly at first, light teasing kisses. As their skin touched softly, their bodies cleaved even closer. Soon Tory sought more, slipping her tongue inside Reese's mouth, hungry now. Moaning softly, she raised herself until her nipples were close to Reese's mouth. Shakily, she whispered, "Suck them, sweetheart."

Tenderly, Reese captured Tory's breasts in both hands, squeezing them gently together as her mouth moved first from one nipple to the other. As Reese sucked carefully, pleasantly torturing the sensitive tips, Tory shifted to straddle Reese's hips, rocking herself rhythmically until her desire streaked wetly over Reese's abdomen. Reese thrust her hips in time to Tory's soft cries of pleasure, hard and full herself and wanting desperately to be touched.

"Stop," Tory panted. "It feels so good. I can't stand it."

"Come up here." Reese's voice was a husky growl. Then she slid her hands down Tory's back to her hips and drew her higher on the bed. The scent of her lover's arousal made Reese's clitoris twitch almost painfully, and she shut her eyes tightly for a second against the surge of need that threatened to steal her concentration. Hoarsely, she whispered, "This okay?"

"Yes. God, yes." Tory leaned forward, braced her palms flat against the wall, and lowered herself onto Reese's mouth. A small cry fluttered from her throat at the first touch of Reese's lips. She tried not to move, not to hurry, but the blood pounded insistently, making her clitoris stiffen and throb with each knowing stroke of Reese's tongue. When she didn't think she could get any harder without exploding, she looked over her shoulder and down the length of Reese's body, taut and trembling against the sheets.

"You're so beautiful." Tory moaned, lifting herself from Reese's mouth. She twisted around, settling once again on top of her lover, this time with her face against Reese's thigh. Desperately she begged, "Come with me?"

"Yesss."

Then Tory parted the engorged tissues with trembling fingers, entering deeply at the same time as she enclosed Reese's clitoris with her lips. Reese jerked and cried out sharply before she took Tory once again.

Boundaries and borders disappeared as their flesh became one, passion a raging flood overflowing the restraints of their desire. They held to one another, dangling on the precipice of surrender, until Tory pulled her face away with a sharp gasp.

"I'm...ready. Have...to come."

"Yes, love," Reese echoed tightly, before drawing Tory in even more deeply.

Tory pressed her lips to Reese's quivering clitoris and trembled as they exploded in unison. Reese held her as she bucked and shook, letting her soar, all the while keeping her safe.

When she gently floated back to earth, Tory found herself once again cradled in Reese's arms, her head tucked securely beneath Reese's chin. She had no idea when she had moved. Reese's chest heaved with the last vestiges of release, her heart hammering beneath Tory's cheek.

"You okay, sweetheart?" Tory questioned softly.

"Hell, yes." Reese laughed shortly, a sound very nearly a sob. "I think I'm still coming."

"Mmm," Tory murmured throatily, her fingers drifting lower. "Go again?"

"No way." Reese grabbed her wrist, stilling her motion. "I'll jump right out of my skin. You're too good. Criminally good."

"So arrest me, Sheriff. I won't try to escape..." Tory's voice trailed off as she slipped into sleep, her hand clasped in Reese's.

"Don't worry," Reese whispered, pressing her lips to the top of Tory's head. "I don't plan on letting you go."

She had worked hard all night not to acknowledge the faint note of caution she'd heard in Wendy Deutsch's voice when Tory's blood pressure elevation was mentioned that afternoon. But the echo of the doctor's words had been there all the time in the back of her mind, a subtle almost intangible warning, like shifting shadows in the mist on night patrol. A good marine learned to heed those silent warnings, because the price of ignoring them was losing the skirmish, or worse. Reese stroked Tory's back, her own breath nearly still in her chest.

*You are everything. Everything.*

# CHAPTER NINE

## April, Manhattan, NY

It was after eleven on Friday night when Caroline walked into the apartment. She gave a small cry of surprise when she saw the familiar figure sprawled on the couch.

"Bri! Why didn't you tell me you were coming?"

Bri stood, shaking the fog of an unplanned nap from her head. It was warm in the apartment, and she'd just closed her eyes for a second. She'd hit the road after her last class and ridden straight through, not even stopping to eat.

"I knew it would take me most of the evening to get here, and I figured if you had plans…" Shrugging, Bri stuffed her hands into her pockets. She'd wanted to come down since the day they'd fought, but it had never happened. First, Reese had been sick, and she'd spent all her free time at the hospital. Then she had classes to make up. Every time she called, Caroline wasn't in. If her girlfriend had called back, she'd never gotten a message. Finally, when the distance stretched into an ache that consumed her days, she'd just decided to come.

"And you thought I'd rather be out doing something else when I could have been waiting here for you?" Caroline shook her head and deposited her portfolio and other things on a small bookcase inside the door. "Do you think I'd want to miss a minute we could be together?"

"You were mad at me," Bri said hoarsely, still not moving. "I'm sorry for what I said about…James."

Caroline came around the couch to Bri. She slipped both arms around her shoulders and pressed close. With her lips against Bri's neck, she murmured, "You're *such* an idiot sometimes. How could you think that for a second?"

"I don't know." Bri rested her cheek on top of Caroline's head. "The longer I'm away from you, the more confused I get. Things don't make sense when we're apart."

"Then come home," Caroline entreated desperately. "Please come back. I'm so lonely without you."

Bri groaned and pulled the smaller woman hard against her. The weather had turned unseasonably warm, as it did sometimes in early spring. Bri was in a T-shirt and jeans, while Caroline wore a cotton blouse open far enough to show the swell of her breasts. Bri caught her breath as she felt Caroline's nipples harden through the thin layers of fabric. They stood there, holding on as tightly as they could, as if the distance between them could be banished by obliterating the air between their bodies.

"I miss you so bad, but I *can't* come back now." Bri was almost pleading. "I'll be through the academy in a few weeks. I *have* to finish."

"Oh, baby, I know. I know." Caroline smoothed her hands up and down Bri's back, turning her face to kiss Bri's neck, the sharp line of her jaw, the corner of her mouth.

Shaking, Bri stifled a cry and found Caroline's lips, aroused and tentative at the same time. She'd never been afraid of the wanting before, because Caroline had always been there to soothe her hunger with a sure touch and certain heart. Now, away from her, the wanting was a torment that haunted Bri day and night. Desire had transformed into loneliness, and it left her aching and lost.

"Bri?" Caroline questioned softly as she drew her head back to search her lover's face. "What's wrong?"

"Nothing. I just missed you."

Sensing Bri's hesitancy, Caroline stepped away. At the look of panic that flickered briefly in Bri's eyes, to be just as quickly extinguished, she smiled softly. "Just stand there for a second." Then she turned and quickly pulled open the sofa bed and smoothed back the sheets. Extending her hand, she said, "Come here."

By the side of the bed, Caroline gently pulled Bri's T-shirt from her jeans and lifted it over her arms and off. Then she sat on the edge of the bed and brought both hands to the buttons on Bri's jeans. When Bri reached to help, Caroline brushed her hands away. "No. Let me."

In another minute, Bri was naked, trembling in a way she could never recall—her skin hot and cold at the same time, her muscles so tight she felt as if she would snap, and yet so weak, she could barely stand. "Carre," she said hoarsely. "What are you doing?"

Caroline looked up, her ocean-green eyes fathoms deep. "I'm reminding you of us."

When Caroline tugged her down to the bed, Bri followed, helpless to resist. Uncharacteristically passive, she stretched out on her back as Caroline leaned over her. When the blond head lowered over her chest and soft lips captured her nipple, she arched upward with a startled cry. She brought trembling hands to Caroline's hair and stroked the soft strands, urgently needing an anchor, feeling as if she might fly apart.

Caroline had her palm pressed to Bri's tense stomach, and when Bri tried to rise, needing the familiar feel of her lover beneath her, Caroline lifted her head and said swiftly, "No."

For a heartbeat, Bri resisted, but then the hand slipped lower, cupping her possessively between her thighs, and she fell back with a strangled groan. Her head was suddenly light; her heart pounded so hard it was pulsing visibly between her ribs. Her hands lay open, palms up by her side, as her friend, her lover, her heart, lay claim to what was hers, stroking every inch of Bri's flesh until she quivered uncontrollably.

"This is where you belong, you know," Caroline gasped at some point. "With me."

And Bri could only moan in response. When she didn't think she could stand it any longer, she pushed up on her elbows and looked down the length of her body. Caroline's cheek lay against her stomach; she stroked her fingers between Bri's legs, touching her teasingly for a few seconds and then moving away, measuring out her torture to the beat of Bri's strangled breathing and the rhythm of her twitching muscles.

"Make me yours," Bri whispered as she rested her fingers beseechingly against Caroline's head and pressed, urging her lower. For a heart-stopping instant, she thought Caroline would resist, but then in one fluid motion the blond head dipped and a warm mouth enclosed her. Bri jerked and cried out, her bones dissolving. She fell back, strength failing as pleasure shot through her. She was hard to the point of bursting, and Caroline's lips were so soft as they licked and tugged at her swollen flesh. The brush of a tongue along the length of her clitoris nearly made her head explode.

"Oh, yeah. Yeah."

Caroline looked up, a satisfied smile on her face. Her voice was like velvet as she purred, "Remember me?"

"Jesus, don't quit," Bri gasped. "I'm gonna come any second."

"Really?" Caroline's tone was ingenuous as she slipped fingers inside.

Bri arched off the bed, thigh muscles straining, her breath tearing from her on a hoarse cry. "Oh, please. Please…"

A wave of nearly painful pleasure swept through Caroline at the sound of Bri's need, and she lowered her head to capture her again with her mouth. Gently, prolonging the moment, she merely held her between her lips, not moving until she felt the sudden swelling all along the shaft. Then, she sucked gently, urging the orgasm to unfold and engulf her lover in one continuous, rolling surge of release. So absorbed in the moment, she was startled when Bri sobbed her name. It was the most beautiful thing she'd ever heard.

Bri didn't return to awareness until she felt Caroline, naked now, stretched out on top of her, moving in the familiar rhythm of desire. Caroline's face was pressed to her neck, her skin slick with urgency, her breath little more than faint broken cries. Bri felt the wet heat as her lover rocked frantically the length of her thigh. She barely had the strength to do more than wrap her arms around her, but she clasped Caroline's hips, adding to the pressure that would bring her off.

"Babe, babe," Bri whispered, her lips to the delicate curve of ear. "I love you."

Caroline's only response was a choked sob.

"That's it, Carre, that's it."

"Oh…I'm coming."

"Do it. Do it." Bri groaned, her heart pounding wildly as Caroline stiffened and whimpered faintly. "Come on me, babe.

Come all over me." Impossibly, Bri felt a second orgasm rise from her depths, a distant thunder eclipsed by the storm raging in Caroline's body. "Oh, yeah. *Yeah*."

Caroline jerked convulsively, her hands desperately clutching Bri's shoulders, and screamed as the climax pummeled her. Bri strained into her, closing her eyes, letting her lover's passion carry her away.

❖

"Man, I've missed that," Caroline mumbled when she emerged from the pleasant torpor that followed. She was still on top of Bri, their arms and legs entangled. "I thought I was going to melt."

"*Meltdown* is more like it." Bri smoothed her hands up and down Caroline's back. Caroline had always been aggressive in bed, but it was rare that Bri let her take control so completely. She was still a little shell-shocked by how helpless—how raw and exposed—she had felt. Laughing a little self-consciously, she added, "You practically gave me a stroke."

"Good." Caroline traced a finger along Bri's neck and down her chest, stopping to cup her breast in her palm. "Feeling better?"

"I can't feel anything at all. I'm pretty sure my legs fell off."

Caroline laughed and snuggled even closer, drawing one leg across Bri's thighs and wrapping an arm around her midsection. "I love you."

"Mmm." Bri ran her fingers through the soft golden hair. "Lucky for me."

"Uh-huh. And try not to forget it, okay?"

"I'm sorry for being an asshole," Bri whispered. When they were together like this, it was hard to remember what made her feel so lonely and so lost.

"It's okay," Caroline said softly. "You're not."

"Yeah, well." Bri sighed as Caroline snuggled closer. "Sometimes I am."

"How's Reese?"

"Good. Better."

"I'm sorry I didn't get up to see her."

"I'll tell her you said hi." As an afterthought, Bri asked, "Have you talked to Tory lately?"

"Not since Reese was in the hospital. It was so crazy—I could never catch her in."

"So you don't know?"

"Know what?"

"Tory's pregnant."

"Oh my God! That's *so* great."

"Yeah. Pretty cool, huh?"

"Oh, I can't wait to see Tory and ask her all about it," Caroline exclaimed. *I want us to have a baby some day.*

"Well, there's a big party in Barnstable the Friday of Memorial Day weekend—kind of like an early graduation thing. Those of us who are done with our class work are celebrating." Bri nuzzled Caroline's ear contentedly. "So if you came up for that, we could swing over and see Tory and Reese after."

Caroline grew still. After a moment, she said, "Uh…it's special, huh?"

"Well, sorta." Bri thought for a second, trying to clear her fuzzy brain. From the way she felt, most of her blood flow was still centered between her legs. "You know, I want you to meet my friends. You're coming for the weekend anyhow, right?"

Another stretch of silence ensued.

"Carre? What's going on?" Bri opened her eyes, suddenly wide-awake.

Caroline's voice was flat, impossible to read. "Part of the scholarship for next year has this work-study thing."

"Uh-huh." Bri's heart started triple-timing. *Jesus, something else? Can't we just forget about that for a while?*

"There's an orientation that whole week. I won't be done until late Friday, and then I'm supposed to go to some kind of reception thing."

"Oh." Bri worked to keep the disappointment from her voice. "So I guess you can't make the party then."

"I'm sorry, I don't think so."

"Well, that's okay. It's just my classmates. No big deal." It felt odd, needing to ask Caroline for a date. It felt even odder to find that things were happening in both their lives that kept them apart. "Work study? What's that going to involve?"

"I'll be assisting one of the profs in the art department," Caroline said quietly. "The problem is…I'm going to be working here for the summer."

"Wait a minute." The significance of what Caroline was saying finally sank in. Swiftly, Bri sat up and reached for the sheet, pulling part of it over herself, searching for some fragment of protection, as if the thin material could shield her heart. "You're not coming home to the Cape for the summer?"

"No."

"And you didn't even *tell* me? Jesus."

"I didn't know until yesterday," Caroline said miserably. "I would have told you sooner—"

"So." Bri cut her off, amazed at how calm she felt inside. No, not calm. Cold. Cold and, mercifully, numb. "So, I'm going to be there, and you're going to be here. And then you're going to be in Europe. For a year."

"We talked about next year." Caroline sat up now, too. She searched around on the floor, found her blouse, and pulled it on. Automatically, she handed Bri her T-shirt. "You said you were okay with it…you *wanted* me—"

"Oh, come on." Bri couldn't take it anymore. She got out of bed, hunted up her jeans, and tugged them on. Her hands trembled as she buttoned her jeans, and she turned away so Caroline wouldn't see. *This is the beginning of the end, don't you see? You go your way, I go mine—sometime in the next twelve months we admit things have changed, and we're done.*

"What are you doing?" Caroline got to her feet and grabbed Bri's forearms. "What's the matter with you? We *knew* this was going to happen sooner or later."

"Not now! Later! We were supposed to have the summer." Bri felt trapped. Powerless. *Don't you see? It's changing already. You didn't even tell me!*

"Do you think I don't care about that?"

"I don't *know*!"

Bri walked to the door and grabbed her helmet and jacket. *But it's happening now, and it's so much worse than I imagined. And what happens when you come back? You'll have a new life, and I'll be part of your old life. I'll be the past. I can't stand around waiting and wondering when that will happen.*

"Where are you going?" Caroline's voice was filled with anger and tears. "It's two o'clock in the morning."

Bri couldn't think of a single thing to say. She couldn't say *goodbye*, because the words would tear her heart out. She couldn't say *I love you*, because the words wouldn't change what was going to happen. In the end, she said nothing.

❖

Bri drove all night and pulled into the parking lot in front of the training center with ten minutes to spare. When she'd left for Manhattan the night before, she'd planned on skipping her Saturday weapons class. Now, school seemed like the only thing that might take her mind off the howling pain that had threatened to swallow her up all night.

She must have sleepwalked through the class, because an hour and a half later, she was surprised to find herself straddling her bike again. She fiddled with her keys, contemplating the rest of the day. The thought of going back to the barren apartment almost made her ill. She could ride to Provincetown, maybe visit Reese. But she should call before she did that. Visit her dad? No, he would only ask her questions that she didn't have the strength to answer.

"Hey," Allie said as she walked up. "You okay?"

Bri raised her head, slightly confused, then smiled faintly in recognition. Allie was wearing an academy T-shirt, tight blue jeans, and expensive-looking hand-tooled cowboy boots. She looked tough and sexy at the same time. "Yeah, sure. Fine."

"I thought you looked a little spacey in class. Rough night?"

"Yeah." Bri laughed bitterly. "Something like that."

"How about I make you breakfast?" The blond moved a little closer and placed a hand on Bri's knee.

Bri didn't even have to think twice. "Okay."

"Excellent." With a broad smile, Allie placed her palm on Bri's shoulder, threw a leg over the broad bike, and snuggled up close. She wrapped both arms around Bri's waist, her hands resting in the curve of Bri's thighs. "Most excellent."

It took only a few minutes to reach Allie's small cottage.

"Is this all yours?" Bri was still feeling a little disoriented.

Allie slid off Bri's Harley, removed her helmet, and hooked it to the bracket on the back. "Yeah, I'm renting it for now. Depending on where I get assigned for my training period, I'll either keep it or sublease it."

"Nice," Bri commented as she followed Allie up the drive.

"Come on in." Allie opened the door and stepped through into a warm and welcoming living room. The furniture was typical for a shoreside cottage, with sturdy wood-framed fabric-covered sofas, matching end tables, and prints displaying seaside vistas on the walls. The compact galley kitchen occupied the rear of the main room and was separated from the living and eating area by a waist-high divider. A door opposite a small fireplace opened into the second room, which appeared to be the bedroom. "Have you put in your request for placement yet?"

"Yeah." Bri waited awkwardly just inside the door, her jacket in one hand. She wasn't used to being alone with another woman. She'd never dated anyone other than Caroline, and although they had a small cadre of male and female friends, they had done almost everything socially as a couple. She'd never had a girlfriend in the sense of a best friend, no one except Caroline, and from the very beginning, it had been more than just friendship between them.

"Sit down," Allie suggested, waving toward the couch. "You want coffee?"

"Yeah, that would be great." As an afterthought, as she headed for the couch, Bri asked, "Do you, uh, need me to do anything?"

"No. Go ahead and relax. You look like you could use it." Allie leaned a shoulder against the open refrigerator door, observed Bri with a small smile, and shook her head. "I can manage this."

Bri clasped her hands between her knees and nodded. Now that she was sitting, she realized that she really *was* beat. A night without sleep and ten hours on the road had left her a little fuzzy. Plus, whenever she fought with Caroline, her world slipped out of focus and nothing quite made sense. There was an ache in her chest that wouldn't quit and an empty feeling in the pit of her stomach.

"Bri?"

"What?" Bri jumped. "Sorry."

"Toast and eggs okay?"

"Sure."

"Just give me a minute."

Bri leaned her head back against the sofa and closed her eyes. When she opened them again, it took her a few seconds to place her surroundings. She was leaning to one side into the corner of the couch, her legs up on the cushions and taking up most of the rest of the sitting area. Allie was seated at the other end, her bare feet propped up on the coffee table, a magazine open on her lap.

"Good nap?" Allie was smiling.

"Oh, man, I'm sorry." Bri jerked upright, rubbed both hands over her face, and searched the wall for a clock. When she saw that it was mid-afternoon, she realized that she had been asleep for several hours. Blushing, she glanced sideways into Allie's dark eyes. "What a jerk, huh?"

"Uh-uh." Allie shifted closer until their shoulders touched, turning slightly so she could meet Bri's eyes. "I thought it was pretty cute when you just conked out. You didn't even flinch when I put your legs up."

"Sorry about breakfast."

"That's okay."

Suddenly, Bri was acutely aware of Allie's body pressing lightly along her side. She was also aware of her light perfume, a scent very different than Caroline's but nice in a pretty sort of way. When she felt the light brush of fingers over her hand, Bri looked down. Allie's hand was small, each nail perfectly sculpted and glossy with a pale pink hue. It was very quiet in the room. The soft rhythm of Allie breathing was soothing and, at the same time, exciting.

A pulse tripped unexpectedly between Bri's thighs, and she caught her breath in surprise. Reflexively, she stood up and stepped away a pace. "I should go. I've got a lot of reading to catch up on."

"Are you going out later?" Allie stood, too. "You know, Saturday night at the Breakers?"

"I don't know," Bri said awkwardly. "Maybe."

"I'll be there." Allie walked with Bri toward the door. "Look for me, okay?"

"Sure, if I go."

When Bri mounted her bike and pulled out onto the highway, she didn't head back to her temporary apartment. She took the highway that wound along the ocean and rode until the churning want in her depths subsided. By the time she returned, it was nearly dark. She didn't go out again that night.

# CHAPTER TEN

## Late April, Provincetown, MA

Tory walked into the bedroom and stopped to watch Reese finish getting dressed. She loved Reese's precise, orderly morning routine. Even today, when Reese wasn't putting on her uniform, but rather chinos and a cotton shirt, she went about the small tasks of getting ready for the day in an efficient, practiced manner. It was one of the things Tory found so comforting about her lover. Reese exuded strength and stability.

It had been frightening at first to discover how quickly she had come to rely on Reese's unwavering presence, how rapidly she had surrendered to the safety and comfort of that love. Now, three years later, she would see Reese sleeping beside her, or propped up in bed reading, or preparing for work, and find herself amazed still that this remarkable woman was in her life. It was at those times when a sudden pulse of fear raced through her, and she remembered what life had been like before Reese and imagined the impossibility of a future without her.

Reese glanced over and caught the contemplative expression on Tory's face. "What are you thinking?"

"Oh…" Tory blushed faintly at being caught in such pointless reverie. "How much I love you."

"Still, huh?" Reese's blue eyes danced as she crossed the bedroom and slid her arms around Tory's waist. Her lips were soft, her kiss gentle. A moment later, she asked, "You okay about today?"

"Just a little bit nervous," Tory confessed.

"Since you always tell me that everything is just routine," Reese reminded her gently, "I never know whether I should worry or not."

"Well, an amniocentesis *is* routine, and thousands are done every day." Tory lightly kissed Reese's jaw. "But it's always a little different when it's you."

"Yes, and it's even harder when it's not."

Tory leaned back in the circle of Reese's arms and studied her intently. "What do you mean?"

"It's hard for me not being able to do anything about you being pregnant."

"Do?" Tory raised an eyebrow. "What would you like to do, sweetheart?"

"I'd like to make sure it's perfect. I'd like to keep you safe." Reese kissed Tory's forehead. "Protect and serve—those are the things I know how to do."

"Oh, Reese," Tory breathed, her smile soft. "You do so much more than you'll ever know—for me, for Bri, for Kate." She smoothed her palm over Reese's chest and kissed her again. "Let's go to the airport."

❖

Two hours later, Reese and Tory arrived at Boston City Hospital, where Tory usually spent her time as an attending physician in the emergency room and not as a patient. When they reached the outpatient obstetrical clinic, they were greeted by a happy cry of welcome.

"Tory!"

"Oh my God, Cath! You didn't have to come in just for this." Tory gathered her sister into a tight hug.

"I haven't seen you in weeks, and this was a great excuse to leave the kids with Danny for the day." Tory's younger sister, a fairer-haired, blue-eyed version of Tory, threw both arms around the pregnant woman and kissed her vigorously on both cheeks. Then she stepped back to allow her eyes to roam over Tory's form. "Look at you. You're gorgeous." She turned to Reese. "Isn't she?"

Smiling, Reese nodded. "Yes. Beautiful."

Blushing profusely, Tory grabbed both Cath and Reese by the hand and pulled them out of the center of the hallway. "Be quiet, you two. You're embarrassing me."

"This is so exciting." Eyes sparkling, Cath looked from Reese to Tory in undisguised delight. "I spoke with Mom and Dad last night, and they can't stop talking about how much they're looking forward to another grandchild. They thought when Danny got his tubes snipped and we were done that they wouldn't have any more. You have no idea how happy you've made them."

Tory slipped her arm around Reese's waist and leaned into her as Reese draped an arm over her shoulder. "I wish they lived closer so we could see them more often."

"Don't worry. I've already been talking to Mom about getting plane tickets so they can come down after the baby is born."

"You mean you actually got Dad to agree to fly?" Tory turned to Reese. "My father doesn't trust anyone else to navigate. Even though they're ten hours away, he always insists on driving."

"I seem to recall him mentioning that the last time we got together," Reese remarked with a grin.

"Well," Cath said, "I think the opportunity to spend more time with his newest grandchild has convinced him that it was worth it for once."

"Amazing." Tory gestured to the sign-in desk. "I should let them know I'm here. I'll be right back."

Cath watched her sister walk away and then tilted her head to study Reese. "How're you doing?"

"Pretty well."

"Nervous?"

Reese nodded.

"Are you going in with her?"

"As long as it's okay with Wendy." The very thought of something being done to Tory while she waited outside in the hall was enough to make Reese's stomach cramp. She didn't get this nervous when she was facing down a drunk with a knife.

"You know," Cath said, taking Reese's hand, "my husband almost passed out when I had my last one. I think it's a normal spousal response."

"I'm glad to hear that," Reese confided softly. "Because I feel that way half the time."

Cath patted Reese's cheek. "You know, honey, you're the best thing that's ever happened to her."

Reese glanced across the room to where Tory was filling out paperwork at the counter. Even from where she stood, Reese could clearly see the swell of her abdomen beneath the loose pullover she wore. Tory's cheeks were brushed a delicate rose, and everything about her seemed fresh and alive—miraculous. When Reese spoke, her voice was husky. "I'm the lucky one."

"I'd say it's mutual." Cath saw Reese's expression change suddenly, her eyes growing focused and intent. She followed Reese's gaze and saw the reason why. Stiffening, she grumbled, "I can't believe it. What is *she* doing here? Son of a...Tory doesn't *need* this now!"

"It's okay," Reese said quietly, placing a restraining hand on Cath's arm. She watched as K.T. spoke to Tory and resisted the urge to join them herself. "She was moonlighting when I was in the hospital. Tory saw her there."

"Tory never mentioned that." Cath had her eyes riveted on the tall, dark-haired surgeon. "She probably knew I'd be stalking through the halls with a gun."

"Tory's okay, Cath," Reese assured her gently.

"Yes, maybe she is. But *I* still haven't forgiven K.T."

At that moment, K.T. turned away from Tory and, glancing in their direction, nodded a greeting.

Reese inclined her head, but Cath merely glared.

Tory rejoined them as the surgeon disappeared down a hallway on the far side of the room. One look at her sister, and Tory knew exactly what was happening. "She saw my name on the outpatient schedule. She just came by to say hello."

"How nice," Cath said acerbically.

"It's okay, sis. Really."

"I know." Cath forced a smile. "So, how long did they say?"

"Wendy is running on time, so it shouldn't be more than half an hour."

They settled in to wait, Tory and Cath catching up on family news while Reese held Tory's hand and tried to relax.

❖

"I just want to make sure the samples get off to the lab." Wendy Deutsch applied a small Band-Aid to the puncture wound in Tory's abdomen just below her umbilicus. "I'll be back in a minute."

"You okay, sweetheart?" Tory turned her head to Reese, who sat by her side on a tall stainless steel stool. Reese's hair was damp with sweat.

"Fine."

"I'm sorry. I couldn't really talk during the procedure."

"That's okay, love." Reese brushed her fingers over Tory's cheek. "I'm pretty sure you weren't supposed to be talking. Wendy explained everything, and I saw as much as I needed to."

As a matter of fact, she'd barely remembered to breathe as she watched Wendy place a long needle through Tory's abdomen and into her uterus. She'd been able to follow the path of the needle perfectly well on the ultrasound monitor. It seemed to pass within millimeters of the baby's head, which, at sixteen weeks, even she could make out without assistance. The whole thing was over in a matter of minutes, but it had felt like an eternity.

"How're *you* feeling?" Reese edged closer so that she could take Tory's hand.

"Fine. Just a little cramping."

"Is that normal?"

"Perfectly," Tory said with a small smile. "Don't worry, sweetheart, Wendy's the best."

At that moment, the obstetrician returned and pulled up another stool next to Reese's.

"That went fine." She had a chart in her hand that she opened and perused for a few seconds. Then she met Tory's eyes. "Your blood pressure's been steadily increasing."

"I know."

"Are you having any other symptoms?"

"No." Tory felt Reese's grip on her hand tighten, and she looked away from her doctor to smile reassuringly at her lover. Softly, she whispered, "It's okay."

"No extremity swelling, no visual problems?"

"None."

"We're not at the point where I'd call this preeclampsia," Wendy said seriously, "but you need to be alert for the early signs, Tory."

"I have been."

"What's going on?" Reese looked sharply from one woman to the other. "Someone explain this to me."

Wendy focused on Reese. "Preeclampsia is a condition which affects some women during pregnancy, particularly women who are nulliparous, meaning they have not previously been pregnant. It's associated with hypertension and, in a small percentage, with other symptoms such as persistent headache, visual abnormalities, abdominal pain, and changes in blood chemistries."

"Is it serious?"

"Reese—" Tory protested gently.

"No. I want to know." Reese's eyes were locked on Wendy's, and her voice was a command. "Go ahead, Doctor."

"It can be, if it progresses. There can be severe hypertension with alteration in renal and liver function and other problems. But—"

"Is it a risk to the baby?"

Wendy continued in a steady, calm tone. "Sometimes if the maternal-fetal blood flow is compromised, there can be intrauterine growth restriction."

"And to Tory?" Reese's voice was even and strong, but there was a roaring in her head that sounded like gunfire.

"*Only* if the condition progresses," Wendy said. "But we're nowhere near that point, Reese. I'm not even willing to call it preeclampsia at this point, but we need to be vigilant."

"I'm already taking my blood pressure three times a day." Tory spoke calmly to reassure Reese. "The diastolic has only risen ten points above my baseline. I've checked my urine daily for protein. There hasn't been any."

"I'll need to see you every two weeks from here on out." Wendy made a few notes in the record. "Keep monitoring your BP and urine the way you've been doing, and add a fingerstick hemoglobin every ten days. Call me at the slightest sign of symptoms. *Even* if you're not sure."

"What about working? Is it safe for Tory to continue?" Reese asked.

Wendy nodded. "Reasonable hours, yes, as long as we don't see any worsening."

"Don't worry," Tory said. "I'll be careful."

"Good. Then I'm satisfied." Wendy stood and smiled at them both. "I'll call you with the lab results as soon as I have them."

Reese was silent as Tory dressed.

"There's nothing wrong, sweetheart, really." Tory took Reese's hand.

"I know." Reese managed a smile, but her eyes were dark. She drew a long breath and straightened her shoulders. "Is it okay for you to eat now?"

"It had better be," Tory said with a laugh. "First of all, I'm starving. And I'm sure Cath expects us all to go to lunch."

Reese slid her arm around Tory's waist and kissed her temple lightly, ignoring the cold feeling in the pit of her stomach. "Then let's not keep her waiting."

## CHAPTER ELEVEN

### May, Provincetown, MA

"Things will start jumping around here over the weekend." At a little before six a.m., Reese poured French roast from the carafe into a travel mug. She was already in uniform, dressed for work. As always, the creases in her shirt and pants were knife-edge sharp, the knot in her tie perfectly positioned below her buttoned collar, her leather belt a polished black. Her weapon was nestled in an equally highly shined leather holster on her right hip.

"Uh-huh."

Reese smiled at Tory, still in the T-shirt she usually slept in—and not much else. Her normally energetic lover looked sleepy and out of sorts. "Want some juice?"

"No," Tory snarled, settling a hip onto a stool at the breakfast counter. "I want some coffee."

"I'll make decaf."

"I don't *want* decaf. I want *real...*" Abruptly, she quieted as her face grew pale.

"Bagel? I can toast—"

"Oh, God..." Tory bolted off the stool.

Heart in her throat, Reese watched Tory rush for the bathroom. After a moment's hesitation, she followed, her insides roiling. *This hasn't happened in weeks. Jesus, God...what's wrong?*

"Tor? Love...can I get you anything?" Reese circled her palm aimlessly over Tory's back as the other woman cradled her head on her arms, her body bent over the sink. Reese's stomach lurched as she felt Tory tremble. "Honey?"

"No," Tory gasped, not looking at her. "I'm fine. Near miss—no eruptions."

"Some water?"

"Yes, fine. Good." With a shaky sigh, Tory straightened up and accepted the glass Reese filled and handed to her. She traced the curve of Reese's jaw with her fingers, smiling faintly. "I'm okay."

"You're sure?"

"Mmm. I am."

Reese asked carefully, "Shouldn't we check your blood pressure?"

Tory was silent a long minute, reluctant to add to her lover's worry. *I want this experience to be a joy for you, not a constant source of anxiety.* "It was just a little blip, sweetheart."

"I need to be part of this, Tor. Please."

Tory'd never seen Reese look so helpless, and her heart twisted to see the pleading in her eyes. "Of course. Come on, I'll show you how to take it."

Reese was a quick study, and five minutes later they looked at one another and smiled.

"No change since my last visit with Wendy," Tory reported. "Okay now?"

Reese nodded. "Can you eat something?"

"I don't think I'm quite ready for that." Tory wrapped her arm around Reese and leaned into her. "You should get to work."

"I'm okay for a bit. You need to eat something. The doctor said—"

"It would be nice if *someone* remembered *I'm* a doctor." Tory heard the temper in her own voice and realized that Reese was just concerned. *In fact, she still looks scared. I never thought I'd see anything that could shake up my marine.* "Sorry. Try not to worry, sweetheart. It was just a bit of leftover morning sickness."

"I'll just read the paper and finish my coffee," Reese said as the two of them walked arm in arm back toward the kitchen. "Then I'll fix you a little breakfast before I leave."

Tory cocked her head and studied her impossibly handsome lover. "Reese Conlon, you *never* read the newspaper in the morning."

"I've never had a pregnant lover before."

"As I recall," Tory said softly, running her fingers lightly down Reese's chest, "*you've* never had a lover before."

"Tory…" There was a warning note in Reese's voice. "I have to go to work in less than an hour."

"So?" Tory remarked innocently, but a smile tugged at the corner of her mouth.

"I don't have time for sex, and I can't work if I'm…aroused all day."

Relenting, Tory kissed Reese swiftly on the lips and moved away to sit on the stool again. "Don't worry. I'm not quite ready for sex this morning myself."

"How about toast instead?"

"God, you're persistent."

"Is that a yes?"

Tory nodded her assent and watched appreciatively as Reese moved efficiently about the kitchen, fixing toast and scrambling eggs. "Thanks," she said when Reese passed the plate to her. Remarkably, it smelled wonderful.

"Tory," Reese began carefully, "what about another person for the clinic?"

The hand that held the fork stopped midway to Tory's mouth. After a second, she finished the motion and then set her utensil down. "I've narrowed it down to two people. I'll have someone by the weekend. I promise."

"That's great." Reese let out a long relieved breath.

Tory didn't say anything.

"Thank you." Reese leaned across the counter and spread her fingers through the hair at the back of Tory's neck, gently massaging the tense muscles. "I know it's not easy for you. But just for this summer."

*No, it's not just for this summer.* Tory turned her head and kissed Reese's palm. "And next year at this time, we'll have a child."

Reese couldn't prevent herself from grinning. "Yeah, we will, won't we?"

"Yes, we will." Tory echoed, smiling now, too. "I know things are going to change. I just need a little time to get used to them."

Reese came quickly around the end of the counter and put her arms around her lover. Brushing her lips across Tory's temple, she said gently, "We'll work everything out. The most important thing for right now is that you're okay."

"As long as I have you, I will be." Tory tilted her face and kissed Reese, a gentle lingering kiss of gratitude and soft desire. When she drew away, her throat was tight with a combination of wonder and need. "Go to work, Sheriff."

"I'll call you later," Reese whispered, her lips to Tory's forehead. "I love you."

❖

Reese was just pulling into the small lot behind the sheriff's department when the call came over her radio. The alarm sounded in front of the fire department in the middle of town at the same time.

"Fire reported, Bradford and 6A."

It was Smith's voice, and as Reese spun the wheel with one hand and floored the accelerator, she flicked her shoulder mike with the other. "Conlon. I've got it."

"Roger, Reese."

The whole of Provincetown is less than four miles long and, sandwiched between the Atlantic Ocean and Cape Cod Bay, even narrower. At that time of morning, just before tourist season, there were barely any cars, and Reese was on scene in less than a minute. The Mooring restaurant, a squat, sprawling ramshackle place at the far end of town, was in flames. She pulled her cruiser diagonally across Bradford and got out, thumbing her mike again.

"I need another car out here to block traffic coming west on 6." As she spoke, she opened the trunk of her vehicle and extracted orange plastic road cones. She placed these across the highway behind her, preventing traffic from approaching the area from the direction of town. Behind her, the fire engine had arrived, and half a dozen firefighters in full regalia were climbing off the truck with loops of heavy hose encircling their shoulders.

"How does it look?" Reese called to the fire captain as he approached. Alan Peterson was technically in charge of the scene.

"It's pretty well involved," he yelled above the roar of the truck engine and the shouts of busy firefighters. "Fortunately, the place is isolated from the surrounding structures by the parking lot on three sides. Unless we get an awful lot of wind, I'm not worried about it spreading."

"What about civilians?" Reese leaned close to his ear to be heard. "Can your people get inside to make sure the place is empty?"

"Negative." He spoke something unintelligible into his handy talkie and then turned his attention back to her. "Too hot."

Reese took a step away from him in the direction of the burning building. She was stopped by a firm grip on her arm.

"Forget it, Sheriff," he said gruffly. "If there were any way to get in there, we would have done it already. I don't want you anywhere near that place. Christ, last time you helped me out, you ended up in the hospital."

"You're not pulling rank on me, are you, Alan?"

"Damn right, I am. As soon as I get an internal assessment, you'll be the first to know."

Reese relented, because she knew he was right. Still, it galled her to have to watch from the sidelines. "Fair enough."

"How are you, Reese?"

"Fit for duty." She answered absently, watching the men and women work in a frenzied but organized fashion to contain the conflagration.

At that moment, Nelson Parker jogged across the street to join them. "What have we got?"

"Structural blaze," Reese informed him. "As far as we know, unoccupied."

"Looks like it's gonna be a total loss." Nelson watched flames lick their way through the cedar-shingled roof and pulse like living beings through the shattered windows into the smoke-clouded air.

"Yeah," Peterson agreed. "A wood building like that, there's no way to stop it. This is a containment exercise, nothing more."

"We'll need the fire marshal's report," Reese pointed out. Fires in empty buildings were always considered suspect, and an automatic investigation was required. Although arson was, strictly speaking, the province of the fire department, it was also *her* jurisdiction because vandalism or vagrancy or malicious behavior might be involved.

"It'll take until tomorrow for the heat to die down enough to comb through the place and probably a couple of days to analyze the forensics, but I'll send along whatever we find as soon as we get it."

"Good enough." Reese turned her attention to Nelson. "We'll need to keep someone from the night shift overtime for a few hours to handle traffic around this place. I'll give Smith a call."

"He's back there on 6. Go ahead and tell him."

"Roger."

"Oh, and Reese?"

"Chief?"

"The new kid is waiting back at the station."

She studied his face but couldn't read a thing in it. "I'll head back as soon as I talk to Smith, then."

"Good."

❖

Within an hour, the fire was out, and all that remained was the cleanup. Reese headed back to the office. When she walked in, the newest member of the department was leaning against the corner of her desk. Reese pushed through the wooden gate and extended her hand to the young cadet in the pristine uniform.

"Officer Parker, welcome aboard."

"Thank you, Sheriff." Bri grinned fleetingly and then straightened. "I would have notified you when I got here, but you were already out on a call."

"No problem. Come on, let's take a ride through town, and we'll talk about the game plan."

When they settled into the car, Reese turned to Bri. "Have you seen your dad?"

"Just for a minute. He told me that my training officer would be along shortly."

"You know, he needs to distance himself a little bit from your training so that there won't be any question of prejudice in your evaluations."

"I know that," Bri said steadily, keeping her eyes forward. *Plus he didn't seem too keen for me to be here. I guess he still thinks I made a mistake leaving...New York.*

She couldn't think about the fact that she hadn't talked to Caroline in over a month. Once she'd finally gotten over some of her anger *and* embarrassment over storming out and worked up the nerve to call her, all she ever got was the answering machine. Eventually, she'd just left a message reminding Caroline of the party this coming Friday and left directions, just in case. *Yeah, sure. You know she's not coming.*

"You know," Reese said, wondering about the distant expression on Bri's face, "some people will still question the fact that *I'm* your training officer, because they know we're friends."

Bri stared at her, clearly surprised. "No *way* will anyone question you."

"Well," Reese worked not to smile, "we'll still need to cross all our t's and dot all our i's."

"Yes, ma'am. I understand." Bri's voice was firm. "That's the way I want it, Sheriff."

"Good. Then let's go to work."

Reese pulled the patrol car to the side of the road across from the smoldering ruins of the Moorings restaurant.

"Whoa," Bri exclaimed.

"Take a look at this scene." Reese led them across the street to the rubble-strewn parking lot. "Then tell me what you want to know about it."

Bri looked around for a second and then began confidently to ask questions. Reese nodded in satisfaction as Bri succinctly elicited the vital information regarding time, circumstances of the call reporting the fire, initial impressions of the fire captain, nature of reported injuries, and other basic data from her.

"Good. You can write all that up when we get back to the station." Reese was in her training mode, and they slowly circled the perimeter, each of them silently studying the scene. "How would you approach the investigation?"

Bri took her time, and when she spoke, she sounded thoughtful but steady. "First, we'll need the fire marshal's report as to whether this was accidental or incendiary."

"Fire by natural causes or intentional," Reese clarified. "Accident or arson."

"Right."

"What do you think the fire marshal is going to tell us?"

Bri squinted at the smoldering remains. "This place has been closed since last summer. As I recall, one of the big resort consortiums has been trying to buy it to build a timeshare here. The land is worth a lot, but the restaurant building had seen better days."

"Uh-huh." Reese realized what a benefit it was for officers to have a history with the community that they policed. She was still a relative newcomer, but after three years, she knew a great deal about the inner workings of the tiny town and its inhabitants. Bri, though, had an advantage that Reese would never be able to match. She had spent all of her life in the midst of these people, and her history was their history.

"Since the restaurant hasn't been functioning in months, it's doubtful that any of the power was on, which lets out electrical origins. Same for the gas." Bri stopped walking and put her hands in her pockets, a gesture that unconsciously mimicked Reese's stance. "No storms lately, so it wasn't lightning. I'd say this is going to be ruled incendiary in nature."

"The fire was man-made, you think?"

"Yes." She didn't waver in her response.

"But it's *not* necessarily arson." At Bri's questioning look, Reese continued, "An abandoned building like this would be a good place for vagrants to camp, and an untended fire could certainly have started this. Incendiary *and* accidental."

"Right." Bri was enthused, captured by the excitement of having a real case to work at last. "So, we need to ask around town and find out if anybody has any info on vagrants—especially where they might be congregating. Could be kids, too." At Reese's raised eyebrow, she blushed. "Uh, when I was…uh…younger, you know… we'd get together in abandoned buildings to…get together."

"Okay, good thought." Reese clapped Bri on the shoulder approvingly while she sighed inwardly. She still had so much to learn about that period of life, which she seemed to have skipped over. Then it suddenly occurred to her that in not too many years, it could be *her* child partying in firetraps like this. Her stomach flipped. "Christ."

"Ma'am?"

"Nothing," Reese said briskly. "We've got several lines of questioning to pursue while we wait for the fire marshal. Let's get started, Officer."

❖

Tory followed the scent of barbecue up the driveway toward the rear of her home. She was surprised to hear the soft murmur of voices and tried to recall if they had made plans with anyone for dinner. She hoped not, because she was beat. But her spirits lifted as she mounted the stairs and saw their visitor.

"Bri!" she cried in surprise. Reese and Bri were both in jeans and T-shirts, and a more attractive pair Tory didn't think she had ever seen. Both of them grinned as she joined them. She paused to kiss Reese before giving Bri a hug. "What are you doing here?"

"I forgot to tell you that Bri was starting her field training today." Reese offered a contrite shrug.

"That's terrific." Tory smiled and tried to hide her weariness. "I'm going inside to change. I'll be right back."

"She looks great," Bri commented as she popped open a beer.

"Yeah," Reese said absently as she followed her lover with her eyes. *And she looks worn out. This new guy can't start too soon for me.*

When Tory returned a few moments later, Reese and Bri set the outside table and piled chicken from the grill onto paper plates. She grabbed a club soda and sat down with a grateful sigh. Jed lay beside her, a hopeful expression in his eyes.

"God, this looks good." After helping herself to salad and chicken, Tory turned to Bri. "Where will you be living? With Nelson?"

Bri blushed. "Uh, I'm not sure yet."

"So where are you staying now?"

"Well, most of my stuff is still in Barnstable. I moved out of the apartment I was sharing this morning and stowed my gear at school. I was going to go up this Friday after work and move it down Saturday." Bri glanced at Reese. "If I can take the morning off? I know it's Memorial Day weekend, but classes just finished and I didn't have ti—"

"It's fine," Reese said. "I'd rather you work nights Saturday and Sunday anyhow. More going on. You need help moving?"

"Nah. I don't have all that much."

"Give a holler if you do."

"I guess you and Caroline will want an apartment for the summer," Tory said as she reached for more salad. "Now is probably a good time to get one."

"Carre's not coming home." Bri stared at her plate.

"How come?" Reese interjected.

"She has a job in New York."

Tory studied Bri's profile, noting the tight line of her jaw. "That's hard."

"Yeah, well…" Bri cleared her throat. "It's a real good deal for her."

"You can bunk here for a while if you need to." Reese glanced at Tory, who nodded silently. "Although I'm sure Nelson would like you to stay at home."

"Thanks. I appreciate it." Bri shrugged. "I don't think Dad and I are ready to be living together right now."

"No problem." Reese stood and stacked some of the plates. "I'm going to take these inside and make coffee. Be back in a few minutes."

"How is Caroline doing?" Tory asked gently, sensing Bri's discomfort.

"Good." Bri sat with head lowered, her hands in fists on her thighs. "She's good. She got a scholarship to study in France next year."

"Why, that's wonderful. The works of hers I've seen are very good."

Bri nodded her head, then reached for her fork and turned it aimlessly on the table. "Yeah, she's terrific. It will be good for her…this next year."

"How long have you two been together? Three years?"

"Four." Bri's voice was barely a whisper.

"It'll take some getting used to—living apart," Tory ventured softly.

"I…" Bri looked away. *I can't get used to it. I don't know how to.*

Tory had never seen Bri look so vulnerable, not even in the hospital after she had been viciously beaten. Bri had been so heartbreakingly strong then, mostly because she'd probably thought Caroline needed her to be. Tory smiled, remembering the fierce look on Caroline's face when she'd stormed into the clinic, insisting that she be allowed to see Bri.

*Tory forcefully interrupted Caroline's headlong dash down the hall.*

*"Wait a minute," Tory soothed, holding the struggling young woman. "It might be better if you see Bri tomorrow, Caroline. It'll be hard to see her like this."*

*Caroline fixed Tory with a contemptuous glare. "You're just like all the rest. You think just because we're young that our feelings don't matter. Last night right about now, she was making love to me. Do you think that doesn't matter either?"*

*"That's not what I meant, Caroline. I know you care about her."*

*"Care about her?" she said coldly. "What if it were Reese in there, Dr. King? Just how long would you wait out here in the hall?"*

*Tory stared at her, knowing that it could easily be Reese under other circumstances. Just the thought made her ill.*

*"You're right. I'm sorry," Tory said softly. "Nothing on earth would keep me away."*

*She watched the pretty young blond, who now seemed so much older than her years, resolutely push through the doors to her lover.*

Hearing the uncertainty in Bri's voice now, Tory realized that all of them, including her, had always assumed that *Bri* was the stronger of the pair. Probably because she looked it, with her swaggering charm and bold good looks. *Appearances. God, how we let them deceive us. You don't know how strong Caroline really is, do you, my beautiful young one?*

"You know," Tory said tenderly, "it will probably be even harder for Caroline, being away from you *and* in a strange new country."

Bri finally looked at her, a question in her eyes. "You think? It just seems like it would all be so...exciting, that she might... forget."

Lightly, Tory rested her fingers on Bri's arm. "No, sweetie, I don't think that will happen."

That slight, affectionate touch and the voice, soft with caring, sliced through the tenuous threads of Bri's resolve. She was so scared most of the time and so lost. It had all seemed so clear just a few months before. Now Caroline was gone...*Oh, that can't be. Not really.*

Suddenly, Bri stood and walked rapidly to the rail. She held on to the wood, polished smooth by hundreds of hands, so tightly that her arms ached—trying to get her breath, waiting until she could speak around the tears crowding her throat. Eventually, in a voice held tightly in check, she said, "Reese showed me the baby pictures."

"Did she?" Tory's own throat was suddenly tight. *Oh, Bri. Baby, what is it?*

"Yeah. It's so neat. I'm...happy for you."

Tory couldn't help herself when she heard the tears in the wistful tone. She crossed the deck, turned Bri around with her hands on her shoulders, and enfolded the young woman in a hug. Brushing her cheek against Bri's, she whispered. "Thank you, sweetie."

For a fleeting second, as Bri surrendered in Tory's arms, nothing hurt at all.

# CHAPTER TWELVE

It was almost ten o'clock Friday night when Bri reached the Breakers, a shoreside restaurant and bar in Barnstable where the party for the recent sheriff academy graduates was being held. Technically, she and her classmates were not graduates; they were on probationary status until completion of their field training. Nevertheless, she was wearing a uniform and carrying a gun and doing what she had always dreamed of doing. It would have been perfect if only Caroline were there to celebrate with her.

She sat for a moment in the parking lot, a long leg down on either side of her motorcycle. The lot was crowded with an odd assortment of jalopies and shiny new luxury cars. She pulled off her helmet and rested it on the bike's gas tank, her hands spread on either side of the smooth round surface. Fleetingly, she thought of the last time she and Caroline had been together, and she thought not of fighting but of making love.

No one but Caroline had ever touched her intimately, and it seemed as if no one ever *would* be able to touch her the way she did. Caroline could make her so excited with just a look that she thought sometimes she'd come in her jeans, and yet when they made love, she felt—more than anything else in the world—safe. At first, it had embarrassed her to realize how much she needed Caroline to make her feel that way. Then, as the weeks had become months and then years, she had gotten used to the feeling, barely noticing that it was Caroline and her love that held her world together.

Without her now, it seemed as if everything was unraveling. They fought more than they ever had, and Bri didn't know how to make it right. The longer they were apart, the harder it seemed to be to get close again. They hadn't seen each other in too many weeks, and during the increasingly rare phone calls, they were both tense and awkward.

*Fuck, this isn't going to do anybody any good. What I need is just to forget about it for a while.*

Nevertheless, the first thing Bri did when she walked through the door into the big room crowded with classmates, academy staff, recent graduates, and the usual locals was to look for Caroline. After a minute or two of fruitless searching, she admitted what she had known all along. Caroline was not there.

"Looking for someone, Bri?" The honey-smooth voice was instantly recognizable.

Bri turned with a resigned smile to Allie. "Not anymore, it looks like."

"Well, glad to hear it," Allie replied, her tone clearly surprised. She tilted her head and studied the faint shadows beneath Bri's eyes. "Did you work today?"

"Uh-huh. Second day. How about you?"

"Me, too. Directing traffic in Town Center. Thrilling." She laughed and took Bri's hand. "Come on, follow me."

Bri let herself be led through the crowd that milled about in the center of the floor, taking care not to be sloshed by the drinks of the already rowdy revelers. A few people called her name, and she yelled hello in passing.

Allie took her out onto the back deck, which was nothing more than a wooden platform in the sand. The area was dimly lit and almost as crowded as inside the bar, but the noise level was lower. Although there wasn't much to see, the air was clearer outside, and the sound of the surf rumbled not far away.

When Allie stopped, Bri asked, "What's up?"

"Got something for you." Allie bent down, dug around in an ice-filled chest, and came up with a beer. She handed it to Bri. "This is the unofficial drinking area for the underage graduates. Technically, we are not in the bar."

"I believe that would be a very loose interpretation of the law, Officer." Bri laughed and took a long swallow. It felt good after the dusty drive, and it felt even better not to be thinking about anything at all.

"It's kind of understood that those of us who aren't quite legal can partake out here—just for the party." Allie helped herself to a beer as well. "It's great to be done with the classroom stuff, don't you think? They're so shorthanded where I am, they don't even treat me like a recruit. I'm on regular rotation with the other officers."

"So you're in Wellfleet for this summer?" Bri took another long pull on her bottle.

"Yeah." Allie grinned. "Fifteen miles from you."

"Some coincidence, huh?"

Allie moved a little closer as the crowd grew denser, her arm brushing Bri's. "You know what they said in Criminal Investigations. There are no coincidences."

Aware of the bare skin against hers, Bri was silent. Allie touched a lot.

"Where are *you* living?"

"Don't know yet." Bri shrugged. "There are usually a lot of single rooms available for summer help—hovels mostly, but I don't need much more than a place to sleep. I figure I'll get something tomorrow."

"You know, I'm moving into a two-bedroom place between Wellfleet and Truro this weekend." Allie sipped her beer and considered Bri contemplatively. "And that's just about halfway between your job and mine. You could always share it with me."

"Uh…" Bri blushed, happy for the dim lighting. "That's…real nice of you, but I'm pretty sure I couldn't afford it."

"I'd bet you could. How does a hundred dollars a month sound?"

Bri laughed. "It sounds like charity, or else you've lost your mind. A room for the summer will go for three or four hundred a week anywhere on the Cape."

"Not charity." It was Allie's turn to shrug. "Consider yourself… um…company for me."

If it hadn't been said with such lightheartedness, or if Allie's smile hadn't been quite so captivating, Bri might have been offended. But for one insane moment, she found herself considering the offer. It would be nice not to be alone, and Allie *was* good company. Then an image of Caroline flashed through her mind and what it was like living with her—*waking up to the sounds of her moving around in the apartment, going to sleep with the heat of her skin under my fingers.* Bri's throat suddenly got tight. "Look, Allie, I really appreciate it—"

"Hey." Allie put her fingers on Bri's arm just under the edge of her shirtsleeve, high on her upper arm. "We're supposed to be celebrating tonight. Don't worry about it. I'll give you my number, and if you don't find something, or you change your mind, the offer's always open. Okay?"

"Sure," Bri said with a smile. Allie was hard to resist. Bri leaned down, fished another beer out of the cooler, and opened it. For the first time in many weeks, she felt almost good.

Forty-five minutes later, the party was in overdrive, with everyone talking too loudly, most everyone drinking too much, and more than a few forgetting whatever social inhibitions they might once have had. Bri and Allie had migrated to the far corner of the deck where they stood beneath an overhanging branch of a nearby magnolia tree. There must have been seventy-five people in a space designed for twenty.

"Let's dance," Allie shouted close to Bri's ear, grasping her hand at the same time.

"*Here?*" Bri looked around at the partygoers, almost all of whom were her colleagues-to-be or, in some cases, her superiors. She wasn't much of a drinker, and she hadn't had all that much, but she felt loose and relaxed. Still…"I don't think this is a great time for us to do that."

"Why not?" Allie moved her hand to Bri's waist, hooked her thumb inside Bri's jeans where they rested on the crest of her hip, and ran her fingers back and forth on Bri's side under her T-shirt. She leaned so close that their thighs brushed. "Do you think they might get the wrong idea?"

Bri could smell her perfume, the same scent she'd noticed that day in Allie's cottage. Even more disconcertingly, she could feel the light press of Allie's breasts against her chest. They were both wearing T-shirts, and neither apparently had anything on underneath. Allie's nipples were hard, and Bri's tightened instantly in response. Totally involuntarily, her stomach clenched and a thrum of pleasure shot down her spine. When the jolt of excitement hit home, she got stiff in the space between one heartbeat and the next.

"What idea would that be?" Bri didn't recognize the low, husky timber of her own voice. Or she did, and she didn't want to think about what it meant. *Christ, I'm getting so hot.*

"Well, if any of them are half the hotshot investigators they think they are," Allie murmured, stepping even closer now, edging one thigh slightly between Bri's legs, "they'll figure out that I'm trying to get you to kiss me."

"I don't...think..."

"Good. Don't then." Allie nudged harder with the leg resting against Bri's crotch, smiling when the unexpected pressure on Bri's rampantly hard clitoris drew a soft groan from her. "And after you kiss me for a long, *long* time, I'd *really* like it if you'd make me come."

"Jesus." Bri blinked to clear her suddenly hazy vision. Then she found herself staring into the most beautiful eyes she'd ever seen. Eyes so warm, so deep, that just looking into them was like the most tender of embraces. Her voice was a mere whisper. "Carre."

Bri had never believed it when people used the expression *time stood still*, but for that brief instant when her eyes met Caroline's, before Caroline turned with a small cry and pushed hurriedly away through the crowd, everything simply stopped. The blood ceased to rush from her heart, the air halted its journey through her lungs, and every thought just...vanished. There was nothing left in her world. Nothing at all.

"Oh my God."

"What?" Allie exclaimed in confusion as Bri suddenly took her by the shoulders and pushed her aside.

❖

By the time Bri managed to force her way through the crowd on the deck into the roiling mass of people in the bar and, finally, to the front door, Caroline was nowhere in sight. Once outside, Bri stood on the gravel path and looked frantically around. The highway was fifty feet away and shrouded in darkness. Caroline didn't have a car.

*Fuck, where could she have gone?* Feeling the effects of the alcohol and not thinking entirely clearly, Bri hurried to the street and peered up and down the deserted road. Nothing. *She couldn't have walked very far. Oh you dumbshit—James! She must have borrowed his car. How else would she have gotten here?*

Bri turned around and sprinted, or rather tried to sprint, toward the adjacent parking lot. She was a little unsteady and realized that she'd inadvertently had more to drink than she'd intended. Plus, it was hard for her muscles to work when there was no blood flowing through her veins. Everything was frozen inside. She'd never been so damn terrified in her life.

The lot was just a gravel-covered patch of dirt, with very little in the way of illumination. Hazy red light filtered out through the beer signs hanging in the dirt-streaked side windows of the bar. Cars were parked haphazardly, and it was still nearly as full as it had been when she'd pulled in earlier on her bike. Then the cough of an engine turning over caught her attention, and, turning in the direction of the sound, Bri saw taillights flicker. She raced toward the car as it backed out from between two trucks, and without even giving it a second thought, slammed both palms down on the trunk.

"Carre! Wait!"

The car came to a jerking halt. The force of the bumper as it rocked against her legs bounced Bri back a step. It hurt but she didn't care. The door flew open and Caroline jumped from the car. Quicker than Bri would have thought possible, Caroline was in front of her, her hands fisted in Bri's T-shirt, shaking her violently.

"Bri, are you *crazy*? Are you completely nuts? I could have killed you. God damn you, what is *wrong* with you?"

"Carre, listen…" Bri began desperately.

"No, *you* listen. I'm sick of it. I'm sick of you pushing me away, and I'm sick of you running away." Caroline was nearly a head shorter than Bri and slender where Bri was all muscle, but anyone watching would have thought that *she* was the stronger of the pair.

Bri stood with her hands loose at her sides and allowed Caroline to manhandle her. "I'm sorry."

"I don't care. That's not good enough. What were you doing in there?" Finally, Caroline stepped back, staring at Bri with wounded eyes and fury in her face. "Is *she* why you moved out? Didn't you even have the guts to tell me?"

"She...? No! God, no."

"Never mind. I didn't have to hear what she was saying to figure out what was going on. I *know* what you look like when you're hot, Bri." Caroline ran a trembling hand through her hair. "You want to tell me that she wasn't making you—" Her voice broke and she turned away.

Bereft, bleeding at the sound of tears in Caroline's voice, Bri took one tentative step forward. She raised her hand but for the first time in their lives together, she was afraid to touch Caroline. "Babe, she's just a friend."

"You're such an idiot, Bri. She was all over you, and you looked like that was just fine with you." Taking a deep breath, Caroline turned back and studied Bri's face as if she were a stranger. "I thought you left Manhattan because of this job. Because you needed something for yourself—something that would make you feel better about yourself. Maybe I was wrong. Maybe it's her—or someone like her—that you really need."

"No. Jesus, no. You're wrong."

"Maybe I'm *not* wrong, and you just haven't figured that out yet." Caroline shook her head unhappily. "I'm going ho—back to Manhattan. Don't call me for a while, okay?"

"Carre, please," Bri begged. It felt like her legs were going to go. In another second, she'd be on her knees. She didn't even care. She'd do anything. "Please, I love you."

"You know what the worst part is?" Caroline slipped back into the car. "I believe you."

As she watched Caroline carefully back the car out again and drive slowly away, Bri thought she might actually die. Caroline didn't look back, not even once.

❖

Bri had no idea how long she'd been sitting on the ground with her back against the rear tire of her motorcycle, her arms wrapped around her knees, her forehead cradled between them. The soft voice finally drew her back to awareness.

"Bri? Hey. Are you sick?"

"No," Bri mumbled without looking up.

"You left in such a hurry, and I couldn't find you anywhere. I thought maybe you came outside because you were gonna be sick." Allie crouched down, resting one hand on Bri's shoulder. "What's going on?"

Finally, Bri raised her head and struggled to focus. "Nothing."

"Jesus, Bri, are you crying?" Allie moved her hand to beneath Bri's chin and lifted it, brushing at the moisture on Bri's face with her other hand.

"No." Roughly, Bri swiped at her cheeks, then got unsteadily to her feet. She was uncertain whether it was the beer or the shock of Caroline leaving that had left her feeling as if she could barely walk. With effort, she swung her leg over her bike and searched in her pockets for her keys. "Listen, I gotta go."

"Uh-uh. No way." Deftly, Allie plucked the keys from Bri's hand when she pulled them from her jeans. "The rules are none of us drive tonight. I mean it, Bri. If you get stopped anywhere tonight for any reason, you'll get busted right out of the academy. Come on, get off the bike."

For a second, Bri hesitated, almost not caring what might happen. But the working part of her brain finally took over and, with a weary sigh, she dismounted. "Okay, fine." She looked around the parking lot as if seeing it for the first time. Most of the cars were still there. "I guess I might as well go back inside and get another drink."

"I've got a better idea." Allie slipped her arm around Bri's waist and said, "Let's go. I've got a ride for us with a designated driver."

It was just easier not to think. Thinking meant remembering, and remembering meant watching Caroline drive away. It was too hard, and she was too tired, and everything hurt so much.

"Okay."

❖

Bri opened her eyes, blinked in the bright sunlight, and immediately closed them. She lay very still, aware that she was in a strange bed and that she was not alone. The crisp cotton sheets felt oddly rough against her bare nipples. Her shirt was off. Her jeans were on. Her fly was open.

*Fuck.*

She hadn't been too drunk to remember now what had happened.

*"Come in with me, Bri," Allie whispered as the car carrying the two of them and several of their friends pulled to a stop in the lane in front of Allie's rented bungalow. "You can stay here tonight."*

*She couldn't ride back to Reese and Tory's. And the prospect of being alone with her pain was more than she could handle. Allie's hand on her thigh was soft and reassuring. "Yeah, okay."*

*They said nothing as they walked down the path to the front door, but Allie had her arm around Bri's waist again. It felt strange. Good, though. Solid. Firm. Alive.*

*Once inside, Allie directed, "This way." She held onto Bri's hand and led her through the dark living room.*

*Bri followed, because it seemed the thing to do. She let Allie draw her down onto the bed, saying nothing as Allie lay beside her, facing her in the dark. A hand came to her cheek and stroked her tenderly, then moved around to the back of her neck and pulled her head close for a kiss.*

*She wasn't thinking of anything. The tongue running lightly over her lips was supple and warm. When it moved inside her mouth, it was the only thing she could feel. There were no thoughts of the past or the future, only that moment and the firm anchor of hot flesh filling her mouth. She sucked it, breathed in the heat, clung to the taste of passion.*

*Dimly, she was aware of Allie's rapid breathing and soft moans. When fingers tugged at the bottom of her T-shirt, Bri shifted and, in the next minute, another barrier was gone. A hand drew her fingers to a full breast and again she heard a small cry in the darkness. Her fingers were closed around a tight nipple, and when she squeezed, Allie whimpered. Bri was sure her heart was beating quickly, but she still couldn't feel it.*

*Fingernails rasped down the center of her belly. Her thighs tightened and didn't relax. She was panting. They both were. She jerked, then lifted her hips when fingers worked loose the snap on her jeans. The sound of her zipper sliding open was so loud in the still room. Soft breasts pressed against her chest, a slender leg slid over her thigh. Fingers pressed inside her jeans. The intoxicating aroma of desire was everywhere.*

"Touch me, Bri," *the honey-smooth voice pleaded, nearly breathless now.* "Please. Oh, make me come."

*She knew the words, but the voice was wrong.* Make me come, baby. Caroline's voice. But not.

*A hand cupped her inside her jeans, fingers closed around her clitoris. The first gripping spasm shot a warning down her legs.*

"Oh fuck," *Bri gasped, rolling away.* "Jesus. Jesus."

"What?" *Allie's voice was a choked cry, thin and desperate.* "Oh, don't stop now."

"I'm sorry. I'm sorry." Carre, God, I am so sorry.

*Fists clenched to her center, Bri turned onto her side. She kept her back to the woman beside her and curled in on herself, closing her eyes tightly. Maybe she slept. Maybe she just disappeared for a while.*

"I can't decide whether I'm mad at you or not," Allie said quietly.

"You should be." Bri turned her head on the pillow and opened her eyes. Allie was sitting up nude against the headboard, inches away. Her breasts, full and firm and rosy-tipped, were beautiful. Bri lifted her gaze to Allie's eyes. "I never should have come here with you last night. I sure shouldn't have gotten into bed with you."

"Why did you?"

Bri hesitated. "I don't know." She was starting to get feeling back. Her body ached where the bumper had grazed her. Mostly, her heart hurt. "I guess I didn't want to be alone."

"Why did you stop when we were making love?"

"I've got a girlfriend."

"Where is she?"

"In…" Bri stumbled on the words. "In New York City."

"Serious?"

Bri nodded. "Yeah."

"You were turned on at the bar. Here, too." Allie smiled softly, her expression dreamlike. "You were so wet when I touched you. You got hard between my fingers. You would have come in another second."

"Yeah." Bri's voice was a whisper. She was wet *now*. But that wasn't the point. She couldn't help what her body did. Only what *she* did about it.

Allie brushed Bri's arm with her fingertips. "You make me crazy hot, you know."

Bri said nothing.

"When you wouldn't touch me last night, I thought I was going to die." Her voice was husky, her eyes slightly glazed. "I had to make myself come. I couldn't help it."

Bri looked away. Her heart hammered wildly.

"Did you hear me?"

"No," Bri rasped, her stomach clenched so tight it hurt.

"It only took one touch. I imagined it was your mouth." Allie drew a trembling breath. "I came so hard—"

Bri sat up suddenly and swung her legs outside the bed. She was shaking. Hoarsely, she said, "I gotta go. I'm sorry."

"I'm not. Next time, though," Allie rested a palm on the center of Bri's bare back, "I want it to be you for real making me come."

## CHAPTER THIRTEEN

Reese came quietly down the stairs, mindful of the blanket-wrapped figure on the sofa. Moving carefully, she crossed to the kitchen and slowly began to assemble the coffeemaker.

"Can I help?" a sleepy voice asked from the living room.

Turning with a smile, Reese shook her head no. "I'm sorry. Did I wake you?"

"Not really." Caroline's eyes were puffy from lack of sleep and too-recent tears. "Is Tory up?"

"Not yet. She's sleeping in." Reese pulled coffee from the refrigerator and unfolded the bag. "I finally talked her into working only a half-day on Saturday. She's going in this afternoon."

"I'm sorry I showed up unannounced last night," Caroline said in a small voice. She slid onto the stool and propped her elbows on the counter, resting her chin in both hands. "I didn't think I could make it all the way back to Manhattan, and I didn't know where else to go."

Reese stopped what she was doing and came around to take a seat next to the young blond. "Don't apologize, Caroline. I'm glad that you came. You can always come here."

"Bri's staying here, too, isn't she?"

Surprised, Reese nodded. "How did you know?"

"Her motorcycle jacket is on the coat tree." Caroline's voice caught on the next words. "She never gets very far away from that."

"You're right. She's supposed to be moving her things over from Barnstable today. I imagine she'll stay here until she finds a place. She can stay indefinitely as far as we're concerned."

"That's good. She'll be…" Caroline had been about to say *safe* and then wondered at herself. *Safe from what? Or from whom?*

"What about you, Caroline? How are you doing?"

"I…" Quickly, she turned away as the tears she *thought* she had finally exhausted began again. In a whisper, she murmured, "Sorry."

"Don't be. Take your time." Reese waited, wanting to comfort her but uncertain if she should. *What the hell is going on?*

Clearly it involved Bri, who had cut out right after their shift had ended the night before, saying she was headed to Barnstable for a class get-together. She'd never mentioned Caroline was coming in for it. And then Caroline had shown up in the middle of the night, clearly shaken and having been crying. When Caroline had said she didn't want to talk, Tory had tucked her in on the couch, kissed her forehead, and said it could wait until the morning.

"Where's Bri?"

Caroline shook her head, keeping her face turned away. "I don't know."

"What's going on with you two?" Reese asked gently.

"I wish I knew." Caroline took a long shaky breath and straightened her shoulders with effort. She turned back to face Reese and met her questioning gaze. "Everything has turned upside down in the last four months. I didn't even realize Bri was unhappy. Maybe I should have."

"She didn't say anything?"

"She hardly ever does. She's always been…she keeps things inside."

"You knew she wanted to be a police officer, though, right?"

"Yes, of course. That's all she ever talked about wanting to do," Caroline replied. "I just thought it would be later. We both thought school in New York would be so great."

"Maybe she did, too, at first." Reese thought of making rounds with Bri the day before. Bri'd looked at home in her uniform—in her new role—strolling down Commercial, greeting people she had known since childhood. She'd looked almost content, which for Bri was unusual. If there hadn't been a shadow in her eyes when she'd smiled, Reese would have been fooled into thinking that she was happy. "Maybe it took leaving here to realize that this is where she belonged."

"Well, I thought we belonged *together*," Caroline said sadly. Her eyes were liquid with more tears, but she stubbornly held them back.

Reese blew out a breath and wished desperately that Tory were there instead of her. She was certain there were things she should be saying, or something that she should be doing. She thought of her own intensely focused, narrow life before she had met Tory. She'd never even imagined having a life with another person when she'd been Bri's age. Just the thought of trying to finish college and NROTC while meeting someone else's needs at the same time seemed overwhelming.

"She must have thought that leaving New York when she did was the right thing to do."

"How could that be? How could it be better for us *not* to be together?"

Caroline's voice was agonized, her confusion so evident that Reese's insides twisted. Sighing, Reese rubbed her face with both hands, searching for a way to explain something she didn't fully understand herself. She had only one point of reference—Tory. She thought about herself and Tory. What it felt like loving her. What she felt every morning when she woke up and found Tory beside her, every time she experienced the wonder of Tory in her arms. It was a miracle reborn with each dawn, and she knew that she would never get over feeling blessed.

"If I were Bri," Reese began as she struggled to put words to the emotions, "I would want to feel as if I deserved you. I would want to feel like...you could be proud of me."

"I've *always* been proud of her," Caroline said, startled. "She's strong and brave and..." The image of Bri with the strange woman the night before flickered into her mind. It was so painful that she lost her voice.

"Maybe," Reese added quietly, "she can't believe that *you* could be proud unless she's proud of herself."

They stared at one another silently until Reese grinned ruefully. "I'm not too good at this, am I?"

"I think you're wonderful," Caroline whispered.

"Look, maybe I can talk to her."

"No." Caroline rested her fingertips on Reese's knee. "Thank you. Really. But *I* need to talk to her."

"She should be back soon. She's got a shift coming up later this afternoon."

"Maybe she's busy." Caroline wondered now, as she had done throughout all the sleepless hours, where Bri had spent the night. *Oh, what am I going to do? Maybe I've already lost her.*

❖

It took Bri close to an hour to walk from Allie's bungalow back to the Breakers and pick up her bike. Then she swung by the academy and collected the few belongings that she had bundled up and left in her locker when she'd moved out of her shared apartment earlier in the week. It was just after ten in the morning when she reached Provincetown.

She hadn't stopped for breakfast or anything else, and she needed coffee and a shower and something to settle the roiling uneasiness in her stomach. The nausea wasn't the remnant of too much alcohol the previous night but the churning disorientation that came from feeling cut off from Caroline. It didn't help that she didn't know what to do with the feelings that Allie had stirred in her the night before and that morning. She'd found other girls besides Caroline attractive before but only in a distant sort of way. Like an *oh yeah, she's cute,* kind of way. No one except Caroline had ever gotten her hot, but Allie did, even when she didn't want her to. She wasn't sure what that meant, and that was even more confusing.

When Bri pulled slowly into Reese and Tory's driveway, her heart leapt at the sight of James's battered Honda. *Carre!*

In the next second, her elation vanished. *Oh, fuck. What am I going to say to her?*

She didn't have any more time to think about it because, as she sat straddling her bike, staring up at the house, Caroline appeared at the top of the stairs leading down from the rear deck. Looking pale and wan, she wrapped her arms around her chest and stared at Bri.

Caroline was wearing one of Tory's sweaters and tight faded jeans, and Bri thought she was the most beautiful girl in the world.

Her mouth went dry and her stomach flipped over. She wanted to run to her, or run away. After pocketing her keys, Bri quickly pulled off her helmet and dismounted. She was shaking, and she didn't think it had anything to do with the lingering vibrations from the powerful engine and the ride down. Taking a deep breath, she walked up the path and climbed the stairs. She stopped one step below Caroline, putting them at eye level, and whispered, "Hey, babe."

"Hi, baby."

They stared at one another, a foot of space between them, a million unsaid words and a thousand unhealed hurts keeping them apart.

"You look like hell," Caroline murmured.

"I feel like that, too." Bri stuffed her hands in her pockets because she wanted to touch her so much. "I thought you had that training thing this weekend."

"I did. I got them to let me postpone it until next week." Caroline smiled sadly. "I wanted to surprise you."

Bri felt like crying. "I'm sorry I fucked up."

"Oh, Bri." Caroline looked away, swallowing hard. "Let's go someplace so we can talk."

"Where?"

"Take me to the first place you ever kissed me." Caroline met her eyes. *If we're going to say goodbye, I want to do it there.*

"Jesus, Carre," Bri moaned. The sadness in Caroline's voice was so much worse than the anger, it was killing her. "I'm sorry."

Caroline just shook her head and walked down to the bike. A minute later, Bri joined her, handed her the helmet from the back, and climbed on. Wordlessly, as she had done hundreds of times before, Caroline settled in behind, wrapped her arms around Bri's waist, and rested her cheek against Bri's shoulder. She closed her eyes as the engine started and held on as if her life depended upon never letting Bri go.

Ten minutes later, Bri slowed and brought the bike to a halt at the far end of the parking lot at Race Point. There were a few cars in the parking lot, but the two of them didn't walk toward the marked trail toward the beach. Instead, they headed down a narrow path that led toward the lighthouse. Ordinarily, they would have held hands, but this time they walked side by side in silence. When they reached the lighthouse, they climbed around to the far side and settled with their backs against the wall, close together but not touching. The dunes spread out along the wild coast below and the ocean filled their view.

"I don't understand what's happening with us, Bri," Caroline finally said. "Why didn't you tell me you were going to leave school? Why didn't you talk to me about it first?"

Bri stared straight ahead, unblinking, until the tears that trembled on her lashes were carried away on the wind. Her voice was low as she answered. "I was afraid you'd talk me out of it."

"I might have tried," Caroline said with a shaky laugh. "You could have waited until the fall, when I...left for France. We could have had all this time together."

"I had to do it when I did."

"Why? I don't understand *why*."

"Because I was afraid once you left I wouldn't be *able* to do it." Bri's voice was harsh, wild.

"Why not?"

"Because I'm afraid when you leave I'm going to..." Suddenly, Bri put her head down on her knees and laced the fingers of both hands behind her neck. Her words were nearly lost in the rush of air that blew off the ocean. "I don't think I'll be able to do anything without you."

"Oh, baby," Caroline murmured, putting her arm around Bri's shoulders. "You can. You can do anything."

"Not without you."

"But I'm not leaving you."

Bri's head jerked up, and her eyes met Caroline's. "You don't know that!"

Shocked, Caroline stared at her. Her first instinct was to protest, because it was unthinkable. But then she realized that Bri didn't know that, didn't *believe* that. "I love you. I have never loved anyone but you. I don't care how long I'm gone, or how far away from me *you* go. I am not going to stop loving you."

"*I'm* not going anywhere," Bri exclaimed.

"No? Where were you last night?"

Bri blinked and her blue eyes darkened. "Jesus, Carre."

"Did you sleep with her?" Caroline's voice was a strangled whisper.

"I…" Bri wanted to make the truth disappear. She wanted the night to do over again. She wanted not to have felt what she felt. "Almost."

"Oh Bri," Caroline moaned. She turned partly away, more in an attempt to expunge the images that came unbidden to her mind than to escape from the sorrow in Bri's eyes. She saw the pretty, dark-haired woman pressed against Bri. The look of hazy need on Bri's face. A look that had only been for her—until last night. "Oh, God."

"Carre—"

Abruptly, Caroline got unsteadily to her feet. She moved a short distance away and stopped. With her back to the wall of the stark white tower, she held herself with her arms around her body, trembling in the chill sea breeze. "I can't…I can't even think about it right now. Take me back to Tory's."

Bri finally found her voice and jumped to her feet. "Carre. I *didn't.*"

"I saw you, Bri," Caroline said softly. "I know you wanted to."

"I don't know how that happened. I didn't go there meaning for it to happen. I was lonely."

"I've been lonely, too. And I wasn't the one who left."

Bri raked both hands through her hair, wanting to pound something. "I know. I *know.* I fucked up. Jesus, Carre, I'm sorry."

"What do you want?" Caroline's voice was calm, her eyes frighteningly empty.

*I want you to come home and live with me—here. I don't want us ever to be apart. I want to be like Reese and Tory.* Bri looked away, her eyes sweeping the shoreline. "I want you to go to Paris next year and study and be a successful artist. And I want to be a cop, here in Provincetown."

"And when I come back? What do you want then?"

"I guess that will be up to you," Bri said quietly.

"No, it won't." Caroline shook her head. "Not now."

Heart sinking, Bri watched Caroline turn and start up the path that led back to the parking lot. For a moment, she considered not going after her. Maybe if they never left this spot, they could turn back time to that magical moment four years before, when a simple kiss had turned on a light in the darkness of her despair.

Eventually, she followed, because there was no going back, no undoing what had been done.

❖

"Caroline?" Tory sat down on the sofa next to the young woman. "Honey? You okay?"

Caroline sat leaning forward, her arms folded on her knees, rocking softly. "Not really."

"I heard Bri's motorcycle earlier. Is she here?"

"Gone." Caroline bit the inside of her lip. *Gone. Gone, and I don't know if she's ever coming back.*

"Can I help?"

"I don't think so. Everything is so...mixed-up." Caroline shifted and looked into Tory's eyes. "Bri...oh God, I can't... Bri was with this other girl—"

*"What?"* Tory exclaimed before she could stop herself. "Oh, honey, I'm so sorry."

"What would you do?" Caroline felt desperate and so very confused. "If...if it were Reese?"

Tory drew a sharp breath, an instant protest on her lips. *It wouldn't be Reese. She would never...*But anything could happen, to anyone. For one heart-sickening second, she remembered how she had felt when she'd found K.T. in an on-call room, in bed with one of the ICU nurses—the horror and shock and incredible sense of betrayal. The way everything had gone cold inside of her. *Reese. Not Reese. Never.* Slowly, she forced herself to think about the unthinkable.

"It would hurt so terribly, I'm not sure what I would do." Tory reached out and took Caroline's hand. "It would depend, I think, on why it happened."

"What difference would it make?"

"Sometimes, when we're confused or a little bit lost, we make bad choices. Sometimes we don't even *choose*, we just *let* things happen. People make mistakes."

"But if she loved me…" Caroline lowered her head, and warm tears fell on the top of Tory's hand.

"Bri loves you. I know that." Tory gently lifted Caroline's chin and then brushed the tears from her cheeks. "I also know you can't make any decisions when you're in so much pain."

"What do you think I should do?"

"I think you should get some sleep. I think you and Bri should talk again, but you both need a little time to settle down."

"I've got to get back to Manhattan anyhow. I keep thinking when I do that she'll…" Caroline took a deep breath. "That she'll start seeing this other girl. I can't stand to think about her with someone else."

"Caroline," Tory said gently. "I don't know what Bri's going to do. But I've seen the two of you together, and I know how much you both love each other. Sometimes even people who love each other go through hard times."

"Do you think it will ever be the same again?"

The hurt in her eyes was so raw that all Tory wanted to do was hold her close and make all her pain go away. But she knew she couldn't. "Do you love her?"

"Oh yes."

"Then I think the two of you can get through this."

Caroline studied Tory, searching her face for assurance. The green eyes gazing back were warm and steady and sure, and some of the aching in Caroline's heart was soothed.

"I never told you how happy I am about your baby," Caroline said shyly. "It's…great."

"Yes. Thank you." Tory's eyes lit up. "We're very excited."

Caroline tilted her head. "Can I ask you something?"

"Sure." Tory nodded. She knew almost everyone was curious about the *how* of it, and she and Reese had already decided that they would answer the technical questions. Well, *she* didn't mind doing it. Reese still tended to shuffle and look for the nearest exit. Her smile widened. "Go ahead."

"Does it bother you that there isn't part of Reese in the baby?"

Tory's lips parted in surprise. It wasn't the question she had expected. Caroline had caught her off guard for the second time. Once again, she considered carefully before answering.

"I would *love* for this baby to have Reese's blue eyes or her gorgeous Black Irish coloring or her wonderful strong body." She turned the gold band on her left ring finger. "But I know without a doubt that our child will have the best parts of Reese *inside*—her strength and her honor and her unwavering love."

Finally, Caroline smiled. Someday, she wanted to have what Tory had. She wanted her art, and a family, and a love of her own.

"Do you mind, can I call you sometimes?"

Tory leaned over and kissed her gently on the cheek. "Anytime you want."

❖

Reese found Tory curled up on the sofa in an old fatigue shirt of hers and a pair of shorts, reading. "Hi, love," she said as she carried two bags of groceries through to the kitchen. "Are Bri and Caroline still here?"

"No." Tory sighed as she tossed the magazine she had been pretending to read onto the end table. "Caroline left around noon to drive back to Manhattan. I thought maybe Bri was with you."

"I haven't seen her since yesterday at the end of shift." Reese joined Tory in the living room after stowing the groceries. "Wasn't she here?"

"Apparently for a minute or two. She and Caroline went off on the motorcycle, and after they talked, Bri hasn't been back."

"Doesn't sound too good," Reese observed with a raised eyebrow. She settled back and slid her arm around Tory's shoulder. Jed plodded in and flopped at Reese's feet. "What's going on, do you know?"

Tory snuggled against Reese's side, threading an arm around her waist as she rested her head on Reese's shoulder. "They're having problems."

"I gathered that from what Caroline said this morning. Did you get a chance to talk to her?"

"Some."

"Thank God. I didn't do a very good job." Reese rubbed her cheek absently across the top of Tory's head, then kissed the fine wisps of hair at her temple. "She's really upset about Bri leaving school, I guess."

"Apparently she's a lot more upset about Bri fooling around with some other girl."

Reese stiffened. "What?"

"I didn't get all the details," Tory said quietly. "It sounds as if Bri has gotten herself involved somehow with someone up here."

"That doesn't seem like Bri. She's always been crazy about Caroline."

"You probably know her better than I do, but the other night I got the sense that this whole thing with Caroline going to Europe has really thrown Bri for a loop."

"That's no reason to fool around," Reese growled. "If she were a recruit and pulled a bonehead stunt like this, I'd have her mopping out every latrine in the barracks. She wouldn't see a liberty until she was ready for retirement."

"She's not a marine, honey," Tory pointed out gently. "And she's scared."

Reese fell silent. Unconsciously, she stroked Tory's back and arm, needing her quiet strength. "Of what?"

"That Caroline will leave her behind, I think."

"So *she* turns around and leaves instead?" Reese blew out her breath, frustrated. "That doesn't make any sense."

Smiling fondly, sensing her lover's struggle to understand something so foreign to her, Tory loosed a button on Reese's shirt, slipped her hand inside, and smoothed her palm over Reese's abdomen. "Emotions don't always make sense, sweetheart."

"If I were worried about losing you," Reese murmured, her lips close to Tory's ear, "the last thing I would do is leave you."

"There aren't many people in the world as solid as you, Reese Conlon." Tory remembered how impossible it had seemed to imagine Reese straying, and although her rational mind argued it could happen, the safety and certainty of Reese's embrace assured her it would not. "God, I got so lucky."

"No." Reese shook her head, pulling Tory closer. "You're my life, Tor."

"And you're mine," Tory whispered, raising her head to find Reese's mouth. She kissed her slowly, savoring the softness of her lips. When she drew back, she felt Reese's breathing hitch and her heart quickened in response. The skin beneath her fingers grew hot. "Reese?"

"Mmm."

"I love you."

Reese groaned softly, arching her hips as Tory stroked a particularly sensitive spot just below her navel. "Don't we both have to work this afternoon?"

"Uh-huh."

"Then I think, Dr. King, that you should remove your hand."

"We have to shower, don't we?"

Reese just grinned.

❖

Tory leaned back into Reese's arms, sighing as Reese reached around her and smoothed warm lather over her breasts and abdomen with both hands. She let her head fall back against Reese's shoulder, closed her eyes, and luxuriated in the heat and the knowing touch of her lover's gentle caress. When Reese palmed her breasts, tenderly smoothing her thumbs across her nipples, Tory moaned softly. "I never want to leave here."

Reese chuckled, holding a full breast in one hand as she ran the other palm down the prominent slope of Tory's belly. "The baby is growing."

"It's really starting to show," Tory murmured, her eyes still closed. "Do you mind?"

"You have to ask?" Reese's voice was husky as she brushed her fingers softly through the downy hair at the base of Tory's abdomen. "It's wonderful. And incredibly sexy."

Tory laughed softly, covering the exploring hand with her own. "I wouldn't have believed it, but I actually feel sexy—in a different way than before, but good."

"How?" It never took more than the sensation of Tory in her arms to arouse Reese. Now, the miracle of what was happening beneath the fragile layers of skin and muscle left her in a constant state of wonder and desire. It was sexual, and yet so much more.

"I feel as if I'm bursting with something so powerful—life, love, I guess. I look at you, and I want you to touch it, touch *me*, some place deep inside."

"I love you." Reese groaned. Tory's soft skin against her breasts and abdomen was like flame to tinder. She was burning, pulsing with excitement. "Take my hand…take me to those places."

"Hold me."

"Always."

Tory drew Reese's fingers between her legs, parting the delicate folds that enclosed her most sensitive places. She led her to the warm pools of her desire, guiding Reese's fingertips gently inside and then upward, until they rested against the undersurface of her clitoris. Her legs were trembling, her breath shallow and fast. "Feel how heavy? How full?"

"Yes," Reese gasped, her head pounding with the effort it took to let Tory guide her. "Beautiful."

Tory pushed against Reese's hand, moaning softly. Then, slowly, she drew her lover inside, resting her weight in the bend of Reese's body as she was filled. "Ah, so good. You feel so good there."

Reese closed her eyes tightly, holding very still as she pressed her mouth to Tory's neck, letting the warm water that cascaded from Tory's skin run between her lips. Nothing ever made her feel quite so humble or so privileged as when she was inside Tory's body. Hoarsely, she whispered, "I want to stay *here* forever."

"You can." Fine ripples cascaded through the muscles enclosing Reese's fingers. Tory tightened involuntarily and the pressure immediately pulsed into her clitoris. She jerked, and Reese's palm brushed over the swollen shaft. She gave a small cry and arched in Reese's arms.

"What is it?"

"I want to come."

Reese gently bit the tender skin below Tory's jaw. "Can you stand?"

"Yes."

When Tory reached behind and braced both palms against Reese's thighs, Reese let the hand that had been encircling Tory's middle drift lower until she could stroke her. Tory was already too close to tease, and Reese started the circular motion that she knew would make her come.

"I love you, Tor," Reese breathed when Tory trembled in her arms.

"Can you feel it?" Tory asked urgently as she began to come.

"Yes." Reese worked so carefully to go slow, drawing out the pleasure as Tory climaxed in her hands.

"Ah," Tory sighed as she slowly relaxed into Reese's embrace. "God, you spoil me."

Reese laughed a bit shakily. She tended to stop breathing every time Tory orgasmed, and her legs had gotten so weak, she'd been worried for a moment that she was going to take them both down.

"Believe me, it's my pleasure."

"Lucky me." Tory wrapped her fingers languidly around Reese's wrists, and gently moved her lover's hands from between her thighs. She turned until her breasts were against Reese's and wrapped both arms around Reese's neck. Resting her forehead against her lover's, she sighed again. "You realize that in another few weeks, I'm going to be too big for us to do that."

"We'll find a way around it," Reese promised, her hands dropping to Tory's hips and caressing her softly. "It will still be okay, right?"

"What?" Tory asked lazily.

"For a little while longer? We can still make love, right?"

Tory laughed and moved one hand between their bodies. "As long as we can find a position where we can reach the important places, we don't have to stop."

"You just need to tell me, okay?" Reese's kissed her softly. "If we shouldn't? If there's a…problem."

Leaning her head back, Tory studied her lover's serious countenance. "You worry too much, Sheriff."

"I love you so much, I just want you to be okay."

"I'm fine," Tory said firmly. She insinuated her fingers into Reese's hair and tugged gently. "Look at me."

Reese fell into Tory's eyes.

"Everything is perfect." As she spoke, she pressed her thigh between Reese's, leaning her weight into her, pinning her to the wall. She knew how sensitive Reese was when they made love. Often, she had to be careful that Reese didn't come too soon from an inadvertent caress. She knew precisely how hard it had been for Reese to make love to her so slowly and so carefully. That her lover would do that despite her own needs moved her terribly. "*You* are perfect."

"Tor," Reese whispered, her vision hazy.

"You can come now, sweetheart." Tory lowered her mouth to Reese's. She pressed harder with her thigh as she slid her tongue into Reese's mouth. She kept her hands in Reese's hair, holding her head still as she searched inside, sucking gently on her. She matched her rhythm to the thrust of Reese's hips and when the fingers gripping her tightened convulsively, she circled her leg faster. As Reese grew rigid, Tory lifted her face away. "Let me watch you."

Reese forced her eyes open, though she was blind to everything except the storm surging through her blood. She crumpled under the onslaught of pleasure, and only Tory's body against hers kept her upright. "Don't...let go," she managed to cry.

"Never. Never."

## CHAPTER FOURTEEN

Reese glanced at the large plain-faced clock on the wall opposite her desk. It was 3:59 p.m. She stood, settled her cap squarely over her brow, and crossed the room to the door. When she stepped out onto the small landing in front of the sheriff's department, she heard the sound of a powerful engine. She looked right toward Bradford and watched the approaching motorcycle streak into the parking lot, spewing gravel and dirt.

Bri climbed off almost before the big bike had stopped moving and jogged over to where Reese waited.

"Officer," Reese said by way of greeting. Bri was in uniform, her shoes polished, although dusty from the ride, and her shirt and pants starched and pressed. Her eyes were hollow and her face pale.

"Sheriff."

"Technically," Reese said shortly, "you're not late. It is customary, however, to arrive at least a half an hour before your shift in the event that there's anything pertinent to relay from the previous shift. In your case, it's mandatory. See to it in the future."

"Yes, ma'am."

"Let's take a ride-through."

They were both silent as Reese drove the cruiser west on Bradford. She slowed as they approached the site of the fire. A deep red Durango SUV was parked on the shoulder across the street from the police barricades that had been erected around the property.

"There's someone walking around back there," Bri observed.

"Yep, I see him." Reese pulled up behind the Durango. "Call in that plate number."

Bri already had the mike in her hand and called for vehicle identification.

"Recognize the vehicle?" Reese thought Bri might know it from around town.

"Nope. Looks to be brand new. Snazzy."

"Uh-huh," Reese agreed as she pushed open her door.

The radio crackled to life and Smith came on, advising them that there were no wants or warrants on the vehicle and that it was registered to an A. Walker of Falls River, Massachusetts.

"Well, let's go see what Mr. Walker is doing poking around our crime scene."

The two officers crossed the street shoulder to shoulder and circled around to the rear of the burned-out shell of the restaurant. Much of the external frame remained, although the building had been nearly gutted. At the location of what had once been the service entrance to the restaurant, a thin figure in blue jeans, a denim workshirt, scuffed work boots, and a baseball cap crouched with his back to them, photographing the interior of the building.

"Sheriff's department," Reese announced as she and Bri walked around one of the yellow and blue sawhorses and approached the stranger. "This is a restricted area."

Slowly, the individual stood and turned in their direction. "I'm an insurance investigator, officers," a mellifluous tenor voice responded.

Reese raised an eyebrow, surveying the emerald green eyes, flawless lightly tanned complexion, and the hint of red hair obscured by the cap. "You have ID?"

"Sure." Approaching them now, the stranger reached into a back pocket with one hand and swept off the ball cap with the other. Thick, luxurious crimson hair cascaded to shoulder level. The strikingly beautiful woman smiled and extended a hand with a leather bi-fold ID case in it. "Ashley Walker."

Reese studied the photo ID on the private investigator's license. Satisfied, she handed it back. "Ordinarily, Ms. Walker, it's wise for a private investigator to check in with the local authorities."

Ashley swept her eyes from Reese to Bri and back again. The two law enforcement agents were disarmingly similar with their dark good looks and nearly matching brilliant blue eyes. The older one was slightly taller and a little more muscular, but in the dark, there wouldn't be much difference between the two. She smiled slowly.

"My apologies. I meant to let you know I was in town, but when I drove by and saw the state of this building, I thought I'd better get a few photographs before it fell down or your town engineers pulled it down."

"Step outside the barricade, please," Reese directed in a tone which implied it was more than a request, "and we'll give you what we have."

"Fine." Ashley returned her ID to her pocket "I didn't get your names?"

"Deputy Sheriff Reese Conlon. This is Officer Parker."

"Pleasure."

Reese nodded in response and glanced at Bri, who was studying the newcomer curiously. "Parker, want to fill Ms. Walker in on the state of the investigation?"

"Yes, ma'am." Without referring to her notes, which she kept in a slim spiral-ringed tablet in her back pocket, Bri recited confidently. "There were no injuries or fatalities associated with the incident. The fire marshal's report isn't expected for at least a week. This being a holiday weekend, most of the labs are closed. At the present time, we are working under the assumption that this is incendiary in nature. The site will remain barricaded until released by the fire marshal for demolition, which we anticipate will be in approximately ten days."

"Sounds routine," Ashley observed, slipping her hands into the back pockets of her jeans.

"And what about your investigation, Ms. Walker?" Bri questioned evenly. "Who are you working for?"

"Just the standard insurance claim." Unperturbed by the mildly suspicious expression on the young officer's face, Ashley produced her wallet, opened it, and slid a business card from an inside pocket. Handing it to Bri, she said, "That's my office address, cell phone number, and pager. Any time you want to reach me, Officer Parker, for any reason, please feel free."

"Finished up here, then?" Reese was curious if the investigator had found something as they started back toward their vehicles.

"I thought I'd stay in town for a while until the fire marshal's report was complete. A busman's holiday," Ashley finished with a soft laugh.

"If you need access to the site, once it's been cleared, let us know," Reese advised.

Ashley rested her hand on the handle of her SUV, hitched one hip against the door, and observed them both with a small grin. "Oh, I'll be sure to do that." Then she stepped into her Durango, started the engine, and drove away with a small wave in their direction.

Bri watched the red truck turn right and disappear around the bend toward Herring Cove. Part of her was irritated at the cocky self-confidence of the private investigator, but she found that the woman's flippant grin stayed with her. "Is that normal?"

"For an insurance investigation? Yeah, pretty much all the time when there's loss of property." Reese opened the driver's side door of the cruiser and slid in while Bri walked around to the other side. "It *isn't* usual to have a PI run the investigation though. Usually, it's one of the insurance company's claim representatives."

"So what do you think?"

"I think we ought to take a very careful look at the fire marshal's report, and I think you're going to have some homework."

❖

When Reese returned to the office an hour later, Nelson was at his desk working on his never-ending stack of paperwork. He glanced up as she pushed through the wooden gate toward her adjoining desk.

"Where's your...trainee?"

"Interviewing some of the neighbors in the area immediately around the fire site. We're looking into the possibility that it was started accidentally by kids using the place to party."

"You think she's okay out there alone?" Nelson carefully straightened his file folders and stacked them on the corner of his desk. "She's only been at this a couple of days."

"It's a simple assignment, Chief. It's just the kind of thing that she needs to do independently at this point."

"You never know what she might run into. She's wearing a gun. That's enough to make some people antsy."

Reese settled behind her desk and took her time answering.

"Nelson, I've read her performance evaluations. She's at the top of her class in all the required areas. She qualified with highest recommendations in firearms and close-range disarmament. She can handle herself."

"You're her training instructor," Nelson snapped. "You're supposed to be *training* her."

A muscle in Reese's jaw jumped. "If you have a problem, sir, with the way I'm conducting Officer Parker's training, I—"

"Oh, stow it, Conlon. She's just a kid. God damn it, I just don't want her to get hurt." He stood up suddenly, his wheeled chair spinning across the small room. *She's all I've got.*

"Chief," Reese ventured in a more reasonable voice. "She's just going to knock on a few doors and ask a few questions. I'm not going to let her patrol alone, at least for a while. This job is what she's chosen to do."

He ran a hand over his hair and grimaced. "Yeah, and she didn't ask my opinion about it."

Reese grinned. "And if she had, do you think you would have been able to talk her out of it?"

"Sure. When pigs fly." Nelson fixed Reese with a baleful stare. "She's not even living at home."

"Uh…" Reese shifted slightly, uncomfortable for the first time. "I think that probably has to do with her being twenty years old, Nelson. She's trying to stand on her own."

"Yeah, I know." He retrieved his chair, pulled it back to his desk, and sat heavily. "But I still wish sometimes she'd waited, at least until she'd finished school."

Reese thought about Caroline's tears that morning, and the desperate anguish she had glimpsed in Bri's eyes that afternoon. *I'm with you there, Chief.*

❖

Reese met Bri several hours later, and they drove into the center of town together for dinner. As they walked toward a small sandwich shop on the pier at Commercial and Standish, Reese asked, "Get anything from the interviews?"

"Maybe," Bri replied cautiously. "The manager of the condominium next door says he thought he saw lights flickering in the restaurant a couple of times late at night in the past few weeks."

"And he didn't bother to call us?" Reese sighed in disgust.

Bri shrugged. "Said he thought it was probably just kids and didn't pay much attention."

"I suppose we're lucky he mentioned it to you at all." Reese was next in line at the order window and put in her request for fish and chips and soda. "I don't suppose he saw a vehicle?"

"Nope. But it fits with our theory that someone's been using the place. If so, they're going to be looking for new digs. I thought maybe we could start keeping an eye on some of the other abandoned places around town."

"Good idea."

After they had both ordered, they moved away to await their dinners.

"There was something else," Bri confided.

Reese raised an eyebrow. "Oh?"

"I talked to maybe a dozen people this evening, up and down the cul-de-sacs off Bradford and along Route 6 toward the Provincetown Inn. At least half told me that I was the second police officer to interview them since the fire."

"Interesting. Hold on for a second." Responding to the shout that their orders were ready, she and Bri collected their food and drinks and walked out of earshot of the tourists and other diners to a small picnic table on MacMillan Wharf. "I don't suppose you got a description of the new member of our force, did you?"

"Yep." Bri grinned. "Red hair, green eyes, late twenties. Female."

"Thorough, isn't she?"

"Would you say that's SOP for an insurance claim?"

"No, I wouldn't." Reese regarded her food absently. Something was off, and the fact that it involved something as dangerous as the possibility of arson bothered her a good deal. "It looks like we need to pay a visit to Ms. Walker."

"Fortunately," Bri announced, patting her chest pocket, "I have all her numbers."

❖

The rest of the shift passed uneventfully. The town was just gearing up for tourist season, and although the population had already doubled with the beginning of Memorial Day weekend, the true crowds would not arrive until July 4th. Nevertheless, all the stores were open up and down Commercial Street, as were most of the restaurants and galleries. Reese and Bri took their time getting reacquainted with the shopkeepers, many of whom had left for the winter and were just returning. They walked through the business district of the tiny village several times, stopping in all the establishments just to say hello. Along the way, they took note of any unoccupied or abandoned buildings. There were at least half a dozen scattered along the length of Commercial Street.

"When you give report to the night shift, make sure you give them the addresses of these places and remind them to do a pass-by several times during the shift."

"Got it." Bri felt a sudden let-down as she realized that her time with Reese was coming to an end. It was five minutes to midnight, and they were on their way back to the sheriff's department to sign out. In another few minutes, Reese would go home and she would be alone. It was Saturday night, she had just finished an exciting shift at work, and she had no one to share it with.

She could go home with Reese, but the small spare bedroom with its single bed seemed too lonely to contemplate. Caroline would be out somewhere with friends, probably having a glass of wine and talking about school, or a film she had just seen, or some project she was involved in. Bri's heart ached as she wondered if Caroline would be thinking about her. *I should call her. But she said not to—that she would call me when she was ready. She said she wanted a little time to think. Think about what? Think about whether she still loves me? Think about whether she still wants to be with me? Think—*

"Bri?"

Bri jumped. They were sitting in front of the sheriff's department. The engine was off and the night was very quiet. She had no idea how long she had been staring unseeing through the windshield.

"Yeah?" she said hoarsely.

"You okay?"

"Yeah." Bri nodded and swallowed hard. "Fine."

"I saw Caroline this morning."

Bri closed her eyes.

"Have you straightened things out with her?" Reese asked gently.

"Not yet." Bri didn't want to talk about it. Just thinking about it made her hurt so much inside she was afraid she would cry. She especially didn't want to discuss what had happened with Reese. She had a sudden sick feeling in her stomach. *Christ, does Reese know about Allie?*

Thankfully, it was too dark in the car for Reese to see her shamed blush. The thought of Reese knowing about the way she had fucked up was almost as bad as Caroline's tears. She felt like dying.

"You need to do that, Bri," Reese said evenly as she opened the door of the cruiser.

"Yeah, I know," Bri replied softly, all the while wondering how to even begin.

❖

When Reese and Bri walked into the office, Lewis, one of the summer recruits who had been hired to work the swing shift, looked up from the dispatch counter and nodded perfunctorily. "There are messages for both of you on the spindle."

Bri looked surprised, and Reese frowned as she asked, "From whom?"

The ruddy complexioned, sandy-haired officer shrugged his heavyset shoulders. "The names are on the slips there. Yours just says to call home."

"God *damn* it," Reese swore swiftly in a tone that made both Bri and Lewis jump. "If you *ever* get a call from my partner or anything remotely *connected* to her again, you call me ASAP."

He stared at her open-mouthed as Reese grabbed the nearest phone and punched in her home number. Her body vibrated with tension.

"Tor?" She worked to sound calm. "Are you all right?"

As Reese listened, her body relaxed, and she settled her hip onto the corner of the nearest desk. A smile slowly eclipsed the worry that had suffused her face. "You're kidding, right?...I thought that was an old wives' tale...Well, I don't know *that* many...No! I'll do it...I'll be home soon."

Still grinning, Reese hung up the receiver. When she glanced up, Bri was watching her intently. "She's fine."

Bri relaxed her tight stance, too. "Good."

"I don't suppose you know Spiritus's number offhand, do you?"

"You're kidding, right? Pizza?"

"That's exactly what I just said to her." Reese shook her head. "She's hungry and pretty cranky about it, too."

"I have to go to the house to change," Bri said with a grin. "You want me to go get it on my way?"

"No, thanks. I know you're good on that bike, but I'd rather you weren't riding while balancing a pizza. If you see Tory when you get home, just tell her that her delivery is on the way."

"Sure thing," Bri replied as Reese picked up the phone again. While Reese got the number and called in the pizza order, Bri pulled the pink message slips from the spindle on the counter. They were two for her. She read them, then read them again. At first, she thought it was a joke, but then realized that it couldn't be. *Who would know to do this?*

Both messages were exactly the same, with one minor difference. Each had only two words, *Call me,* followed by a phone number. They were signed Ashley and Allie, respectively.

"Everything okay, Bri?" Reese noted the confused expression on Bri's face.

Blushing, Bri rapidly stuffed the notes into her pants pocket. "Sure. Perfect."

❖

"Oh, thank God," Tory said vehemently as Reese walked in the house. "Hurry."

Reese grinned at her lover, who was curled up on the sofa in a shapeless button-up pajama top and what appeared to be striped boxers. "You know, I can remember a time when you only said that in bed."

"Shut up, Conlon, and give me my pizza."

Laughing outright, Reese put the box down on the coffee table in front of Tory and walked through to the kitchen for plates and napkins. "Is Bri here?"

"No," Tory said around a mouthful of pizza. "She came in, changed her clothes, and went right back out again."

"At this hour?" Reese frowned as she carried a bottle of beer for herself tucked against her side, a glass of seltzer for Tory in one hand, and plates, silverware, and napkins in the other. She carefully set them all down, settled on the sofa, and slid a slice of pizza onto a plate. "What is she doing out?"

"It's Saturday night, love."

"So?" Reese regarded her with a raised eyebrow.

"Try to remember Saturday night when you were twenty."

"I remember perfectly well, and I was either studying or, more likely, sleeping." Reese shook her head. "ROTC students got up early, because we had PT first thing in the morning. Every morning."

"I forgot." Tory ran her hand affectionately up the inside of Reese's thigh. "You were a most unusual twenty-year-old, sweetheart."

"Oh yeah?" Reese said challengingly. "So what were *you* doing?"

For a second, Tory was quiet. "I met K.T. that summer."

Hearing the sadness Tory couldn't quite hide, Reese slipped her arm around her lover's shoulder. "If I could take her out and thrash her, I would do it cheerfully."

"She was good with you in the hospital," Tory pointed out with a smile as she rested her cheek against Reese's shoulder. "She was good to me then, too."

"That notwithstanding," Reese said with a low grumble. "She hurt you, and that's not acceptable."

"It doesn't matter anymore."

Reese kissed her gently, lingering for a moment to savor the incredible softness of her lips. "I missed you."

"Mmm, me, too," Tory murmured.

"Did you and K.T. talk about the past at all, when I was sick? I can't remember very much of the first couple of days."

"Not really." Tory drew a shaky breath as her throat tightened. It was still hard to think about how very close she had come to losing Reese. She moved closer on the sofa, her pizza forgotten. "You were all I could think about. I was shocked to see her at first, but I didn't really feel anything."

"I can't imagine ever seeing you and not wanting you, not loving you," Reese whispered, resting her chin on the top of Tory's head. "No matter what."

"Sometimes there's so much hurt it drives the love from your heart."

Reese tightened her hold on the woman in her arms. "I'm not sorry that you're not with her, but I'm sorry that you were hurt."

"I know, sweetheart. But loving you makes up for any pain I ever had."

"You think Bri and Caroline are going to be okay?"

"I think they *can* be," Tory said quietly, "if they come back together soon and don't do anything more to add to the pain."

"Do you think I should go look for Bri before she gets herself into more trouble?"

"Let's give her a chance to find her own way." Tory felt Reese stiffen. "She needs to come to her own realization of what she wants and needs."

"I just don't want either of them to suffer any more." Reese closed her eyes. "You didn't see Bri today. She's...lost."

Tory tilted her chin and pressed her lips to Reese's neck, then reached a hand back to curl her fingers into the thick, black hair. Tugging gently, she pulled Reese down for a proper kiss. When she lifted her mouth away, she whispered huskily, "You're going to make the most wonderful parent."

❖

By the time Bri rode back to the center of town and parked her bike, most of the stores were closed and the bars were beginning to empty. As was often the case, Commercial Street between the Pied, one of the popular lesbian bars, and Spiritus Pizza was crowded with men and women who were not yet ready to end their Saturday night revelry. It was a cruising ground and general meeting place, and it had been a common location for her clandestine late-night rendezvous throughout high school.

As she approached the gathering throng, she remembered Reese coming upon her and Caroline in the narrow alley between the ramshackle restaurant and the adjoining storefront one night when they'd been seventeen. They'd been making out in the shadows when Reese had walked up on them, her flashlight beam illuminating them in the midst of passion. Stunned, Bri had thought for a second that they had been busted. She'd stepped in front of Caroline to hide the fact that Caroline's lace-up vest was open and the snap of her jeans unbuttoned. All she could think of in that second was to protect Caroline from whatever threatened them. *God, I was scared. But Carre never flinched. She's never backed down from anything.*

Thinking about that night, she felt anew how desperately she had wanted Caroline, physically and emotionally, and how unbelievable it had been to actually have her—to be able to touch her, to be able to express physically how much she loved her. She still couldn't believe her luck. Out of all the people Caroline could have had, she'd chosen her. Sometimes she had expected to wake up in the morning and look into Caroline's eyes and see the realization there that Caroline had made a mistake. *That she didn't love me after all. That she finally realized that I had nothing to offer her.*

Bri's chest ached just remembering how sweet those first few months had been, and how desperate the last. *I miss you so much, babe.*

"Unless I'm wrong," a deep melodious voice announced very close to Bri's ear, "I believe you're looking for me."

*Jesus Christ. I'm walking around not paying attention to a damn thing I'm doing. Some alert cop.*

Hoping that her involuntary flinch hadn't been noticed, Bri turned to the woman by her side as they continued navigating slowly through the wall-to-wall people. "You *did* say to meet you here."

Ashley Walker was wearing a sleeveless black T-shirt tucked into figure-hugging black leather pants and black ankle-high riding boots. Her crimson hair was down and glinted like fire as she casually brushed it back with one hand. "I didn't think you'd call me."

"I'm working the same case you are," Bri reminded her. The two messages folded inside her right front pocket had felt hot enough to burn as she had ridden the short distance from the sheriff's department to Reese and Tory's home just on the border between Provincetown and Truro. At first, she'd thought she would ignore them both. The idea of seeing Allie was a little scary. Things seemed to happen that she didn't plan on when they were together. The more she'd thought about it, however, the more it seemed that Ashley Walker could only have business on her mind. After all, *they* didn't even know one another. "You said you might have some information for me."

Ashley slowed and nodded toward the Pied. "We can probably still make last call."

"No thanks." Bri wasn't interested in drinking, and if she was, she wouldn't be doing it in a bar in Provincetown. Not for another couple of months, and probably not even then.

"All right, then." Ashley sighed and pretended to look disappointed, but her slightly lopsided grin gave her away. "So I'm guilty of mixing business with pleasure. We *can* do both."

Bri blushed. *Work. Keep the conversation on business.* "Have you been conducting interviews with the neighbors around the Moorings?"

"I see you *have* been working," Ashley observed with a new note of respect in her voice. "Come on. Let's get out of this crowd."

Bri followed as Ashley turned down one of the sandy access paths to the beach. Once there, they both settled onto a pile of sun-bleached, wind-weathered pilings that had once been part of a fishing pier. Ashley drew one knee up, wrapped both arms around it, and leaned a bare shoulder lightly against the outside of Bri's arm.

"Yes, I've been asking around a bit." Ashley confirmed what Bri already knew. "I thought maybe we could pool our resources."

"Share information, you mean?" Bri moved an inch away. The touch of skin contacting hers was unexpectedly warm.

"Could save us both some time," Ashley pointed out. She noted the subtle shift in Bri's body and tried to decide if it was intentional. The young officer looked even better out of uniform than she did in one, and that was pretty damn good. The white T-shirt hugged her torso, doing little to hide the swell of her breasts and hint of hard nipples, and the low-riding jeans seemed designed to invite a hand inside.

"So," Bri remarked, watching the mooring lights of the sailboats anchored in the harbor flicker on the water as the boats rocked on the quiet tide. "Did you find out anything?"

"Not so fast, hotshot." Ashley laughed softly. "I'll show you mine *if* you agree to show me yours."

Bri turned until she could search Ashley's face. Up close, moonlight danced in her eyes. "I don't think it works that way. See, *I'm* the law and you're private. So I don't have to share what I know with you. But I'm pretty sure *you're* not supposed to keep secrets."

"Somehow I thought you were going to be more cooperative." Ashley studied Bri, looking for some indication that she might be able to tease her into revealing if the local authorities had uncovered anything pertinent to their common investigation.

"Why would you think that?"

"I had a feeling you might want to get ahead—impress that formidable partner of yours." Ashley shrugged. "Breaking a case always helps the reputation."

"I wasn't aware there *was* a case. We don't even know if the fire was intentionally set." Bri waited a beat. "Do we?"

"You're pretty slick, hotshot. Nice try." Ashley laughed again. "Are you trying to *pump* me?"

"Me? I'm just a rookie."

"Uh-huh. Sure 'nuff." Ashley rocked her leg playfully against Bri's thigh. "Well, this won't be the first time I've misread a situation. You *look* young, but you're sure not naïve."

Bri wasn't entirely certain of that, because she was pretty much feeling her way along by instinct, but she was damn certain that if she talked about the case with a private investigator, Reese would kick her ass. She didn't need years of experience to know that. "So, I guess that means you're not going to be sharing, huh?"

"Well, at least not information. Not right now." Ashley stood and dusted off the rear of her leather pants, then slid both hands into her back pockets and looked down at Bri. She tilted one hip and stretched, the thin shirt outlining her high breasts and taut nipples. "Want to take a walk on the beach?"

Bri regarded her steadily, then stood. "Sure."

## CHAPTER FIFTEEN

Reese turned over in bed, awakened by the low rumble of the motorcycle in the driveway. The bedside clock read 3:45 a.m. For a moment, she contemplated getting up.

"Go back to sleep, sweetheart," Tory whispered as she rolled toward Reese and slipped an arm around her waist. Curling against her lover's back, she nuzzled into the soft warmth of Reese's neck and kissed her softly. "She's okay."

Reese sighed and laced her fingers through Tory's, where they lay against her breast. "I hope so."

❖

At five minutes to seven, Reese knelt to one side of the forty-by fifty-foot room with her eyes closed, her hands resting palms up on her thighs. Tory and four students ranging in age from fourteen to twenty-five lined up on the tatami mats in a single line, barely an inch separating them. They knelt, too, facing the front of the room where the ceremonial altar stood on a small hand-carved wooden bench. The room was very still as each student mentally prepared for class.

Reese stiffened, as she had only hours before, when she heard the sound of an engine drawing near. Intent on maintaining her own focus, she did not glance over as Bri came into the room, hastily tying her belt before taking her place to Tory's right.

At precisely seven, Reese moved to the center of the room, knelt, and bowed. Ordinarily, the class proceeded with no conversation other than when Reese announced the attack and corresponding defense to be performed. Once she called upon a student to assist her in demonstrating the techniques, the students paired off with no regard to rank and repeated the drills. Senior-level practitioners worked with beginners as well as each other. Within each pair, the students alternated offensive and defensive positions until Reese called a halt.

Bri had practiced only briefly with the class during her last visit home, and Reese watched carefully as Bri worked with the first student. It was not unusual for students who left a dojo to practice elsewhere to learn variations in the techniques and to incorporate habits that very often might be at odds with the philosophy or style of their previous school. Aware that Bri had very recently been practicing hand-to-hand combat skills with her colleagues in the academy, Reese wanted to be sure that she could temper her physicality when training with inexperienced beginners. And even more importantly, that she was careful with Tory.

After their last visit with Wendy, Reese had gently suggested that Tory suspend her workouts until after the baby was born, but Tory had merely smiled and said that the physical exercise was good for her. Reese was always careful not to choose techniques that involved shoulder lifts or throws, but still, every defense in jujitsu finished with a takedown to the floor. And every time a student took her lover to the mat, no matter how gently, Reese's heart lurched. The first time Tory bowed to Bri in invitation to practice, Reese quickly crossed the mat to them. Before Bri and Tory could begin, Reese extended a hand to Bri, indicating that Bri should perform the technique with her.

If Bri kept on schedule, she would be ready to test for black belt before the end of the year. It was time for her to be challenged. When Bri launched the first punch toward Reese's midsection, Reese pivoted, grasped the punching wrist, then turned tightly counterclockwise and threw Bri to the mat. Following her student down, she quickly immobilized Bri with a wrist lock. When they practiced the technique with positions reversed, Bri executed smoothly and with controlled force.

Reese was pleased. She bowed, dismissing Bri, and moved to Tory to repeat the same technique. Although Tory was a black belt in hapkido, that style was more akin to tae kwon do than jujitsu. And though not equal in rank, Tory and Bri were of nearly equal experience in this class.

When Tory threw her punch, Reese repeated the defense and smoothly guided Tory to the floor. As she cradled Tory's elbow between her knees and applied force on her wrist, effectively pinning her, she leaned forward slightly over Tory's supine form and murmured, "Everything okay?"

"Yes, *sensei*."

"Be careful with Bri. She's very strong."

"I will be." For the briefest instant, she smiled directly into Reese's eyes and murmured faintly, "I'm fine, sweetheart."

Reese nodded briefly, her gaze a caress, and moved away.

At the end of class, Reese approached Bri, who was carefully folding her *gi* jacket and brown obi. "It's good to have you back."

"It's great to be here." Almost shyly, Bri looked quickly at Reese, then away. "Can I talk to you later?"

"Sure." Reese glanced at the clock. "It's about breakfast time. I was going to take Tory to Café Heaven. Want to come along?"

"That's okay. I don't want to…get in the way."

Reese laughed. "It's just breakfast, Bri."

"Well…"

"Come on, Bri," Tory said as she joined them. "I heard that. You're coming, and that's all there is to it. You can leave your motorcycle here, and we'll bring you back after breakfast to pick it up."

❖

The tiny restaurant was situated just up the street from where Bri had met Ashley the night before. It had only a dozen or so tables and was always crowded, but luckily it took only a few moments for them to be seated. Even more fortunately, the waitress recognized them as regulars, so it took only another minute to place their orders.

"So how is the new guy working out?" Bri asked Tory after finishing a large glass of orange juice in three big gulps. "What's his name?"

"Dan Riley." Tory's response was precisely neutral. "He's only been here one day."

"Is he just here for the summer?" Bri reached for the basket of bread. She didn't notice that her conversational inquiries made both Reese and Tory look uncomfortable.

"That was the plan. I can't imagine that we would need two doctors full-time during the off-season."

"Yeah, but I guess you'll be pretty busy with the baby, huh?"

"Fortunately," Reese interjected, "Jean and my mother have already offered to baby-sit while Tory's at work. As soon as she and the baby are ready, Tory will be able to get back to her regular schedule at the clinic."

Under the table, Tory slid her hand around Reese's knee where it rested against her leg and squeezed gently. "We still have a few of the logistical details to work out. Like who is going to run the breast milk back and forth."

Bri colored and looked quickly out the front window. "Oh. Right. That."

"So," Reese said casually as she peppered her omelet, "how was your night?"

"Uh…it was…fine."

"Much activity in town?"

"It was crowded right around closing time, but after that, it emptied out pretty quickly."

"Uh-huh. Not much going on after one-thirty or so." Reese raised an eyebrow and regarded Bri steadily.

"Well…" Bri'd wanted to discuss the encounter with Reese, because it still bothered her, and she couldn't quite work out why. That is, she wanted to tell Reese about *most* of it, anyhow. "I met Ashley Walker, and we talked about the case for a while."

Reese stiffened almost imperceptibly. "You talked about the case?"

"Not about the case, exactly. Well, I mean, *she* wanted to talk about the case."

"I'll bet she did," Reese muttered.

"Who, by the way, is Ashley Walker?" Tory looked from one to the other and tried to figure out what, precisely, was going on. Reese was acting as if Bri had done something wrong. Her lover sounded very much like an attending about to come down hard on a new intern who had made a moronic mistake and hadn't yet figured it out. Her first instinct was to rush to Bri's defense, whatever her transgression might have been, because she knew that Bri worshiped Reese. She couldn't bear the thought of anyone else whom Bri loved hurting her, even unintentionally.

It took all Tory's willpower not to say anything. Bri had chosen Reese to be her training instructor, and Tory knew how great that responsibility was. For the first time, she wondered if perhaps it had been a mistake for Reese to accept the position. Bri needed a good training instructor, but what she needed even more right now was a friend.

Aware that they were in a public place, Bri lowered her voice and leaned across the small table close to Tory. "She's a private detective who's working for an insurance company."

"I see. This is about the fire, I take it?"

"Yeah."

"What did the two of you discuss?" Reese's eyes were steady on Bri's face, her voice flat.

"*We* didn't discuss anything," Bri said with a faint hint of disgust. "She was fishing for information about our investigation. I was hoping she'd tell *me* something. So we both came away with no satisfaction."

"Does that tell you anything?" Reese speared a strawberry with her fork and waited. *You're good at this, kiddo. Let's see what your instincts are like.*

"I've been thinking about that." Bri took her time, her eggs and linguica forgotten. "If she was trying to find out what we knew, then there must be something *to* know. More than just a fire. It's only been a couple of days, and no one would expect us to have much on it yet. She was trying to see if we had information on something else."

"Uh-huh." Reese moved on to the bananas. "Like what?"

"Like…" Bri hitched her shoulders, worried about looking dumb. "Like *another* fire?"

"Mmm. Could be."

Tory relaxed and leaned back in her chair, enjoying the Socratic exchange. She'd seen Reese work dozens of time. But she'd never seen her quite like this. Usually, when Reese was in the field, she was in command mode. She issued orders, then expected them to be followed without question. She rarely explained, because she saw no need to do so. She had been bred and raised in a military family, where the power was clearly delineated and the authority unquestioningly accepted. However, watching her lead Bri through this algorithm of deductive reasoning showed Tory a fascinating side of her partner that she had never before observed.

Suddenly, she had an image of Reese with their child, patiently teaching him or her how to think about the world. To her absolute chagrin, she felt her eyes fill with tears. *Oh my God, this pregnancy is doing the strangest things to me.*

"Tor?" Reese glanced with concern at Tory, feeling her lover grow tight against her side. "What's wrong?"

"Nothing, sweetheart." Tory shook her head and smiled wanly.

Reese kissed her cheek softly, then looked back to Bri. "So, what's your plan?"

By the time Tory composed herself, she caught only the tail end of the conversation.

"I agree," Reese said as she finished her cottage cheese. "After we finish our first tour through town this afternoon, I want you to start looking for similars."

"I can make some calls, too," Bri said eagerly.

Reese nodded thoughtfully. "Might not be a bad idea to check personally. Sometimes we don't get all the reports, and if they're late with the data entries in the other divisions, we might not pull it up on the computer yet."

"It's a holiday weekend," Tory pointed out, suddenly feeling much more herself. "I imagine you'll have a hard time tracking people down, if it's anything like it is around here. You hardly have anyone in the office, and the ones who *are* there don't seem to know a lot about what's going on."

Grinning, Reese ran her fingers lightly down Tory's forearm and squeezed her hand. "Well, our guy Lewis knows a lot more about it now than he did last night. The next time you call, I've got a feeling you'll get priority treatment."

"Good." Tory bumped her shoulder softly into Reese's. "And rightly so, too."

The three of them laughed and finished breakfast, speaking no more of medicine or law enforcement.

❖

On Wednesday morning as Reese and Tory were both preparing for work, Tory asked casually, "So, did Bri find anything out from her computer searches about the fire in town?"

Reese was halfway through tying a precision knot in her tie and finished before answering. "Not yet. I think today will probably be more productive. You were right. We had a hard time connecting with anyone the last couple of days, especially with all the traffic leaving the Cape after the holiday. Everyone was in the field."

"So, what's this investigator like?"

"I can't say for sure. She seemed confident, and the fact that she picked Bri to question also suggests that she's clever."

"Because Bri is a beginner, and she thought Bri was a likely source of information?"

Reese nodded. "I'm sure she knew she wouldn't get anything from me."

"It could be she was just using it as an excuse to see Bri socially, you know. Did she look like the type who might be interested?"

"I didn't really notice."

Tory smiled fondly. "How lucky for me. Describe her for me."

"I thought that didn't work," Reese protested. "Besides, wouldn't you have to see her to get…you know, some kind of vibe or something?"

"Talk about old wives' tales." Tory laughed out loud. "Just tell me about the way she looked and what she said when the three of you first met."

Reese complied as Tory listened intently. When she finished, Tory shook her head knowingly. "Just what Bri needs is another woman interested in her. She sounds cute, too."

"I don't know." Reese shrugged and clipped her badge to her left breast pocket. "I guess so."

"Do *you* think there's an arsonist at work?"

Surprised by the sudden change in topic, Reese turned from the mirror and regarded her lover. "I don't have any evidence to suggest that."

"But you're worried about it, aren't you?"

"I do think it's odd that a private investigator has been assigned to cover what is usually a straightforward insurance claim. The fact that she was trying to get information from Bri makes me suspicious that there's more going on than we realize." Reese threaded her belt through her trousers and clipped her holster above her right hip. She met Tory's eyes and blew out a breath. "Yes, I think that this fire is going to turn out to be arson."

Tory sat on the edge of the bed and patted the place next to her. "Sit down for a minute."

Immediately, Reese moved to her side and took her hand. "What is it?"

"We haven't talked about this very much." Tory began carefully, holding Reese's left hand in hers. Absently, she turned the wedding band on her lover's ring finger. "You know I wouldn't change anything about you, don't you?"

"Tor," Reese breathed. She turned her head and kissed the tip of Tory's shoulder, which at the moment was exposed where the nightshirt she still wore had fallen down her arm. "What is it, love?"

"I'm not sure *what* it is exactly. I don't know if it's my pregnancy making me a little sensitive or the fact that…" She swallowed and waited a beat to make sure her voice was steady. "Or the fact that you almost died less than three months ago."

"Ah, love, it's over now." Reese turned fully and drew Tory into her arms, cradling her as she rested her chin against the top of her head. "I don't want you to worry."

"That's just it. I *do* worry. I've always worried a little about you getting hurt—I don't think anyone whose lover does what you do for a living doesn't. If you'll recall, sweetheart, it was a gunshot wound that finally brought us together."

Reese tilted Tory's chin up with two fingers beneath her jaw and kissed her, a long, slow possessive kiss. When she drew back, she murmured, "I remember everything about it. But that was three years ago, and nothing serious has happened since."

"That's not precisely true," Tory objected gently. "If you remember, two years ago you had to break up a bar brawl, and one of the drunks pulled a knife."

"That was just a scratch, and if she hadn't come at me while I was stopping the bleeding on the first victim, she never would have gotten that close."

"Yes, but if you hadn't been as quick and as well-trained as you are, that knife would've been between your shoulder blades in another second."

"Tor—"

"My point is, Reese, that you *do* have a dangerous job. It would scare me under any circumstances, but now..." Again, she drew a shaky breath. "I keep thinking how important you are. You're everything to me. I wouldn't want to live without you. But now, it's even more vital that you're safe, because there's going to be another life depending upon you."

Reese's chest tightened. "I'll be careful. I promise. You don't have to worry about that, Tor. My family means more to me than anything in the world. I won't do anything to risk it."

*I know you mean that, sweetheart, but I know you won't be able to help yourself. You'll do your duty because that's who you are.*

Swiftly, Tory wrapped both arms around Reese's waist and pressed hard against her, needing to feel her, needing to know the solid reassurance of her unwavering presence. "I love you so much."

"And you can count on it," Reese whispered.

"Good, because I do."

"Don't we have a doctor's visit coming up this week?" Reese asked gently.

"You don't need to come with me every time. Wendy is just going to check fetal growth and monitor my hemoglobin and do the usual routine prenatal things like that."

"What about your blood pressure?" Reese tried not to ask her about it very often, but it was on her mind every day.

"It's okay." Tory smoothed her palm over Reese's chest and drew away. "You need to get ready for work, sweetheart."

Reese stood and caught Tory's hand. "Tor? Remember, you promised."

"Okay." Tory sighed. "There's still a persistent elevation, but nothing approaching critical."

"I'm going with you." Reese tried hard to sound unconcerned, but her insides turned to ice.

"Reese—"

"I'm going with you. Friday, right?"

Tory threaded her arms around Reese's neck and kissed her. Amazingly, as her breasts and stomach brushed against Reese's hard body, she felt a swell of arousal. She kissed her longer than she had meant to, because Reese's lips were soft and full and her mouth was so warm. The strong hands moving the length of her back and gently rubbing the muscles below the swell of her hips urged her blood to run faster and her muscles to tense. When Tory reached the point that she knew she needed to stop or go forward until she had satisfied her rapidly escalating desire, she pulled her mouth away, gasping shallowly.

"Can you be late?"

Breathing rapidly herself, Reese shook her head regretfully. "I shouldn't. Bri will be expecting me."

"Oh, damn." Tory tightened her hold and rested her face against Reese's shoulder. "I suppose this is good practice."

Aware that her thighs were trembling faintly, Reese laughed hollowly. "Practice for what?"

"Coitus interruptus." Tory leaned back, her eyes dancing. "I have a feeling that we're going to experience that a little more often once we have a third person in the house."

"You know," Reese quirked a brow, "there may be a few aspects about this baby thing we should have discussed in a little more detail."

Tory kissed Reese's chin. "Regrets, Sheriff?"

Smiling softly, Reese ran one finger along the edge of Tory's jaw, ending with a light caress along her lower lip. "Not a one, Dr. King."

## CHAPTER SIXTEEN

When Bri walked into the station house thirty minutes before her split shift was due to begin, her father and Gladys were the only two people present.

"Hi, sweet cakes," Gladys called. She'd called Bri that all Bri's life and apparently wasn't about to stop now.

Bri grinned and sketched a small wave in the air. "Yo, Gladys."

"What say we take a ride," Nelson suggested mildly before Bri had a chance to sit down.

"Yes, sir." Bri tried to hide her surprise. She'd been assigned to her father's command for almost a week, and he'd done little more than nod to her and give a perfunctory "How're you doing" in passing. She hadn't been able to tell if he was angry with her or not. Since the night she'd told him she was leaving school, the only time they'd really spoken had been when Reese was sick. Then it was as if they had both understood that what was happening with Reese was something bigger than their differences. They had tacitly agreed not to talk about anything personal. Her dad had come to the hospital every day, but most of the time he stood in the hall outside Reese's room, getting updates from Bri or Tory that way. He had clearly been uncomfortable visiting Reese while she was sick.

Once, when Bri had walked in unexpectedly and seen her father leaning over Reese's hospital bed, she'd had a flashback of seeing him with her mom in the last weeks of her life. Suddenly, she thought she knew why he didn't like to visit.

When they got into the patrol car, Nelson backed out onto Shank Painter Road and silently headed toward Route 6. Bri didn't know what to expect and tried desperately to remember if she had done anything wrong in the last few days. She supposed he could've

found out about her late-night stroll on the beach with Ashley
Walker, but it wasn't like he didn't know that she was gay. And it
wasn't like they'd ended up under a pier making out somewhere.

She and Ashley had walked and talked until, eventually, they'd
made a complete circuit of town. When Ashley had taken her hand
and asked her to come upstairs to her rented room for the night,
Bri had just said no thanks, and that was the end of it. Then she'd
ridden out to Herring Cove and sat astride her bike watching the
moonlight on the water and listening to the surf. She was lonely,
but this time she knew exactly who she was lonely for. She didn't
need to wake up next to Ashley Walker to know that it was Caroline
she wanted to lie down beside.

Bri jumped when her father cleared his throat and gazed her
way. *Jesus, I've got to pay more attention when I'm working.*

"Caroline called me this morning," Nelson announced without
preamble. He spun the wheel and turned into the lane that led to the
ranger's kiosk at the entrance to the parking lot at Herring Cove.

"Is she okay? Has something happened?" Bri was unable to
keep the alarm from her voice.

"She's okay, as near as I can tell." He pulled into a spot in the
parking lot facing the ocean. The scene was familiar to everyone
who had ever spent time in the small seaside town. A few fishermen
lingered, sharing the sand with the early-morning sunbathers. It
was almost June and the air was still cold, but nothing seemed to
keep people from the beach, even when they had to wear jackets as
they sat on their beach towels.

"Then why did she call?"

Nelson fixed his attention straight ahead, his hands curled
around the steering wheel. "She sounded pretty upset, though."

"Dad—"

"I didn't get you out here to lecture, Bri," Nelson said gruffly.
"God knows, I'm no expert at this kind of thing. She asked me if
she could stay at the house for a while this summer."

"What?" Bri shot up straight in the seat and stared at him in
amazement. "She has a job in Manhattan this summer! She's not
coming home. That's how this whole thing got started."

"What whole thing?" Nelson was pleased that he managed to sound calm while pretending to concentrate on the activity along the shore. Bri hadn't said this much to him in months.

Bri blushed. "This whole...mess...between Carre and me. I thought she was coming home for the summer before she went to Europe, and then she told me that she was going to stay in Manhattan. When I heard that, I...I got a little crazy."

"A little crazy?"

"I...we had a fight. It was my fault. It was stupid."

"Well," Nelson said, finally turning to his daughter, "she wants to come home now. She said she got a job with one of the artists in town...something about a special deal she arranged with the chairman down there."

"She's coming home," Bri whispered, her heart sinking as she tried to understand what that meant. *And she didn't call me.*

"You know, Bri, I think a lot of her. Hell, I love her." He cleared his throat again and searched his shirt pocket for his Tums. When he found one, he pulled it out, tore off the wrapper, and chewed it vigorously. "I know she doesn't have anywhere else to stay here, not with the way her old man always treated her. But...you're my daughter. If it's going to be a problem—"

"No!" Bri shook her head. "No, it's no problem. It's fine."

"Because I thought," Nelson persisted, "maybe, you'd be moving back in sometime."

"Uh...I planned on getting an apartment. I just...haven't... yet." There was something about being at Reese and Tory's that felt right, comforting. And living at home would make her feel too much like a kid again.

"You could visit, you know." His voice was soft, his eyes uncertain.

"I will," Bri said quietly. "I'm sorry...about the thing...about school."

"Well, Reese says you're not half bad in the field, so maybe you made the right decision."

"Yeah?" Bri almost grinned, but her thoughts were still on Caroline. *Is she coming home to be with me?* It killed her that she didn't know anymore.

"So you're okay with Caroline staying with me?"

"Absolutely. This is her home, too. And I don't want her going anywhere near her old man."

"Is there something I don't know about Caroline and her father?" Nelson regarded his daughter steadily. "I know the guy is a grade-A asshole, but is there something you two never told me? Because if there is—"

"He hit her a couple of times," Bri said abruptly. Just the thought of anyone touching Caroline made her insides twist. "But he never went near her...sexually." Bri laughed mirthlessly. "If he'd ever tried, Carre would've killed him...or I would have."

Nelson believed her. "I don't know what's going on between the two of you, Bri. But if you...if you love her, you should try to make it right."

Bri was momentarily speechless. It was the most he'd ever said about her and Caroline's relationship. He'd given them a home and given them his protection when they'd needed it, but he'd never really said very much about their being together. His saying it now brought unexpected tears to her eyes, and she had to look out the window and blink.

"I love her," she whispered, watching a gull bank steeply toward the ocean's surface and disappear under the crest of a wave.

"That's good then." He started the engine and backed out of the parking place. "Good she's coming home."

❖

When Bri and Nelson returned to the office, Reese was there at her desk leafing through a stack of papers. She motioned to Bri to join her. "We're getting some feedback from the feelers you sent out."

"Oh yeah?" Bri pulled over a chair and raised a questioning eyebrow. "What's up?"

"There have been three suspicious fires on the Cape in as many months." Reese pulled out several sheets of paper and passed them to Bri. "In addition, there were four others, all in a cluster around Providence or lower Massachusetts, in the past six months."

"So," Bri rapidly scanned the pages, "do you think we have a serial arsonist?"

"I don't know. But I think we need to put that question to Ashley Walker."

Slowly, Bri raised her head and met Reese's eyes. "Do you think she has something to do with this?"

Reese shrugged. "I don't think *anything* yet. But there's more we need to find out. How're your computer skills?"

"Pretty good." Bri grinned.

"All right then. Make a spreadsheet with what we know about each fire—owner of record, insurers, net value of the properties, amount of the policy, policy beneficiaries—"

"Wait." Bri flipped to a clean page in her notebook and wrote rapidly. "Okay, go ahead."

"...and intervals between events. Pull up all the fire marshals' reports and look for a pattern—time of day, incendiary method, anything indicating a signature. Review any witness statements. And let's run a background check on Ashley Walker."

Bri looked up from her notes. "Uh...any particular reason?"

"Not specifically. But information is our most potent weapon." Reese studied her trainee intently. "Do you have a problem with looking into Ms. Walker?"

"No, ma'am," Bri said crisply. "Not at all."

"Would you happen to know where she's staying in town?"

"Yes." Now Bri blushed.

Reese stood and settled her cap down over her brow. "Then let's go, Officer Parker."

❖

Ashley, barefoot and in a sleeveless red T-shirt with gray gym shorts, opened the door after the second knock. She had obviously just gotten up. Her hair had been hastily finger-combed, and her eyes were still hazy with sleep. Looking from Reese to Bri, she grinned lazily. "Come on in."

Reese removed her cap and tucked it under one arm. Bri did the same.

"Sorry I can't offer you coffee," the redhead remarked, "but this place doesn't have a kitchen."

"No problem," Reese replied. "Sorry to disturb you so early, but there are a couple of things I want to check with you."

"If you don't mind," Ashley poured coffee from a thermos into a Styrofoam cup, "I'm going to finish this. I haven't had my second cup yet, and it usually takes at least that much for me to get started in the morning. Thank God that Espresso Joe's is just across the street." She carried her coffee to a worn overstuffed chair and regarded her visitors, who were both still standing. "Somehow, I don't think you came here to fill me in on the investigation."

"Actually, Ms. Walker," Reese used her official voice, "we were hoping that you could provide *us* with some assistance."

She shrugged, curled up in the chair with her feet tucked beneath her, and smiled. "It's your town, Sheriff. Your game."

"That's true," Bri said before Reese could reply. "But we're just coming into the inning, and you've been playing for a while."

"I'm not sure I follow." Ashley leaned back and regarded Bri over the top of her coffee cup as she slowly brought it to her lips. "What's your point, Officer?"

"We wondered if you might have any information on similar occurrences." Bri hooked one thumb over her gun belt and raised a dark brow.

"Now, how could I answer that when I don't know anything about *this* occurrence?"

Reese smiled. "Were you a lawyer in a previous life, Ms. Walker?"

"No," Ashley replied carefully, "as a matter of fact, Sheriff, I was a cop."

"Then you appreciate our situation." Reese didn't miss a beat. "It would help us if you'd share whatever pertinent information you might have."

Ashley blew out a breath. "I don't know that I *have* any. I called the fire captain first thing this morning, and he promised me a look at the fire marshal's report tomorrow. If I learn anything that has any bearing on your case, I'll let you know."

"That easy?" Reese raised an eyebrow.

Ashley's gaze flickered to Bri and slowly traveled the length of her body. "Let's just say it's a favor."

As they walked down the street toward the patrol car, Reese stopped Bri by her arm. "Is there anything you want to tell me about you and Ashley Walker?"

"No, ma'am," Bri replied stiffly.

"This isn't personal, Bri. This is business."

Meeting Reese's eyes, Bri said steadily. "There's nothing going on of a personal nature. I told you everything that happened the other night."

*Except what you were doing out until quarter to four in the morning. And that's none of my business. And I still want to know.*

Reese drew a long breath and let it out slowly. "Good enough. Let's go hunt down Alan Peterson. If he told Ms. Walker that he'd have something for her on the fire *tomorrow*, he has something today."

Once they were settled in the car, Reese began to drive slowly through town. They did this run multiple times throughout their shift, just watching the traffic flow and the various pedestrians roaming in and out of the many small shops.

At length, Bri commented quietly, "Carre is coming back for the summer, after all."

"Well, when did this happen?"

"She called my dad this morning. She's going to stay with him."

"How do you feel about that arrangement?" Reese kept the surprise from her voice.

"I'm okay with it."

"And how do you feel about her coming back here for the summer?"

Bri turned her cap aimlessly in her hands. "I wanted her to come before, but she said she couldn't. Now she's coming, and we're not even speaking."

"There's a fairly simple way to change that."

Bri cast Reese a questioning glance.

"Bri." Reese shook her head and smothered a small smile. "Call her on the phone."

❖

Bri hooked a boot heel over the bottom rail of the split-log fence that ran between the Meeting House and the building next door. Leaning a shoulder against the side of the pay phone kiosk, she listened to the repetitive ringing on the other end. Her heart pounded and her palms were damp. She could've called from Reese and Tory's, but she wanted to be alone. In the middle of Commercial Street at eight at night, she was hardly alone, but somehow the anonymous faces passing by made her feel invisible.

"Hello?"

For a second, Bri couldn't speak.

"Hello?"

"Carre?" Her throat was so dry it came out barely a whisper.

"Bri?" Uncertain, hopeful.

"Hey, babe."

"Hi, baby."

There was silence again, and Bri thought she could hear Caroline breathing. Finally, she forced herself to speak. "My dad told me that you're going to stay with him this summer."

"Uh-huh."

"I thought…I thought you had a job in the city?" Bri cradled the phone between her head and shoulder and stuffed her hands into the pockets of her leather motorcycle pants.

"I did. I mean, I was *going* to have one."

"So, what happened?"

Caroline laughed shakily. "*You* happened, Bri."

"Huh?"

"*You* happened to me—about four years ago. I took one look at you, and I thought you were the hottest girl I'd ever seen in my life."

"Jesus, Carre," Bri murmured, barely breathing. From three hundred miles away, the sound of Caroline's voice made her skin flush.

"And then these last few months, you've been different. Gone, sort of. And I didn't even realize that I'd let you go."

"No, you didn't…I—"

"But you're there, and I'm here. Isn't that what you said would happen when I went to France?" Caroline's voice was stronger now.

"That I'd be there and you'd be here, and everything would change? Well, it already *has* changed, Bri."

"I don't know how it happened," Bri said desperately.

"Neither do I. But it's not going to get any better unless *we* do something to change it."

"But what about school? Your job?"

"I talked to my adviser and the chairman. I told them that I had a family emergency and that I needed to be home for the summer. They found me someone to work with…a preceptor kind of thing."

Bri blinked, her eyes suddenly burning. Unconsciously, she brushed moisture from her cheeks with the back of one hand, reaching for the phone with the other and gripping it tightly. "I'm sorry. I didn't mean for you to have to do that."

"What *did* you mean, Bri? For me just to go away and that would be the end of it?"

"I thought…" She ran a shaking hand through her hair and tried to ignore the queasy roiling of her stomach. "I thought you would go away and when you came back, if you still wanted me, then it would be like it was before."

"If I still wanted you?" Caroline's voice was cold. "You didn't think I would?"

"I was afraid you wouldn't."

"It hurts to know you didn't believe in me, Bri. That you didn't have any faith in what we have together."

"That's not it," Bri protested fervently.

"Isn't it? Think about it, Bri."

Bri was silent for a long moment. Then, her voice broke when she spoke. "Can I see you when you come home?"

"Not if you're seeing anyone else."

The pain and tears in Caroline's voice made Bri bleed inside. "I'm not. I swear."

"I'll be moving to Nelson's the second Saturday in June. Call me sometime."

"I love you, babe," Bri said softly.

"Take good care of yourself, baby."

The soft click signaling that Caroline had hung up was like a lifeline being severed. Adrift, Bri stood for a long time listening to the dial tone, thinking about faith.

# CHAPTER SEVENTEEN

Bri leaned back in the large overstuffed chair, her hands resting on the threadbare arms, her legs spread to make room for the woman kneeling in front of her. She wore only an unbuttoned shirt, parted down the center. A pale arm stretched upward over the length of her abdomen to enclose her right breast. Fingers rhythmically squeezed her stone-hard nipple as a soft tongue encircled the swollen prominence of her clitoris, working her slowly and carefully, keeping her on the edge, aching, but not allowing the elusive release.

Her irregular breathing was the only sound.

The room was nearly dark, and it was difficult to see more than shadows shifting in the hazy half-light. The chair where she sat, however, was speared by a shaft of moonlight, and when she looked down, she caught glimpses of the woman's eyes gazing upward, avidly watching as the effect of what she was doing with her mouth rippled across Bri's face in the flickering illumination.

As the pressure coalesced into a fist deep inside, Bri's thighs quivered and her fingers clenched. With each long sweep of the warm tongue, the muscles in her abdomen contracted. She arched her neck and groaned softly as the escalating strokes beat against a particularly sensitive spot. Staring into the mesmerizing eyes, Bri watched the golden head rock between her thighs.

"Carre," she whispered.

There was no answer.

Relentlessly, the perfect rhythm drove her ever closer to explosion. When her hips lifted and white heat spiraled along her spine, she muttered hoarsely, "I'm gonna come in your mouth."

The insistent lips sucked at her, pushing her beyond volition. Her body tensed, grew rigid, then crumpled as she shouted sharply in surrender. Gasping, she twitched helplessly as the orgasm ripped through her.

"Bri!"

Thunderous pounding on her door pulled Bri awake, the last remnants of her nocturnal climax still humming through her veins.

"What?" she croaked. She glanced around the room in confusion. The night through her window was pitch black. She cleared her throat and sat up quickly. "Yeah?"

"Un-ass that bed, Officer," Reese ordered. "We need to roll."

Still a bit shaky, Bri grabbed the nearest thing she could find, which turned out to be a pair of faded blue jeans, and slid them on. Getting her feet under her finally, she grabbed a corduroy shirt from over the back of a chair and shrugged into it. Buttoning it with one hand, she jerked the door open with the other and stared up at Reese. The sheriff wore jeans as well, with a khaki uniform shirt. Her badge was clipped to the shirt pocket, her automatic holstered on her right hip.

"What's going on?"

"Grab your equipment. There's a fire in Truro, and they're asking for help."

❖

Well before Reese and Bri screeched to a halt behind a long row of official vehicles, it was easy to see the flames shooting into the sky from a totally fire-engulfed building. Fire trucks fronted the burning structure, a confusion of hoses spewing water in crisscrossing arcs onto the disintegrating roof. Firefighters, EMTs, and law enforcement officials hurried back and forth in the parking lot in front of what had once been a three-story structure.

"That place has been abandoned for a couple of years, hasn't it?" Reese shouted as she and Bri raced on foot toward a knot of Truro and Wellfleet officers.

"Yeah," Bri yelled back. Then she pointed across the parking lot to the adjacent buildings. "But *they're* not."

At that moment, the Truro police chief spied Reese and waved her over. "Conlon! Good Christ, this place has gone up like a matchbox in less than five minutes. We haven't had time to evacuate the neighboring motels. I've got people working on both sides of the street, but the main priority is that motel right next door. They've got forty-five units, most of them full, and we're not sure everyone's out yet. I don't have enough people for a room-to-room."

"Roger. We're on it."

Bri followed Reese as they ran toward the adjacent motel. People streamed past them carrying suitcases and belongings in a mad exodus. A cluster of cars inched along bumper to bumper trying to get out of the narrow parking lot, creating a logjam at the exit to Route 6.

"Bri!" a familiar voice called.

Bri looked to her right and saw three other officers rushing toward her, one of whom she knew well. "Allie!"

"What's the plan?" Allie asked breathlessly, falling into step alongside Bri. "We're with you, my chief said."

"Reese will let us know when we get there."

Just at that moment, Reese stopped suddenly and started issuing orders. "You two," she pointed to the two officers in Wellfleet uniforms, "start on the far end of the ground floor and check every unit. *Every* unit. Break the doors down if you have to. Tell anyone still in there *not* to bother with their cars, but to proceed on foot to the highway." She looked at Bri and Allie. "You two take the upper floors," she indicated with a nod of her head toward the outdoor hallway running the length of the second floor of the motel. "Make it fast. The wind's picking up, and there are already sparks on the roof."

"Got it," Bri snapped.

"Let's move, everybody."

Within minutes, men, women, and children in various stages of undress scrambled from the last of the occupied motel units as officers pounded on doors and shouted instructions. In the distance, approaching sirens signaled that more fire trucks and emergency personnel were en route.

"Bri, look at the roof," Allie cried as they jogged down the corridor connecting the units.

Glancing up, Bri was shocked to see almost the entire cedar-shingled surface dancing with flames. "Jesus, it's moving so fast. Hurry up!"

Smoke poured from the units where doors stood open, but there were at least a dozen rooms still closed and presumably occupied.

"Why aren't they coming out?" Bri shouted as her eyes began to burn with the thickening clouds of smoke that roiled around them.

Coughing, Allie replied, "Maybe some of them partied too much tonight and didn't hear the sirens. Or maybe there's more smoke in those rooms than we think. Maybe they *can't* get out."

"There's just a couple more." Bri was gasping. "Let's get them open."

From the ground, coordinating the evacuation efforts, Reese watched Bri and Allie race toward the last four units on the end of the building most heavily involved by fire. She turned to the motel owner who had been pacing anxiously by her side. "Are those units occupied?"

"Just the one on the far end." His voice was high-pitched with tension. "I can't remember who's in there."

As they spoke, part of the roof fell in.

Reese grabbed a megaphone from a nearby fire captain and raced toward the stairs leading up to the second floor exterior hallway about fifty feet from where she had last seen Bri and Allie.

"Parker," she yelled into the megaphone. "Parker, clear the area ASAP! Parker, do you copy?"

By the time she reached the second floor, Reese's lungs were burning and her eyes were streaming with tears. The smoke was so thick she couldn't see through it, so she ran in the direction she had last seen the trainees.

From the ground, the fire captain couldn't see anyone at all on the second floor when the rest of the roof collapsed in a plume of sparks, flying debris, and ash.

❖

Tory was on her way to her Jeep when the cruiser pulled into her driveway. Reese had only been gone twenty minutes when Tory had decided that if the fire was serious enough to require reinforcements, the situation might call for her skills as well. In the past, she would have followed Reese immediately, but when Reese had insisted she stay home, she hadn't argued. She hadn't been sleeping well the last few nights and *was* exhausted. But before long, she realized that she would never be able to get back to sleep. That was when she had pulled herself from the bed and gotten dressed.

"Nelson," Tory called as he stepped from the car and walked toward her. "I was just getting ready to go."

The security lights had come on under the eaves of the house when he had pulled into the driveway, and she could see his face clearly in the falsely bright illumination. His expression caused a cold hand to close around her heart.

"What is it?" Tory cried, trying and failing to keep her voice level. She braced her hand against the side of her vehicle, her legs shaking nearly uncontrollably. *This can't be happening. Not again. I can't do this again.*

"There are four buildings involved already." Nelson's voice was flat, his eyes eerily empty. "A lot of minor injuries. The motel next to where it started is almost gone."

"Nelson," Tory said harshly, recognizing that he was very nearly in shock. She wanted to scream, feared that she might. "What's happened?"

"Bri…"

"Oh no," Tory gasped, sagging slightly against the Jeep. *We can't lose Bri.*

"Bri and another girl…another cadet…they were evacuating the upper floors…when the roof collapsed."

Forcing herself to act, to *think* despite the panic eclipsing her reason, Tory went to him and put her hand on his forearm. "Nelson, is she hurt?"

"Missing," he rasped. His hands were trembling as he rubbed them over his face. "She…didn't come out."

"Let's go," Tory urged, but before she could move, the rest of it hit her. *Nelson* had come for her. She drew a sharp breath as pain lanced through her. *If Bri is missing, then where is...but you know, don't you? Reese would go after her. She would never leave her injured in the field. Especially not Bri. Reese would never leave Bri.*

"Oh God, Nelson...not *both* of them!"

He could only nod, his terror boundless.

As Nelson rocketed the cruiser east on Route 6, covering the few miles between Tory's home and the scene of the conflagration, Tory stared straight ahead through the windshield, one hand on the door handle, the other beneath her sweatshirt, resting against her abdomen. Beneath her fingers, hope swelled even as an agony of despair hammered at the edges of her consciousness. *Reese won't leave me. She promised.*

"Can't you go any faster?" she whispered desperately.

"Not and get us there in one piece," Nelson grunted, his foot already heavy on the gas pedal.

The radio crackled and a male voice cut through the static. "Chief, you copy?"

Nelson grabbed blindly for the mike. "Go ahead."

"We've got a body in the building, Chief. No ID yet."

Wordlessly, Tory focused on the scene emerging ahead. She could see the fire now, the dozens of rescue vehicles, and great clouds of dark smoke billowing into the night sky. *Don't leave me, sweetheart. I can't do this without you. Please, darling, please.*

Nelson slammed to a halt, and Tory was out of the vehicle almost before it had stopped. Then she faltered, realizing she had nowhere to go. The scene was one of barely controlled pandemonium. Men and women rushed back and forth between EMS vans, fire rescue trucks, patrol cars, and civilian vehicles. There were officers with flashlights standing in the highway directing a stream of cars and RVs that presumably belonged to tourists who had been able to evacuate before the traffic from the parking lots had become hopelessly snarled. Frantically, she searched for someone recognizable and finally saw Jeff Lyons, one of the officers from the Provincetown force.

"Jeff!" Tory rushed toward him as quickly as her unfamiliarly heavy body and her cumbersome leg brace would allow. "Have you seen Reese or Bri?"

He shook his head, his expression dazed. "Not since they went off to evacuate the Gull Crest Motel. What does the chief say?"

"He doesn't know anything either." Impatiently, she turned away. Panic threatened to choke her. "God, isn't anyone in charge around here?"

As if by instinct, she made her way through the masses of milling people and ended up near the EMS transport vehicles. There were at least a dozen EMTs and paramedics rendering emergency care to civilians and rescue personnel alike, the bulk of whom appeared to have burns or smoke inhalation from the quick glance Tory got as she peered at the faces of the victims. *Where are you, Reese? Where in God's name are you?*

After five fruitless minutes of searching, her hair was drenched with sweat, her face was covered with soot from the ash-filled air, and her control was in tatters. A horrific surge of desolation swept through her, and tears overflowed her stinging lids without her even being aware of them. *I can't do this. I can't. I can't.*

From close by, a firefighter shouted, "Somebody get a gurney. We've got walking wounded coming."

Tory jerked around at the sound of his voice and frantically searched the edges of the beach forest that bordered one side of the access road where most of the rescue vehicles had parked. It was difficult to see through the haze created by the combination of emergency lights and swirling smoke, but eventually she could discern a lone figure emerging from the artificial mists, carrying some kind of bundle. She blinked the tears and smoke from her eyes and was able to make out that the bundle was a person, and the grime-covered apparition carrying the victim was Reese.

For one brief instant, Tory thought she might faint. The relief was so acute that she couldn't breathe. Even seeing her lover more clearly with each step wasn't enough to banish the terrible ache that had seized her heart. She started forward as quickly as she could.

The EMTs reached Reese well before Tory and relieved the sheriff of her burden. Still, she had barely relinquished the frail, elderly man to the care of the rescue team before Tory flung herself into her arms.

"I thought you were dead," Tory gasped. Her hands were all over Reese, stroking her chest and her back and up and down her arms, searching for injury. "Are you hurt? Are you hurt?"

"Tory, I'm all right." Reese grabbed Tory's hands, stilling her frenzied motion, and then gathered her close. Tory's heart was beating wildly against her chest, and with her lips close to her lover's ear, Reese said gently, "Tory, listen to me. Stop, love. Stop. I'm all right."

The sound of Reese's voice, low and steady and calm, brought instant surcease to Tory's terror. Suddenly, she regained control and, after taking a long slow breath, was able to separate herself enough from Reese to look into her face.

"Where's Bri?"

"Back in the forest. She's with an injured officer. Bri wouldn't leave her, and I had to get this fellow to the EMTs." Reese framed Tory's face with both hands and kissed her swiftly. "Sweetheart, I need to go back for Bri."

Blindly, unthinkingly, Tory grasped Reese's shirtfront with both hands. "*No.*"

"It's all right, love. There's no danger. I'll be right back."

"Yes, I understand. Of course," Tory said, swiftly quelling her involuntary reaction. "I was just so scared."

"I know. God, I'm sorry. I didn't think you'd be here."

"Go get Bri, darling." With every second, Tory was feeling stronger, more in control. Reese was safe. And there was still much work to be done. *Her* work. "I'm going back to the ambulances to see if I can help out."

"You shouldn't even be here. You sure shouldn't be working." Reese grabbed for her hand. "Go home, Tor. Please. It's crazy out here."

Finally, Tory smiled. "You're a fine one to talk, Sheriff. Go do what you have to do and come back as soon as you can." She rested her palm for an instant against Reese's cheek. "Please don't be gone long. I can't stand it right now."

"As soon as I get Bri and the other cadet squared away, I'll find you. I promise."

Tory watched her walk away, believing her promise to return because without that, she couldn't go on.

❖

Tory straightened up and pressed both hands to her lower back. It felt as if she'd been bending over patients on stretchers, and others who had slumped onto every available surface, for hours. In reality, it had probably only been two. Fortunately, most of the injuries were minor—burns sustained by rescue personnel or bumps, bruises, and lacerations acquired by the evacuating tourists as they fumbled around in the near-dark while attempting to flee the scene.

One firefighter had broken an arm falling from a crumbling balcony, and there had been at least one fatality. The body was still awaiting the medical examiner from Orleans and lay on the ground covered by a tarp, watched over by a CSI tech. In addition, a young female officer had sustained a leg injury after jumping from the second floor of a burning building.

Tory glanced to her right to check on that particular patient. If she hadn't been so busy, and so tired, she might have wondered more about what she saw. As it was, her concerns would have to wait until she could catch her breath.

❖

Allie sat with her back against the tire of an EMS van while Bri crouched beside her, holding a cup of coffee.

"Are you sure you're not cold?" Bri asked worriedly.

Allie smiled wanly. "Not really. Besides, if I drink any more of that I'm going to have to pee, and there's no way I can walk."

"That's okay. We'll figure something out," Bri said firmly. "Tory said you should keep your leg elevated and stay warm."

"You don't have to stay with me, you know." Allie shook her head in disgust. "Boy, I'm never going to live this down. My first big assignment and I end up falling on my ass."

"I don't think anyone is going to put you down for twisting your ankle while jumping from a burning building." Bri swiped sweat from her face and grimaced as she brushed against the burned spot on her neck. "Besides, it could happen to anybody."

"Oh sure," Allie said sarcastically. "You and Reese not only managed to do it, but Reese did it with that old man over her shoulder."

"That's Reese." Bri shrugged. "She can do anything."

Allie regarded Bri intently in the gray light of early dawn. "You really believe that, don't you?"

"Yeah."

"I wouldn't mind being like her someday," Allie said thoughtfully. She watched the pregnant doctor instructing an EMT about something involving the patient they were both caring for. When Bri and Reese had carried her from the woods, she'd seen Reese and Dr. King together for a few minutes. The two of them had looked at one another as if there was no one else on earth. Even soot-streaked and disheveled, Dr. King was a beautiful woman. "I wouldn't mind having someone like *her*, either."

Bri followed Allie's gaze, saw Tory, and laughed shortly. "Who wouldn't?"

"Don't you?" Allie questioned softly.

It was a few seconds before Bri replied. Then quietly, she said, "I don't know. I hope so."

"You haven't called me. I kind of thought it might be because of that girlfriend you mentioned."

"Yeah."

"Because, you know, I thought things were pretty hot between us."

Flushing, Bri thought about waking up with Allie naked beside her. She remembered it almost as a dream, and the memory was exciting. Her eyes moved slowly over Allie's face, appreciating how attractive she was. Even scratched and sweat-streaked, she was sexy. "Yeah, it was hot. *You're* hot. Totally."

"But?"

"But I'm in love with someone."

"It wouldn't have to be anything real serious, you know." Allie brushed Bri's hand with her fingertips. "Just a little fun. I think about you…a lot."

"I can't," Bri said. And it didn't feel like a sacrifice at all.

"Okay." Allie acquiesced with a rueful grin. "I gave it my best shot. If things change, call me, okay? Because we've got unfinished business."

"I'm going to find Reese and see what else needs to be done. It looks like everything's kind of under control now. I'll be back soon."

"Sure." Allie closed her eyes, giving in to her fatigue and discomfort. "I'm not going to be running off anywhere."

❖

"Tory," a male voice said from behind her.

Tory turned, frowning, and then exclaimed, "Dan! What are you doing here?"

The solidly built dark-haired man shrugged, grinning a bit shyly. "Reese called me and said that you might need relief about now."

"Oh, she did, did she?" Tory raised an eyebrow, uncertain whether she was actually angry or not. She *was* tired, and she had a headache. It must be after five in the morning, and she was working on very little sleep. Nevertheless, she hadn't quite gotten used to anyone interfering with her professional life. That was the one area where she had always had complete control, and for so many years, medicine had been the only area where she felt competent and, somehow, safe. *But things are different now. I'm married; I have Reese; I have a different life. I'll still be me, even if I'm not always doing this.*

Dan Riley frowned as he took in his new employer. She was clearly exhausted and the fingers that brushed absently at the strands of damp hair clinging to her cheeks trembled faintly. "I would have come sooner, but to tell you the truth, I slept right through all the sirens. Even if I'd I heard them, I probably wouldn't have realized that they meant anything serious. In New York City, sirens are just part of life."

"If I'd had any idea how many people were going to need attention here," Tory admitted, "I would have called you myself. Then I got busy, and I just forgot."

"Well," he said briskly. "I'm here now, so let me finish triaging the remaining patients. You should go home."

Before Tory could respond, another voice interjected, "A very good suggestion, Dr. Riley." Reese stepped closer to Tory and kissed her cheek. "Hello, love."

Smiling despite herself, Tory touched her fingertips to Reese's chin, brushing at a trickle of dried blood. "You've cut yourself, Sheriff."

"Nothing major," Reese assured her. She glanced to the side and inclined her head toward Allie. "How's she doing?"

"I think the ankle is just sprained, but she needs to be x-rayed." Tory leaned her shoulder against the side of the fire rescue truck. "She wouldn't let me send her off to Hyannis to be evaluated because she said the civilians should go first. I thought I'd bring her back to the clinic and shoot a film there."

"Fine," Reese said. "There's not much left to do here except cleanup. The fire's under control, and all the civilians have been moved to temporary housing at the high schools in Provincetown and Wellfleet."

Reese turned to Dan Riley and murmured something. Then to Tory, "As soon as I collect Bri, check in with the chief, and make sure that the rest of my people know what they're supposed to be doing, we can get out of here."

As Tory watched Reese hurry off yet again, Dan said, "Let me take your pressure, Tory."

"What?" Tory asked in surprise.

"Let me check your BP." His eyes were kind as they met hers. "You've been on your feet all night."

"Did she ask you to do that?"

"I know how she feels." He deftly avoided the answer, then pulled a blood pressure cuff from inside the truck and wrapped it around Tory's left upper arm. "When my wife was pregnant the first time, I had morning sickness every day for five months. I felt completely helpless and equal parts ecstatic and terrified. You can't blame her for worrying."

"I don't blame her," Tory said seriously. "I just don't want that to be all she feels about this." If she hadn't been so tired, she probably never would have admitted that out loud, particularly to someone she barely knew at all. But it was out before she could stop it.

Dan smiled. "I'm sure she feels a lot more than that."

A minute later, he took the cuff off and regarded her steadily. "One-forty over ninety-two. Is that unusual?"

Tory drew a shaky breath, and then shook her head. "It hasn't been consistent, but for the last few days, it's been in that range."

"Does your obstetrician know?"

"Generally, yes, but I haven't called her about this."

He sighed, sliding his hands into the pockets of his chinos. "It's none of my business, but you should call her."

"I will. Listen," Tory said quickly, "don't say anything to Reese, all right, Dan? There's nothing to worry about just yet. That's been the only symptom."

"Of course. Like I said, it's not my business."

At that moment, Reese and Bri returned.

"Everything okay?" Reese looked from Tory to Dan.

"Everything is fine." Tory took Reese's hand. "Let's take Officer Tremont back to the clinic so I can evaluate her properly."

The four of them trudged through the water-soaked, litter-strewn fire site toward the highway where Reese had left her Blazer. She and Bri supported Allie between them.

Halfway there, Reese noticed someone on the outskirts of the crowd and said quickly, "Let's stop for a second. Bri, make sure you've got Officer Tremont."

"No problem." Bri slipped her arm more firmly around Allie's waist. Allie curved her arm around Bri's neck and leaned into her.

"I'll be right back," Reese said as she moved away.

Tory watched Reese approach a woman and speak to her briefly. "Who is that?"

"That's Ashley Walker," Bri said.

"The private investigator?"

"Yes."

After a minute, Reese and the redhead turned and walked back to where the others were waiting.

"Officer Parker," Ashley said with a slow smile when she recognized Bri.

"Ms. Walker," Bri said with a small tilt of her chin.

"I thought we might have a chat with Ms. Walker while Tory checks out Allie's ankle, Bri," Reese said neutrally. She didn't think it necessary to mention that it hadn't been a request when she had told the private investigator to accompany them. She wanted answers, and she intended to have them before very much more time had passed.

"Hello," Allie said, extending her hand to the newcomer. "Allie Tremont."

"Ashley Walker," the redhead replied languorously, her throaty tenor slightly raspy from the smoke, her green eyes flickering downward once before returning to Allie's face. "Are you all right?"

"I will be." Allie never took her eyes from Ashley's.

Tory watched the exchange, which, although completely innocent, held a note of intimacy that almost made her feel like a voyeur. "If we're all done with the introductions," she interjected dryly, "perhaps we can get back to the clinic so *I* can decide how Officer Tremont is doing."

Reese laughed, noting the irritation in her lover's voice. "Good idea, Dr. King." She slid her arm around Allie's waist from the opposite side and glanced at Bri. "Ready?"

Bri, who had been completely silent during the exchange between the two women, just nodded. "You bet."

"I'll follow you in my car," Ashley said.

"Don't get lost," Reese advised.

"I wouldn't think of it."

## CHAPTER EIGHTEEN

"You can use my office," Tory said to Reese as the small group proceeded down the central hallway of her clinic toward the x-ray room at the rear. "Just help me get Officer Tremont up onto the table so I can get these films."

After Reese and Bri lifted the injured officer onto the narrow x-ray table, Reese followed Tory to the opposite side of the room where the control panels that operated the machine were located. Too quietly for the others to hear, she murmured, "Is it okay for you to take the x-rays?"

Tory smiled fondly and grasped her lover's hand briefly. "Don't worry, sweetheart. I've got a very large lead shield."

"Sorry."

"No need to be. I love the way you love me."

"Good." Reese brushed her fingers across Tory's cheek. "We'll be in your office. Just give a holler when you need us."

"No problem."

Reese, Bri, and Ashley Walker left the small radiology room and crossed the hall diagonally to Tory's office.

"Sit down, please, Ms. Walker," Reese instructed while pointing to one of the two chairs in front of Tory's large wood desk. She leaned her hips against it, but remained standing. Bri stood also, a few feet away, off to Ashley's right.

Without preamble, Reese stated, "This is now a murder investigation. The presumptive conclusion here is arson, with either intentional homicide or unintentional manslaughter. That distinction will need to be determined by the coroner and the fire marshal."

Ashley Walker watched Reese's face as she spoke. The two women made eye contact and neither allowed her gaze to waver.

Walker said nothing and sat relaxed in the chair, her booted right foot crossed over her left knee.

"I want to know exactly what you're investigating, Ms. Walker. If I find in the future that you have information pertinent to this investigation which you do *not* reveal to me now, I will arrest you for obstruction of justice. Not only will that be unpleasant for you, but it will also seriously jeopardize your PI license." Reese's tone was even and nonconfrontational. She was reciting the facts, and it was very clear that she meant every word.

After a moment's deliberation, Ashley Walker nodded slightly. "Up until last night, every suspicious fire has been set in unoccupied buildings. Not only that, there has never been any risk to surrounding structures or individuals. There's never even been a serious injury."

"And because of that," Bri said quietly, startling both Reese and Ashley, "you thought you could keep what you knew to yourself. Right?"

"My job is to protect my client." Walker shrugged. "If in the course of doing my job, I can help out the police, I do. On the other hand, I'm not obligated to do so."

"Things have changed now," Reese persisted quietly.

"Yes, I know." Ashley shook out her thick red hair and eased her shoulders slightly. "I'm looking for a man named Stanley Morris. He was a claims investigator for the company that hired me."

"The insurance company?"

"Yes. Six months ago, he was forced to leave, ostensibly due to downsizing. If there were other reasons, I don't know about them. Shortly thereafter, the first of what would turn out to be a series of fires occurred in buildings that were insured by the company."

"Some kind of retribution?" Bri asked.

"That's what we think. Morris's area of specialty was fire investigation, and the timing seemed right. But the company didn't have any proof."

"So they hired you," Reese surmised.

"I worked missing persons when I was a cop in Providence," Ashley informed them. "I do a lot of skip tracing, and Morris had dropped out of sight soon after he had been let go. That was one of the reasons that he came under suspicion to begin with. They hired me to track him down and, hopefully, to clear him of these arsons."

"But?" Reese could hear the word in her tone.

Ashley blew out a frustrated breath. "But I haven't been able to find him, although it seems like I'm always close."

"What about his movement patterns?" Bri interjected. "Does he fit for the suspicious fires?"

Again, Ashley nodded. "He's been running through his credit cards pretty fast in the last few months. He uses them a few times and then stops. By the time I get on to him, he's gone. But he's been in the vicinity of at least a couple of the fires which we suspect to be arson."

"Do the authorities know about this?"

"No."

"Christ," Reese muttered in disgust.

"Come on, Sheriff." Ashley showed her first hint of ire. "You know how much attention the police are going to pay to a *possible* suspect with no concrete evidence to tie him to the crimes, and no indication of where he is or where he might be going. He's moving around, and the entire case crosses too many jurisdictional borders."

Reluctantly, Reese agreed. "You're right. If he's crossing state lines, only a federal investigation would be able to keep track of him."

"Right. And I certainly don't have enough to interest the feds."

"Can you place him anywhere around here?"

Ashley shook her head. "No. The last place I can put him is in Falls River six weeks ago. But that doesn't mean he's not here on the Cape, paying with cash and lying low."

"All right. We'll get an APB out to the other divisions on the Cape today," Reese said in her command mode. "Is there anything *else* we should know about this guy?"

"When he lost his job, his wife left him. He's angry, and I'm not sure he's entirely stable. I would consider him violent and recommend caution if he is to be apprehended." She hesitated.

"I'm not sure it's relevant, but he was an explosives expert in the Army."

"So noted." Reese pushed off from the desk and glanced at her watch. "I'll get this out on the wire as soon as we square away Officer Tremont. Are you going to stay around for a while?"

"Yeah, for a while. If this new fire is his doing, it would be the first time he struck again so close in time and geography." Ashley stood as well. "Maybe he's coming undone. I might as well stay here until I can pick up some trace of him."

"Just be sure that if you learn anything further, you share it with us," Reese said in a tone that left no room for negotiation.

"Understood, Sheriff."

The officers and the PI walked back to the radiology suite, where they found Tory placing a soft cast on Allie Tremont's left lower leg. Tory looked up when the others walked in.

"There's a very small chip fracture of the distal fibula. It shouldn't be a problem long term, but it needs to be immobilized for three or four weeks."

When Allie started to slide down off the table, Tory said quickly, "No weight bearing, Officer Tremont. Not for at least a week. I'll see what I can do about finding you some crutches."

"Great. This is gonna be *real* simple considering that I live by myself." Allie looked frustrated as well as worn out. "I don't even have any way to get home."

"I can take you," Bri said quietly.

"Why don't I do it," Ashley Walker volunteered. "I'm sure that you have work to finish up, Officer Parker. I can drop you off somewhere, too, if you like."

Bri looked at Ashley in surprise, but she didn't argue. "Okay. Fine."

"Well then," Tory said briskly. "Now that we have that all sorted out, perhaps one of you can help Officer Tremont out to the waiting area."

"I'll do that." Bri moved to Allie's side.

Ashley dug in her pocket for her keys. "I'll get my car and bring it up to the door."

"And I should take *you* home, Dr. King," Reese said quietly.

For a brief instant, Tory thought about protesting, as patient hours were to start at the clinic shortly. But she didn't argue because she couldn't deny that she was exhausted. At the very least, she needed a shower and something to eat. Nodding her head tiredly, she said, "All right, Sheriff."

"I'll check in at the station," Bri said, "and see you later, Reese."

Reese tenderly took Tory's hand. "That sounds like a plan."

❖

"Tory, love. We're home." Reese gently shook her lover's shoulder.

Tory mumbled and stirred, then opened her eyes. "Reese?"

"Time for you to get some sleep." Reese softly stroked Tory's cheek.

"Time for me to take a shower. God, I'm grimy."

Reese got out and walked around the front of her SUV and opened Tory's door. She extended a hand and said, "I've got an even better idea."

"Oh?" Tory raised an eyebrow. "I love you beyond imagination, Sheriff. But I couldn't make love right now if my life depended upon it."

"Really?" Reese slipped her arm around Tory's waist. "Actually, I had something else in mind."

Jed was waiting for them at the rear door, and they let him out to explore.

"Why don't you go upstairs and get undressed," Reese said. "I'll put some food for him on the deck, and then I'll be right up."

Five minutes later, Tory, clad only in an old T-shirt of Reese's, since hers no longer fit comfortably, was tiredly brushing her teeth in front of the bathroom mirror. Reese came in behind her, lifted the hair at the back of her neck with one hand, and kissed her on the ultrasensitive spot just below her hairline.

"Mmm," Tory murmured, closing her eyes. "God, that feels good."

"Just wait," Reese whispered. She nuzzled Tory's ear before moving away.

The next moment, Tory heard the bath water running and turned as Reese began to strip. She rested her hips against the counter and watched as Reese unsnapped her jeans and pushed them off. Reese was halfway through the buttons on her shirt when Tory murmured huskily, "You are *so* gorgeous."

Reese grinned. "No sex, remember?"

"The heart is willing…" Tory laughed. "But the body is weak. Actually, not weak, just damn tired."

For an instant, Reese's eyes darkened with concern, but then she forced a smile. "I've got just what the doctor ordered."

Naked now, Reese reached down to test the water temperature and then opened a small bottle that rested on a ledge on one side of the tub. She poured the vanilla-scented essential oils into the water, capped the bottle, and replaced it. Turning with a smile, she held out her hand. "Your bath awaits, my lady."

With an appreciative groan, Tory pulled off the T-shirt, then steadied herself on Reese's shoulder to step into the tub. As she lowered herself into the soothing heat, Reese pulled the shades and quickly lit several candles that stood on the bathroom counter.

"Wet your hair." Reese sat on the edge of the tub and reached for the shampoo.

Lids half closed, Tory tilted her head back until her hair was below the surface of the water. When she pushed herself up, Reese leaned forward and massaged the shampoo into her hair.

"You have the best hands," Tory murmured, closing her eyes completely. Reese's fingers were strong but gentle. In their years together, those hands had touched her everywhere, inside and out, but each time she felt them on her body, a small surge of excitement rippled through her.

Reese took her time, smoothing the lather down the back of Tory's neck and over her shoulders, massaging the tense muscles. Eventually, she directed softly, "Go ahead and rinse."

Once again, when Tory lifted herself from the water, Reese was waiting, this time with a body sponge that she used to spread a fragrant bath gel over Tory's back. When she'd finished massaging her from shoulders to hips, Reese stepped into the tub behind Tory and settled down with a leg extended on either side of her.

"Lean back," Reese whispered in Tory's ear.

The tub was deep, and the water came to just above Tory's breasts as she reclined in Reese's embrace. Allowing her head to fall back against Reese's shoulder, she closed her eyes.

Tenderly, Reese reached around and spread the soothing lotion over Tory's upper chest and down the swell of her breasts. Tory groaned faintly and lifted her breasts into Reese's palms.

"Remember," Reese murmured, "no sex."

"God, you're evil," Tory muttered, even as she realized that she wouldn't be able to follow through with the distant pulse of desire in her depths. The sensation of want was pleasant, nevertheless.

When Tory opened her eyes again, she realized that she had been asleep, cushioned within the curve of Reese's body. Astonishingly, the water was still warm.

"How long have I been asleep?"

"About twenty minutes." Reese rested with her back against the wall and her chin on the top of Tory's head. "I've been turning the water on now and then to keep it warm. You didn't even realize when I recycled it."

"I can't remember the last time I was this out of it." She sighed deeply.

"Let's go to bed now, love."

Tory shook her head, then found Reese's hand where it rested on the edge of the tub. She squeezed it gently. "Sweetheart, it's Friday. I need to go to the clinic."

Reese didn't move. "Stay home today, Tory. Dan can take care of things."

"We're supposed to see Wendy this afternoon, too."

"I know. Can it wait until Monday?"

"I don't see why not," Tory said softly. "What about you? Are you going to work? You were up all night, too, Sheriff."

"I thought I'd lie down with you for a while." Reese hoped that would entice Tory to stay home.

"You know that's an offer I can't refuse, don't you?"

Smiling to herself, Reese kissed the top of Tory's head. "That's what I was counting on."

❖

An hour later, Reese slipped from the bed, moved quietly across the room, and collected her clothes. She stepped out into the hall and carefully closed the bedroom door. She dressed quickly and stepped stealthily down the stairs. Bri was sitting at the kitchen counter, drinking orange juice and eating a bowl of cereal.

"Did Ashley get Allie squared away?"

"Yep," Bri said.

Halfway around the counter toward the kitchen, Reese stopped, turned, and walked back to Bri's side. "You've got a pretty big burn on the side of your neck."

"I just realized it. I guess that happened when that drape caught on fire as we were going out the window."

"You did a fine job back there," Reese commended. "Both you and Allie. I'll make sure it goes into your record."

Bri blushed. "We didn't do anything that everyone else wasn't doing."

"Not everyone would've been willing to go into a room that was already in flames. The two of you did that." Reese rested her hand on Bri's shoulder. "I'm proud of you."

"Thanks." Tears stung Bri's eyes as she murmured huskily, "And thanks for coming after us. I'm not sure I could've gotten him out of there."

"You could have." Reese was certain and wanted Bri to know. She walked into the kitchen and found a coffee cup. "As soon as you're done eating, report to the clinic and have that burn looked after."

"Yes, ma'am."

"And then take the rest of the day off and get some sleep."

"What about you? Are you taking the day off?"

Reese shook her head. "I want to follow up on what Ashley told us about this guy Morris. Plus, I want to be there if we get an ID on the body. Maybe it was him."

"Then I'm coming in, too."

Reese finished pouring her cup of coffee and regarded Bri steadily. "I don't want to see you before two this afternoon."

"Roger," Bri replied, her eyes alight. "I'll get over to the clinic now, then."

"Good idea."

Reese watched Bri jump from the stool, grab her motorcycle jacket, and hurry out. Smiling, she shook her head and tried not to think about how close she had come to losing not one but two cadets earlier that day.

❖

When Bri returned to the house an hour and a half later, Reese was gone but Tory's Jeep was in the driveway. Knowing that Tory must be upstairs still asleep, Bri grabbed the portable phone from its cradle on the breakfast counter and took it with her into her small room. She pulled off her clothes and got naked under the sheets. Holding her breath, she punched a number and waited. A minute later, the familiar voice answered. "Carre?"

"Bri?" Almost as if she could hear something in Bri's voice, Caroline asked anxiously, "What's wrong?"

"I know I'm supposed to wait until you get here to call, but I just—"

"Are you hurt?"

Bri stretched out on her back, careful not to brush the side of her neck against the pillow where the medicine had been applied. "No, not really. Just a little bit of a burn."

Caroline took a deep breath. "There was a fire?"

"In Truro. A big one." Bri hesitated, then said very softly, "I love you, babe. I miss you so much."

"Something happened, didn't it?" The concern was still sharp in Caroline's tone. "Tell me what happened."

"Nothing," Bri said quickly. "It was crazy for a little while, and we almost got trapped in this burning room, but we went out the window—"

"And you got burned," Caroline interrupted in an unnaturally calm tone of voice. "Where?"

"Just the side of my neck and a little bit on my shoulder."

"Has Tory looked at it?"

"She's upstairs asleep. Her associate checked it. I'm okay."

There were a few seconds of silence as they listened to each other breathe.

"If something happens to you, Bri, I'm not going to be able to stand it," Caroline said softly. *I still haven't forgotten the first time.*

"Nothing is going to happen. It's just…I thought about you when, for a minute there…"

"It was really bad, wasn't it?"

"It happened so fast, I didn't have time to be scared." Bri took a long breath. "I just wanted you to know that you're the only girl I've ever loved. And the only one I want."

The silence returned, to be broken a few seconds later by the sound of tears.

"Hey," Bri whispered, her heart twisting in her chest. "Please don't cry. I never meant to hurt you."

"I know."

"When you get here," Bri avowed, "I'm going to make sure you know how much I love you."

"Promise me you'll be careful."

"I promise." Bri closed her eyes. *I promise never to hurt you again. I promise to love you forever. Please let me.*

"I'll see you soon, baby," Caroline whispered.

"Okay."

When the dial tone signaled that Caroline was gone, Bri pushed the off button, curled onto her side with the phone still in her hand, and fell asleep with the image of Caroline in her mind.

## CHAPTER NINETEEN

### June, Boston, MA

"I can't believe how much she's moving," Reese whispered to Tory. She was sitting at the head of the exam table, her cheek resting against the top of Tory's head, and they were both watching the ultrasound image as Wendy Deutsch moved the probe over Tory's abdomen. "Can you feel all that?"

"Mmm." Reese's arm rested around Tory's body, just below her breasts, and Tory had laced the fingers of her left hand with those of Reese's right. Tory squeezed gently and nodded. "Most of the time."

"I don't know if she'll be a rower, but she's sure gonna be a swimmer," Reese murmured with a small laugh.

"Fetal size and movement look excellent." Wendy smiled at Tory. "You're both doing beautifully."

Reese kissed the top of Tory's head, her eyes still watching the image on the screen.

Wendy removed the probe and set it aside. "Come on back to my office when you're ready."

A few minutes later, Reese and Tory were once again seated in front of Wendy's desk.

"Everything seems fine with the baby at this point," Wendy reiterated and steadily held Tory's gaze. "We need to talk about your blood pressure, though."

"I know."

"The elevation is persistent and substantial, although still in a range that I would consider mild hypertension. We have to consider this preeclampsia."

"Yes." Tory's voice was very calm.

Reese's heart plummeted, but she managed to sit absolutely still, and she knew that nothing showed on her face. When she glanced at her lover, she could read nothing in Tory's expression either.

"Most experts agree that at your stage, the only management is expectant." Wendy shrugged. "Salt restriction and plenty of rest can't hurt. I don't ordinarily treat my patients with anti-hypertensives because they haven't been shown to be of any value in terms of the outcome."

"I've read the same thing," Tory said. In fact, she'd been searching the literature for the last few weeks, ever since she had first noticed the slow progression of her gestational hypertension. She probably knew as much as Wendy about preeclampsia at this point.

"As long as there's no progression of the symptoms," Wendy said, her eyes still solemn and riveted on Tory, "I'm willing to manage this on an outpatient basis."

"As opposed to what?" Reese asked sharply.

Wendy switched her gaze to Reese. "As opposed to bed rest, either at home or in the hospital for fetal and maternal monitoring."

"Hospitalization? For weeks?" Reese was unable to keep the note of incredulity from her voice as she looked from Tory to the obstetrician. "We still have almost three months to go, right?"

"In all likelihood, we'll induce labor at thirty-seven weeks if conditions are optimal," Wendy noted mildly. "But yes, we're a ways away from that at this point."

"So let me get this straight." Reese needed accurate information to make sense of what was so important to her, and so far from her usual area of expertise. "As long as nothing changes, we just wait until the baby is big enough to be delivered, right?"

Tory smiled and reached for Reese's hand. "Right."

"And if the other things develop," Reese persisted, "the protein in the urine, or headaches, or visual disturbances or abnormal blood tests—then Tory is admitted to the hospital until the baby can be delivered?"

"That's possible, yes," Wendy confirmed.

"Okay then." Reese took a deep breath. "That's the plan."

"Yes, Reese." Wendy smiled. "That sounds like the plan." She looked at Tory again. "Weekly visits. No excuses. Take your blood pressure every four hours and twice-weekly blood screening."

"Done."

"And I want you to cut your hours at the clinic." Before Tory could respond, Wendy added, "You're in the last trimester now, Tory. It's time to slow down a little bit."

"Yes, all right."

"Good," Wendy said briskly. "I'll see you next week."

❖

On the plane ride back to Provincetown, Reese sat in the window seat with Tory leaning quietly against her shoulder. They held hands, but they didn't speak. When they landed at the small airstrip at Race Point, it was still early afternoon.

"How're you feeling?" Reese leaned close as they walked through the tiny terminal.

"Fine." Tory took her hand again. "It was nice to be away with you, even for a checkup."

"How about I drive over to the beach, and we take a look at the ocean."

"Nice. I'd like that."

A few moments later, Reese parked in front of the ranger's station and helped Tory climb from the Blazer. "Do you want to walk down to the beach, or to the lighthouse?"

"The lighthouse, I think."

They held hands and took their time walking down the winding sand path between low scrubs to the lighthouse that stood at the curve of the tip of Cape Cod as it stretched out into the Atlantic Ocean.

Reese smoothed the sand free of pebbles and needles at the base of the stone structure. "Is this okay?"

"Perfect." Tory eased down with a sigh.

Reese settled beside her and slid an arm behind Tory's shoulder. For a few moments, they were silent, basking in the June sun and watching the sailboats and larger crafts track across the ocean in front of them.

"Tell me how worried I should be about what's happening," Reese said at length.

"For now, not too." Tory rested her cheek against Reese's shoulder. She turned slightly so she could thread her arm around Reese's waist, drawing her knee gently over Reese's thigh until she was reclining in her lover's arms. "Everything has been stable except for the blood pressure, and that hasn't really changed very much."

"How long until the baby has a good chance?"

"God, you always go right for the heart of things, don't you, Sheriff?"

Reese tightened her hold. "I don't know the things you know. But I need to, because I want to be prepared."

"Like Wendy said, thirty-seven weeks is usually the point when labor is induced in situations like this. But many times, a few weeks earlier and the baby will do fine."

"So, we need at least another eight or nine, right?"

"That would be good."

"I don't want you to train anymore." Reese gently massaged Tory's back.

Tory was still for a moment, and then she tilted her chin and kissed the underside of Reese's jaw. "Okay."

"And you'll do half-shifts at the clinic?"

"Yep."

"Do you know how much I love you?" Reese asked, looking into Tory's eyes.

"I do." Tory kissed her, slow and deep and thoroughly. When she drew her head back, she smiled, knowing from the way Reese's eyes had darkened that the kiss had had its intended effect. "Do you know how much I love *you?*"

"I can make a pretty good guess," Reese murmured softly, running her free hand up and down Tory's arm.

"Make sure you get home on time from work tonight, and you won't have to guess."

❖

"Everything okay?" Nelson questioned the instant Reese walked into the office just after four p.m.

"Yep. Perfect." Reese nodded to Gladys, who responded with a thumbs-up gesture and a smile. Reese removed her hat, put it on the corner of her desk, and looked around the room. "Is Bri out on patrol?"

"Yep." Nelson closed one folder and opened another. "She's out on a call with Smith, checking out a complaint about a noisy dog."

"Now, Chief," Reese said with a grin, "she could handle that by herself."

"I know that. I wanted to make sure *Smith* had some backup." He laughed. "Don't forget the time Smith had the seat torn out of his pants by a pit bull he was trying to corral."

"I remember. I'm sure he does, too." Chuckling, Reese settled behind her desk to examine the pile of memos in her intake box.

"Anything new on the firebug?" Nelson asked.

"No." Reese frowned. "We've got his description out to all the departments on the Cape. We still haven't identified the body from the fire in Truro, but it's probably going to turn out to be a vagrant, if we ever get an ID on him at all."

"Any reason to think the perp's still around here?"

"Not that I can figure out." Still, Reese had a niggling feeling in the back of her mind that their arsonist hadn't moved on to greener pastures. "There's nothing in his background that targets this particular location, as far as I can tell. The insurance company he used to work for insures properties all over New England, with a concentration in lower Massachusetts and Rhode Island. If there's something keeping him around here, I don't know what it might be."

"You know how it goes. Usually it's some trivial detail that you never find out until you catch the guy," Nelson observed. "It could be something as simple as he used to vacation here every summer. Who the hell knows? The guy is nuts."

"Yeah."

"So…Bri graduates, formally, in a couple of weeks." Nelson squared the papers on his desk into neat piles.

"I know." Reese looked up from her own paperwork and studied him.

He met her eyes and grinned sheepishly. "I put in for her to be assigned here permanently."

"Good." Reese grinned back. "I was going to suggest it, if you didn't. She's a good officer, Nelson, and this is her home. She's good with the people, and she's happy here."

"Is she?" His voice was solemn and his expression serious. "She's been coming around for dinner a couple times a week, but she never says much."

"She's doing okay, Nelson," Reese replied to his unasked question. Since the fire in Truro, Bri had done nothing but work hard every day, performing in an exemplary fashion. She spent her evenings at home with Reese and Tory, trained in the dojo every morning before work, and seemed to have found some new level of peace.

"Caroline's going to be here the end of this week."

"Then I'd say that might be the only thing Bri needs to be really okay."

"Jesus," Nelson said wistfully. "I hope so."

❖

When the door to Bri's room opened a little after seven on Friday night, Tory looked up from the couch where she sat reading a magazine. Her young house guest crossed the room toward her, a faintly uneasy look on her face.

"Nervous?" Tory asked kindly. They were alone in the house, because Reese was at the dojo teaching a class. Ordinarily, Bri would have been with her assisting, but tonight was an exception.

"Jesus, yes." Bri's voice was tight and clipped. "Dumb, huh?"

"No." Tory shook her head. "I don't think so. I think it's pretty sweet."

Bri blushed furiously. Then, almost shyly, she asked, "Do I… uh…look okay?"

Giving the question due respect, Tory took in the new black jeans, the polished black boots, and the crisp white shirt. Bri looked like Bri always looked, lean and sleek and slightly dangerous. "You look great. I'm sure the only thing that's going to matter to Caroline is that you're there to see her."

"It feels pretty weird visiting her at my own house, where we used to sleep in my bedroom together. And now she lives there and I don't."

"Things have changed now, Bri. You were kids then, and you're not any longer."

Bri settled a hip on the arm of the sofa and regarded Tory solemnly. "If you were Carre, what would you want from me now?"

Tory almost smiled, but she managed not to. Sometimes, Bri was so much like Reese—totally guileless and without a clue as to how attractive that was. No wonder every young lesbian with a heartbeat on the Cape was after her. "Caroline loves you, Bri. I'm sure all she needs to know is that you love her, too."

"I do." Bri searched Tory's eyes. "But I've messed things up, and now I'm not sure she believes me."

"Trust is a terribly fragile thing," Tory said gently. "You know that, right?"

Bri nodded. She had become very still and every ounce of her attention was riveted on Tory's face.

"The first step is to tell her what you feel, *everything* that you feel, as honestly as you can. If you're scared, or not sure of how you feel, or even if you're not sure if you love her—"

"No," Bri interrupted vehemently. "I *am* sure."

"Then tell her all those things." Tory waited a beat, and then continued softly, "But sometimes, sweetie, when we've hurt someone or shaken their trust in us, it just takes time for that to get better."

"Do you think it will ever be okay?" Bri's voice was hoarse with the effort to hold back tears.

"I do." Tory's voice was certain and sure. "I have faith in you. Both of you."

## CHAPTER TWENTY

B ri walked down the gravel path, zipped her leathers, and straddled her motorcycle. She tried not to think too hard about what she should say; she was afraid that if she did, she'd blow it. The house she had grown up in was only a mile from Reese and Tory's. Going west into Provincetown, just before 6A split to become Bradford and Commercial, a narrow street ran north into the scrub pines. The Parkers' tidy two-story Cape Codder with its small yard and tiny front porch was one of several on the street. A sheriff's cruiser was pulled over in front of the house, so she knew her dad was home.

She parked in the narrow driveway and walked up the familiar front steps. There she hesitated, uncertain whether to knock or go in. It felt strange even coming to the front door, and stranger still to be picking up her girlfriend for a date. Before she could make up her mind, the door opened, and she was face to face with her father.

"Hi," she said quickly.

"Hey, Bri." Nelson made a motion with his head toward the interior of the house. "Caroline said she'd be right down." He looked at her awkwardly for a second. "You...uh...want to come in?"

"Yeah, sure." Bri followed him into the living room. The television was on in one corner, turned down low and tuned to some kind of reality program. She stared at it as her father sat down, but she had no idea what she was seeing. She rocked uneasily from foot to foot. It had been almost two months since she'd seen Caroline.

"Hi, Bri," a soft voice said from somewhere quite close by.

Bri jumped, startled, and looked toward the stairs that led down from the upper floor, separating the living room and dining room. Caroline stood halfway down, dressed in a scoop-neck black Lycra top and hip-hugger blue jeans. A thin silver belt of interlocking links was looped around her waist. The end trailed down one thigh.

Bri's mouth was suddenly dry. How could she have forgotten how hot Caroline was? Only when a puzzled expression replaced Caroline's initial tentative smile of welcome did Bri find her voice.

"Hi, ba—uh, Carre."

Nelson cleared his throat and stood up from his recliner in front of the television. Christ, he felt like he was watching his kid on her first date, and come to think of it, he guessed he was. When Bri had been a teenager, she'd kept her relationship with Caroline a secret, and by the time he'd found out about it, they'd been well past the courtship stage. He'd never seen them together in the beginning, and he was just now realizing how glad he was to have a second chance. The funny thing was, looking from Caroline to Bri, he couldn't decide which one he wanted to protect more. Hell, he loved them both.

"So, you two doing anything interesting?"

"Uh..." Bri's eyes devoured Caroline even as she stood rooted to the spot. "I was wondering if you'd like to go to the movies? They're showing *Bound* again at the Cinema Arts, and I know you've seen it, but—"

"I'd love to go," Caroline said quickly. She descended the stairs and crossed the small room to Bri's side. She wanted to throw her arms around her. If it had been any other time that they'd been apart, she would have. Now, she felt shy and uncertain. Bri had said that there was no one else, but it seemed like forever since they had been together. She knew hardly anything of what had happened to Bri in the last few months, and she couldn't quite bring herself to touch her. "Eight o'clock?"

"Uh-huh." Bri lifted a hand, automatically reaching for Caroline's, and then stopped. Softly, she said, "We should go now."

"Okay," Caroline replied, her eyes holding Bri's.

Nelson coughed and broke the spell. "Well, you two have fun. And be careful." As the two young women turned and started toward the door, he cleared his throat. "Just so I know, uh, should I expect you back tonight?"

He'd left the question intentionally vague, because he couldn't quite figure out what was going on. His daughter was living with his second in command, and her girlfriend was living with *him*. The two of them had lived together here for several months before leaving for college. He'd known then they were lovers, but it had all been so new to him that he had managed to avoid really thinking about the particulars. Now, it was pretty clear that what kept these two together was the same thing that kept a man and woman together— love and everything that went with it, including sex. Except they weren't married, so he had no idea what the protocol was now.

"*I* will be back later," Caroline said immediately.

"Okay then." He tried to act as if he hadn't seen Bri flinch slightly at the answer.

"I'll see you at work tomorrow, Dad," Bri said before closing the door.

Once outside, they walked to the motorcycle and Bri climbed on. A few seconds later, Caroline followed, as she had done hundreds of times before. When she wrapped her arms around Bri's waist from behind, automatically sliding warm palms over Bri's stomach, Bri shivered and dropped the keys. When Caroline tightened her hold and rested her cheek against the back of Bri's leather-jacketed shoulder, Bri spoke without turning around. "You look beautiful."

"You look great, too."

Bri's entire body twitched as she felt Caroline's hot breath against the back of her neck. Then she put one leg down and leaned over, groping on the ground for her keys. When she found them, her hands were shaking so badly she barely managed to get them into the ignition. "Hold on."

"Oh, don't worry, I will."

The sound of the engine drowned out Caroline's reply.

❖

The small theater in the center of town was crowded, mostly with gays and lesbians, but also with a fair number of ordinary tourists as well. Caroline and Bri found seats near the back just as the show started.

Fifteen minutes after the movie had begun, Caroline reached between the seats and found Bri's left hand, linking their fingers together.

Bri stared straight ahead at the screen, but her entire focus was riveted on the small points of contact between her body and Caroline's. Where the outside of her thigh rested against Caroline's leg, where the point of her shoulder touched Caroline's arm, where the insides of her fingers fused with Caroline's smaller ones. It was as if life flowed into her through those small areas of connection—a sensation more exciting than anything she had experienced in weeks.

Her breathing suddenly ragged, Bri struggled with a mass of conflicting emotions. It was so good to be with Caroline again, but being this close to her and unable to touch her was making Bri crazy. She wanted to kiss Caroline more at that moment than she had *ever* wanted to kiss her in her life. Even when they had first been together, she hadn't felt this deep, aching need. Back then, as a teenager, she had been neither sure of her welcome nor certain of her worthiness. All she had known was the pain of being different, and it had been hard to believe that Caroline really wanted her. The desire that consumed her then had been almost desperate—often foreign and unfocused—even to her.

Now, her mind and body held the memory of Caroline's mouth and hands and skin, the smell of her, the soft sound of her in the night. Now Bri wanted *her*, wanted what they'd had and lost, with an intensity that left her breathless. The muscles in her legs were so tight they were cramping, and the crotch of her jeans was soaked with urgency. Somehow, she managed to sit still through the entire movie.

As she and Caroline walked out onto the still-busy streets a little after ten p.m., Caroline tugged on their linked hands. "Do you want to walk on the beach?"

"Yeah. Okay." To Bri's great relief, Caroline did not let go of her hand.

They walked through town with their fingers interlinked until they reached the beach access path between the Boatslip and the Martin House, one of the oldest buildings in town that housed one of the most popular restaurants. A few minutes later, they reached the water's edge, not far from the tumbled-down pier where Bri had sat that night with Ashley.

Moonlight glinted on the water and the surf frothed white just inches from their toes. The sand was black where the ocean had bled onto it.

It was Caroline who broke the silence. "How's work?"

"Good," Bri said quickly. The nights were cold by the water, even in summer, and Bri removed her jacket and draped it around Caroline's shoulders. "I like it."

Caroline turned, snuggled into the jacket, and luxuriated in the heat left behind by her lover's body. Tentatively, she lifted a hand and ran her fingers tenderly down the side of Bri's neck. "I can see where you got burned."

"It's all healed. Tory said it would just be red for a while."

"So you're glad about the decision that you made?" Caroline's voice trembled slightly with the question.

"Well, I'm glad that I went to the academy when I did." Cautiously, Bri placed her fingertips very lightly on either side of Caroline's waist beneath the bottom of the jacket. Now, only shadows separated them. "I'm not happy I left you, though. I'm sorry for screwing up."

"I knew something was wrong for a while, and I should have made you tell me." Caroline automatically slid her hand around Bri's hips and hooked her thumb into Bri's back pocket, a gesture so ingrained she didn't notice it. Her movement brought them closer together until their thighs touched.

Bri swallowed, concentrating on what she needed to say while trying to ignore the swift surge of arousal stirred by the press of Caroline's body. "I should've told you sooner. It's not your fault."

"Why didn't you tell me?"

"I knew how much you loved living in New York City." Bri shrugged. "I knew how excited you were about going to Europe. I was afraid if I told you that I really wanted to come home, you would think..."

"What?" Caroline pressed closer. "You thought I would think what?"

"I wanted to fit in with your life. I didn't want you to think I was too...ordinary."

Caroline rested her forehead against Bri's chest. With a laugh, or what might have been a sob, she said, "Oh, baby, you are *so* not ordinary."

"I think I'm going to be assigned to the force here permanently." There, she'd said it. Tory said to tell her everything.

"So you'll be living here...for good?" Caroline grew very still. *What does that mean for us?*

"Maybe." Bri's words came out a whisper, and she was unable to ask the question that she so desperately needed answered. *Will you live here with me?*

"Have you been seeing anyone since you've been here?" Caroline spoke quietly, so quietly that her words were nearly carried away on the night wind.

"No. Not once," Bri replied vehemently. Then, steeling herself, she forced herself to ask, "You?"

When Caroline didn't answer, Bri feared her legs might desert her. She had to lock her knees together to stay standing, but as it was, she was trembling. Desperately, she whispered, "Babe?"

"One night...one night a few weeks after I saw you in the bar with that...girl..." Caroline pressed her cheek to Bri's chest and closed her eyes. Unconsciously, they held more tightly to one another. "I...can't."

Just thinking about that night with Allie, knowing that *Caroline* knew, made Bri feel sick. Still, she managed to speak through a throat tight with dread. "Go ahead. It's okay."

"I was at a party with some of my friends from school...and some other people I didn't know," Caroline went on, her voice pitched low. "There was a woman there who was...hitting on me. I'd had some wine, but I wasn't drunk. That's not what this was about. I think...I think I wanted to find out if I could be...without you."

"Oh babe," Bri moaned, burying her face in Caroline's hair. *This must be what dying feels like. Please, please, please don't let me lose her.*

"It got late, and we were alone, and...she started kissing me. I let her. I didn't kiss her back, but I don't think she even noticed." Caroline's voice faltered for a second, and then she continued more firmly. "After a few minutes, she...touched me. I asked her to stop, and she did."

Bri's breath rasped harshly in and out of her chest. She hurt everywhere inside. Tightening her hold on the woman in her arms, she said hoarsely, "I love you, Carre. I won't ever hurt you again. I promise."

"I've missed you so much, Bri," Caroline said softly.

"I love you, babe. Do you believe me?"

"I've always believed you."

"Is it enough?" Bri was holding her breath. She wasn't even certain her heart was still beating.

Caroline turned her face and pressed her lips to the spot where she could feel Bri's heart pounding. "I always thought it *would* be... before. I'm not sure now. But we'll find out."

❖

Tory was asleep on the couch when Reese walked in. The sound of the door and Jed's boisterous welcome woke her, and she turned with some difficulty onto her side to watch her lover approach.

Smiling, Reese leaned down and kissed her softly on the mouth. "Hi, love. How are you doing?"

"Other than feeling like a narcotized whale, I'm doing just fine."

"You don't *look* like a whale," Reese commented as she lifted Tory's feet, sat down, and settled her lover's legs onto her lap. She began to massage Tory's feet, which elicited of groan of pleasure. "You look verdant."

"Verdant?" Tory raised an eyebrow.

"Lush, ripe, filled with life..."

"Are you trying to seduce me?"

"Do I have to try?"

"No." Tory nudged her heel between Reese's thighs, eliciting a groan from her. "But I don't mind if you want to give it a shot."

"Aren't you supposed to be losing interest or something?" Reese was only half joking. Somehow, she had assumed that being pregnant would mean Tory would become less interested in sex, especially now that she was clearly physically uncomfortable much of the time. As it was, Tory became more enticing to *her* every day, and she had to work at tempering her frequent desire. She didn't want Tory to feel pressured.

"To tell you the truth," Tory said somewhat irritably, "I feel like sex a lot, but more and more of the time, some part of my body or another isn't up to it."

Reese leaned sideways until she was reclining next to Tory, taking care to support herself on one arm so that she didn't put her weight on her lover's body. "Whatever you want, whenever you want. You're the boss."

"I don't want you to be deprived," Tory said softly, suddenly serious.

"What?" Reese shook her head, smoothing her palm down Tory's arm and then sliding her fingers beneath the loose blouse she wore. "There isn't anything in the world I want except you, just like this."

As she spoke, Reese ran her fingers over the swell of Tory's belly, and then brushed lightly over the curve of one full breast. "You get more beautiful every day. And when I feel the baby move, it's just about the most thrilling thing I've ever experienced." Reese continued to draw her fingers tenderly over Tory's abdomen, then bent her head and placed a gentle kiss on Tory's mouth.

Tory closed her eyes and sighed. "This is heaven. But once in a while, Sheriff, I miss the wild sex."

Reese laughed out loud. "I need to shower. Then what do you say we get in bed and see what happens?"

"See? I knew you were trying to seduce me."

When Reese emerged from the shower a half-hour later, Tory was propped up in bed, naked, the covers just barely covering her breasts. She was apparently asleep.

Quietly, Reese crossed to the bed and reached for the bedside light.

"Just turn it down low, but leave it on," Tory murmured. "I want to see your face."

"Okay." Reese slid carefully beneath the sheets.

Tory turned on her left side, the position Wendy had recommended as the best one to enhance blood flow through her uterus. "You know what I love about sex with you?"

"What?" Reese's eyes were fixed on her lover's. Tory's expression was both whimsical and tender.

"You don't hold anything back."

"'Cause I love you with everything I am," Reese whispered, gently resting her palm on the arch of Tory's hip. "You own me."

"Mmm. I love *that* about you, too." Tory nestled her cheek in the bend of her own arm and ran her other hand over Reese's abdomen. "I also happen to love your body."

"That's good." Reese drew a slightly shaky breath as Tory's fingers traced light circles on her skin. "Because I love it when you touch me."

"I want to watch you come," Tory said steadily, running her fingertip between Reese's breasts, then fleetingly over her nipples. She gave a murmur of satisfaction as they hardened to her touch.

"Aren't you tired?" Reese was having trouble keeping her breathing steady or her legs still. There was something in Tory's expression—her eyes were so intense, searching inside of her—that every nerve in her body tingled.

"I said I wanted to *watch*." Tory's voice was low, husky, and her eyes were wide with desire. As she spoke, she moved her hand to Reese's. Slowly, deliberately, her gaze holding her lover captive, she drew Reese's fingers down the center of Reese's body and between her thighs. "Okay?"

Reese's lips parted with a soft groan as Tory pressed down on Reese's hand, urging her fingers against the base of her own clitoris. Throat tight, Reese murmured, "I said anything you wanted."

"I want."

Tory eased her hold on Reese's hand, keeping her fingers lightly in contact so that she could feel Reese move. In her mind, she saw the strong, sure fingers as they slid over warm, engorged tissues. She felt the faint lift of Reese's hips as Reese's eyes darkened to purple. Her own heart beat faster as she watched the tension grow in Reese's face. Beneath her palm, Reese's hand circled gently.

"Are you hard?"

"Christ, yes." Reese found it almost impossible to talk because it was even harder to get a full breath. It wasn't as much the pleasure spiraling from beneath her fingers, but the look of hunger in Tory's eyes that was making her so heavy and hard. She'd give

Tory anything, knowing it would never be enough to show her how much her love meant.

"Slow down," Tory said softly.

"I don't...think I...can," Reese said through gritted teeth. The muscles in her stomach danced in anticipation as her attention narrowed down to one pounding point. She was swollen, stiff, preparing to explode. "Oh fuck, Tor. It feels so good."

"Make it last," Tory urged, wanting desperately to touch her, but knowing if she did, Reese would come immediately. She enjoyed watching the pleasure ripple through Reese's body too much to end it too quickly. "You're so beautiful right now."

"I want...to come," Reese gasped desperately, her vision dimming. "Can I?"

"Hold on as long as you can." Tory shifted her fingers lower, gliding over Reese's fingertips as Reese fondled herself. "Tell me when you're coming."

"Soon...oh, yeah, soon."

"Wait...wait, baby."

"Tory," Reese said sharply. Her eyes opened wide, then the pupils flickered rapidly as her limbs grew rigid. "I'm gonna come."

"Yes, sweetheart," Tory murmured as she slid into her in one single motion. "You are."

Reese choked out a cry as she flung her head back, forcing the orgasm on with each frantic stroke of her hand. When the convulsive contractions were almost over, Tory withdrew nearly completely and then entered again, setting off another round of spasms.

"Jesus," Reese gasped, pressing her forehead to Tory's shoulder.

"Keep going," Tory ordered urgently. "Keep going until you come again."

Reese begged, "Stay inside," as she teased herself hard again.

"I'm here," Tory soothed. "I'm here."

Reese was so sensitive, it only took a few tugs and her entire body began to tremble. "Oh...it's coming." It hit her fast, and she moaned, folding in on herself as the force of it pounded through her.

Dimly, Reese heard Tory's voice close to her ear. "Again?"

"I can't, I can't." Sweat streaked her face as she pressed her cheek to Tory's breast. She still cupped herself with her palm, but Tory had withdrawn. "God, I'm wasted."

"You're gorgeous," Tory said thickly, running her fingers through Reese's damp hair. "Thank you."

Reese managed to move enough to tilt her head back and look into Tory's face. "You don't need to thank me for anything. There is nothing in me you can't have."

"I adore you." Tory pressed her lips to Reese's forehead, then drew her lover's head back to her breast. "Now go to sleep, sweetheart."

With a sigh, Reese slid her arm over Tory's hips and closed her eyes, doing as her lover bid.

❖

After the beach, Bri and Caroline went to Spiritus for pizza, then just walked through town together, stopping in shops with no particular destination in mind. Something they had done hundreds of times before, something so familiar and yet so new. They were together, but the easy confidence that had always existed between them was missing.

When Bri looked at the woman who had been her lover and a critical part of her life, it was as if she were seeing her for the first time. Caroline seemed separate from Bri and her reality in a way that she never had been before. The chance to be with Caroline this way, just strolling and talking, felt so much more precious to Bri now, because she was also acutely aware of the distance that shadowed their relationship.

A little after midnight, Bri walked Caroline to the door of what she now thought of as her father's house, not hers.

"Can I see you tomorrow night?" Bri stopped at the top of the stairs and leaned a shoulder against the railing post. Five more feet, and Caroline would be inside and gone. She desperately did not want her to go.

"I'm supposed to meet with Gianelli tomorrow to find out what he needs me to do at the gallery. I don't know how late I'll need to work."

"That's okay. You can call me, or I can stop by."

Caroline stepped closer until she was nearly between Bri's legs. Curling her fingers around the outer edge of Bri's left hand, she circled her thumb over the top and traced the middle finger down to the wide silver band that she had placed on Bri's hand when they were sixteen. "I'd like that."

"Carre," Bri whispered just before she kissed her. The kiss was nearly as tentative and tender as the first time she had dared to put her mouth on Caroline's skin. Their thighs brushed lightly, and they joined fingers, clasping hands as their lips met.

Bri had no idea how long the kiss lasted. She had no awareness of anything except the way Caroline smelled, and the incredible softness of the inside of her mouth, and the warmth that flowed from Caroline into her very core. This time, every time. It was so right.

Slowly, Caroline pressed closer until the front of her body pressed snugly against Bri's, her hips sheltered between Bri's thighs, her pelvis rocking softly in time with her slowly thrusting tongue. She whimpered quietly and Bri moaned.

Abruptly, Bri broke off the kiss and pulled her head back. "Babe," she whispered urgently.

"What?" Caroline was breathless, too.

"I have to stop."

"We're just kissing," Caroline teased gently.

Bri shook her head. "You feel too good. I've missed you so much. If we keep it up, I'm gonna come in my jeans."

Caroline laughed quietly, hooking her fingertips just inside the waistband of Bri's pants. "I've always loved it when you do that. It's so hot."

"Yeah, right." Bri managed a self-conscious shrug. "But I want to save it."

"For what?" Caroline tilted her head and studied Bri's handsome face, dark now with tension and desire.

"I want the first time to be special," Bri whispered, resting her forehead gently on Caroline's.

"The first time?"

"The first time we're together again."

With a small cry, Caroline wrapped her arms around Bri's waist and pressed her cheek to Bri's shoulder. "I love you."

It was true what they said, Bri thought as she locked her fingers together at the base of Caroline's spine and held her as close as she could. Some words *were* the sweetest sound you could ever hear.

They were still wrapped up in one another when the front door opened and Nelson stuck his head out.

"Maybe you two should get a room," he suggested mildly.

Caroline turned in the circle of Bri's arms, her hands finding Bri's again and clasping them against her stomach. "We were just saying good night."

Bri rested her chin on the top of Caroline's head.

"Careful on that motorcycle, Bri," Nelson said.

"Yes, sir," Bri called as the front door closed. "Jesus. Do you think he was watching us?"

"No. Nelson wouldn't do that. He probably heard the motorcycle and got curious after a while about what we were doing." Carefully, Caroline stepped away and turned around to face Bri. "Besides, we were just kissing."

"Well, yeah, but he's my father. Jesus."

"Baby, he knows we sleep together. We slept together in the house almost all one summer."

"Well, he never *saw* us," Bri said pointedly.

Caroline laughed. "You are so fucking cute."

"What happened to hot?" Bri demanded almost petulantly, but she couldn't help grinning.

"Hmm. That, too." Caroline ran her fingers lightly along the edge of Bri's jaw. "I should go in. Be good, okay?"

"You mean I can't go home and take care of myself?"

"I'd rather you waited for me," Caroline replied, her voice soft and low.

"Does it count against me if I come in my sleep?"

Caroline seemed to give this some thought, her smile widening. "Depends on who you're dreaming about."

"Babe," Bri whispered, completely serious, "I only dream of you."

## CHAPTER TWENTY-ONE

Just before one p.m. the following Friday, Reese stopped by the clinic to pick Tory up after her half-day shift was over. The waiting room was unusually quiet, with only a mother and two small children waiting. Randy was nowhere in sight, so Reese walked around the reception desk and through the door that led to the examining rooms and Tory's office. As she passed an open room on her right, she automatically glanced in and saw Dan Riley bending over a woman lying on the examining table. Reese stopped abruptly, her pulse suddenly spiking.

The woman was Tory.

"Tor?" Reese inquired sharply as she stepped inside.

"Sweetheart?" Tory lifted her head, clearly surprised. "What are you doing here?"

"What's the matter? Are you all right?" Reese walked around the far side of the table and grasped Tory's right hand. "What happened?"

"Nothing," Tory said quickly. "Dan was just checking my pressure."

"Lying down in here?" Reese asked suspiciously. She raised her eyes to Dan's, but his gray ones revealed nothing.

Tory sighed. "I had a bit of a headache, and Dan insisted that I lie down."

"Headache." Reese said the word very calmly as she studied Tory's face. Inside, the roaring in her head was making it hard for her to think. *Headache, visual disturbances, protein in...* "Did you call Wendy?"

"It's not necessary." Tory shook her head and sat up on the side of the table. "My pressure hasn't changed. It's just an ordinary headache. It happens." She spoke very slowly and kept her eyes fixed on Reese's. "Sweetheart, everything is fine."

Finally, Reese shifted her gaze back to Dan, and he nodded slightly before speaking.

"Her pressure's high but no higher than what she tells me it's been for the last few weeks." He smiled, the kind of smile doctors give patients to reassure them. "But…her shift is over, so I recommend an afternoon of taking it easy. I think that will probably solve the problem."

"Well, that's what we'll do then." Reese forced a smile of her own. "Let's go home, love."

"Aren't you working now?" Tory protested.

"It's no problem. I'll split the shift and go back in later." Reese's tone left no room for argument.

❖

Fifteen minutes later, they were home.

"Do you want to lie down upstairs?" Reese asked once they were inside.

"No," Tory replied quietly. "I'm not really tired. I'll just sit out on the deck."

"How about lunch?"

"Just something to drink would be fine."

"There's some lemonade left. Okay?"

Smiling, Tory kissed Reese on the cheek. "Sounds wonderful."

Reese filled the glasses with ice and homemade lemonade and carried them outside on a tray with crackers and cheese. Tory was stretched out in a lounge chair, her eyes closed. Reese set the small lunch down on the table between the chairs, then turned to slip away quietly.

"I'm awake," Tory murmured.

"Are you sure you don't want to take a nap?"

Tory stretched out her hand and Reese took it. "I'm really fine. Every now and then, I think my body rebels because I can't drink caffeine. That's all it was."

"Well, it won't be that long before you can drink coffee again."

"That will depend on how the breast-feeding goes," Tory said, smiling faintly as she closed her eyes.

"Oh yeah, I forgot about that." Reese sat beside her on the chaise and stroked Tory's hair. "I guess you're going to have to get used to being decaffeinated for quite a while."

"Mmm. Apparently."

"Will you be all right? I'll be back in a bit. I'm going to make a phone call."

"You don't usually announce something like that." Tory opened her eyes and searched Reese's face. "Who are you calling?"

Reese hesitated. "My father."

"To tell him about the baby?" Tory pushed herself upright on the chair with some effort.

Reese nodded.

"Why now?"

"Because it's going to be soon," Reese said. "And it's time I stopped protecting him from who I am."

"Sweetheart, you don't have to do this for me."

"I know."

"Call him from out here, then," Tory said softly.

"Why don't you just rest, okay? I'll only—"

"Sweetheart," Tory interrupted, "this is about us, and I want to be with you."

After a few seconds, Reese nodded. "All right."

She carried a portable phone out to the deck and sat back down on the end of Tory's lounge chair. Without hesitating, she punched in the number and waited wordlessly.

"Lieutenant Colonel Conlon for the general." Reese assumed a military demeanor just saying her name. Then, straightening perceptibly, she continued, "Hello, sir. How are you, sir?...Fine, sir...Yes, sir. The reason I'm calling is of a personal nature, sir... A family matter. No sir, I wouldn't expect you to understand. If I may, sir...My partner, Tory King, and I are expecting a child at the beginning of September."

Intently, Tory watched her lover's face, trying to gauge Reese's father's response from her expression. A muscle along the edge of Reese's jaw jumped, and her fingers tightened on the phone. Automatically, Tory laid her palm gently against the center of Reese's back and traced tiny circles with her fingertips.

"No, sir. I didn't call you to make an official statement, sir. I called you...because you're my father, and I wanted you to know about this." Reese's blue eyes glinted, brilliant as chips of glass in the sunlight. "If you feel it's necessary to do that, sir, that's certainly your prerogative...No, sir, I will not, under any circumstances."

Abruptly, Reese stood and walked to the edge of the deck. She rested the phone carefully on the top railing. When a few minutes had passed and she neither spoke nor turned in Tory's direction, Tory got to her feet and went to her side.

"What did he say, sweetheart?" Tory gently replaced her hand on Reese's back. The muscles under her hand were board stiff.

Reese turned slightly until she could meet Tory's eyes. Her voice was low and rough. "He threatened me with a court-martial if I insisted on acknowledging my relationship with you."

Tory drew a sharp breath. "Will he do it?"

"I don't know," Reese replied quietly. "I don't know anything about him, it seems."

"Oh, sweetheart, I'm so sorry." Tory leaned against Reese's side and slid her arm around her waist. "I love you."

Reese returned the embrace and pressed her face into Tory's hair. For a few moments, she merely stood, eyes closed, allowing love to fill her senses—the smell of Tory's shampoo, the soft strands of hair that caressed her cheek, the thud of Tory's heart against her own chest, and most of all, the promise of life growing between them.

When she straightened, Reese's eyes were clear and her smile was soft. "I love you, too. Both of you—more than anything in the world."

Tory kissed her. "Let's call Kate and Jean and invite ourselves to dinner tonight."

"That sounds like a great idea."

❖

"Go ahead to work, Reese," Kate said. "We'll take Tory home in a little while. You'll be late for your shift if you don't leave now, and I want to talk some more about baby things with Tory."

"Okay, if you're sure. Tory?"

"Its fine, sweetheart. I'll see you later at home."

Reese frowned faintly. "Don't wait up. It'll be after midnight before I get back."

"Then wake me up," Tory murmured as she put her hand behind Reese's neck and pulled her head down for a kiss. "Now get out of here, Sheriff."

Kate and Tory settled in the living room of Kate and Jean's bungalow. Jean was clearing dishes in the kitchen after their early supper.

After Reese left, Kate confided quietly, "I could just kill him for hurting her."

"I know," Tory agreed. "So could I. Do you think he'll go through with it?"

"I don't know. Somehow, I don't think so. My gut instinct is that he's holding the threat of court-martial over her head in the hopes that she'll come back into the fold."

"She hasn't really left, you know." Tory sighed. "She still thinks of herself as a marine, and she's still in the reserves. I'm sure if war were to come, she would go active immediately."

Kate shook her head. "She might have before, but if she had any choice at all, I don't think she would now. Not with the baby coming."

Tory was silent for so long that Kate tilted her head and raised her brows. "Is something wrong?"

"Do you and Jean have any plans to be away in the next few weeks?"

"We were going to go to Jean's brother's for Fourth of July weekend. He and his family live near D.C." Kate rested her hand on Tory's knee. "Is there some reason we should cancel?"

"I really hate to ask you," Tory began hesitantly.

"What is it?"

"Hopefully, nothing, but I'm having just a bit of a problem with the pregnancy, and I might go…early."

"What kind of a problem?" Kate's blue eyes were gentle on Tory's.

Tory explained while Kate listened calmly.

"Could this be dangerous?"

"Not likely, but the possibility of complications with the delivery does exist." Tory smiled wryly at the question. "Reese is so much like you."

"Thank you." Startled, Kate blushed with pleasure.

"Kate, in case anything were to…happen to me, Reese…" Tory's voice trailed off, and she had to wait a few seconds before she could continue. "Reese would need help for a while."

"Listen, my sweet," Kate said tenderly, taking both of Tory's hands in hers. "We're not going to let anything happen to you. You or the baby. But no matter what, I promise that Reese will be fine. This time, I'll be there for her."

"I know you will," Tory said softly.

"You look tired. Let me collect my lover, and we'll take you home."

"Thank you, Kate. For everything."

❖

Bri raised her head and whispered, "Did you just hear a car?"

Caroline, who reclined between Bri's legs on the sofa, murmured breathlessly, "No. Don't stop."

"I think Reese is home," Bri insisted, sitting up a little. "Besides, if we keep making out like this, I'm going to have some kind of serious nerve damage. I'm walking around permanently hard."

"Poor baby," Caroline teased. "You're the one who wanted to watch TV here instead of going out, and you know what happens when we lie down together."

"Yeah. I know." Bri nuzzled Caroline's ear. In a throaty voice, she murmured, "Why do you think I suggested it?"

Caroline slid her hand under Bri's T-shirt and let her fingers drift just below the waistband of Bri's jeans. She smiled at Bri's swift intake of breath and the rapid tensing of the abdominal muscles. "Then it's your own fault if you're suffering. I could fix that, but you keep saying no."

Bri was about to protest when the front door opened and closed quietly. "Hey," she said as Reese walked toward them.

"Hi, you two." Reese put her hat and keys on the breakfast counter. "Tory asleep?"

"It was all quiet when we got here about ten o'clock," Bri announced.

"Good." Reese headed for the stairs. "I'll see you in the morn—"

The phone rang and, turning back quickly, Reese grabbed for it.

"Conlon." She listened without expression for a few moments, and then said, "Maybe we should talk now. Where are you?"

Bri sat up completely, swinging her legs to the floor so that Caroline could move beside her. Intently, she watched Reese's face, some instinct resonating to her training officer's sudden tension.

"You are actually closer to me here than the sheriff's office. Come to the house." Reese recited the directions and hung up the phone, then turned to Bri. "That was Ashley Walker. She says she knows where Morris is."

"Holy shit." Suddenly Bri had an uncomfortable realization. "Is she coming here?"

"She's just outside of Wellfleet. We're closer, and since you and I are both here, it makes sense."

Bri glanced to Caroline. "Maybe I should run you home real fast."

"Why? I'll just wait in your room if you don't want me to hear what's going on."

*I don't want you to be here if Ashley is going to be...Ashley. I don't want you to get the wrong idea. Not now, not when things are so much better between us.*

"What's going on?" Tory called from the top of the stairs.

"Nothing, love," Reese said quickly. "Just a call from work."

"Do you have to go back out?" Tory, wearing a loose top and baggy sweatpants, descended to the living room and made her way into the kitchen. She opened the refrigerator, drew out a carton of orange juice, then pulled a glass from the dish drainer by the sink. "Hi, Caroline. How are you?"

"I'm good. How're you?"

"Doing fine," Tory responded as she carried her juice around the counter and balanced one hip on the stool. "How're things working out with Gianelli?"

"Just great." Caroline smiled brilliantly, resting her hand on Bri's thigh. "I'm really supposed to be there to help out, but he's been taking me out with him in the mornings when he paints. I've been doing some work then, too, and he's been great about giving me feedback."

"That's terrific," Tory said with genuine enthusiasm. She watched Reese check her watch for the second time, and repeated, "What's going on, sweetheart?"

With obvious reluctance, Reese replied, "We might have some information on the arsonist. Ashley Walker is on her way over."

"Really." Tory did some quick calculating. Considering the hour and Reese's expression, it was clear that something important was happening. "Can I talk to you out on the deck?"

"Of course."

Once outside, Tory asked, "Do you expect some kind of action soon?"

Reese hesitated.

"You can't keep these things from me, sweetheart."

"It depends on what Ashley has to say," Reese conceded. "If it sounds as if she has a good lead, the sooner we apprehend him the better."

"Will you take Bri?"

"Yes."

"Is she ready for this kind of situation?"

"Technically, she's still a trainee, but for all practical purposes, she's done with her training, and in a week or so will be a full-time officer. If I don't take her, she's going to feel I don't trust her."

"Do you?" Tory sensed a rare hint of uncertainty in Reese's voice.

"Yes," Reese said immediately, then frowned. "But, you know, when I think about it, I get tight inside. I never do that. Hell, I've commanded people in situations a lot tougher than this one."

"Yes, but did you *love* any of them?"

"I don't lo—" Reese sighed. "Yeah, I do." She rested her forehead against Tory's and closed her eyes. "But I care about them all."

"She's special," Tory murmured softly. *Like you.*

"Yes." Reese wrapped her arms around Tory. "We'll be fine."

"Will you tell me what's happening after you talk to Ashley?"

"Will you promise to go back to bed and try to get some sleep if I do?"

"God, you're difficult." Tory's voice was a mixture of frustration and tenderness. "Yes, I promise. As long as you promise to come home unscathed."

Reese pressed her lips to Tory's forehead and then her mouth. When she drew back, she whispered huskily, "I promise."

"Then we have a deal." Tory rested her cheek against Reese's shoulder, then sighed. "I think that was the doorbell."

❖

Caroline walked out onto the deck carrying Tory's sweatshirt. She was wearing Bri's leather jacket. "Do you mind company while they're talking?"

"Not at all." Tory smiled and reached for the sweatshirt. "Thanks, sweetie."

"Ashley Walker is a knockout," Caroline remarked as she sat down in the lounge chair next to Tory.

"Uh-huh. She's very attractive."

"Bri is being real careful not to look at her." Caroline pulled the leather jacket around her. Even though it was the end of June, it was still jacket weather in the middle of the night. "I'm not going to ask if they went out, because Bri told me she hasn't been seeing anyone. But she has that guilty look she gets when there's something she doesn't want me to know about."

Tory laughed softly. "Bri has no idea how easy she is to read."

"Don't tell her, okay," Caroline said with a small smile. Then she asked shyly, "Is Reese like that?"

"Most of the time, her feelings are so clear." Tory gave the question some thought. "She can be very good at hiding the things that bother her, though. But I can usually tell when she's doing that, and if I ask her, she always tries to explain."

"I should've done that with Bri last winter."

Tory heard the sadness in Caroline's voice. "Honey, you're not responsible for the entire relationship all by yourself."

Caroline turned on her side and curled one arm behind her head so that she could watch Tory as she spoke. "I don't think Bri would have ended up going home with another girl if I'd really known what was going on with her."

"Maybe not," Tory agreed. "I don't know all the details, but I get the sense that whatever happened was over pretty fast. Bri has done nothing but pine for you since she's been here. She's head over heels in love with you."

"She hasn't asked me to live with her when I finish school," Caroline said in a small voice.

"Do you want to?"

"Of course. I've always wanted to live with her. I love her."

"What about your career?"

"What about it?" Caroline laughed. "Provincetown is famous for its artists. I might never be famous, but I can't imagine why I couldn't do what I want to do here."

"Have you told her that?"

"No."

"Why not?"

Caroline was silent for a long moment. "I guess because…I'm still mad at her for making plans without me. For leaving me alone for the last four months."

"Then I guess you two have more to talk about."

"Yeah, I guess so."

"Do me a favor, okay?"

"Sure," Caroline said with a hint of surprise.

"Don't wait too long." There was something almost regretful in Tory's tone. "Time is so precious."

"Is there something wrong?"

"No, sweetie." Tory produced a tiny laugh, trying to chase away the persistent sense of foreboding. "Everything's fine. I just know you two love each other, and I want to see you happy."

The sound of the kitchen doors sliding open caught their attention, and both women looked back toward the house.

Reese stepped out onto the deck. "Bri and I are going in to work in a bit."

Caroline got up suddenly and started toward the house.

"What is it?" Tory sat up on the lounge chair, making room for Reese next to her.

"We have a possible location for Stanley Morris," Reese said as she sat and took Tory's hand. "Ashley has been running deep background checks on everyone in Morris's family, as well as his wife's relatives. She turned up something on an Internet search tonight."

"Must be pretty important to get you all out in the middle of the night."

"Morris's wife's great-grandfather was a photographer. Apparently, a pretty famous one, at least locally."

"Locally?"

"Yes. He was one of the early 20th-century Provincetown art colonists."

Tory stared at Reese. "He lived *here*?"

"He did." Reese's eyes glinted in the moonlight. "In a dune shack."

"Oh my God," Tory said. "Do you think that's where Morris is?"

The dune shacks were just that, ramshackle structures built in the shelter of the dunes on the opposite side of the narrow strip of land at the very end of Cape Cod from the village. Provincetown itself was nestled in the harbor, while two miles across the barren dunes was the Atlantic Ocean. Writers, painters, and photographers had built rustic shelters in this isolated location and often returned to them summer after summer for decades. Most were only accessible on foot. Many of the shacks had been lost to weather and neglect, but some still remained. They were only rarely occupied in recent years.

"It would make sense," Reese acknowledged. "According to Ashley's paper trail, Morris disappeared somewhere on the Cape a few weeks ago."

"What are you going to do?"

"Nelson is waking up the museum curator right now so we can study the dune shack maps. Once we're certain we know which one we're dealing with, we're going to take a ride out to check."

"Tonight?" Tory's heart pounded with sudden apprehension.

People thought that small-town policing was a safe job, and most of the time it was. But there was never any guarantee that the drunk at the corner bar wouldn't have a gun, or that the simple car stop for a broken headlight wouldn't turn violent. And now Reese planned to apprehend a man who by all reports was unbalanced and had already killed someone, intentionally or not.

"At dawn." Reese shifted and slid her arm around Tory's waist. "It shouldn't be anything too much. We'll take the four-wheel-drive up the access road most of the way and then go by foot. He won't expect us. Besides, the guy is an arsonist. He's not likely to put up a fight."

"Of course," Tory said evenly, knowing Reese would go, regardless of her fears. This was what Reese did. "Who else is going?"

"Bri, Ashley, and Nelson."

"Ashley?" That was a surprise.

"She's been chasing this guy a long time, and she's an ex-cop. She's probably better trained for this than Lyons or Smith. I cleared it with Nelson already, and she's earned it."

"Is that enough manpower?"

"Should be," Reese replied. "Any more and we'll run the risk of announcing ourselves."

"When are you going?"

She checked her watch. "We're supposed to meet at two a.m."

"Soon then." Tory took a slow steadying breath. "Will you call me as soon as it's over?"

"I don't suppose there's any chance that you'll be able to sleep, is there?" Reese lifted Tory's chin with her fingertips and kissed her softly. "Maybe just a little?"

"I'll lie down when you go," Tory murmured, her mouth against Reese's. She wanted to fist her hands in Reese's shirt and keep her safely at home forever. "But I might not sleep until you get back into bed."

"Then I'll be home as soon as I can." Reese sealed her vow with a kiss.

❖

When Caroline stepped inside, she immediately saw Bri and Ashley leaning against the breakfast counter on the far side of the room, facing one another as they talked. She also noted in one quick glance that Ashley had placed her left hand on Bri's forearm where it rested on the back of a chair. The gesture might have been innocent, but the sight of another woman touching Bri made Caroline's stomach hurt and her head pound. She'd had quite enough of other women pawing at her lover. Without hesitation, she walked to them and put her arm around Bri's waist.

"Hi, baby."

"Hey, babe," Bri said softly, resting her hand lightly on the back of Caroline's neck.

"Reese says you two are going into work."

"In a little bit," Bri acknowledged with a nod. "That's what we were just discussing." Suddenly realizing her oversight, Bri added hastily, "Uh, Carre, this is Ashley Walker."

"Hi. I'm Carre, Bri's girlfriend." She extended her hand.

Ashley nodded, her eyes searching the pretty young blond's. If she hadn't been too busy with her own love life to pursue the sexy sheriff's officer, the look in Bri's girlfriend's eyes would have been enough to dissuade her. "Got it."

"Well," Bri said, looking from one to the other a bit uncertainly. "I should get ready."

"I'll come with you." Caroline smiled at Ashley. "Nice to meet you."

"Same here," Ashley said good-naturedly. She picked up the phone and dialed as Bri and Caroline walked away.

Caroline heard Ashley say "Honey?" as she pulled Bri's bedroom door closed. She sat on the side of Bri's bed and watched her lover change. "Who's she calling?"

"Uh—her girlfriend, probably." Bri slid her belt through the loops of her uniform pants and reached for her gun. *Allie, I'll bet.*

"Huh." Everyone seemed tense, and it struck Caroline for the first time that Bri was *really* a police officer. She could leave for work and be hurt. Not come home. Even Reese had been shot once. "We should go apartment hunting."

Bri stopped abruptly and regarded Caroline in the dim light of the bedside lamp. "We should?"

"Uh-huh. You can't stay here forever, plus I don't think we can make love in here without waking up Reese and Tory. It doesn't make sense for both of us to move back to Nelson's. We need our own place."

"We do?" Bri's throat was dry, and her heart was beating two hundred times a minute. "*Our* place?"

"Yes, absolutely." Caroline rose and crossed to Bri. She brushed the jet-black strands of hair off Bri's forehead, then threaded her arms around Bri's waist. "So I can visit on weekends from school."

"Weekends." Bri felt incapable of full sentences. *What are you saying?*

"Uh-huh," Caroline said quietly, her eyes on Bri's. "Until I finish school and move back."

"Here?"

"This is where you'll be, right?"

Bri nodded. She had to go to work. Reese had said ten minutes. But the world had stopped, and all she knew was the thudding of her pulse and the warmth deep in her belly. This was what mattered. *This* moment.

"You'll live here…with me?"

"Of course." Caroline's lips were soft against Bri's cheek. "I love you. I can't live anywhere else."

"Carre—"

"Shh," Caroline murmured gently just before she kissed Bri thoroughly.

## CHAPTER TWENTY-TWO

Reese, Nelson, Bri and Ashley drove toward Race Point just before dawn. When they reached the ranger's kiosk, Nelson put the vehicle into four-wheel drive and turned onto a narrow trail in the sand that ran parallel to the ocean and beach. After a mile, he cut the lights and drove another quarter of a mile before stopping.

He glanced at Reese in the front seat opposite him. "Think we should proceed from here on foot?"

She nodded. "He's probably asleep, but nevertheless, vehicles out here are unusual. He's likely to be suspicious about anything he hears."

Reese turned in the seat to face Bri and Ashley, who sat in the rear. "I'll take point, and when we get there, Nelson will circle around to cover the rear."

Both women nodded.

"You two," Reese said, looking pointedly at Bri, "watch my back. I'll be going through the door first. Questions?"

No one had any.

It took fifteen minutes of scrambling up and over sand dunes and skirting low cranberry bushes and scrub before they reached the vicinity of the shack that had been identified on the archival museum maps as once belonging to Albert Reims, Stanley Morris's wife's ancestor. There were no lights, no vehicle, nothing to indicate that the one-room structure was occupied.

As they approached, Reese directed the small group with hand signals. She counted off five, holding up one finger at a time, indicating to Nelson that they would give him five minutes to get into position on the far side of the shack before moving in. Once he disappeared from sight, she hunkered down, checked her watch, and drew her weapon.

Her mind was not blank, but she had no fixed thoughts. Every sense, however, was completely engaged, on full alert, as she listened for some sound to indicate that they were not alone, looked for some clue that something was not as it should be. All was quiet. Nothing was amiss.

When Reese checked her watch again, exactly five minutes had passed. She held up her left hand, the fingers closed. Behind her, she heard the faintest shifting as Bri and Ashley drew their weapons. Slowly, she extended three fingers, one at a time.

On three, she was up and running.

Reese hit the door with her right foot, her weapon in two hands at shoulder height as she pushed through shouting, "Police!"

There must have been a sensor on the door. The instant it flew open, a blinding light struck her full in the face. She didn't even have time to search for a target through the glare. There was an explosion and an impact to her chest so powerful that her body was blown back through the doorway.

The next thing Reese knew, she was lying on her back, staring into the sky, completely unable to breathe. Her chest was on fire; it felt as if her lungs were exploding. She couldn't move her arms or legs, and when she tried to speak, she couldn't make a sound. The sky tilted, and she finally realized someone was dragging her over the sand. Distantly, over the ringing in her ears, she heard thunder. Incongruously, she wondered if it was going to rain.

Bri's face came into view, white and terrified. Her lips were moving, but Reese couldn't hear anything. Her vision was blurry, and every sensation was eclipsed by searing pain. She was aware of her stomach and chest muscles straining, contracting violently, as she desperately fought for one breath. Suddenly, air blasted into her chest as if a vacuum seal had been released, and she groaned with a combination of relief and agony.

"Reese!" Bri shouted. "Jesus Christ, Reese!"

Reese focused on one thought. Only one. Still struggling for air, she whispered, "Don't…call…Tory."

❖

Tory was awakened by the sound of the front door closing. She blinked, trying to get oriented. Her neck was sore and her back ached. There was a weight against her left side that she realized, after a moment, was Caroline, asleep against her shoulder. A morning news show was playing on the television. *God, we must have fallen asleep with the television on.*

"Reese?" She groggily sat up. Caroline stirred beside her and sat up as well. "Honey? I thought you were going to call?"

"Thought...you might...be asleep," Reese said deliberately as she walked carefully to the breakfast counter and deposited her keys. Bri was behind her, carrying a duffel bag.

"What time is it?" Tory rose, running her hands through her hair. "God, my head is fuzzy."

"A little after eight," Bri replied hoarsely.

Tory stared at the two of them, abruptly wary. Bri was white as a sheet. For some reason, Reese wouldn't look at her. "What's going on?"

Sensing something amiss as well, Caroline moved to Bri's side and threaded her arm around her waist. "You okay, baby?"

"Yeah. Fine." But she trembled as she draped her arm around Caroline's shoulders.

"Where's your shirt?" Tory was increasingly suspicious as she suddenly realized that Reese was wearing only the dark green T-shirt that she often wore beneath her uniform shirt.

"Tory," Reese said gently. "We've all...been up all night. What do you say...we go to bed, and I'll...give you all the details later."

"Fine." There was something wrong, and whatever it was, it needed to be discussed in private. Tory's eyes were riveted on Reese. One thing she was certain of, however, was that something had happened to her lover.

Bri cleared her throat. "I'm going to take Carre home."

"And she's gonna stay with me for a while," Caroline added quickly.

Bri glanced at her in surprise, but said nothing.

"Fine," Tory said again, not looking at them as she walked to Reese and rested a hand lightly on her lover's back. Reese was shaking.

"I'll call in later," Bri said as she and Caroline headed for the door.

Once they were alone, Tory regarded Reese quietly. "You're hurt, aren't you?"

"Just bruises," Reese said as firmly as she could. It hurt to talk, and she was sweating with the effort to keep her voice level.

"How badly?"

"I'll be fine…after I lie down…for a few hours."

"C'mon then. Let's get you upstairs."

In their bedroom, Reese began to slowly undress. Moving methodically, she unbuckled her belt, unzipped her trousers, and let them fall to the floor. She didn't bother removing her briefs. The T-shirt was going to be a challenge. When she tried to raise her arms, she grunted involuntarily at another swift surge of pain.

"Let me do that," Tory said stiffly, her stomach in knots. "Just tell me what happened."

"He was…prepared for us. I took a round, but I…was wearing a vest. I'm okay."

Tory's heart clenched. *I took a round.*

"Just hold still until I get this off." Tory's voice rang hollowly as she focused on her task. When she finally managed to lift the shirt over Reese's head, she drew a sharp breath, shocked at the sight of a fist-sized bruise in the center of her lover's chest. The skin was already darkening to purple, and the area around it was swollen and edematous. "Oh my God."

"Tory—"

"Oh my God, Reese!" Suddenly dizzy, Tory placed both hands on Reese's shoulders. "Why didn't someone call me?"

"I'm okay," Reese insisted, putting her arms around her lover. "C'mon, let's…sit down on the bed."

"Don't you dare patronize me, Reese Conlon." Tory's eyes were blazing. "*Why* didn't someone call me?"

"Because I didn't want…you to be scared," Reese said steadily. *The last thing I wanted was you racing around in the middle of the night, worried about me. Wendy said you should take it easy.* "The vest stopped it. It's just a bruise."

"Have you seen Dan?"

"No. I just wanted…to get home."

"We need to go to the clinic *right now*." Tory stepped away. Her tone was frigid. "You need an EKG and a chest x-ray. For all we know, you could have a cracked sternum or cardiac contusion."

"Tory, please," Reese pleaded. "I just need a little sleep…and so do you. I promise I'll go later if you…still think I should."

"For God's sake, Reese, what were you thinking? Look at you!" For a moment, Tory was too angry and too frightened to think. She knew very well that there was ammunition capable of piercing body armor, and that it was probably only good fortune that Reese hadn't been shot with something that could have penetrated her vest. From the location of the bruise, it would've been fatal. "I can't stand this."

Tory turned away, trembling.

Tenderly, Reese placed her hands on Tory's shoulders and rested her cheek against the top of Tory's head. "It's okay, love. I'm fine. Let's just go to bed. I need to lie down…and I need you beside me."

"Yes, all right." Tory reached up and took one of Reese's hands. She couldn't keep arguing with her when she was hurt. They were both too exhausted.

Together, they walked slowly to the bed and slipped beneath the sheets. Tory settled into a comfortable position and Reese fit her body to her lover's.

"I love you, Tory," Reese murmured, her eyes already closing.

Tory found Reese's hand and enclosed it in her own, drawing it between her breasts. Closing her eyes, she held the heat of Reese's skin against her heart. "I love you, too. You're my life."

❖

Bri kicked the stand down on her bike and settled her right foot on the ground. She turned slightly and looked at Caroline. "My dad is going to be in the office all morning taking care of the paperwork from the…thing…with Morris."

Caroline regarded her steadily, hands still loosely clasping Bri's waist. Bri's blue eyes were almost black, wounded looking. "You don't have to go right back to work, do you?"

"Not till this afternoon."

"Come inside."

Mutely, Bri nodded and dismounted. She followed Caroline into the house and up the stairs to what had once been her own bedroom. She stopped inside the door, suddenly at a loss. "Uh, I should probably take a shower...or something."

"I'll take one with you."

"Okay." Voice eerily flat, Bri had a strange numb feeling, like her insides were frozen. "Sure."

Once in the bathroom, Caroline turned on the shower, and the room filled with the mist of hot steam. They hadn't been naked together since the last time they'd made love, weeks before, and they were both quiet as they undressed.

Bri bent to strip off her briefs, and when she straightened, Caroline stepped close and wrapped her arms around Bri's neck. Caught off guard, Bri moaned faintly, closing her eyes as the heat of Caroline's skin scorched along her body. Breathlessly, she murmured, "You feel so good."

"Mmm," Caroline sighed, resting her cheek on Bri's shoulder. "Are you okay, baby?"

"Yeah, pretty much."

"Are you gonna tell me what happened?"

"Later." Bri palmed Caroline's hips and pulled her tighter. The sweet rush of arousal chased the horror from her consciousness. "I can't think right now."

"Are you sure you want a shower?" Caroline's voice was husky, and her hips had begun a subtle undulation that was totally involuntary. Her nipples tightened as she brushed her breasts lightly against Bri's.

"Oh man," Bri groaned, twitching with urgency. "Let's jump in fast, because I can't wait very long."

Trying to stay joined, they scrambled into the shower and soaped each other quickly in a tangle of arms and legs. They stopped frequently to kiss, their hands hungry—touching, teasing, tormenting. Then, they hurriedly stepped out and grabbed blindly for towels, still exploring one another with their mouths. In another minute, they were in bed.

"I don't want to hurry," Bri gasped. She caught Caroline's hand as it slid down her belly, stopping her. "It's been so long. I want to show you how much I love you."

"I can't do slow right now," Caroline muttered, opening her legs as Bri fit her thigh between them. "I'm already too excited."

"So am I." Bri's lips moved over Caroline's neck, and she braced herself on one arm as she squeezed a stone-hard nipple with her other hand. "I'm so ready it hurts."

"I wanna come." Caroline arched her hips, pressing hard against Bri's thigh.

"Me too." But Bri rolled off her lover, breaking the exquisite contact. She ignored the warning pulsations between her legs, fighting back the urge to orgasm.

Caroline cried out in protest and turned on her side to face Bri. Her pupils were huge, unfocused, hazy with need. "Please, baby."

Bri stroked a finger down Caroline's cheek. "Let's hold on… as long as we can."

"I can't," Caroline pleaded, her lids flickering as her breasts heaved with each erratic breath.

"Kiss me for a while," Bri urged as she brought her mouth to Caroline's. The heat sent a jolt of pleasure down Bri's spine, and her hips jerked in response. She grunted in surprise as her clitoris stiffened further, aching for release. She was in danger of climaxing without being touched, and she struggled to hold back.

Caroline was whimpering steadily, writhing against Bri frantically as they drank one another's passion. Abruptly, Caroline pulled her head away and grabbed Bri's hand, forcing it between her legs. "I have to. Oh, I have to."

"I love you, babe," Bri cried as Caroline thrust against her palm, hot and hard and wet. Bri kept her eyes open through sheer force of will, watching in wonder as Caroline's face dissolved into orgasm. Her own head was spinning, the muscles in her stomach and thighs clenched tight, her clitoris pounding.

"Oh, I'm coming," Caroline cried.

"Yes, yes," Bri whispered urgently, pressing hard with the heel of her hand as she slid her fingers into Caroline's depths.

Caroline cried out again, and her head snapped back, her body jerking. Bri stroked her lover through her climax, then stayed inside her, thrusting gently as the internal spasms gradually abated. Eventually, Caroline quieted in Bri's embrace, her head tucked into the crook of Bri's neck.

"Oh my God," Caroline murmured. "You're so good."

"I love you so much." Bri's voice was choked and rough.

"Good." Caroline was barely moving, almost stuporous in the aftermath of her orgasm. "Did you come?"

"No."

Caroline tilted her head back, her eyes cloudy and her lips smiling softly. "Playing hard to get?"

"I wanted to watch you."

"Wanna now?"

"Oh man, yeah." Bri moaned, shivering as Caroline licked her neck.

Laughing softly, Caroline slid her fingers between Bri's thighs, gliding under and around and over the blood-engorged tissues. "You're so hard."

Bri couldn't speak. She couldn't even breathe. Every sinew and cell was poised to explode. When Caroline touched her in just the right place, with just the right pressure, as only she could do, Bri gave one hoarse shout and came. The near-crippling waves of pleasure seemed endless, and by the time she could think again, her body was slick with sweat and her face wet with tears.

"Oh baby," Caroline crooned, pressing Bri's face to her breasts. "It's okay. It's okay."

"I was so scared," Bri whispered. "I was so scared."

Caroline wasn't sure what she was talking about, but she could feel Bri tremble, and that was enough to scare *her*. She held her lover as tightly as she could. "Everything is going to be okay."

Bri was lost. The orgasm had stripped her defenses bare. The long weeks of loneliness when she'd feared she'd lost Caroline, and the terror of seeing Reese on the ground with a hole in the center of her chest, came crashing in on her. She sobbed helplessly.

With no idea what to do, Caroline did the only thing she could. She stroked Bri's hair and face, kissed her forehead, wrapped her arms and legs around her so that every inch of their bodies touched. If she could have taken Bri inside her and sheltered her from the pain, she would have. Her own heart ached to the point of breaking, and her tears fell on Bri's tightly closed eyelids. "I love you, I love you," she said over and over and over.

Eventually, Bri quieted and managed a long shaky breath. "Sorry."

"S'okay."

"The fucker had the whole place rigged," Bri said, keeping her cheek pressed to Caroline's breast. The steady thud of her lover's heart was comforting. "Motion detectors, light sensors, infrared cameras—the whole works. Fucking paranoid nut case."

"What happened?" Caroline asked gently as Bri faltered.

"It happened so fast. So fast." Bri shuddered. "One second I was running, and the next thing I knew, there was a shot—Christ, it sounded like a cannon—and Reese came flying back through the doorway. Her body hit me and knocked me down."

Caroline bit her lip to stop her cry of horror. Bri needed to talk, and she didn't want to do anything to stop her.

"I thought she was dead, Carre," Bri whispered, the anguish raw in her voice. "She wasn't moving, and there was a hole right in the middle of her shirt. I thought for a second she was dead."

"I'm so sorry, baby." Caroline ran her fingers through Bri's hair, petting her.

"I couldn't think. I froze. I fucked up."

"No," Caroline said with certainty. "Just tell me what happened."

Bri pulled far enough away to be able to meet Caroline's eyes. "I forgot all about the guy still inside the building. All I could think about was Reese. Ashley shot Morris as he was coming through the door with a fucking automatic in his hands. If she hadn't been there, he would've killed me *and* Reese."

Caroline's heart almost stopped beating then, and everything inside her turned to ice. It was too much for her to let in—the terror Bri must've felt, the chaos and confusion, the single second that could have changed her future had it turned out differently. "Oh Jesus."

"I blew it, babe," Bri said miserably.

"Oh, baby, you don't know that." Caroline forced herself to concentrate on Bri. "If Ashley had been the one right behind Reese, *she* might have been the one caught off guard. And *you* might have been the one to shoot him."

"Maybe," Bri said dubiously.

"Is he dead?"

"Yeah."

"And Ashley and your dad are all right?"

Bri nodded again.

"Reese will be okay, too, right?"

"She'll be hurting for a few days, but she says it's not serious."

"Then everything turned out fine." Caroline felt Bri stiffen and try to move away, but she pulled her close again. "What did Reese say?"

"She said I did good," Bri acknowledged reluctantly.

"Then believe her, because I know she wouldn't lie to you. No matter what."

Bri sighed and closed her eyes. "I'm so tired, babe."

Caroline shifted a little and settled Bri against her side, cradling Bri's head against her breast. Most of the time Bri held *her* while they slept, and it felt so special to hold her protectively now. "I love you, baby. Go to sleep now."

❖

When Reese awoke, it was night. Tory lay close to her, her hand resting on Reese's hip. Slowly, Reese drew a deep breath. It hurt, but she could manage it.

"How do you feel?" Tory asked from out of the dark.

"Sore, but nothing feels broken."

"I've been lying here listening to you breathe. You sound okay."

"I can't believe I slept more than twelve hours."

"You needed it." Tory softly stroked the length of Reese's thigh. The silence stretched between them. "I know you were trying to protect me."

"Yes." Reese found Tory's hand and linked their fingers. "Are you still angry?"

"Mostly still scared."

With effort, Reese rolled onto her side, ignoring the shaft of pain that started in her breastbone and penetrated through to her back. In the pale moonlight, she could just make out Tory's face, luminous in the silvery shadows. "I told you I wouldn't take any chances, and I didn't. I wore the vest."

"I know," Tory whispered. "And we both know if it had been a few inches higher, it could've been your throat."

"Tor—"

"It's okay, sweetheart. It didn't happen, and I know you'll be careful." Tory raised their joined hands and kissed the top of Reese's. "It's just that sometimes, especially when you're hurt, I get scared."

"Oh, love." Reese sighed, moving closer until she could put her arm around Tory. "I'm sorry."

"It's just that I love you so much," Tory murmured. She kissed her with the gentle, tentative touch of a first kiss, amazed at how precious their love still felt.

When they drew apart, Reese sighed again, this time with pleasure. "You do the most amazing things to me."

Softly, Tory laughed. "I can't believe you're still saying that. I'm so big I can barely reach you."

"You don't have to touch me." Reese was absolutely serious. "All I have to do is look at you."

Tory gasped, taken aback as always by the depth of Reese's devotion. "You, Reese Conlon, are a heart-stopper."

"Yeah?"

"Yeah. And the sexiest woman I've ever met."

"Glad to hear it," Reese murmured. "Because I'm afraid your future opportunities in that area will be severely limited."

"I'm quite sure you'll be able to keep me occupied indefinitely." After a second, Tory was more serious. "Can you tell me about it now?"

"Tor," Reese said tenderly. "You might not want—"

"I want, sweetheart. Knowing is always better than wondering."

After another kiss, Reese outlined the morning's events. She spoke concisely, as if she was giving a report, until she reached the point where she went through the door. Then her tone grew guarded.

"When I was first hit, I wasn't entirely certain what had happened..." Reese's voice trailed off, and for the first time, she considered her words before speaking.

"Go ahead, sweetheart," Tory said gently. "I'm okay."

"I couldn't move, and I couldn't get a breath, and I wasn't sure how badly I was hit."

Tory struggled to keep her voice even. "Were you frightened?"

"Not for me, so much. I was worried about Bri, because I couldn't see her. I was worried about you, because..."

"Because?"

"I didn't want to leave you alone." Reese sensed Tory tremble and moved closer to her. "You know I never would, right?"

"I know that," Tory whispered, blinking back tears that she didn't want Reese to see.

Reese drew a breath and winced at another surge of pain.

"Are you all right?"

"Yeah," Reese grunted. "I just have to breathe easy. When I finally realized I was pretty much okay, the only thing I could think of was that I didn't want an officer showing up at our door, because I knew what you would think."

"If you're hurt," Tory said firmly, "I want to know about it."

"I don't want anything to upset you. Not now." Reese was adamant. "I just want us to get through the next few months, and for you and the baby to be all right."

"We will be," Tory assured her, then kissed Reese again. "I promise, sweetheart."

As Reese sighed and closed her eyes, Tory desperately hoped that she could keep her promise.

## CHAPTER TWENTY-THREE

### July, Provincetown, MA

"I don't think spending the evening in town is exactly what Wendy meant by bed rest." Reese was in uniform, having stopped home in the middle of a Saturday, ostensibly for lunch. Mostly, she'd wanted to see how Tory was doing with her new routine.

"She didn't say *strict* bed rest," Tory pointed out irritably. She got up from the couch with some difficulty and started to pace. "She didn't even say *bed rest*. What she said was 'rest at home.'"

"I know what she said." Reese leaned against the counter and tried not to raise her voice. "She said your blood pressure had edged up another five points, and it was time for you to cut back on *everything*."

"I stopped training last month. Now I've agreed not to work for the rest of my term. I can't be any more sedentary without risking a psychotic break." Tory ran her hands through her hair and strode to the glass doors overlooking the deck, her back to Reese. "You should know I wouldn't do anything dangerous."

Reese considered how far she could push. The visit to the obstetrician two days before had scared the hell out of her. Wendy had as much as said that as soon as there were clear signs of fetal maturity, Tory would need to be sectioned. There were traces of protein in her urine now. The preeclampsia was worsening, and they couldn't wait for the full term.

Reese felt as if she was living with a ticking bomb. And she knew that her anxiety was probably making Tory crazier than the forced inactivity. Sighing, she crossed the room and rested her hands lightly on Tory's shoulders.

"I know you won't take chances. I'm sorry." Reese rubbed her cheek against Tory's hair, then kissed her temple. "It's going to be a madhouse with the fireworks at the monument tonight."

Tory reached up and covered Reese's hands with her own. With a sigh, she leaned back into her lover's solid presence. "I know this waiting is as hard on you as it is on me. I'm sorry I get difficult sometimes."

"No," Reese whispered, closing her eyes and breathing in the scent of Tory's hair. For a minute, she forgot everything. "You're not difficult. You're beautiful."

"I feel fine, sweetheart." Tory went on quietly, watching the sailboats in the harbor glide by, thinking how much she missed being out on the water. "Since I haven't been going to work this past week, my pressure is steady. I don't have any progression of my symptoms. Let's just go out tonight, okay? I promise just for a little while."

"Sure." Reese wrapped her arms around her lover from behind.

"Cath and crew will be here tomorrow. I promise I'll let you do all the shopping *and* the barbequing."

"Now *there's* a deal." Reese laughed.

Tory turned and put her arms around Reese's neck. Heavy now with child, she found it difficult to get as close as she wanted. "It's Saturday night—date night. I want to do something fun with you."

"I know it's been tough lately," Reese said softly. The bruise on her chest had finally faded. She had hoped that the last of Tory's fears had disappeared along with it, but she wasn't sure if it was the awkwardness of pregnancy or the lingering worry for Reese's safety that was keeping Tory up at night. But she knew that her lover wasn't sleeping well. "I'm really happy about the baby, Tory. And I love you so much."

"You always know what to say, don't you, Sheriff?" Tory's eyes darkened, and she pressed closer. Voice husky, she murmured, "Do you think sex counts as bed rest?"

"I think it might fall under the vigorous exercise category," Reese answered, her lips against Tory's neck. "But let's try it at bedtime, nice and easy. Okay?"

"I was thinking *now*, and a little more along the lines of wild and crazy."

Reese kissed her, lingering on her mouth, softly caressing her breasts and belly. Tory's heart beat hard against her palm, and then the baby kicked beneath her fingers. The love was so precious, so profound, that when she drew away, her heart actually ached.

"I'm going into work for a little while more, because I can't trust myself around you. Will you promise to take a nap?"

"Yes," Tory whispered, and then she raised her head for another kiss. She didn't let Reese go until she'd drawn a groan from her. "That's better."

"For *you* maybe," Reese gasped. "But I'm going to suffer all afternoon."

Tory smiled and ran her hand down the center of Reese's chest. "Just remember, sweetheart, I've got the cure."

Laughing, Reese stepped away, collected her keys, settled her hat low over her eyes, and headed for the door.

Once Reese had departed, Tory stretched out on the couch with a sigh and put her feet up. She hated to admit how tired she was, even to herself. Within minutes, she was asleep.

❖

Reese slid in behind the wheel, started the engine, and pulled out of the department parking lot. Glancing at Bri, she asked, "Are you and Caroline pretty much settled in the new place?"

Bri grinned. "Other than the fact that we don't have any furniture, we're doing fine."

"You two need anything? Because, you know, Tory and I can help out with—"

"No, we're okay, but thanks. My dad has a bunch of extra stuff he said we could take."

Reese nodded as she turned left onto Bradford and headed toward the east end of town for the first part of the tour. "Good."

She hesitated just a second. "I'm glad to see that you two are doing okay."

"Not as glad as me," Bri said with conviction. "Now that I'm working, I think that the two years until Carre can move back will go really fast."

"So, you're all right with Paris?"

"It still...scares me some. But I love her." Bri shrugged and blushed. "And I know she loves me."

"You must be really proud of her."

"Yeah, I am," Bri said, meaning it.

Reese watched the road while simultaneously scanning passing cars, checking out the yards that they passed, and looking over the pedestrians who crowded the sidewalks. Quietly, she said, "I'm proud of *you*, Bri."

"You are?"

"You made a tough decision when you left school, and you saw it through. You're a fine officer."

"I messed up a few things." Bri's voice was pitched low as she stared straight ahead. "With Carre." She took a breath and turned to Reese. "Out there in the dunes that morning with Morris, too."

"No," Reese said steadily, looking quickly at Bri, meeting her eyes with absolute certainty. "You made some mistakes with Caroline, but you owned up to them, and you worked it out. As far as Morris is concerned, you took care of your wounded. You trusted your partner to cover your back, and Ashley came through. You both did fine."

"Thanks," Bri whispered.

"Have you heard from Ashley or Allie?"

"I talked to Ashley the day the final report on the shooting was filed. She said she was headed back to Rhode Island." Bri grinned. "She also said she expected to be around a fair amount this summer, because Allie is going to be assigned permanently in Wellfleet."

"Huh. Guess that worked out too, then." Reese pulled to the curb and rolled down her window. "Ma'am. You can't leave your car there. You're in a yellow zone and the sightseeing trolley won't be able to get by. There's a public parking area a quarter mile down Commercial Street on your left."

Reese waited until the tourist had dutifully pulled away, then eased back into traffic. "As I was saying, I guess everything tur—"

The radio crackled to life, and Gladys's voice filled the car. "Reese?"

"Go ahead."

"There's an emergency call for you. It's Tory."

"Patch her through to my cell phone." Reese braked sharply, pulled off the road, and snatched the mobile from her belt. It rang an instant later, and she snapped it open. "Tor?"

"I just called the paramedics," Tory reported, her voice tight. "I'm having some bleeding."

"I'll be right there." Reese jammed the phone back onto her belt, flicked on the lights and siren, and slammed her foot down on the gas pedal.

When Reese careened into her driveway, the EMS van was already there. She swerved around it, jammed on the brakes, and jumped from the cruiser. As she ran toward the stairs, she yelled back to Bri.

"Call Tory's sister. The number's on my rolodex at the station."

The door to the living room was open, and as she pushed through, the paramedics were just strapping Tory onto a stretcher. Just seeing Tory like that made Reese's stomach twist, and for one terrible second, she thought she might be ill. Then, Tory turned her head, their eyes met, and everything inside of Reese settled.

"Hey, love," Reese said gently as she crossed quickly to her lover's side, reaching for the hand that Tory extended. "How are you feeling?"

"You need to call Wendy," Tory said urgently, unable to keep the anxiety from her voice. "She's going to need to talk to whoever is on call in Hyannis, because I can't make it to Boston."

"I'll do that while we're en route." Reese walked alongside the stretcher as the two men in the blue paramedic jump suits maneuvered it through the door and outside. "But you need to tell me what's going on so I can tell *her*."

Tory bit her lip and squeezed Reese's hand so hard that the band on Reese's ring finger pressed painfully into the bone.

"Tor?" Reese unsuccessfully tried to keep the panic from her voice. "Baby? What is it?"

"I'm having...some pain."

Tory's face was white and her skin clammy.

Reese looked at the two men. "I think we need to hurry here."

"Don't worry," one of them grunted as he pulled open the back of the ambulance. "We'll be flying in just a minute."

Reese punched in Wendy's number as the two men engaged the hydraulic lifts on the stretcher, raised it up, and then slid it into the back of the van. She was forced to leave a message when she couldn't get through to the obstetrician's office.

Once the EMTs had Tory secured inside the van, the older of the pair climbed out and ran around to the driver's compartment. Reese knelt by Tory's side on the corrugated floor, one hand cradling Tory's head and the other gripping her hand. Within seconds, they were rocketing east on Route 6.

"Put the fetal heart monitor on now," Tory instructed the EMT.

"Let me get you lined up first," he said calmly.

"Check the baby's heart rate *first*." Her tone left no room for discussion.

"Sure, Doc. Just try to relax, okay?"

"Hurry," Tory gasped as another wave of pain began. "Then call ahead and tell them...you have an abruption coming in."

The EMT hesitated, his expression darkening. "You sure?"

Tory gritted her teeth and sweat broke out on her forehead. Finally, when the cramp passed, she gasped, "Yes."

"Tory..." Reese was frantic. "What's happening?"

"I—" Tory clenched her jaws as another wave of pain coursed through her abdomen. "I think the placenta is separating from the uterine wall. That's what's causing the bleeding."

Neither of them spoke for a moment as the EMT situated the external fetal heart monitor. The seconds it took for him to get a reading seemed endless. "Heart rate's normal."

"Watch it carefully for decelerations," Tory instructed as she drew a shaky breath. She looked into Reese's eyes. "They're probably going to have to section me quickly, especially if the baby's heart rate drops."

"Can we wait for Wendy?"

Tory shook her head. "We could try to wait, but there's a danger for the baby if the hemorrhage worsens."

"What about you?" Reese whispered, her insides so tight she could barely breathe. *It's you, Tory. Only you. You're my heart. My soul.*

"I'll be okay."

The EMT hung an IV bag and connected it to the intravenous catheter he had previously inserted into Tory's forearm. Then he pumped up the blood pressure cuff on her left arm and checked another reading. "Your pressure's through the roof, Doc. I'm gonna call for instructions to treat you."

"You can't lower my pressure very much," Tory objected. "Hypotension will decrease the blood flow to the baby. We can't risk that now."

"We can't chance you stroking out either," he said bluntly as he reached for the mike. "You need meds."

As he rapidly relayed Tory's vital signs and medical situation to whoever was monitoring at the base station in the hospital, Reese rested her forehead against Tory's. Quietly, she murmured, "Tor, we can't risk something happening to you."

"We have to do what's best for the baby." Tory placed her palm against Reese's cheek. "Trust me."

Reese had never been so scared in her life. She had to rely on what Tory was telling her, because she didn't understand what was happening. Still, she had a terrible feeling that Tory's only concern was the baby, and Reese was terrified for them both.

"They've called the OB guy to come in," the EMT reported as he pulled a syringe and medication vial from the red tackle box that contained his emergency drugs.

"What is that?" Tory asked.

"Mag sulfate."

"What's it for?" Reese felt as if she was in the dark on an unknown battlefield.

The EMT hung the drip. "Helps prevent seizures from the hypertension and premature labor."

*Seizures. Jesus Christ.* Reese thought her head might explode. "What about her blood pressure?"

"As soon as I get this drip going," he said calmly, "I'll give her a dose of nifedipine. That should take the edge off."

"No," Tory said forcefully. "Not until we're in the emergency room. If my pressure drops and the baby becomes hypoxic, we need someone who can section me stat."

"You're still bleeding at a pretty good rate." He regarded her solemnly. "That might settle down some if your blood pressure were a little lower."

"We'll be there soon, won't we?" Tory's face tightened at yet another surge of pain.

"ETA six minutes."

"Then we wait."

Tory closed her eyes, attempting to gather her strength.

Reese lifted her lover's hand to her lips and held a kiss against the pale skin. The only comfort she could find in the nightmare world of the rocking van was the steady, rapid beat of the fetal heart monitor.

❖

The instant the EMTs shoved the stretcher through the double doors into the emergency room, both men started shouting. Reese was so busy keeping pace with the stretcher and holding on to Tory that she could only catch snippets of what they were saying.

"…placental abruption…"

"…hemorrhage…"

"…hypertension…"

"…thirty-three weeks…"

"…OB stat…"

A tall, thin balding man in a white coat approached on the run. "I'm Dr. Saunders, the emergency room physician. I called the OB attending. He should be here in forty-five minutes."

"That might be too long," Tory gasped. "Is there an OB resident in the house?"

"A second-year," the ER physician advised. "Not senior enough for what you need. I consulted the in-house general surgeon, just in case."

"I'm expecting her obstetrician to call any second," Reese stated as several nurses assisted the EMTs in moving Tory to a gurney. "When I tried to reach her earlier, I got her service."

"Fine," Dr. Saunders said distractedly as he instructed one of the nurses to draw blood for a type and crossmatch. He turned to another ER tech. "Alert the operating room to prepare for an emergency Caesarean section. And call in the pediatric intensivist from home. Tell her it's a high-risk delivery."

"What have we got?" a deep voice questioned from behind Reese.

Reese turned as K.T. O'Bannon's dark eyes fell on Tory. There was a flicker of recognition, and then something far more personal flashed in the surgeon's face before the impenetrable professional mask returned. Reese experienced an instant surge of relief. K.T. wouldn't let anything happen to Tory—she still loved her.

"She's bleeding," Reese murmured quietly, almost choking on the words.

K.T. nodded to Reese, then leaned over the bed and briefly ran her fingers over Tory's cheek. Gently, she said, "Hi, Vic. I thought it had to be you when I heard that a pregnant doctor was coming in. I always seem to be on call when you roll in."

"Just your luck," Tory whispered.

"What's the situation?"

"I think I'm getting ready to deliver this baby," Tory gasped, her green eyes almost all pupil, her brow running with sweat. "I'm bleeding pretty rapidly."

"Pressure's up there too," K.T. murmured as she quickly scanned the monitors surrounding the bed. She glanced at the OB resident, a freckle-faced, blond-haired boy who looked to be about fifteen, as he hurried up to the bedside. "Can you give me a status check on the baby?"

With a surprising degree of aplomb, the young man dragged over a portable ultrasound, checked the monitors, and did a quick evaluation. "Can't tell the extent of the abruption. Fetal heart rate's good with no dips, though. And there's movement."

Reese rapidly searched the faces clustered around Tory, frantically trying to decipher the medical shorthand. "What does that *mean*?"

"It means the baby's alive," the resident said flatly.

Reese felt as if she'd been shot...again. It took her a second to get her breath. "You mean there's a chance she might *not* be?"

"With a moderate to severe placental abruption, the fetal mortality rate is very high," the resident dutifully reported.

"Christ, will you shut up," K.T. snapped. "All I want *you* to do is stand here and monitor the baby. If you see a problem, tell me. Otherwise, I don't want to hear *anything* from you."

Purposefully, she turned partly away from him and looked steadily into Reese's eyes. "The baby's fine. The baby's going to *be* fine as long as we keep a careful watch on things."

"What about Tory?" Reese clutched the bed rail so hard her fingers ached. In a strangled voice, she repeated desperately, "K.T., what about Tory?"

"I'm not going to let anything happen to Tory." K.T. angled back to Tory. "First, we need to get you hydrated, and then we'll control your pressure a little bit better. We may not be able to wait for a phone consultation with Wendy. You ready for that?"

"Yes," Tory said tersely. "I'm having regular contractions, and I'm still bleeding." She struggled with pain and fatigue and fear. She took a deep, calming breath. "K.T....can you do this?"

"Of course I can," K.T. said with absolute certainty. She tilted her chin toward the OB resident. "I'll bring Junior here along for backup."

"Then go ahead." Tory closed her eyes.

"I won't let you down, Vic," K.T. murmured. Then she gestured to Reese. "I need to speak with you over here."

Reluctantly, Reese released Tory's hand, stepped away from the stretcher, and followed.

"I have to take Tory to the operating room very soon," K.T. said. "She could start bleeding more heavily at any minute, and that's not only a risk to *her* life, but also to the baby's."

"Okay," Reese said hoarsely. "Whatever you need to do."

K.T. nodded. "Good. I'll need you to sign the consents."

Reese put a hand on K.T.'s forearm. "If something happens... if you have to...make a choice between them..." Reese faltered, then said steadily, "I want you—"

"Save it, Sheriff," K.T. interrupted curtly. "That's not a choice you're going to have to make. I don't plan on losing either one of them."

Reese believed K.T. because she had to. Because any other possibility was unthinkable. She walked on wooden legs back to Tory's side and gently enfolded her hand again.

"I love you, Tory."

Tory's lids fluttered open. She smiled softly. "You've given me everything I've ever wanted, sweetheart. If...if I—"

"Don't." Reese stopped her with a kiss. When she drew back, her blue eyes were calm. "We're not saying goodbye. Not now. Not ever."

"I lov—"

"We've got a dip in the fetal heart rate," the OB resident called out.

"That's it," K.T. said firmly, grasping the bottom of the stretcher and propelling it out of the small cubicle as the resident grabbed hold of the other end. "Let's move, everybody."

Reese ran beside the gurney, trying to hold Tory's gaze. Her lover's eyes were clouded with pain and worry. The elevator doors slid open, most of the people piled on along with the stretcher, and Reese was forced to step back.

When the doors closed with a quiet swoosh, she was left alone in the suddenly still hallway. She had never felt so empty in her life.

## CHAPTER TWENTY-FOUR

K ate stood in the doorway of a small waiting room down the hall from two windowless, gray metal doors marked with a red sign that proclaimed *No Admittance—Labor and Delivery.* The beige-carpeted floor, framed prints on the wall, and shaded lamps on matching end tables were a well-meant but unsuccessful attempt to make the space appear less institutional. Her daughter was the only person there.

Reese sat with her head down, elbows on her knees, fingers laced behind her neck. She was still in uniform, but her bowed figure held none of the command presence she usually projected.

"Reese?" Kate said softly as she approached. "Honey?"

"Mom?" Reese looked up, her eyes hollow pits of pain.

"Any news?" Kate slid onto the vinyl sofa beside her daughter and put an arm around her waist. "They told me downstairs that Tory was in delivery."

Reese shook her head. When she spoke her voice was rusty, as if she hadn't used it in a long time. "What are you doing here?"

"Bri brought me. She and Caroline are outside in the hall. It helps to know a cop. Bri put the siren on."

"I'm glad you're here," Reese whispered. "I...I don't know what to do."

"What happened?" Kate pulled her daughter close, aware that Reese was shaking.

"Christ, I don't *know*," Reese said desperately, running both hands through her hair. "It all happened so fast. One minute, she was fine. Earlier, we were joking about making love..." She closed her eyes and groaned. "Jesus, what if..."

"Reese!" Kate's tone would have snapped a seasoned veteran to attention. "Let's deal with what we know."

"Yes," Reese said dully. "Okay. Right." Briefly, she recounted the whirlwind events, then glanced toward the empty doorway. "They've been in there half an hour. Shouldn't they…shouldn't something have happened by now?"

"I'm sure they're all busy, honey." Kate's voice was gentle now as she slowly rubbed her hand up and down Reese's back. "It doesn't mean a thing."

Reese met her mother's gaze. "I don't want Tory to die. I don't care about anything else—God, not even…" Her voice broke, eyes flooding with tears. "She'd hate me if she knew."

"No, honey, she wouldn't. Tory would understand. I know she loves you that much, too."

"But *she's* all I can think about—"

"It's natural for you to fear for your lover's life. There's nothing to feel badly about."

"I understand now what you must have gone through when you left," Reese said softly.

Kate drew a swift breath. "Oh, Reese, sweetheart. Thank you."

Smiling faintly, Reese cleared her throat and made an effort to focus. "Did you say Bri was here?"

"Just outside with her girlfriend." Kate stood. "Shall I get them?"

"Yes, please. Where's Jean?"

"On her way—she was in Orleans. I reached her on her cell phone. Tory's sister Cath is flying in, too." Kate turned toward the door. "I'm going to call Jean again. I won't be far."

"Good."

A minute later, Bri and Caroline entered.

"Hey," Bri said quietly, stopping a few feet from Reese, her hands in her pockets.

Caroline leaned down, kissed Reese on the cheek, then settled close to her on the couch. She rested one small hand lightly on Reese's forearm. "Any word on Tory and the baby?"

"Not yet."

When Caroline linked her fingers through Reese's, Reese held on gratefully, then met Bri's eyes. The young officer looked worried but steady, and Reese found her familiar presence a comfort. "Who's working?"

"I called Dad. He said not to worry, it's covered."

"Thanks for contacting everyone."

"No problem." Bri didn't know what the hell else to say. It made her insides turn to water to see Reese looking so scared and trying to pretend she wasn't.

Caroline must have seen the edge of panic in Bri's expression, because she held out her other hand. "Sit down, baby."

Bri reached for Caroline and did as she was told. The three of them were sitting pressed together in silence when K.T. appeared in the doorway.

"Reese." Bri noticed the surgeon first and urgently pointed.

Reese jumped to her feet and rushed across the room. The surgeon murmured something and Reese sagged, then steadied herself with a hand against the doorjamb. After a second's hesitation, K.T. put a hand on the back of Reese's neck, leaned close, and spoke into her ear. Reese nodded, squared her shoulders, and disappeared around the corner.

"Oh fuck." Bri stared at Caroline. Her voice was high and tight. "What do you think is going on?"

"It will be okay, baby," Caroline said gently, putting an arm around Bri's waist. She kissed her temple. "Nothing will happen to Tory."

Bri closed her eyes and leaned into Caroline's certain strength. "I'm so glad you're here," she whispered.

"Me, too." *And I always will be.*

❖

Tory was the only patient in the small recovery room. Reese stepped inside, a yellow cotton cover gown over her uniform, and swallowed hard when she saw how pale and still her lover appeared. Slowly, she crossed the green tiled floor to the side of the steel-enclosed bed, reached over the rail, and lifted Tory's left hand in her palm.

"Tor?" she whispered softly.

Tory moaned faintly and opened her eyes with effort. Her pupils were dilated and unfocused.

"Re...Reese?"

With her free hand, Reese smoothed Tory's damp hair gently back from her forehead. "We have a baby daughter." Reese managed a smile. "K.T. says everything went fine."

*Tory and the baby are stable. Tory bled heavily but the hemorrhage has stopped for now. If we can keep her pressure down, she might make it without a transfusion. The baby was a little slow to breathe, but she seems okay now. The neonatologist is evaluating her.*

"What...was...her...Apgar?"

"I don't know what that is, love." Reese stroked Tory's cheek. "You just rest, okay?"

"Have you...seen her?"

"Not yet. The pediatrician has her right now."

Tory blinked, and her eyes seemed clearer. "Can you get me some water?"

"I'll ask one of the nurses." Reese started to move, and Tory tightened her grip on Reese's hand.

"No. Not yet. Just stay here. Tell me about...our baby."

"I'm going to go see her in a few minutes. The doctors have to check her out first." Reese leaned over and kissed Tory's forehead. "You did great, Tor."

"Might have been better...if I'd waited a bit longer," Tory said with a weak smile. "Maybe...next time...I'll do better."

Reese's heart lurched. *Oh no. Never. I'm not risking you ever again.*

"You okay, sweetheart?"

"Yeah." Reese's voice was husky. "Fine."

A nurse approached with a practiced smile. "I'm sorry. Dr. King needs some rest. You can come back in a little while."

"All right," Reese replied, although she made no move to leave. She was uncertain if she would be able to force herself away from Tory's side. She wasn't yet convinced that something wasn't going to happen to take her away. "You'll be okay?"

Tory smiled again and squeezed Reese's hand harder. "I'll be fine. Go see our daughter...come back...and tell me."

"I love you," Reese whispered.

"Love you, too." Tory barely got the words out as she closed her eyes.

❖

In yet another sterile anteroom, Reese scrubbed her hands and donned a green gown. This time when she stepped into the neonatal intensive care unit, she stopped in shock and not a little bit of trepidation. There were as many nurses as bassinets in the crowded room, along with a mountain of blinking machines and beeping monitors. It was intimidating in the extreme.

"Can I help you with something?" A dark haired, middle-aged nurse in pale blue scrubs sounded just a bit suspicious.

"I'm looking for...uh...baby...uh...baby girl King."

"And you are?"

From behind them, a deep alto voice answered, "The other mother."

"Oh," the nurse exclaimed brightly, her smile genuine. "She's in the isolation room with Dr. Newman."

"The isolation room?" Reese repeated. Now the knots in her stomach tied themselves into yet another configuration. *What now?*

K.T. put her hand on Reese's shoulder. "It's standard, especially with a baby this small. Come on. I'll take you back...unless you don't want me to."

Reese met K.T.'s eyes. "I owe you. And I think Tory would like you to see the baby."

K.T. blushed, an almost reportable event where she was concerned. When she spoke, her voice was low and thick. "I'd like that. I was too busy earlier to do more than hand her off."

A minute later, the two of them stared wordlessly into the heated, plastic-enclosed bassinette at the tiny red face, nearly obscured by the small knit cap on her egg-sized head and the cotton receiving blanket dwarfing her miniature body. An IV ran into her impossibly small foot, which was taped to a wooden tongue blade no bigger than a Popsicle stick for support.

Reese blinked and then unself-consciously wiped at the tears that suddenly appeared on her cheeks. "She's beautiful."

"Yes. She is." K.T. cleared her throat. "I'll check with the pediatrician and give you an update in a minute or two. Congratulations, Reese."

"Thanks," Reese said, her eyes still fixed on the baby. When she looked up, K.T. was gone.

❖

Upon awakening, Tory was immediately aware of the sharp pain in her abdomen. She drew a surprised breath. Then she remembered. *C-section. Incisional pain. Okay. Not too bad.*

She opened her eyes. Reese was in a chair by her bedside, her head back, eyes closed. There were circles under those eyes. She wore jeans and a scrub shirt. She was gorgeous.

"Sweetheart?"

Reese jumped, her lids flew open, and she blinked. Then she grinned—a blazing smile that set every worry in Tory's mind at ease.

"Is she all right?"

"She's great," Reese exclaimed, sitting forward and taking Tory's hand. "She weighs almost four pounds. The doctor says her lungs are mature, and she's absolutely perfect."

Tory bit her lip, but she couldn't stop the tears.

Reese eased onto the edge of the bed and put her arm behind her lover's shoulders. She kissed Tory's forehead, her eyes, her lips. When she drew back, she murmured, "You want to go see her?"

"God, yes."

Reese rang the bedside bell and when a nurse appeared, she asked for a wheelchair. Very carefully, the two of them helped Tory from the bed into the chair.

"Ready?" Reese leaned down and smiled at Tory.

"Let's go lights and siren for this trip, Sheriff."

Reese laughed. "Anything you say, Dr. King."

❖

Reese squatted on her heels, scarcely breathing. There were some things so beautiful they hurt to look at. Tory's face as she gazed at the baby in her arms was one of them.

When Tory finally raised her head, her eyes were filled with wonder. She reached out her free hand and stroked Reese's cheek. "Can you believe it?"

"No," Reese whispered. She edged closer, resting one hand on the baby's back as Tory cradled her. "I can't. If I look at her too long, I'm afraid something is going to explode inside of me, the feelings get so big."

Tory brushed her fingers through Reese's hair. "I love you so much."

At that moment, the infant's eyes, unfocused but a brilliant blue, opened wide.

Tory stroked the baby's cheek. "Hello, Regina."

"Hey, Reggie." Reese grinned large.

## EPILOGUE

### August, Provincetown, MA

Nelson looked up as the door opened, then frowned in surprise. "What are you doing here?"

"Chief?" Reese appeared equally confused.

"I thought you were going to get the baby."

"Oh!" Reese couldn't suppress a big smile. "We are. But they aren't signing her out until after morning rounds, so I've got a few hours."

"Jesus, Conlon, you don't have to come to work *every* day, you know." He shook his head in mock disgust, but he was smiling, too.

"Well, Tory and my mom are out getting last-minute baby things, so I didn't have anything to do anyhow." She tossed her hat on her desk. "Bri around?"

He hesitated. "Took Caroline to the airport."

"Right," Reese said quietly. "She leaves—what? For Boston now, then tonight for France?"

"Uh-huh." He cleared his throat. "I already said my goodbyes early this morning. Hate to watch the plane take off."

"You think I have time to catch them?" Reese checked her watch. "Things have been so busy since Reggie was born, I completely forgot Caroline was leaving so soon. What with Tory needing to be at the hospital so much of the time, and then the pediatrician telling us that the baby was going to be able to come home two weeks sooner than we thought, I lost track of which end was up."

Nelson snorted. "You have no idea how bad it's going to get. For *years*."

"Well, Bri sure was worth it."

"Yeah," he said softly. "She was." He looked at the clock. "You should make it if you use the siren."

"I'll call in later." She grabbed her hat and darted out.

❖

Reese pulled her cruiser into the tiny airport parking lot beside Tory's Jeep and sprinted toward the small terminal. Once through the doors, she easily picked out the group she was looking for. Tory and Kate stood with Bri and Caroline on the far side of the room. Bri and Caroline appeared to be glued together.

"Hey," Reese called as she hurried over.

"You just realized, too, huh?" Tory kissed Reese on the cheek.

"Yeah." Reese turned to Caroline. "You all set?"

"Yes." Caroline's eyes were red-rimmed and her voice feathery. One arm was wrapped tightly around Bri's waist, her thumb hooked over Bri's belt at the hip.

The PA system crackled to life and the flight to Boston was announced.

"That's you, babe," Bri said unnecessarily, since it was the only departing flight scheduled. She had her hand on Caroline's neck, stroking her softly.

"Well," Tory said with a smile, stepping forward to slide an arm around Caroline. "Have a wonderful time, sweetie. Send us pictures."

"You, too. I want to see Regina photos every week."

"I'll take care of that," Kate said. "You have a good flight, honey."

To Reese's surprise, Caroline released Bri and threw her arms around Reese's neck. In a voice too low for anyone else to hear, she murmured, "Take care of Bri, okay?"

Reese hugged her, then kissed her cheek. "You bet I will. Don't worry."

Then Bri and Caroline were in each other's arms, and Tory, Kate, and Reese all studied the tarmac while the two young lovers kissed. Finally, Bri stepped away and reached for one of Caroline's carry-on bags. "I'll walk you out."

"Don't forget how much I love you, baby," Caroline whispered as they approached the small plane.

"I won't. You neither, okay?"

"I'll miss you so much."

Bri bit her lip, then forced a grin. "The time will go fast. You'll be so busy. Work hard…and have fun. Okay?"

At the base of the steps leading up to the cabin, they faced one another.

"I'll be home for Christmas." Caroline blinked back tears.

Bri held her gaze, then traced a finger down her cheek. "I'll be right here waiting."

❖

"Are you sure she's okay back there?" Reese asked anxiously as Tory slid into the passenger seat of the Jeep.

They both turned and surveyed the tiny bundle in the car seat belted into the rear. The pale yellow blanket moved faintly as their daughter kicked and stretched her miniature limbs.

"Maybe you should sit with her," Reese muttered. "In case she needs…anything."

"I just fed her." Tory rested her palm on her lover's thigh. "She's fine, sweetheart. It's safer back there, and she's going to go to sleep as soon as you start driving."

"Okay." Reese pulled out onto Route 6 and wished for the hundredth time that she'd brought the patrol car so she could put the lights on and make the traffic ahead pull over and out of the way. She didn't like having moving vehicles anywhere near them, not with Reggie in the car. *What if some idiot runs into us?* "This is awful."

Tory laughed. "Honey, she's not made of glass. She's one strong little girl. Look how quickly she made her minimum safe weight. Almost three weeks early."

"You think she's gonna do everything early?" Reese dared a quick glance at Tory. "'Cause I'm still playing catch-up. Am I ever gonna be prepared?"

"Probably not." Tory linked her fingers through Reese's. "That's part of the fun."

"Yeah, right." But Reese was smiling.

"I was thinking that Women's Week might be a nice time," Tory mused. "Regina will be settled in by then."

"For what?"

Tory brought their joined hands to her lips and kissed Reese's fingers. "For the wedding you promised me."

"Oh." Reese slowed for a light, then met Tory's eyes. Her voice was suddenly husky. "That."

"Mm-hmm." Tory's face was soft with love and contentment. From behind them came a small hiccough, and then what sounded very much like a tiny laugh.

"And they say honeymoons don't last forever," Reese whispered.

*The End*

# About the Author

Radclyffe is the author of numerous lesbian romances (*Safe Harbor, Innocent Hearts, Love's Melody Lost, Love's Tender Warriors, Tomorrow's Promise, Passion's Bright Fury, Love's Masquerade, shadowland,* and *Fated Love*), as well as two romance/intrigue series: the Honor series *(Above All, Honor* revised edition, *Honor Bound, Love & Honor,* and *Honor Guards)* and the Justice series *(Shield of Justice,* the prequel *A Matter of Trust, In Pursuit of Justice,* and *Justice in the Shadows),* selections in *Infinite Pleasures: An Anthology of Lesbian Erotica,* edited by Stacia Seaman and Nann Dunne (2004) and in *Milk of Human Kindness,* an anthology of lesbian authors writing about mothers and daughters, edited by Lori L. Lake (2004).

A 2003/2004 recipient of the Alice B. award for her body of work as well as a member of the Golden Crown Literary Society, Pink Ink, and the Romance Writers of America, she lives with her partner, Lee, in Philadelphia, PA where she both writes and practices surgery full-time. She states, "I began reading lesbian fiction at the age of twelve when I found a copy of Ann Bannon's *Beebo Brinker.* Not long after, I began collecting every book with lesbian content I could find. The new titles come much faster now than they did in the decades when a new book or two every year felt like a gift, but I still treasure every single one. These works are our history and our legacy, and I am proud to contribute in some small way to those archives."

Her upcoming works include the next in the Provincetown Tales, *Distant Shores, Silent Thunder* (2005); the next in the Justice series, *Justice Served* (2005); and the next in the Honor series, *Honor Reclaimed* (2005).

Look for information about these works at www.radfic.com and www.boldstrokesbooks.com.

# Other Books Available From
# Bold Strokes Books

**Change Of Pace:** *Erotic Interludes* (ISBN: 1-933110-07-4) Twenty-five hot-wired encounters guaranteed to spark more than just your imagination. Erotica as you've always dreamed of it.

**Fated Love** (ISBN: 1-933110-05-8) Amidst the chaos and drama of a busy emergency room, two women must contend not only with the fragile nature of life, but also with the mysteries of the heart and the irresistible forces of fate.

**Justice in the Shadows** (ISBN: 1-933110-03-1) In a shadow world of secrets, lies, and hidden agendas, Detective Sergeant Rebecca Frye and her lover, Dr. Catherine Rawlings, join forces once again in the elusive search for justice.

**shadowland** (ISBN: 1-933110-11-2) In a world on the far edge of desire, two women are drawn together by power, passion, and dark pleasures. An erotic romance.

**Love's Masquerade** (ISBN: 1-933110-14-7) Plunged into the often indistinguishable realms of fiction, fantasy, and hidden desires, Auden Frost discovers a shifting landscape that will force her to question everything she has believed to be true about herself and the nature of love.

**Beyond the Breakwater** ISBN: 1-933110-06-6) One Provincetown summer three women learn the true meaning of love, friendship, and family. Second in the Provincetown Tales.

**Tomorrow's Promise** (ISBN: 1-933110-12-0) One timeless summer, two very different women discover the power of passion to heal and the promise of hope that only love can bestow.

**Love's Tender Warriors** (ISBN: 1-933110-02-3) Two women who have accepted loneliness as a way of life learn that love is worth fighting for and a battle they cannot afford to lose.

**Love's Melody Lost** (ISBN: 1-933110-00-7) A secretive artist with a haunted past and a young woman escaping a life that proved to be a lie find their destinies entwined.

**Safe Harbor** (ISBN: 1-933110-13-9) A mysterious newcomer, a reclusive doctor, and a troubled gay teenager learn about love, friendship, and trust during one tumultuous summer in Provincetown. First in the Provincetown Tales.

**Above All, Honor** (ISBN: 1-933110-04-X) The first in the Honor series introduces single-minded Secret Service Agent Cameron Roberts and the woman she is sworn to protect—Blair Powell, the daughter of the president of the United States. First in the Honor series.

**Love & Honor** (ISBN: 1-933110-10-4) The president's daughter and her security chief are faced with difficult choices as they battle a tangled web of Washington intrigue for…love and honor. Third in the Honor series.

**Honor Guards** (ISBN: 1-933110-01-5) In a journey that begins on the streets of Paris's Left Bank and culminates in a wild flight for their lives, the president's daughter and those who are sworn to protect her wage a desperate struggle for survival. Fourth in the Honor series.